Arms of Deliverance is a compelling novel giving the reader an accurate portrayal of the anxieties and threats facing the airmen in the war against Nazi Germany. As a co-pilot who parachuted from a burning B-17 and witnessed the mayhem in the sky over Berlin, I found this novel both gripping and exciting.

—Glenn Howard Hale,
former 2nd. Lt., 390th Bomb Group, 8th Air Force.
MIA 2Mar45 on Dresden raid, parachuting into Poland

It was a fascinating pleasure to watch the development of the author's courageous young reporter. The description of airbase activities and flight in a B-17 bomber out of Bassingbourn, England brought back poignant memories of my personal wartime experiences. I too flew with the 91st Bomb Group out of Bassingbourn as a Pathfinder Navigator. The descriptions of flight conditions are thought-provoking and accurate. Further, the author has pieced together an intriguing story with different segments. She skillfully guides the reader through peaks and valleys of why we fought, the struggle to win, nail-biting suspense, divine guidance, and . . . sweet victory. Tricia Goyer has effectively captured the robust 'Can Do' spirit of World War II.

—John Howland, Pathfinder Navigator,
91st Bomb Group

I found the book by Tricia Goyer brought back a lot of memories of WW2. It was very interesting how she wove the story around all the characters. Also, her research adds to the authenticity of the characters and times and places involved.

—Jack Gaffney,
91st Bomb Group

As a veteran of the 8th Army Air Corp and the 91st Bomb Group, 401st Squadron, years 1943 and 1944 completing my tour of 31 missions by mid 1944, I can appreciate the preparation Mrs. Goyer attained to get the details so accurate that she brought back the vivid details of each incident she included in portraying the actual flight experiences of the crew and positions of responsibility during the heat of battle.

> —George Parrish,
> 8th Army Air Corp and 91st Bomb Group

War-weary WWII Europe sets the stage for *Arms of Deliverance*, a powerful novel that weaves the lives of ordinary men and women who become extraordinary heroes. Their stories grip the heart with the powerful emotions that only war can bring. Love and hate, life and death, and those misguided passions that could only know defeat. Between the pages, I was there. Lived it and felt the surge of freedom that only true sacrifice can bring.

> —DiAnn Mills, bestselling author of
> *Leather and Lace* and *When the Lion Roars*

Tricia Goyer's *Arms of Deliverance* is a great read. Fast paced, beautifully researched and touching, it brings the years of World War II to life.

> —DeAnna Julie Dodson, author of
> *In Honor Bound, By Love Redeemed* and *To Grace Surrendered*

ARMS OF
Deliverance

A STORY OF PROMISE

A Novel

TRICIA
GOYER

MOODY PUBLISHERS
CHICAGO

© 2006 by
TRICIA GOYER

Scripture quotations, unless otherwise noted, are taken from the King James Version. Scriptures marked NLT are taken from the *Holy Bible, New Living Translation*, copyright 1996. Used by permission of Tyndale House Publishers, Inc., Wheaton, Illinois 60189. All rights reserved.

Editor: LB Norton
Cover Design: LeVan Fisher Design
Cover Image: Steve Gardner, pixelworksstudio.net and istockphoto
Interior Design: Ragont Design

Library of Congress Cataloging-in-Publication Data

Goyer, Tricia.
    Arms of deliverance : a story of promise / by Tricia Goyer.
        p. cm.
    ISBN-13: 978-0-8024-1556-1
    ISBN-10: 0-8024-1556-3
    1. Women journalists—Fiction. 2. Jewish women—Fiction. 3. World War, 1939-1945—Belgium—Fiction. 4. Eugenics—Germany—History—20th century—Fiction. I. Title.

PS3607.O94A89 2006
813'.6—dc22

                                                              2006008109

We hope you enjoy this book from Moody Publishers. Our goal is to provide high-quality, thought-provoking books and products that connect truth to your real needs and challenges. For more information on other books and products written and produced from a biblical perspective, go to www.moodypublishers.com or write to:

Moody Publishers
820 N. LaSalle Boulevard
Chicago, IL 60610

1 3 5 7 9 10 8 6 4 2

Printed in the United States of America

To Leslie Joy

Your care and compassion for others pales only to your
passion for God. I'm proud to be your mom.

"You guided my conception and formed me in the womb.
You clothed me with skin and flesh, and you knit
my bones and sinews together.
You gave me life and showed me your unfailing love.
My life was preserved by your care."
Job 10:10–12 NLT

CHAPTER ONE

Katrine squared her shoulders and instinctively pressed a hand to her stomach as she stepped through the open doors of the café, past the yellow sign that read NO JEWS ALLOWED. She paused as the strong aroma of coffee and cigarette smoke hit her face. Men and women clustered around tables. Beautiful people in the height of their glory.

Looking around at the room's flocked wallpaper, ornate light fixtures, and marble flooring, she found it hard to believe that not too far away a war stormed. Not only battles for land and power, but a war against a people—her people . . . or what used to be her people.

Tucked between France, Holland, and Germany, Belgium had fallen to Nazi control in 1940, four years earlier. Yet many acted as if the war were not more than a minor disturbance—especially the Germans who filled and controlled the streets, embracing the country as their own.

Katrine had come here too, to escape, to blend in with the

numerous transplants on the Belgium streets. More than a year had passed since she was Rebecca Lodz. With the right connections and right papers, she'd hidden herself well. Perhaps too well.

She had visited this café and sipped coffee with her lover only the day before. Yet today she looked upon the scene differently. Now when she glanced at the other women with their fine clothes, red lips, and fancy hats, she realized what she'd become, and whom she'd betrayed. Heaviness burdened her chest the same way it had when she was hiding in that dark, smelly barn.

Only this time it wasn't rotten potatoes that pressed upon her, animal fodder that for a time had protected her from death. Her burden now was shame—for she was to birth the child of a man who wouldn't hesitate to kill her if he only knew the truth.

She sucked in a calming breath, wishing she'd called to cancel their meeting. But it was too late. Hendrick had spotted her and waved her toward the secluded table. Two glasses of red wine sat on the glass surface, one half empty. Katrine could tell from the foggy sheen of his gaze that this glass wasn't his first.

"Sweetheart, you look beautiful tonight. That new dress brings out the blue in your eyes." He took her face in his hands and pressed his lips against hers. There was possession in his kiss, and a hunger she had come to know well.

"Sit, we will eat, and then take a walk along the river. It's beautiful this time of year, don't you think?" His voice was deep and throaty, and Katrine knew what he wanted.

Although Hendrick Schwartz was an officer in Hitler's army and a wealthy man with a fine furnished apartment, he was also an outdoor enthusiast like none Katrine had known. No doubt he had in mind finding a secluded corner of the park and laying her down in the soft spring grass to take what they both had come to understand was rightfully his.

Katrine stared across the table at her lover. Though twenty years her senior, Hendrick, with his tall, thin frame and chiseled features, turned the heads of many beautiful women. He'd caught her attention, after all.

They'd met one of the first times she'd dared venture out

with her new identification papers. Though Katrine now lived a thousand miles away from the village of her birth, and though she looked as Aryan as the women highlighted on Hitler's posters promoting racial purity, she wasn't used to being out in the open.

After a year of hiding, she'd walked out of her home that afternoon still longing for the safety of darkness. "People can hide better in a crowd than in the safest dark hole," said the resistance worker who'd come up with the plan to "Germanize" any Jews who looked the part.

Katrine was riding the tram to the market in Brussels when the handsome officer sat down beside her. She answered his questions bluntly. Yes, she was new to the city, having recently taken a job as a nanny. No, she hadn't had time to see much of the Belgian capital. Yes, she did have Sunday afternoons off. Before she realized what was happening, she found herself agreeing to a picnic in Parc de Laeken the next Sunday afternoon.

When Katrine told her protector about the invitation from a German officer, the woman had been pleased. "If you can fool him, you'll fool them all. No one would dare question the girlfriend of a dedicated SS man."

Now, mere months later, she not only hated herself for falling in love with the handsome soldier, but for tying herself to him through this child—their child. She picked up her wine glass, swished it, then set it back down, her eyes focusing on the grouted lines of the tiled table.

Hendrick took her hand in his. "What is it, darling? Your favorite song is playing, and you didn't even comment. Are you ill? We don't have to go for a stroll tonight, after all. Perhaps we can return to my apartment, and I can rub your feet." Hendrick winked at her. "I told you, you shouldn't work so hard. Are the Pfizer children acting up again?"

"Hendrick, I'm pregnant." The words escaped her lips, and Katrine lowered her head, unwilling to meet his gaze. She'd been meaning to wait. To find the right time, the right words. Although she hated what she was, Hendrick's mistress, what scared her even more was the thought of being alone, forced to raise a child on the little income she made.

"Pregnant?" Hendrick rose and swept her into his arms. "Yes! A child. My child." His voice rose and his laughter echoed in the room. He spun her around once and set her down gently in her chair. Then he lowered his face toward hers and placed a dozen soft kisses across her forehead, acting as if they were the only two people there.

"A child. My child!" he repeated, louder.

With trembling fingers, Katrine pushed back the stray curls that had escaped from her pinned-up hair. "You're happy?" Her eyes searched his.

"Happy? I'm overjoyed. No, jubilant!"

"But what of your . . . wife?" Katrine mouthed the last word rather than speaking it aloud.

Hendrick laughed again and sat back down. "Oh, sweet Katrine, you think she does not know? I am with you nearly every day of the week. Our picnics, the gifts." He took a long drink of wine. "Oh, my naïve girl, this is a new Germany. A land of innovative ideals. Haven't you heard Himmler himself: 'All women might not have the opportunity to become wives, but all should have the chance to become mothers.' My darling, I've given you that chance. And you, my dear, will give me the son I long for."

Mary Kelley sprinted down Sixth. The soles of her black-and-white saddle shoes barely touched the littered sidewalk as she wove through the crowd with the same urgency as when she was ten and Mr. Stein chased her, broom in hand, after she'd stolen a pack of gum from his corner grocery.

Only this time she was running *to* something, not away. For if she got the scoop today—the true story from the senator concerning the future of veterans' benefits—then she'd really be going places. Away from her past as the illegitimate, big-dreaming daughter of a cleaning woman. Away from the gangly girl who'd lived her whole life dreaming of escape from the tight-knit German neighborhood in which the home country wasn't simply missed, but rather revived in the New York streets with an abundance of sausage, beer, and song.

The dense crowd slowed Mary's steps, and she noted that the entourage of black sedans had nearly made it to the corner. If she didn't hurry, the senator would slip inside the hotel before Mary could get a chance to speak to her.

"Excuse me, sir. Pardon, ma'am." Mary straightened her pleated black skirt and white blouse, then reached into her small satchel and pulled out two pink ribbons. She quickly parted her hair and formed two ponytails. Then she stuck a pencil behind her ear, clutched a composition notebook to her chest, and made her way through the mass of journalists already forming a semicircle at the end of the parade route. "Excuse me. May I squeeze in? Thanks so much."

The crowd parted, body by body, until Mary had made her way to the front of the line.

Two black cars were just pulling up. Shiny Rolls-Royces with tinted windows, looking as if they'd just rolled off the assembly line. They parked in front of the Wall Street hotel where a press conference would be held tomorrow. Yet somehow news of the senator's early arrival had leaked out, drawing lines of veterans, educators, and others who wanted either to bend the senator's ear or get an early scoop.

Mary cocked her head to get a view of the occupants, but a wide man with a suit coat that smelled of cigar, sweat, and ink blocked her view. He stepped back and nearly bowled her over.

The tall, lean reporter standing next to Mary spoke up in her defense. "Hey, Mac, stop getting so pushy, will you? You most knocked o'er the girl here."

Mac, or rather Chester McWilliams, reporter from the *Times*, hardly gave her a second glance. "That's no girl. It's Mary Kelley from the *Sentinel*. Sorry, Mare, the schoolgirl gag isn't going to work this time."

"Wanna bet?" With a duck and a leap, Mary dodged under Chester's arm and slid her thin form between the two yellow-and-white-striped barricades.

A security guard approached with quickened steps. "Sorry, miss. Can't let you pass."

She slunk back as he gently wrapped a hand around her arm.

"But, mister, I promised I'd get this interview. What am I gonna tell my teacher if I don't? I mean, I only need five minutes." She twirled one of her ponytails between her fingers and smiled. "Please?"

"Let her through," called a voice.

Mary turned her head to see a woman climbing from the stretch limo.

"What are you doing manhandling a young woman like that? You're lucky I don't take down your name."

The woman walked over and motioned the security guard out of the way, then cradled Mary's elbow. "I already promised an interview to the daughter of a friend, but I appreciate your interest and spunk. If you behave yourself, I'll let you sit in."

The senator led Mary through the front doors of the lobby, then turned and paused. As if on cue, the door to the second limo opened, and a tall, attractive young woman climbed out. Dressed as impeccably as the senator herself, she slid from the passenger's seat, smoothing her sky blue suit with manicured fingers.

"Lee O'Donnelly. I should have known," Mary whispered, hugging her notebook tighter to her chest.

"So you know her?" The senator straightened her collar. "Of course you do. I hear from her father she's only been away from *Vogue* for a few months and has already made a splash in city reporting. I just love women with gumption."

Lee approached, offering a bright smile to the doorman, who opened the glass door wide for her entrance. Her heels clicked on the polished lobby floor, and gold bracelets jingled on her wrist. Lee smiled at the senator, but the look faded when she noticed Mary. One lone eyebrow jutted up as if to say *What are you doing here?*

Mary stepped forward before Lee could say a word. "Miss O'Donnelly, so nice to see you. I read your column every day and find myself in awe of the extent of your family connections.

And here you are again. I was invited to join in. I hope you don't mind."

"Mind? Of course not. Any friend of the senator is a friend of mine." She placed a hand on the senator's shoulder. "Or should I call you Lovey?" Lee's lips curled in a coy grin.

"Your mother told you, didn't she?" The senator laughed. "I made her swear not to breathe a word of my nickname . . . and you look so much like her, dear. Being in your presence takes me back twenty years." The senator hurried through the lobby and toward the lounge, her arm entwined with Lee's.

Takes me back too. Mary felt twelve years old again. *Find a corner and sit in it. Not a peep, remember?*

"You coming, dear?" the senator called back over her shoulder. "No time to dawdle. As Lee here can tell you, reporters must not only keep up, but blaze the trail if necessary."

"Coming!" Mary quickened her steps to reach the senator's side, but it didn't change anything. She was just a tagalong, allowed to come along for the ride. Just as she'd always been.

School had been out for two weeks, and the thought of spending another day in their stuffy apartment alone while her mother worked was enough to cause twelve-year-old Mary to resort to begging.

She could hear the stirring in the Heinzes' kitchen, just on the other side of theirs. The odor of Cousin Velma's spicy sausage, onion, and eggs nearly caused her stomach to heave. Hadn't the woman ever heard of pancakes? And if she had to spend one more day listening to the constant playing of German folk songs—

As if on cue, the phonograph started up. Mary pressed her hands to her ears as the familiar voice sang. Jetzt kommt die fröliche. Sommerszeit, die. Stunden voller Lust und Wonne . . .

Her mother hummed from the next room, then joined in. Her mom's soft voice was much prettier than the German lady's husky one.

Yes, begging was definitely worth a try.

Mary walked to their bedroom and sat on the rumpled covers, watching as her mother applied her makeup. "Mom, do you have to go to work today? Can't we go to the park or the zoo? It's such a nice day outside."

"You know I have to work. The guys wouldn't know what to do without me picking up their carbon and sweeping their ashes. And you want to have a new outfit when school starts again, don't you?"

Though Mary's father wasn't around—never had been—her mother had faced every obstacle in their path with rolled-up sleeves, a cocked jaw, and a narrow gaze that Mary was sure even President Roosevelt himself would back down from.

She crossed her arms. "Then let me come with you. I'll be good. I'll just sit in a corner and watch the reporters work. They won't even know I'm there, I promise."

"You don't understand. It's more complicated than that. . . ." Her mother looked out the window, pressing her lower lip between her teeth.

"Ple-ease. If I'm not good, I'll never ask again." She held her breath.

Finally her mother nodded, as if coming to some resolution within herself. Then she stood and placed her hands on her hips. "All right then. Get your shoes and run a comb through your hair. But don't be whining halfway through the day if you're bored."

They hurried out of the apartment. Her mother glanced at her watch, then took Mary's hand, leading her through the busy streets toward the large office buildings downtown.

Mary didn't say a word. She knew that if the wrong thing escaped her lips, her mother would send her back to the thin walls, smelly cooking, and German music.

Thirty minutes later, they approached the Sentinel *building. Her mother stopped and turned to her. "Don't speak unless you're spoken to. Just find a corner and sit in it."*

Outside the newsroom she paused once more, straightened Mary's collar, and stepped back, obviously satisfied. "Remember, not a peep."

Mary nodded. Even from the other side of the closed door, she could hear the curious rhythm of fingers pounding on typewriter keys.

They stepped inside, and she was met by a bustling scene of white-collared men in motion, of words and confusion, black ink and white paper. Some men sat at long wooden desks, pounding their fingers against typewriter keys. Others leaned against the wall near the stand-up telephones, taking notes. And some hunched over semicircular desks that read COPY in bold letters on the front. These men wore green shades over their eyes and seemed intent on the white papers spread before them. One man was so round, Mary didn't understand why the wooden chair didn't break under him. Another tall man sat sideways because he couldn't fold his long legs under the desk.

Mary didn't know any of them or their various roles. But her heart pounded as fast as the typewriter keys, with rising excitement and expectation.

The young woman's mouth opened wide, a cry bursting from her lips as Hendrick plunged the lethal injection into the white flesh of her breast, stabbing it into her heart. The needle slid deep, and Hendrick released its contents, then stood back to wait. In a matter of seconds the poison would take effect. He had performed the task a hundred times before. He'd witnessed the way death washed over a body—frantic movements soon stilling—as the feeble soul slipped away.

A group of men circled behind him, chosen officers of purification. They waited in anticipation, prepared to learn from the master, the expressions of their faces a mix of horror and thrill.

Yet still the mouth remained open. The screams continued.

A hand grasped Hendrick's shoulder. "It's happening again. You must stop her."

Hendrick reached for the woman's mouth, attempting to cover it with his hand, but she would not be silenced. *Die, you must die.*

It wasn't a joyous task, but one of necessity. Only valued life deserved the Fatherland's valuable resources, and this dim-witted female was not worthy. She continued to struggle. Then her face washed out in a stream of bright, white light.

"Hendrick, wake up! The child, she screams in her sleep. *You* brought her here. You silence her."

His eyes adjusted to the brightness, and he realized he was in his family home, on the outskirts of Brussels. It was Onna, his wife, lying wide-eyed next to him. And the screams—they filtered in from the room attached to theirs. The ornate door did little to muffle the cries.

They're the screams of a child, he realized. Yet their intensity was the same.

"Curse you, woman. I thought you found a nanny for her. I'm tired of these late-night episodes."

"It's Magie's day off. What do you expect? You said—"

His look silenced her.

Hendrick jumped from the bed, slid on his satin robe, and strode across the room, still attempting to push the feebleminded woman's face from his mind's eye. Was she one of the hundreds he'd disposed of in his duty of carrying out the required ethnic cleansing? Had her face somehow become imprinted on his conscience? Hendrick wasn't sure, but he refused to allow guilt to accuse his honored work.

Taking a deep breath, he stopped just short of the door and allowed his heartbeat to settle. He closed his eyes and pictured the angelic face, the wide blue eyes, the blonde curls. This was the second child he'd chosen. *Aryan blood reclaimed from Polish soil.*

"Poor thing, what nightmares she must have from her past life," Hendrick muttered as he pushed the door open. Soon, he knew, the girl would adjust to her new destiny—just as her sister had. Soon the nightmares would cease.

"Stella," he whispered, his bare feet sinking into the plush carpet of the room. A shaft of light angled through the doorway onto his new daughter's face and outstretched arms. With three steps, Hendrick was at her side. He sat upon her bed and pulled her close.

"Papa, Papa, Papa," she cried in his ear. He pulled her tighter, allowing her four-year-old frame to fold into his.

16

"Shhh, Papa is here. All is well, my Stella. All is well." Hendrick patted her back, but at his words the girl's body stiffened. Her cries stopped, and with a small gasp she pulled back from his arms.

"Papa is here," he repeated.

Stella pushed against his chest and shook her head. "No," she whispered. Her blue eyes darted, glancing around the pink and lace room with the same horror as the woman in his dreams.

"Papa is here." Hendrick's voice rose, growing in strength. He laid Stella back on her white cotton sheets. "I will not let them take you back, child. Close your eyes and rest now."

She shivered, and he tucked the blankets tight under her chin. "Sleep now. Sweet dreams, Stella."

Even in the dim light, he could see her squeeze her lids tighter.

"Good girl. Good, obedient child." He patted the top of her blonde head, yet still her shoulders trembled. He leaned over to the lamp on the nightstand and flipped it on. Golden light cascaded over the bed and her small frame. "It is the darkness that scares you," he whispered, wondering if she understood his German words. "It will be better in the morning."

Hendrick returned to bed to find Onna curled to her side— her back to him—pretending to sleep. He slid into the sheets beside her and curved his body next to hers. Though arousal stirred within his flesh, he refused to let himself give in. It was Onna's fault, after all, that the child in the next room was not of his blood. It was her body that refused to provide children—the pride of every officer of the Reich.

Sweet Katrine, he thought, wishing it were her within his sheets tonight. *Katrine is giving me the child I so desire. Even now my blood pumps through the heir of the Reich growing in her womb.*

"Sweet Katrine," he whispered. Onna's body stiffened in his arms, but Hendrick didn't care. "It is she who will give us *our* child," he said louder, tightening his grasp. "It's a name you should love as much as I, my dear. For through *her* my strength will live on."

Though the quartet in the foyer was practicing one of her favorite melodies, Lee O'Donnelly wasn't in any hurry to go downstairs and greet guests. She had thoughts of deadlines and finding the next big story on her mind.

She sighed as her pink satin robe slid off her shoulders, folding into a puddle on the marble floor. With quick movements, she pinned her shoulder-length hair to the top of her head and stepped into the water, drawn and awaiting her arrival. It was the perfect temperature and scented with lavender. Jane always prepared it right.

Thank goodness for good help.

Lee sank deeper into the warmth, leaned against the cushioned headrest, and closed her eyes.

Thank goodness for middle-of-the-day baths to melt away the tension.

She had barely been at the newsroom two hours when her mother called the office, reminding her of the afternoon tea and charity event with two dozen of their family's closest friends. The Queen of the Known World, as Lee referred to her mother behind her back, had demanded her daughters attend. Demanded, not asked. As if they were still children who must obey her every whim.

The music's volume rose, and Lee visualized the upbeat notes climbing the polished, winding staircase and sliding under her door, seeking her out in the deep recesses of her private bath and urging her to put on a happy face.

Music meant parties. And parties meant people. Rich people. Arrogant people. People who lived as if this worldwide war didn't affect them in the least. People who instead expected one to smile and entertain with witty and complimentary conversation.

Yesterday, before heading to the tailor's for a fitting of a new Dior dress, Lee had scanned the guest list. More money would be assembled on their patio this afternoon than was held in the Bank of New York. Close friends indeed.

She allowed her arms to float to the top of the water, determined to relax and take her time. After thirty minutes, her fingertips began to shrivel, and she expected Jane—in black uniform and white cap—to arrive with a summons.

Sure enough, not five minutes later a soft knock sounded.

"Jane, tell Mother to go ahead and start without me. It's been a hard day at the office."

"I'm not the help," a husky female voice said through the door, "but I *was* sent up to urge you to hurry."

The door swung open, and a leggy brunette entered. A flattering fuchsia dress clung to her sister's frame. Though two years older, Rondi looked enough like Lee that people often thought they were twins.

Lee continued to soak as her sister perched herself on the marble countertop and lit a cigarette. She flicked a red-painted toe at her sister, splashing a spray of water but carefully missing. "Dad will kill you if he discovers those *hideous* things in the house. He just paid a fortune to have the drapes cleaned, remember?"

Rondi let a thin trail of smoke curl from her lips and grinned. "I'm sorry, *Lenora*, but I'm not the one in the hot seat today. I'm afraid it's your rear firmly planted on Daddy's bad side. But at least you're giving Roger a break."

"Yes, well, next time I see him, I'll encourage our dear brother to write a thank-you note." Lee rose from the water, stepping over the satin robe and reaching for the white cotton one hanging on the wall hook. "I don't understand why Daddy isn't over it. I thought after seeing my byline on the front page a few times, he'd be willing to give me some slack."

"Could it be, one, he hates reporters? Two, his shining hope for the future, our brother, turned his back on the family business to work as one. Or three, his darling daughter left a reputable establishment to do the same."

Lee sighed. "It was either a new career or death from monotony. What was I supposed to do?"

"He's not going to back down on this one, Lee. Where do

you think you got your strong will from? At least we know you're not the child of the milkman." Rondi laughed. "And I actually think he's even more upset today than he was three weeks ago. After all, the whole city now knows it's Marvin O'Donnelly's daughter bucking the system, attempting to do a man's job."

"Attempting? More like succeeding." Lee cinched the cotton belt around her waist, patted her neck with a plush hand towel, and then released the clip holding up her hair. Dark, thick strands fell on her shoulders. "My reputation precedes me, and my editors are coming to understand that I indeed have all the right connections."

Rondi took one more puff, then turned on the sink faucet and ran her cigarette underneath.

Lee smirked as her sibling walked to the bathroom window and opened it wide, waving her hand to dissipate the smoke.

Rondi sighed. "So you have your name on the front page. But is it really worth it? It's not like you didn't have a good job at *Vogue*. And just think of all the fringe benefits you gave up—lavish parties, fascinating interviews, generous gifts . . . a smile on Daddy's face."

Lee strode out of the bathroom and to her wardrobe, opening it wide to discover her chiffon rose-hued dress pressed and waiting. To most women such a garment would be a luxury beyond imagining; to her it was just another evidence of being trapped in an archaic system dictated by her parents.

"I've had it with his hardheadedness." Lee dressed hastily. "I want to do more with my life than give socialites tips on the best places to look for designer labels in patriotic shades of red, white, and blue. There's a war going on, for goodness' sake, with men fighting and dying. What about reporting that?"

Rondi glanced in the vanity mirror and then pinched her cheeks to give them more color. From the look on her sister's face, Lee was sure Rondi would rather be pinching her.

With a final sigh and shake of her pretty head, Rondi stalked toward the door. She paused at the threshold. "Well, there's no war in New York, but *your family* is here. Think about that.

Because sometimes harmony in the home is more important than one person's crazy dreams. Sometimes striking out solo just isn't worth it, sister."

CHAPTER TWO

The city room was a man's world. Spittoons graced the corner of every desk. Cigar stubs, half-smoked cigarettes, and crumpled papers littered the floor. Massive Underwood typewriters topped rows of oak desks—a man sitting behind each one.

Mary had gotten her story in over an hour ago—beating Paul Bramley by a mere thirty seconds. It was a game they played every day, seeing whose text would hit the editor's desk first, and guessing how close to the front page each story would appear. To win both meant a slice of pie at Brenda's Café at the expense of the loser. Anything less than a complete win was a wash, not worth a free cup of coffee.

Paul glanced up from his whirring black typewriter keys. His brown fedora was pushed back from his forehead, his press pass tucked into the band. When he saw her, his fingers stilled, and a key froze in midair. "Gee whiz, girlie. You made me lose my train of thought." His green eyes sparkled. "Good work on the senator's story. Your ingenuity never ceases to amaze me. It seems she's on to something with that Servicemen's Readjustment Act. Or what was it you called it—the GI Bill?"

"It was an easy story, really. All I did was sit back on that white leather chesterfield and take it all in." Mary smirked. "And I couldn't have timed it better—I mean, what were the odds of a surprise meet-up with that bomber crew just back from overseas? Their hopes of starting their own businesses and attending college added a special touch, don't you think?"

"What are the odds? C'mon, Mary, what source tipped you this time?"

Mary eyed her friend and shook her head. "A girl never tells her secrets. Now, speaking of secrets, let me see what you came up with."

She peered over Paul's shoulder and read silently.

Mary Kelley looks like a New York City high-schooler with her blonde hair and pretty face—reminiscent of the girl all the boys had a crush on. And while this unassuming reporter often wears knee socks and oxfords to work, the others on her beat are on to her, and rightly so. For in that pretty little head of Mary's is a mind her co-workers claim to be one-half Florence Nightingale and the other half Sherlock Holmes. Her stories not only find the facts—sleuthing for the crux of the story—they make readers care. Which is exactly the type of person needed on the front lines of this war.

Dear sirs, the people of this country have heard enough of the facts. They're ready for heart. Although war production is at an all-time high, our men are still in need of more if we're going to rise victorious. How can we empower our dockworkers to put in more hours, or encourage our Rosie the Riveters to give a little extra? By reminding them of their brothers and sons who need their support. Mary Kelley can do the job of providing the heart behind the headlines, and because of her pretty face on the masthead she'll become America's Sweetheart as well.

Mary cleared her throat as she rolled the sheet of paper from the machine. "It sounds a little over the top, Paul. America's Sweetheart? Increasing war production by writing stories with heart? I want a job overseas, not to become the next Shirley Temple."

Paul tipped the high-back wooden chair onto two legs and entwined his fingers behind his head. "Obviously, doll, you have no idea of the stuffiness of the review board. Yeah, it may be a little much . . . until you remember these guys probably read a dozen applications each day—every one of them with well-written, moving stories attached. There are plenty of reporters worthy of the assignment, but what's Rule Number 7 of Paul's Pointers?"

"Use your words to paint a picture in the reader's mind, so they're not just reading about an event, they're living it too." Mary lifted her fingers as if reciting a Girl Scout pledge.

"You get an A for the day," he chuckled. "My advice *and* recommendation are going to take you places. Heck, soon you'll be *invited* to those private interviews instead of crashing them. Speaking of which, did you read the piece by that high-society chick? Isn't she with *Vogue* or something?"

"Lee O'Donnelly? Used to be, but lately she's been trying her hand at hard news, which in my opinion still needs work. I mean 99 percent of the questions she asked the senator had to do with catching up on old times."

"Sounds like she's clued in on Rule Number 25."

"Rule 25?"

"It's not what you know, it's who you know."

Mary grinned and crossed her arms over her white blouse. "Yeah, yeah. You're right. But it's still my guess she won't last another month."

Mary scanned Paul's letter of recommendation one more time, then folded it and slid it into a plain white envelope. "Okay, I'll include this with my application. But if this sweetheart thing doesn't pan out, I swear you're gonna owe me more than a slice of pie. More like a whole meal."

Paul rose, unfolding his tall frame from the chair. He wrapped an arm around her shoulders, and she leaned into his embrace.

"Your faith in me means so much."

The news phone let out a shrill ring. Paul squeezed her

shoulder, then grabbed his pencil and pad. "Good luck. I just hope running your application down to the main office doesn't take too much time away from tomorrow's deadline."

"You kidding? I have a scoop in the same neighborhood." She winked, then slid on the blue blazer that Paul always complained reminded him of the ones worn by the students at St. Francis Boarding School for Girls.

He pulled out a cigar from his shirt pocket and tucked it between his lips. "Get outta here, kid. There's an assignment over the big blue pond that has your name all over it. And whether you like it or not, you're already a sweetheart in my book."

Eddie Anderson slung his musette bag over his shoulder and hurried toward the large brick barrack, noting stares from other officers lounging around the manicured lawns and checking out new arrivals.

As a member of the 91st, his new home was AAF Station 121, Bassingbourn, England—thirteen miles from Cambridge and a short distance from Royston. The truck ride to the base had driven them through a typical rural farming area, and Eddie had been surprised to find the accommodations more civilized than he'd expected.

Since the 91st had been one of the first bombing groups in England, they'd been lucky enough to be stationed at a permanent RAF base. Other B-17 crews whom Eddie met his first night in London had warned him about cold Quonset huts and other temporary buildings hastily plopped down on the English countryside.

Bassingbourn looked more like a country club than a temporary airfield. It had substantial brick construction, which included an Enlisted Men's club, an Officers' Club, steam heat in the buildings, and even indoor toilets.

"Looks like we'll be fighting the war as gentlemen," Eddie's buddy, José Garcia, had stated with a smile and a low whistle when they climbed out of the truck upon arrival.

With the rest of his crew still in line waiting for supplies, Eddie volunteered to go on ahead to find their assigned quarters.

Four men lounged in the sunshine—some of the first sun he'd seen since their ship docked. One guy whittled with his pocketknife, his eyes on Eddie instead of the stick. Another looked from the clear blue sky to Eddie and back to the sky again, as if expecting approaching aircraft any second.

Eddie made eye contact with each one, nodding at their glances, still trying to take in where he really was. He'd never imagined finding himself in Europe. Once, right after high school, he'd driven from Montana to Spokane, Washington, to give a friend a ride to college. He thought that was far.

He'd faced basic and navigational training in the States, and before that he'd been a normal high school kid floating on wooden rafts with his brother on Whitefish Lake. As they basked in the sun, they'd watched the bald eagles spread their wings, catching a ride on the updrafts, swooping and rising through the clouds. Now he was doing the same.

He entered the barracks and spotted the officers' assigned room. Eddie paused. Stuff was everywhere, piled on the long rows of iron cots. Clothes, shaving kits, letters opened and stacked. The smiling face of a girl—captured in a glamour shot reminiscent of Betty Grable—stared up at him from where it rested on a pillow. Every bunk appeared taken. Had he misunderstood the clerk's directions?

He took two tentative steps backward.

"Sorry about this, buster." The voice spoke from the doorway behind him. "The cleanup crew hasn't been by yet."

A lieutenant, whom Eddie recognized as the whittling man, strode up. He was nearly Eddie's height, but stockier, with reddish hair that looked as if it hadn't been combed in a week.

"Took off yesterday . . . was their tenth mission."

The man sank onto an unmade cot, and Eddie suddenly understood. He had a dozen questions about the guys who'd left their letters half written and their laundry unwashed, fully expecting to return. But as he opened his mouth to speak, he realized maybe it was better he didn't know.

"They were just one of a dozen planes lost," the officer said. "It was a hard hit." He sighed. "The privates haven't had time to empty this place and clean the bunks." He pulled a cigarette from his shirt pocket, then reached over and stuck his hand under the pillow of the cot closest to the door, pulling out a silver lighter. "I'm Clifford, by the way."

Clifford lifted the silver rectangle toward a warm shaft of light. "Used to be mine till I lost it in a poker game. James Buch always did have luck with cards. Too bad he wasn't as fortunate flying."

He lit up his Chesterfield and inhaled nearly a quarter of it on the first drag.

"That his bunk?" Eddie cocked his chin toward the cot.

"Was." Clifford spoke without removing the cigarette from his lips. He glanced at the lighter one last time, then tossed it back onto the pillow. "Doesn't seem right taking it back. You can have it or any other stuff you find useful. Only personal items will be sent home."

Eddie dropped his bag to the floor, uncertain of what to do, what to say.

"The rest of your crew here?"

"They're still collecting supplies. I was lucky to be first in line."

"You a navigator?"

Eddie furrowed his brow. "How d'ja know?"

"The ink on your fingers gives you away—doing all those calculations, you know."

Eddie glanced again at the silver lighter but refused to pick it up. "Were they shot down by ground artillery?"

"Nah. Another plane got hit and started falling before *Lucy Lou* could get outta the way. She split open like a ripe watermelon. I didn't see one lousy chute. Dang Krauts."

"I'm sorry you lost your friends." Eddie's sentiments sounded lame, even to himself.

The man rose and kicked the toe of his boot against the floor. "I'm from Kentucky, horse country. Dung is a part of life." He took a musette bag from under the second cot and began to fill it.

Eddie did the same with the items on the cot closest to the door. He swallowed the large lump in his throat and tossed the lighter in with the rest.

"Just in from the States?"

"Yup." Eddie unfastened a photo of a young, dark-haired girl that had been pinned to the wall. He hardly gave it a moment's glance before tucking it between the pages of a book of English poetry. Then he stuck both into the bag, wondering whose hands would unpack it—a father, a mother, the girl?

"Yea, though I walk through the valley of the shadow of death, I will fear no evil: for thou art with me; thy rod and thy staff they comfort me," Eddie whispered to himself as he gathered the rest of the guy's things.

He wasn't sure if Clifford heard him and really didn't care. Eddie needed the comfort those words provided. And despite the prayer, he wondered just what he'd walked into. After all, the average crew only made it fifteen missions . . . yet it took thirty before they could go home.

This place cast a shadow of death that couldn't be denied, even on the days when the sun dared shine.

———————————

Lee glanced at the address, matched it up with the weathered apartment building, and motioned to her driver. "Right there, Jimmy. Pull over next to that police vehicle. Meet me here in fifteen minutes."

From the front seat, her driver nodded his graying head and swerved through traffic as if on a mission from MacArthur himself.

When the car stopped, Lee quickly jumped out. A green glob of something spattered onto the right toe of her brown leather pumps.

"If that's not the end-all," she muttered. "Curses!" Without further hesitation she hurried toward the front entrance.

"Hold that door, please," she called to a police officer who'd just exited.

"No way, lady. No admittance." He held out an arm.

"Lee O'Donnelly, *New York News*. I've already talked to Baker. He gave me the okay."

"Chief Baker?" The cop tilted his cap back on his head.

Lee thrust both hands on her slender hips. "No, *Chef* Baker . . . of course the chief."

"Okay, lady. But I swear, if you're pulling my leg . . ." He took a step back.

The glass-inset entry door swung shut, and Lee was alone with the panel of mailboxes, the odor of dust and age, and a worn set of carpeted steps leading to the crime scene. Narrow steps creaked with each hurried footfall over one, then two flights of switchbacked stairs. Curious neighbors peered past chain-restrained doors as she alighted on the third floor landing, and a distant radio supplied a crooner's song to the surreal scene.

A pudgy hand held the second door on the left open partway, and she approached. A stocky police officer was exiting, along with a man dressed in a suit—undercover for sure. Lee recognized him from another story she'd recently covered. He didn't even bother a second glance as she slid past them into the doorway.

Investigators swarmed one of the back rooms, and a tall man in a suit stood in the immaculate white kitchen, scribbling in a leather-bound notebook. With his shoulders slouched and his face narrowed in a deep frown, he looked twenty years older than he had just this morning.

"Well, hello, Roger. What a pleasant surprise."

Her brother's blue eyes flashed her direction, and he sighed. "Sorry, can't say the same, Sis. Aren't you supposed to be at a fancy party?"

Lee shrugged, realizing she still wore a strand of sapphires around her neck. Surely they clashed with the chocolate-colored suit. "Mother was trying to steer the conversation toward dessert when I got called away. She didn't say a word, but you should have seen the look on Daddy's face. I swear, if looks could kill . . ."

"Uh, do you remember who you're talking to? I invented that look."

Lee chortled as she scanned the amazingly tidy apartment. She stepped into the dining room and spotted a notepad and fountain pen resting on the polished table. There was no mail. Not even the Sunday paper. Nothing out of place. She lifted the pen.

"I wouldn't—"

Her brother's words were cut short as she realized it wasn't a pen, but a knife fashioned to look like one. And the wet substance on the tip was definitely not ink.

"Ugh." She glanced down to spy more of the red substance pooled on the floor just inches from her green-globbed shoe. A thin red trail led to a back room.

Lee's stomach lurched, and she dropped the knife. "Thanks for warning me."

"As if you would have listened . . ."

She eyed her brother, who was still taking notes, and sucked in a deep breath.

Roger glanced up at her. "You okay, sis? I was only foolin'. But don't touch anything else. We can come in, but we're not supposed to mess up the crime scene."

Lee regained her poise, tilted her head, and smiled. If anyone besides Roger were standing there, she would have hurried to the sidewalk, waited for her driver, and then told her boss that she hadn't been admitted. At least those years of etiquette class had been useful for something.

"You're right. I don't know what I was thinking. And thank you for being concerned."

Leaving her brother behind, she hurried through the rooms, inspecting scenic photographs, neatly arranged socks in the top drawer of the bedroom dresser, and tidy stacks of *Life* magazines sorted by date of publication.

Lee interviewed a few of the officers, and within fifteen minutes she had enough to write the story. She bypassed the back room with the body. It was the owner of the apartment. But from what she'd heard from the boss, he was being treated more like a suspect than a victim, a spy of some type.

I've seen enough without having to bother with the dead guy.

As her brother watched her every move, Lee jotted down one final note about the white cat with large green eyes on the sofa. The feline watched her movements with curiosity, then yawned and curled into a ball.

"You done already?" Roger asked.

"You know me, always eager to get on to the next thing."

He scratched his reddish brown hair under his gray hat. "Yeah, and you know me. I'll still be here for hours." He flipped through his notebook, showing her the pages he had already scribbled on. "I can't write if I don't have a feel for the whole thing. I mean, this was somebody's life. A person's dead, and I can't dismiss the thought that I'm responsible for giving him a fair shake."

"Take your time then. I'll tell Jane to save you a plate."

Lee gave Roger a small wave as she left the apartment, then hurried down the stairs.

As she climbed into her waiting car, she felt sorry for Roger. He usually spent more time on stories than they were worth. *It's only one dead guy who most likely will be forgotten by his neighbors in a week's time. And he was on the wrong side of the fence, after all.*

Lee smiled, realizing perhaps this gift for throwing a story together had to do with her training in the society pages. She'd learned to catch the slightest intricacy, such as which of the four kings—Gable, Heflin, Cooper, and Steward—was on the brink of yet another romance. Or why the leading man's hand was placed on Rita Hayworth's elbow rather than the small of her back as she was led down the red carpet. And what the slightest spark of interest glinting in the eyes of Rockefeller meant. These small particulars were hints of gossip-inspiring events that would soon splash through the papers—under her byline.

Her colleagues joked, "Here comes Lee; when's the story gonna start?"

She glanced out the car window, eyeing the tall skyscrapers

that filled her vision as they headed into the center of town. She noted the fading light reflecting off the numerous glass windows, casting a lighted hue over the city, and her mind returned to the apartment.

The man was said to be a spy, and the police believed he'd been working alone. Lee knew that wasn't the case. Some of the magazine clippings she'd noticed in the apartment were from *Vogue*—she recognized the photos. And then there were the pocked imprints in the carpet. High heels to be sure. Lee knew there was at least one more person involved, despite how well *she* hid herself. And Lee was certain it was something Chief Baker would be interested in hearing.

"On second thought, can you drive me by the police station first? I need a few minutes with the chief."

While Jimmy slowly maneuvered the car through the busy New York traffic, Lee rested her head against the back of the upholstered seat as the words of tomorrow's headline arranged themselves in her mind. "BOY NEXT DOOR" DISCOVERED TO BE GERMAN SPY

Not quite.

FRIENDLY NEIGHBOR LEADING DOUBLE LIFE

Hmm.

SINISTER SIDE DISCOVERED TO FRIENDLY BOY NEXT DOOR

Almost.

SECRET LIFE OF BOY NEXT DOOR . . . AND COULD HIS PARTNER BE SPYING ON YOU?

Yes, that had a nice ring to it.

No doubt every paper would state the facts of the dead man's undercover work: How he got into the country. Who he was working for. What could have leaked out.

Only her story would be different. It would bring a human side to the enemy. A man who enjoyed nature photography, cared for animals, and no doubt was part of a larger network. A man who fooled even those closest to him, proving loose lips do sink ships and it never pays to deceive.

Yes, this would be the story to prove, finally prove, what Lee had been telling her editor all along. She was ready for big news—the front lines.

CHAPTER THREE

The scent of cleaning supplies and cigar smoke replaced the fresh spring breeze as Hendrick stepped from a Brussels street into the building of the Office for Race and Settlement. With quick steps he moved to the third door to the right and unlocked it. Four doors down, another SS officer walked through the doorway into the space Hendrick had previously occupied. It was there Hendrick's duties had encompassed racial cleansing— washing away the impure blood that tainted the health of their national body. And while Hendrick had performed his job efficiently, he was thankful for his promotion, moving him from an angel of darkness to a provider of hope and light.

Entering the room, he flipped on the light switch and placed his briefcase on his desk. Then, as he did every day, he strode to the wall of children's photographs, noting the new ones added. These captured images encouraged him and prodded him on in his work.

The sound of a woman's high-heeled shoes clicking down

the hall filtered through the open doorway. He knew it was Lydia, his new secretary. She always dressed for him, pampered him. He made the effort to turn his eyes to the doorway as she entered, allowing her to see that he appreciated her efforts.

"In every system of purification there are four types of people," he said as she entered. "The cleansers and those cleansed. The bystanders and those honored to rescue others."

Lydia approached, her eyes daring to meet his, and handed him a file. "And aren't we thankful, Officer Schwartz. They're beautiful. Perfect."

"Yes, they are." He winked, noting the blush rising up Lydia's cheeks. "Blonde, blue-eyed, fair-skinned, and perfectly featured."

"Especially those two." Lydia turned to the wall and pointed to the image of Hendrick's two daughters—the photo Onna had surprised him with the week prior. Yet even Sabine's smile could not make up for the forlorn look on Stella's face.

Poor child. Soon, Stella. Soon you will forget that dark past.

"Are they handling the adjustment well?" Lydia tucked a blonde strand of hair back into the knot at the base of her neck and turned to the files stacked on Hendrick's desk.

"It will take time, especially for the younger one. Perhaps Onna was right. Perhaps we should have taken her to one of the children's centers first." He sighed, remembering Stella's screams. And his dream. *Or was it a memory?*

He glanced to the top file in his hands. More requests from German officers on the new frontier. And additional shipments to fulfill them.

"But still." He strode to his desk, which faced the room's lone window. "I couldn't bear the thought of parting with her. Once I'd chosen her, I had to have her close, lest she forget my position in her life."

Lydia responded with a soft smile and set about filing his important documents in the tall gray cabinets.

Hendrick studied the large oak just outside the glass and wondered about the new buds just starting to crack open. How good it would be to examine their unfolding. How wonderful to escape this desk and walk among spring's gifts. Yet the files, the reports, the requests could not wait. More important than Hendrick's curiosity and his longing for the outdoors was his duty to his country. To screen. To sift. To discover amongst the genetic muddle those racially valuable.

Hendrick sank into his leather seat and again looked at the faces on the wall. His chest grew warm with pride. He was their rescuer. The valuable blood in their veins had been preserved— no matter the means of coming by it.

Katrine rubbed her belly, imagining the baby inside, still having a hard time believing *she* would be a mother. She then turned her attention to the child in her care, hoisting the chubby toddler from the polished dark wood crib. Two plump arms wrapped tightly around her neck.

She carried one-year-old Arthur through the large, quiet house. Her shoes were the only sound echoing through the long hallways. That and Arthur's cooing attempts at words.

Who knew where the boys' parents were? Perhaps off for a day in the country or shopping at the boutiques still doing business despite the war. Mrs. Pfizer's "Mother's Cross," which hung over the dining room mantel, proclaimed that she'd birthed six offspring for the Führer. Yet Katrine hadn't seen the family all together once—even on weekends when the older children were home from school.

Perhaps the Führer was more concerned about German mothers birthing Aryans than raising them. Katrine's mind wandered to her grandmother's round, joyful face and her father's deep, sincere voice as he prayed over the Sabbat meal. A lump formed in her throat, and she quickly pushed those thoughts out of her mind.

Instead Katrine sucked in the warm spring air as she stepped outside onto the mansion's long driveway. She choked down nausea as she settled Arthur into his pram. "In you go, little guy." Last week Hedda, one of the maids, had overheard Katrine retching in the toilet and expressed her concern that she'd get the baby sick. Hedda no longer seemed to worry. Katrine had not confessed her condition, but no doubt the woman knew. She had seen the handsome SS officer walking Katrine home after their regular evening outings.

"Oh, quiet now. We'll be moving in a second." Katrine tucked the blanket around Arthur and pushed it toward Grote Markt, known to be one of the most beautiful squares in Belgium, and even all of Europe. The pram's wheels trundled over countless cobblestones as she enjoyed the figures atop the Maison du Roi, a Gothic style building with pointy spires jutting into the air. Yet the rest of the square seemed rather lifeless. Everything was crafted white and gray stone, causing her to ache for the pastel colored buildings of Prague's Old Town Square.

Was it only a few years ago she'd walked home from the synagogue, through the streets of the beautiful Czech capital, unafraid and content with her place in the world? Had that really been her . . . or some other girl?

Katrine—or rather, Rebecca—wasn't sure.

"Live," her father had told her. "For us, for our people, you must survive. And someday you will tell your children, my grandchildren, about our joys and our struggles. Do not allow our name to be forever lost."

Her father's dark head had bowed low, placing a kiss upon each cheek. Of course, his instruction had failed to consider *whose* child she would bear.

A grandchild of the great teacher Samuel Lodź conceived by a soldier of destruction? Katrine's stomach churned. She reached in her pocket for a hard biscuit.

A large German tank rolled down the street, interrupting her thoughts. The sidewalk beneath her feet rumbled, and she fanned her nose against the smelly exhaust. Its once shiny exterior was now dented and pocked with holes, yet she could not deny the machine's power. From the open hatch, a soldier lifted his hand in a *Heil Hitler* salute. Katrine quickly looked away, refusing to meet his gaze.

Instead she glanced at the pram, smiling at little Arthur's wide-eyed gaze as he watched the monster roll by. His head was bald, except for the light blond fuzz at the nape of his neck. Arthur smiled, showing his two front teeth, and his attention moved to the wood larks chirping in the ancient oak overhanging the boulevard. As they walked beneath, Katrine breathed in the scent of its new leaves just budding—the scent of spring was the same despite the war that waged.

This war that had altered her life's path. This war that caused her to betray father, mother, grandmother. And, most of all, betray herself. She never thought she would do such a thing. Never thought—

The stoplight changed, and Katrine pushed the pram more quickly now, as if in the vain attempt to escape her thoughts. Wasn't this the very thing Moses and the holy prophets spoke against— mixing the godly with the ungodly? Becoming one with an uncircumcised gentile?

Katrine spotted Hendrick waiting for her up ahead. His warm smile displaced her thoughts of the prophets' warnings. Instead of sitting on the park bench and reading news of the latest Nazi conquest, as he usually did during his lunch hour, Hendrick sat halfway up in a tree, studying the buds preparing to unfold into new leaves.

He smiled and waved, then jumped to the ground, straightening his shoulders and striding with straight-legged steps, the curious naturalist transforming into a soldier before her eyes.

On reaching her, Hendrick gently removed her hands from the pram and wrapped them around his waist, pulling her close. Katrine's face pressed against his rough, uniformed chest. She breathed in the spicy scent of his cologne, then shifted her head slightly and studied the embossed image on his gold buttons. The death's-head skulls smiled at her, mocking her. She closed her eyes and instead focused on his beating heart as she'd done so many times before.

The news phone rang, and Paul answered it as usual. But from the look on his face Mary knew it wasn't a news report coming in. Instead of pulling his pencil from behind his ear and scribbling notes, he glanced toward Mary and nodded. Then he set down the handset with a smile.

"It's those overseas government news service people. They want to see you right away . . . *sweetheart.*"

Mary straightened in the wooden chair and slid her fingers from the typewriter's keyboard. "But my deadline. I'm almost done." She glanced at the carbon in the machine, suddenly realizing she had no idea what she'd even been working on.

"Go now, will ya, kid?" Paul slid a cigar from his front shirt pocket and placed it between his lips, lighting it. The red glow bounced up and down as he spoke. "I'll finish it up for you. I can make up fluff as well as you can."

She still didn't budge.

Paul waved his hands toward the door. "What are ya waitin' for? From what I hear, they're not going to hold up the action until you get there. This is Europe we're talking about. The war. The big stuff. Now go."

Mary stood by her mom's side, shoulders straight, as the elevator carried them to the newsroom again. Yesterday she had watched all day long as men had hustled in and out of the room, pounding out stories, getting a call, and then running out to chase another lead.

They'd hardly noticed her tucked away in the corner, but that was okay. She liked watching the frenzied pace of the newsroom, the chaos of the reporters frantically trying to create the most gripping story possible. Wouldn't that be amazing, to write a story and then see people in restaurants reading it with their morning cup of coffee?

The elevator man opened the doors.

"Gerta!" a voice called to her mother as they stepped into the hall.

A thin woman with red hair and a pink suit approached and placed a hand on her mother's arm. "I just wanted to thank you for that tip. The red wine came right out—"

*Mary's mother cleared her throat, and the woman's words
stopped short.*

*"I'm glad my trick was useful. Have you met my daughter?
Mary, this is Yvonne. She's the secretary of, uh, one of the editors."*

*Yvonne took a step closer to Mary and lifted her chin. "What
beautiful eyes, child—the most amazing aqua color. In fact, I know
only one person with eyes like. . . ." Her words trailed off, and she
looked at Gerta. "There I go, putting my foot in my mouth again."*

*"Most people say she looks like me." Mother grabbed Mary's
hand and pulled her down the hall toward the newsroom. "Glad you
were able to remove that stain," she called back over her shoulder.*

*"Mother, wait. That lady said I look like someone. That I have
the same eyes. Did she know my father?"*

*Her mother brushed the blonde curls from Mary's shoulders. "She
did know him, and she does. And I knew that bringing you here
would lead to this." She took a deep breath and looked down the hallway. "Walk to that stairway and see for yourself. He always takes
the stairs.*

*"You don't need to talk to the man, but heaven help me if you
aren't old enough to see him. After all, I have to see him every day."
Her mother seemed to be talking more to herself than to Mary. "I
stand here and he sees me. Then he turns and just keeps walking."*

*The sound of footsteps echoed in Mary's ears, and she felt her
throat drop to the pit of her stomach as she turned to follow her mother's gaze.*

Mary arrived at the Main Office of Foreign Correspondents
with eager anticipation, out of breath from her quickened steps.

"Miss Kelley." The receptionist's face brightened as Mary
approached. "They're waiting for you in Conference Room One."

Mary glanced down at her disheveled skirt and knee socks,
and suddenly wished she'd kept her good suit at the office for an
occasion such as this. She quickly combed her fingers through the
large, loopy curls that fell just to her shoulders, took a deep
breath, and stepped into the conference room.

The director sat at the head of the table, and one other reporter sat beside him. Lee O'Donnelly.

Lee's lavender suit was freshly pressed. A pillbox hat sat upon her straight black hair, and she looked as if she'd just stepped out of one of New York's top salons—as she probably had.

"Mary Kelley, good to have you. Take a seat." Gerald Walker motioned to the chair on his right.

Mary sat, curling her legs to the side and hoping to hide her scuffed Buster Browns.

"Ladies, tomorrow morning the *Queen Mary* will set sail for England. I've asked six other reporters—male reporters—to be on board. And I'm extending the same offer to you."

Mary's fingers curled around the armrest, and she leaned forward in her chair, hanging on his every word.

"The foreign correspondents have decided that our nation needs more uplifting news of its boys. Too often V-mail is smudgy and hard to read—not to mention heavily censored. Family members are complaining. We're hoping that more correspondents will help get news to the folks back home. And we're not only eager for news of the front line, but news of our boys themselves—their life overseas, and how they're faring so far from home. That's why we've chosen the two of you."

Mary's lips lifted in a wide grin, and she had a sudden urge to jump out of her seat and give Mr. Walker a hug. Lee only nodded and smiled demurely, as if she'd expected this assignment all along.

"Now, just to let you know the command structure . . . authorization for your position comes from the European Theater of Operations U.S. Army. Officially, it's referred to as the ETOUSA, but most of the time it's just ETO." Mr. Walker folded his hands on the table in front of him, and his voice grew stern.

"Because the war department wants to keep tabs, every reporter and photographer moving into the war zone has to first be accredited to a particular branch of the service. Ladies, as of tomorrow you'll be considered part of the U.S. Army. We've already done extensive background checks on both of you." He flipped through the file folders on the table before him. "I see you both have taken it upon yourselves to receive overseas inoculations. Wise thinking. I like that initiative."

Mary cocked an eyebrow at Mr. Walker's words. She thought she'd been creative and ahead of the game—getting her shots in the mere hope of being accepted. She glanced at Lee. *Perhaps the high-society chick is smarter than she looks.*

Lee took the director's hands in her own. "Thank you so much for this opportunity, sir. I am honored to be asked to serve in this way." She held his hands for a moment before releasing them with a squeeze.

"And, Miss Kelley, do these arrangements agree with you?"

"Yes, of course. Wonderful. I agree it's a wonderful opponent—I mean opportunity. I'm thrilled to be chosen." She accepted Mr. Walker's firm handshake, but instead of proving her confidence, her sweaty palm flopped like a dead fish in his hand.

Mr. Walker cleared his throat. "Fine then, I'll see you both at the pier at 7:00 p.m. tomorrow. And pack light. You're lucky to get to hitch a ride with the troops. Don't make the officers regret their decision."

When the two women stepped into the hallway, Lee turned to Mary. Her smile disappeared like a light switch flipping off. "We may be colleagues, but don't think we have to be friends. And don't expect me to help you with your stories. I'll have my own to write. What you *can* expect is this: I'll fight for the front page. No hard feelings, of course." She gave Mary a half smile.

"No, Lee. No hard feelings. You're above that, aren't you? After all, you've been in the newspaper business for what, two weeks?" Mary turned and strode toward the staircase. Let Lee take the elevator. She'd walk.

As Mary strode away from the Main Office of Foreign Correspondents, she thought about how far she'd come. She'd always known that women could do anything as well as men, and the article she'd written a few years ago about Helen Richey, the first woman employed as an airline pilot, had been her first realization of that.

It was one of her first big assignments, and her mentor, Paul, had liked what he'd read. Said it was a good description of women in jobs normally held by only men, even though he'd teased that it was a fluke, that women would never be accepted into all the roles men claimed. She'd given him a big slug in the arm for that comment.

When Mary had read it to her mom that evening, deepening her voice for impact, her mother leaned forward on the sofa, nodding and smiling with each point, and ending with wild applause. That's why Mary didn't understand the next day when it showed up in print, it had been hacked in half and used as filler next to ads for denture cream and a "cure-all" tonic.

She'd gone to bed stone-faced, telling herself to suck it up, that all reporters must pay their dues. Her mother had made her favorite dinner, meat-loaf sandwiches, but it hadn't helped.

"I told you he doesn't care," Mary finally said as they sat on the stoop watching the local kids play kick the can in the street.

"Or maybe he cares too much." It was her mother's day off. Instead of wearing her hair up for work, it cascaded down her shoulders to the middle of her back. She looked younger, especially with the wistful gleam in her eyes.

"Yeah, right. And how's that? He cares so much that he's going to forever chain me to insignificant stories that are diced to pieces before being hidden away in obscure parts of the paper—"

"Hold it right there." Her mother held up her hands. Unlike her pretty face, they were old and raw from the chemicals she used to clean. "Do you think giving you special privileges would make you feel any better? I mean, what if you made the front page and everyone in the office knew it was because you were the editor's daughter?"

Mary lowered her gaze. "I guess I wouldn't like it."

They sat there silent, perhaps both thinking of what could have been.

CHAPTER FOUR

Lee slid her hands into the pockets of her sky blue traveling jacket, hoping to hide their trembling. Seven reporters were circled on the wooden pier, awaiting their orders to board the troopship *Queen Mary*. There were supposed to be eight reporters in total—isn't that what they'd been told? Yet someone hadn't made it.

Maybe whoever didn't show up had decided that reporting the news far from the tanks, big guns, and bombers was a better option. And perhaps it *wasn't* the nippy night air that caused the trembling to travel up her arms.

Thousands of GIs lined the pier, sweating in their brown wool uniforms. They laughed, joked, and shuffled along, lugging their bulging barrack bags with each step. Wandering among the troops were numerous Red Cross workers, handing out coffee and doughnuts. They laughed at the jokes and asked questions about the men.

The reporters and other officials waited off to the side, away from the ragged lines, but not far enough to miss out on the stench of sweat and cigarette smoke that joined with the saltwater air and heavy oil smell.

Lee covered her nose with her kerchief. She glanced at the correspondents as they chatted about the latest news of war and the families they were leaving behind. They laughed and joked like old friends, and most of them were—or at least acquaintances. Even that girl reporter, Mary Kelley, was nearly doubled over in laughter as one of them joked about a rookie reporter who mixed up his quotes, causing an uproar in city hall.

"He called the phone number he was given and assumed the man answering the phone was the mayor. It never occurred to him that it had been perhaps *too* easy to catch the big guy on the first try."

More laughter.

Lee glanced behind her, wondering where Jimmy was with her luggage. Then she looked to the gangplank, hoping they'd board soon. Anything to escape the torture of listening to this nonsense. Didn't they connect the dots and realize she'd only been working in hard news for a few months? That she could be considered a rookie? Or maybe that's why they did it—to put her in her place.

She said nothing, but the others glanced over every so often, and she imagined what they were thinking—*who does that Lee O'Donnelly think she is, taking the spot of someone more worthy?*

Lee opened her leather purse and reread the note from her brother one more time, hoping to distract her thoughts.

Safe passage and knock their socks off. You're a shining star. Glow bright. Glow long. And remember, it's not what you know, it's who you know that counts.

Love, Your Brother

On the second sheet of paper was a list of names and address of some of his close friends in England. "It's who you know," Lee whispered to herself, hoping it would prove as true overseas as it did here.

Then we'll see who will be ignoring whom, she smirked to herself. *And we'll see just who wants to be friends.*

A chill traveled up Mary's arms as she strode up the gangplank, a suitcase in each hand. A sailor walked behind her, hauling her prize possession, an Underwood typewriter that she'd saved up six months to buy.

The *Queen Mary* was a former luxury liner converted to a troopship. And so far her majesty's luck had been good as she made twice-monthly, highly nerve-racking, five-day crossings to South Hampton, England.

A thick cloud of cigarette smoke coiled around the deck. Equally as thick was the cacophony of men's voices as they called out to each other and banged around, taking their last breaths of fresh air and lumbering into the hold.

Mary had reported many crossings. She'd interviewed numerous young soldiers, then waved her good-byes from the dock. Now it was her turn.

She watched as Lee jotted notes in a small notebook, dressed as if she'd just stepped off a runway. Her trademark heavy gold bracelets clinked on her slender wrists as her pencil scribbled across the paper. Mary also noted how the woman's high-heeled black pumps nearly caused her to trip more than once—the pointy heels catching in the slits between the polished wooden floorboards.

She attempted to stifle a giggle as Lee marched past, wondering how that outfit would hold up in the field. Surely the woman understood there was no maid on the front lines to press her garments.

Once all had boarded, the liaison for the International News Services gathered their small group together, handing out room assignments and instructions for the trip.

The ship's horn blared and sailors swirled around them—men in motion—each busy at his assigned task. The New York skyline seemed to take on an ethereal glow in the sunset as the liaison spoke hurriedly in his high-pitched voice, as if afraid the ship would embark too soon, trapping him for the journey.

"In your rooms you'll find your press cards, uniforms, and contact information for the news service overseas," he said. "Any additional questions can be handled by the staff there. Enjoy the trip and make us proud. Remember, America hangs on your every word."

The sailor standing next to Mary led them to their cabins. The door he directed her to was partly ajar, and Mary kicked it open with her foot, attempting to balance her load of two small suitcases and the typewriter. The heavy machine nearly pulled her shoulder out of socket as she swung it into the room.

A soldier on deck had offered to carry it down the rest of the way for her, but Mary had declined. "You have your job to do, and I have mine. Besides, I'll need to get use to hauling this thing around Europe."

She dropped her suitcases on one of two twin beds and flopped onto the freshly laundered duvet cover. "Finally, alone," she muttered, kicking off her loafers.

"Not quite," a voice called from the open doorway. Lee entered with an entourage of sailors carrying her things. "In fact, *alone* won't be in your vocabulary for the next five days. I hope you don't snore."

Lee thanked the men, then paused, staring at the musette bags at the end of the bed. "Looks like they left us gifts."

Ignoring Lee, Mary dug into her bag. Helmet, fatigue outfit, green coveralls with white hood, a gas mask, insect powder, sunglasses, mosquito netting, a canteen, and gloves bearing a sticker stating they'd been treated for gas.

She held up the coveralls. "By golly, Lee. I think this color brings out the green in your eyes."

They finally embarked at midnight, the darkness protecting them from the German U-boats that lay in wait in the black waters just off the United States coastline. Unable to sleep, Mary tiptoed out of the cabin and joined another reporter at the rail, gaining one last glimpse of American soil. For more than an hour the ship maneuvered through the congested harbor, past the shipyards with their giant cranes, until finally turning out to the open seas. A few other night owls also lined the railings to watch the Manhattan skyline slip away.

Mary pulled her green field jacket tighter around her shoulders, shielding herself from the brisk salt spray.

"Well, if it isn't Goldilocks herself. What's wrong, Queen Mary? Your bed too hard? No, wait, too soft?"

Mary turned toward the curly-haired man whose thin moustache made him appear as if he had a dirty lip. He was handsome, she had to admit. In fact, Clive James from the *Herald* had a way with the ladies even more famous than his way with words.

She crossed her arms over her chest. "Actually, it's the snoring coming from the other bed. I only *wish* it were Baby Bear." Mary sighed. "But I suppose five days will pass soon enough. I mean, we're on a ship, crossing the ocean, heading toward adventure and real news. It's worth it, right?"

"Yeah, I'm excited about going, but I hope the war ends quickly. I'd rather be writing stuffy old business reports any day." Clive dug his hands deep into his pockets and stared at the floorboards of the deck as though his gaze could penetrate to the troops sleeping in the hold. "Overseas news doesn't count for much without bloodshed on one side or the other."

Mary cocked her head, surprised to find that Clive could actually be serious. Yeah, war was tough, but America was involved for a good reason, right? She didn't want to tell him that she hoped the war would continue for at least a little while. Long enough for her to witness some action and make a name for herself as a *top* overseas female correspondent.

Her gaze drifted over the dark waters. "It's weird, you know," she finally said, "that the bad guys are out there somewhere, lurking in these very waters." A shiver ran down her spine.

"You're right." He leaned farther over the railing. "From

here on out nothing is certain. Well, almost nothing." He scooted closer. "The war's heating up. Reporters are being sent into more dangerous situations every day. I'm sure you've read the stories of correspondents losing their lives. Word has it I'll be sent to cover the front."

His voice was solemn, and she almost heard a quiver in his tone. His hand moved from the rail to the top of hers, and suddenly Clive's serious nature made sense.

"Oh, you have to be joking!" Mary blurted out, her voice catching on the cold ocean breeze. "Schoolgirls may fall for that *I might never be coming back* business, but who do you think I am?" She took one last glance at the tall man, then stalked away. "News flash," she called over her shoulder. "I may look like I'm sixteen, but I know the games guys like you play."

It wasn't until she had nearly reached the stairwell that Mary noticed Lee standing in its shadows. For a brief moment, the white glow of a lighter flickered, illuminating her face.

"Barely out of port and already being pounced on." Lee took a drag and blew it out slowly.

Mary paused and watched as a sly smile curled the woman's lips.

"I suppose it's not what's lurking *out there*, in those waters, that we should be worried about," Lee continued.

Her own burst of laughter caught Mary by surprise. "Yeah, I guess you're right."

"Men. I swear they think one good line will make a woman swoon." Lee flicked her ashes to the deck. Her face had been washed clean of makeup, and her hair was pulled back in a tight bun. For the first time she seemed approachable.

A cool wind came up, and Mary pulled her jacket tighter around her thin frame. "I hope I didn't wake you, getting out of bed and all."

"Nah, I was awake. I guess this sharing a room will take getting used to." She took another drag from her cigarette and blew it out slowly. "Did I really snore?"

"More like heavy breathing, with a little nasal whine."

"Sorry. No one's told me that before."

Mary pushed the whipping strands of her hair off her face, wishing Lee would step out of the shadows.

"Oh, I've heard all about my sleep habits. Until I got my own apartment a couple years ago, my mom and I shared a bed." Mary chuckled. "We lived in a small apartment with drafty walls, and we stayed warmer by cuddling. It actually took some getting used to sleeping alone."

"Well, isn't that quaint." Lee tossed her cigarette to the deck and smashed it with the pointy toe of her shoe, and walked toward the railing.

Quaint? Mary felt a tightness in her chest as she headed down to their cabin alone. How could she expect Lee O'Donnelly to understand? Lee's mother never had to sweep up the cigar ashes or wipe the muddy shoeprints of a building full of careless workers, just to keep food on the table. And Gerta had done it without the help of the man in the large office on the third floor.

"Mother," Mary had gotten up her courage to ask one day, "how can you do it? How can you go back to work day after day seeing him there? Don't you ever wonder if things could have been different? Don't you imagine the life you could have had— we could have had—with him?"

Her mother seemed to be studying the ground. "At first, I guess I kept working there because I had hope. I thought he'd marry me, especially once he knew I was carrying his child." She took a deep breath. "But I kept going back because that place was all I knew. Besides, at least they knew . . . still know that he loved me once. I guess knowing that helped me to feel it wasn't just some dream."

"I would have always reminded you."

"I know, sweetheart. And you do. You're the best part of our rocky relationship. In the world's eyes, what happened may have been considered a thing of shame, but God can turn even the shameful things into good."

Mary got ready for bed, softly singing. *Jetzt kommt die fröliche. Sommerszeit, die. Stunden voller Lust und Wonne . . .*

"Now comes the merry summertime, the hours full of joy and endless delight. We leave behind our home, we freely, gladly roam. . . . So happy to be in the warm sunlight."

That's what I've done, Mary thought as she turned out the light, *left behind my home to gladly roam . . . although I'm not exactly heading for warm sunlight and endless delight.*

CHAPTER FIVE

The warm summer sun shone down on Katrine as she stretched out on the picnic blanket at Sablon Square. Now that the days were warmer, wandering through the cultural areas of Brussels had become Hendrick's passion. Even this moment, Hendrick stood in a wide-legged stance, his gaze intent on one of the forty-eight statues representing a medieval guild that lined the park. In this closest one, the statuary-man carried a ladder with a dozen birds perched on it.

The air smelled of freshly cut grass and the pink blossoms that grew on the hedges. Katrine didn't know their name, but they smelled like candy—a nice touch to the beautiful afternoon.

She lay on her side, resting her head on her hand, watching Hendrick. Her other hand instinctively caressed her stomach, which was already pushing out into a small bump. For the past few evenings she'd laughed to herself, feeling the fluttering of the child within. She lay extra still, hoping it would do the same today. She could already imagine the delight in Hendrick's eyes if he were able to feel the baby's kicks.

Hendrick moved to the next statue down the line, then turned ever so slightly in her direction. "Darling, I'm sorry we can't stay long today. I just heard this morning that I must go into work this evening. A new shipment will be arriving."

"A shipment, like of weapons?" Katrine's mind flashed to the uniformed German soldiers who'd guarded the streets of Prague, her home. Her stomach lurched at the memory of their shiny metal guns pointed at anyone wearing a yellow star.

"Weapons?" Hendrick laughed. "Katrine, how many times have I told you, my position is with RuSHA, Office for Race and Settlement. The shipment from Poland, my dear, is children— those we've found acceptable for Aryanization."

Katrine sat up, shielding the sun with her hand as she looked into Hendrick's face. "You mean children who are not German? I just assumed they were German orphans from the war." She shook her head. "I don't understand. Why would parents agree to send their children away?"

Hendrick moved toward her, squatted down, and took her hands in his. His face grew as cold and emotionless as the statues staring down upon them. "I told you my wife wasn't able to conceive, but my work made it possible for her to have two daughters. They're from Poland, but I assure you that by looking at them you'd never know the difference. What matters most, of course, is that they have no Jewish blood. It would never be proper to mix the holy with the unholy. We keep only what is valuable to our cause."

"And the rest? The children who are not pure?" Katrine pulled her hands from his.

"Let's not talk about that, shall we? It's such a beautiful day." Hendrick glanced away.

Katrine's stomach heaved. On hands and knees she quickly crawled across the grass, vomiting under a small shrub. Even when the retching stopped, the trembling of her shoulders and arms wouldn't cease. Surely she'd misunderstood. Surely . . .

She thought of her younger brother and sister, and a cry

caught in her throat. Abram and Ruth had been innocent, chubby toddlers the last time she'd seen them. Maybe she'd understood Hendrick's work before, but just hadn't wanted to believe it. Now she had to face the facts. Hendrick was involved in "eliminating" children. Beautiful children, like her brother and sister. Children like the one she carried inside her.

Katrine felt his hand upon her back, and she instinctively jerked away.

"Darling." Hendrick's voice was gentle. "Please forgive me; I'm a foolish man. I've forgotten your condition. We must get you out of this sun before you have heatstroke. Come, take my hand."

Without a word Katrine obeyed, allowing him to pull her up from the ground. He led her to his military vehicle, and she slid onto the leather seat and waited in silence as he returned to the manicured lawn to retrieve their picnic things.

As she watched him pack up the food and neatly fold the blanket, Katrine took in deep breaths, willing herself to calm down. But her mind refused to ignore what she'd just heard. *How can I do this? It's one thing to hide behind my blonde hair and fair skin to save my life, but . . .* A flutter tickled her middle, and she bowed her head. *But, little one, how can I hide my fear of his finding out about you?*

Eddie jumped from the army's uncovered six-by truck, where he and the others had been packed in like cattle, seated on benches with their personal gear piled in front of them. His boots smacked onto the asphalt runway with a thud, and he set his briefcase next to one of the stand lights, shaded for blackout conditions. Then he zipped his B-10 fleece-lined green jacket to his chin. Though not as stylish as his leather flight coat, it kept him warm. Just what he needed when huddling in the B-17's open-air fuselage at 30,000 feet, a virtual 30-below wind tunnel.

Besides, the jacket was nice protection from the rain present nine out of ten days here in England. It pelted windows, rattled tin roofs, dripped from ledges, and gathered into puddles and pools. Sometimes it fell in sheets, but thankfully today it lingered as a mist so fine Eddie couldn't feel the distinct drops.

Words drilled into him at navigation school ran through his head. *Five minutes of work on the ground takes care of thirty minutes of work in the air.* So after the briefing, he'd made his way to the navigators' ready room to lay out his charts for the mission. With maps spread over several big tables, he penciled in every checkpoint and course change—even the assembly and departure points and times over England. He also checked the flak-charts and drew crosshatched red circles corresponding to the danger areas they'd soon be flying over.

Eddie was the last crew member to arrive at the plane, just a few minutes before engine time. *Destiny's Child* waited patiently for him, and he glanced up at her with respect for the job she was about to do.

On the nose of the plane, her name was written in large yellow letters. A baby dressed in a diaper, reminiscent of the popular cartoon character Uncle Rafe, strode across the words, illustrating it. The baby had a pipe and carried a gun, and his face was set in determination as if he were off to get some Germans.

Above the script, bomb symbols had been painted—one for each mission *Destiny's Child* had flown with Eddie's crew and those who'd come before. Forward of the cranky baby, swastikas proudly displayed her kills. And though her patched-up body was evidence that those missions hadn't been easy, she wasn't about to give up. Even now the ground crew tended her like a prizefighter being readied for a championship match.

Eddie glanced around at the nine-man crew as they prepared for their third mission, and he realized how much he'd grown to appreciate them in the short time they'd been together—through flight training at the Overseas Training Unit in Kearney, Nebraska, and now the real thing.

In the dim glow of the shaded lights, Lt. Martin DeBorgia, the twenty-seven-year-old pilot and "old man" of their group, circled the plane for the preflight check and gabbed with the mechanics as if he were preparing for a Sunday drive. He was the most experienced of the group, having flown B-24s before being transferred to the 17s. Low-key and rugged, he was their calming factor, and despite his *It'll be fine* attitude, or maybe because of it, Eddie was grateful that Marty was leading them into battle.

Lt. Adam Haugan, the copilot, followed Marty around the plane, mimicking his every move to the stifled belly laughs of the rest of the crew. This boy-next-door nineteen-year-old with the peach-fuzz beard reminded Eddie of Mickey Rooney, which meant it was very hard to take him seriously.

Adam caught Eddie's gaze. Grinning under the attention, he continued to tail Marty, overemphasizing every gesture. As Marty stepped back to observe the patch job on the body of the plane, Adam did the same, shielding his face against the nonexistent sunlight and silently counting the patched shrapnel and bullet holes. Adam's eyes widened as the number increased.

Eddie couldn't hold back any longer, and let go a loud burst of laughter.

Marty turned and playfully punched his copilot's shoulder. "And this is what we have for second-in-command?" He grabbed Adam in a headlock.

Not far from their horseplay, Lt. José Garcia, their bombardier, climbed up to get a closer look at the engine. Eddie noted the jiggle of the ladder and hurried over, grabbing hold to steady it.

Trained as an airplane mechanic before the war, José was warm and outgoing. And his most prized possession, a photo of his wife, Maria, and their son, Manuel, peeked out of the top of José's jacket pocket as it did every mission.

"It never ceases to amaze me," he called out to anyone who cared to listen, "that such a huge hunk of metal could ever get us airborne. What a beautiful machine."

As Eddie steadied the ladder, T. Sgt. Carter Taft, the second youngest of the group, sidled up beside him, taking hold of the other leg of the ladder. If any of them could be considered a loner, it would be Carter. While others played cards or wrote letters home on their days off, Carter read English novels and jotted notes for the book he one day hoped to write.

A tough nut to crack, Eddie thought.

Yet during their missions, Carter was a different person. He came to life monitoring the power instruments and fuel consumption and operating the top turret with boyish enthusiasm. Even now his coal-black eyes brightened as the mechanics rolled the stands away from the plane.

José climbed down, and Eddie, shivering in the cold morning air, retrieved his briefcase. Inside were the tools of his trade, including a Weems plotter, pencils, and E-6B computer. Made of aluminum, the E-6B was small enough to slip into his jacket pocket, yet with it he could compute fuel consumption, distance-rate-time calculations, the effect of altitude and temperature upon indicated airspeed, and the effect of wind on the flight path of the airplane.

"Time to load up, boys." DeBorgia pointed to the craft as if he were a tour guide, and the guys lined up next to the hatch.

"Look, we're a chorus line," Sergeant Vinny Rosario called out, swinging his arms over the shoulders of the two guys closest to him.

Eddie chuckled as Vinny twirled around with a sway of his hips, emulating the dancing girls at the local pub.

When his turn came, Eddie swung his briefcase into the open nose hatch, then paused. A pink dawn now cast a warm glow over the air base, and just beyond the black asphalt strip of runway a herd of cattle grazed on lush, green grass.

Not far beyond that, a small English cottage sat seemingly undisturbed by the bombers preparing for flight. A single line of smoke wafted from the chimney, and Eddie knew that soon the farmwife would be out to milk the goat and gather eggs. It was one of the quaintest sights Eddie had ever seen, and he wished he could impress the image into his mind, just in case. . . .

He climbed in, pushing that thought away, and went about setting up the navigator's station. Through the window he noted S. Sgt. Wallace English, their ball turret operator, still outside pacing their staging area and rubbing his hands together.

Wally studied their B-17 as if checking off a mental list, and Eddie's stomach churned as he watched him. The belly-gunner's job was the most dangerous of all, his life depending on the ball-turret's overly intricate mechanism. Eddie was glad he wasn't the one hanging from the bottom of the aircraft in a plastic bubble.

Each man had a different way of handling the fear that greeted them at the hardstand. Some, like Marty, acted as if it weren't a big deal. Then there were those like Vinny and Adam, who ignored the gnawing fear by clowning around. Then there were others who refused to hide it. No mask could shield the apprehension in their eyes.

Eddie placed his logbook on the small workstation as Vinny's rendition of an English chorus loudly flowed out of the radio room. Always eager to help, Vinny had already assembled and checked Eddie's 50-caliber machine gun and brought along Eddie's parachute and helmet, saving him a trip to the equipment room.

In contrast to Vinny's singing, the three gunners filed past Eddie stone-faced and silent. Chancey Buckston, Glen Cromwell, and Reggie Mullans were the veterans of the group, having been part of a previous crew in the *Mississippi Maiden*, which was lost over France. They'd been assigned to a different crew that day—and had witnessed their plane being shot down.

Though four months had passed without word of their friends' fate, they still hoped the others would surface—Eddie saw it in their eyes whenever a new jeepload of men arrived at the base. But on days like today, those hopeful faces solidified into looks of resolve. If they didn't do their job, someone else would have to. Besides, each mission meant one less they'd have to do before reaching the required thirty.

Throughout the plane, the rest of the crew had finished setting up and checking their equipment, including guns, radio gear, ammo belts, and oxygen. Eddie did the same, finally donning his final layer of gear: the flak vest, two pair of gloves, helmet, oxygen mask, and throat mic.

As usual, Vinny had also laid out Eddie's seat-pack parachute on the 50-caliber ammunition box that served as his chair in front of the navigator's table. As he secured the chute's system of straps and snapped the helmet strap under his chin, Eddie's mind couldn't help but flash back to the previous raid.

Their fighter escort had barely gotten them across the Channel when their aircraft was forced to return to base due to a mechanical problem. As they retreated, instead of spotting a neat formation of planes out the tail window, cruising their way over France, they instead witnessed scattered scores of parachutes floating downward—evidence of a slaughter they'd barely missed.

The crews who'd left Bassingbourn that day full of expectation, and part of a trusted team, had been left to fend for themselves. And if it weren't for a sputtering engine, Eddie's crew would have wound up in the midst of it. Fighting. Falling. And then attempting to somehow make it back across enemy lines.

That night they'd been the lucky ones sleeping—or at least attempting to sleep—in the comfort of their own barracks with photos of their loved ones peering down at them from the rickety shelves above their beds.

Who knew what the other guys had faced? Were they still running from the Germans? Had they been captured? Had they even made it to the ground alive?

At the appointed time, *Destiny's Child* taxied out to position in the long line of thirty-seven B-17s waiting to take off. There was one extra plane for the possible abort or early loss. And it was anyone's guess how many would return that evening.

They approached the head of the runway, turned onto its center line, and Eddie felt the brakes set. Even though he couldn't see the pilots from his position, in his mind he watched them checking gauges once more, an arm reaching out, the hand grasping all four throttles and pushing them all the way to their stops. The engines roared to full power, and he imagined them waving to the guys at the tower and closing the cowl flaps to reduce drag.

He scooted the ammunition-box chair forward as the brakes

released and the aircraft started to roll, slowly at first, then picking up speed, hurling down the runway. His hands gripped the edge of the navigation table, which was fastened to the wall of the plane. As they approached their minimum airspeed, the tail wheel lifted off the runway, and soon the entire aircraft was no longer earthbound.

There was very little chatter on the interphone as the plane lifted from the ground and skimmed the trees at the end of the runway. Eddie let out a slow breath as thirty-seven B-17s were airborne in a matter of minutes. Their next task was to form into squadrons. During the briefing, the pilots had been told at what time on an imaginary clock the squadron would form and at what altitude and distance from the field the lead plane would be hovering.

Today, as they slowly climbed, Eddie and the other crew members watched for flares to be fired from the lead plane as a signal for the others to take their places in the formation. Within a minute, two red flares and one green—the signal of the 324th squadron—burst in the air like shots out of a Roman candle. *Destiny's Child* slid into her assigned position on the right wing of *Sky Blazer*, which was leading the left three-plane element.

A day's work was about to begin, and Eddie glanced at his watch, jotting down the assembly time. *Right on schedule.* It was simply one of the first entries in the day's logged events.

When he had finished writing, Eddie prayed a silent prayer that even though they flew through the valley of death, the Lord would be with them. To guide. To protect. To bring them home.

Hendrick tucked the keys to the flat in his pocket and walked through the living room and down the hall to the first door on the right. He clicked on the lamp. Light flooded the room, and his eyes fell on the oak cradle in the corner. He caressed the smooth wooden frame, remembering his spontaneous trip to the furniture store the day Katrine announced her pregnancy. He'd chosen this cradle above the rest. Appreciated the swastika carved near the head of the bed. Only the finest should rock his child.

For months it had taken all his self-control to keep this flat a secret from Katrine. A hundred times, as they'd walked down the boulevard arm in arm, he'd wanted to point to the third-story window and confess his gift. *See what things are given to those who give their greatest gifts to their country.*

Still he'd waited, wanting everything to be perfect. Just this morning he'd planned on wrapping the key to the front door in a box for her birthday. But now?

Hendrick pushed the crib violently, knocking it to its side, the image of Katrine's condemning gaze bearing down on his mind. The horrified look had flashed in her eyes the moment he'd explained the shipment of children. Instead of pride in his work, there'd been distaste—no, revulsion—in her eyes.

"Does she not realize I do this work for our child?" he shouted, not caring if the neighbors heard him through the walls. "It is my work for all the generations to follow, including the generation of our offspring!"

Hendrick's fist slammed into the light-blue painted wall. Pain shot through his knuckles and up his arm. He bared his teeth and shook his hand, the memory of the Reichsführer's words confirming his righteous task. *"One only possesses a land when even the last inhabitant of this territory belongs to his own people."*

How many times had Himmler said those words? How much time, effort, pain had Hendrick sacrificed to fulfill just that?

And now? *Doesn't she realize those shipments represent lives redeemed?*

Hendrick shook his hand harder as he strode from the room, slamming the door behind him and refusing to pay attention to the swelling knuckles. The living area was lit with a single lamp, yet the warm glow over the exquisitely furnished room mocked him. Instead of seeing a symbol of his favor, the place proved his stupidity in placing his affection in the hands of someone who lacked understanding.

Katrine has no idea what sacrifice means, Hendrick thought, striding to the phone. He sank down onto the cushioned wing-back chair, realizing he had work to do still—even at this late hour.

He lifted the phone and asked the operator to connect him to his office. A smile curled on his lips as Lydia's soft voice answered.

"Have they arrived?"

Lydia's voice hinted of weariness. "They're here. But it's late now, and . . ."

Hendrick interrupted. "I'll be there in fifteen minutes. Tell the guards I wish for the children to await my arrival," he stated in a commanding tone. "I'll do the final inspection myself, tonight. Not one of them lies down for the night in the comfort of a state home until I confirm their worth!"

The brick offices looked different in the light of the moon, Hendrick realized, as he took the front steps two at a time. Even before he opened the doors, the children's whimpers met him, grating on his nerves.

One day they will appreciate how I saved them, how I kept their blood from crying from amongst the ashes. They would have no hope, no future, if it weren't for me.

Instead of moving down the hall toward his office, Hendrick turned to the left into the reception area. Lydia waited with two transport guards. Over a dozen children lined the wooden benches, yet despite the late hour, none of them slept. Instead they huddled together, filthy from travel, eyes wide with fear. Thankfully, his uniformed presence was enough to halt their cries.

Hendrick moved to the child closest to the door. One of the guards approached, pulling the boy to his feet and holding him tight.

"Age?"

"We assume seven, Officer Schwartz."

Hendrick grabbed the boy by the chin and tilted it toward the light.

Blue eyes. Well spaced.

He jerked the face to the right, then left, to examine the profile.

Hendrick didn't need to compare the child's features with the charts hanging on the walls to know the size and shape of this boy's nose fit well within the specifications.

"Stretch your arms, boy!" Hendrick lifted his arms in example, knowing the child couldn't understand his words. The boy's shoulders trembled, and he muttered something Hendrick couldn't understand. Yet he mimicked Hendrick's actions, and his frame appeared strong.

"Fine, good specimen. Perfect for Nazi Youth," he stated to Lydia, who was taking notes. With determined steps, he moved to the next child in line.

An older girl, nearing puberty, clenched a toddler to her chest. The older one's nose was slightly hooked, and her hair was darker than what he usually saw in shipments.

"Sisters?" Hendrick asked, noting black-and-blue bruises on the older child's face.

"No. Neighbors, we believe." One of the transport guards poked at her shoulder. "The older child put up quite a fight. She refused to release the younger one to us. We thought it was easier to bring her along."

Hendrick squatted to get a look at the toddler. Her face scrunched, and she burst into tears as he neared. But even still he could tell she was as Aryan as they came—in fact, she looked almost as if she could be related to his own Stella.

"The younger one is good. Send her to the Ardennes home. The older one—well, that's your problem."

Hendrick paused as the words replayed in his mind. *Ardennes home . . . Lebensborn.* The place designed for mothers-to-be to be cared for. The place for children to receive the best upbringing under the guidelines of the Nazi state.

Why didn't I think of that before?

Hendrick knew what he had to do, but first he focused his attention back on the work at hand. He continued down the line, scrutinizing with swiftness and skill.

"Fine shipment. Good work, men." He gave a straight-armed salute, then hurried toward his office. Already Hendrick's mind was calculating which German families on his list should be first to receive a child once the Germanization was complete.

Herr and Frau Hiedl wish for a third. That first boy might be a good fit.

And intermingled with those thoughts were plans for his own trip to the beautiful Ardennes home. Wegimont bei Lüttich.

"Officer Schwartz?" It was Lydia's voice that halted his steps. "Do you need me for anything else?"

Hendrick turned and noticed she'd changed her attire since earlier today in the office. Her gray work jacket had been replaced by a red sweater that clung to her curves.

"Actually, I was hoping you could help me with a few files." Hendrick unlocked his door and turned the knob. Lydia followed, and his heart pounded at her nearness.

Sounds of movement drifted down the hall. More cries. The shuffling of feet. Shouts of guards. Then the screams of the older girl and the toddler's cry.

"You'd think one girl wouldn't cause so much commotion." Hendrick's voice was husky.

"They'll be fine." Lydia smiled. "See, they have her outside already. They should have her in the van any minute. Then we will not be forced to consider her again." She took a step toward him.

Lydia was pretty in a simple way. And though she did not have the stunning beauty of Katrine, there was something about her that intrigued Hendrick. The light of the hall hit her face, and he dared not turn on the office lamps for fear of breaking the trance.

Yes, that is it. The key to her beauty. Hendrick focused on her blue eyes. Large, round . . . adoring.

"Officer Schwartz." She lifted an eyebrow. "Don't you think we could work on those files tomorrow? I should get home, and I was hoping you would walk me."

"You're right." He stepped back into the hall, motioning her to follow. Then he allowed the door to click shut behind him. "On one condition."

"What's that?"

"You tell me your birthday."

"I just had it, last month. I'm twenty now. Why do you ask?"

Hendrick shrugged, then offered his arm to her. "Oh, nothing. I have a gift I hope to give to someone, someday." He patted her hand on his arm. "A gift for a special woman, appreciative and worthy."

The army jeep jerked to a stop, and Mary stared wide-eyed at the ornate, gray stone structure that rose before her. Nothing had prepared her for this; she'd expected to be housed in some army tent encampment.

"The Savoy? I can't believe it. Do you realize the Russian Prima Ballerina Anne Pavlova first danced in cabaret here? I've read about this place, but never imagined I'd see London—let alone stay at the Savoy." She jumped down from the back of the jeep, since there was no rear passenger door, and looked up at the face of the world-renowned hotel, shielding her eyes from the noon sun.

"Oh, yes, Pavlova. I saw her dance here in '29." Lee waited in the jeep until the army private jumped from the driver's seat. With a very southern "There y'are, miss," he extended his hand to help her out.

Lee cast a sweet smile. "Yes, I think it was her last season before her death. I was too young to appreciate it really. I fell asleep halfway through the performance."

Mary rolled her eyes. "Oh, yes, Pavlova, " she muttered, then swung her musette bags over her shoulder and stalked toward the front door. Inside she was welcomed by a refuge of Victorian elegance. Plush burgundy carpet, polished wood furniture, and artwork worthy of a gallery. Only instead of tuxedoed men and elegantly dressed women, the Art Deco mirrors reflected the hurried movement of American military men and women.

Somehow Lee's trunk and two suitcases were unloaded and stacked in the hotel foyer in less then a minute. Surprised, Mary turned to see a group of young soldiers circled around the elegant reporter. With a small wave, Lee dismissed them, assuring them the porters would take her things the rest of the way to her room. Then she approached Mary, scanning the room with one upraised eyebrow.

A distinguished-looking porter with Winston Churchill jowls approached, handing Lee and Mary slips of paper with the room assignments. "The lady reporters. Two beautiful starlets. Come, follow me."

Mary readjusted the bags hanging from her shoulders and followed the porter and Lee through the lobby and up the elegant staircase, anticipating Lee's reaction when she discovered what Mary had already figured out.

The porter opened one door and handed them each a key.

Lee turned to Mary, her smile fading. "You too?"

She nodded. "Me too."

Lee moaned, then handed the porter a tip, shooing him away. "I knew it—that they would see us as a package deal." She kicked open the door with a force Mary wouldn't have expected, and it banged against its stop, bouncing halfway back. "Can't just send one naïve reporter over the big, bad seas, can we? Have to make sure there's someone there to buddy up with." Lee strode inside and set her handbag on the bed closer to the window.

Mary took two steps in and did a small turn, taking in the rose-patterned walls, velvet drapes, and fluffy feather pillows. Then she hurried to the window. "Is that the Thames?"

Lee barely glanced up as she tugged off her uniform cap. "Yeah, I suppose." She undid her French twist and let her dark locks fall past her shoulders.

"Do you, uh, mind if I have the bed by the window?" Mary quickly unhooked the latches and pried it open, eager to get a better look at the famous British river. "I would just love to write Mom that I was having English tea overlooking the Thames."

The chill from the window caressed Mary's cheek as she gazed down at the river below, then beyond to the city. While evidence of bombings could be seen in every direction, the thought of exploring one of the places she'd visited in the pages of a novel caused her stomach to flip. Her mind raced as she considered where to visit on her first day off: Piccadilly Circus, Downing Street, Scotland Yard, Houses of Parliament.

"Sure. Have the window." Lee snatched up her handbag and strode across the room to the matching twin bed. "Knock your socks off. I don't plan on sticking around this joint very long anyway."

"And just where do you plan on going?"

"The front lines, of course."

"Of course." Mary stood, prancing to the door. She flipped her shoulder-length blonde hair, mimicking Lee. "And I'm going someplace too. To dinner."

By the time she returned from eating downstairs, the place looked as if Lee was planning an extensive sojourn. On the desk a stack of white paper, a cup with pens, and a blotter had been arranged. In the center of it all, a Hermes Baby typewriter.

The nerve! Mary thought. *She's not the only writer in this room.* A sarcastic complaint popped into her mind, but she stopped short when she glanced at Lee, who hadn't turned when Mary entered. Her slumped shoulders suggested that maybe this wasn't as easy for her as she let on.

It was only their third bombing run—this one over Belgium—yet from the moment *Destiny's Child* flew through the clouds during assembly, Eddie knew it would take a miracle to get them home.

The mission began on the ground with intermittent haze. But as they rose, attempting to reach their desired altitude, the cloud cover was thick, making visibility difficult. No, make that nearly impossible.

Eddie pressed his oxygen mask to his face, breathing deep slow breaths. *Keep your eye on your wingman,* he wanted to tell the pilot over the interphone. *Don't lose sight of your wingman.*

Midair collisions during assembly were a common fear due to

the gray mountains of clouds that deterred visibility. It was painful enough to lose a crew due to enemy fire, but losing them because of weather was a double blow.

The haze thinned slightly and the oxygen in Eddie's mask began to flow easier—or at least it seemed that way as his beating heart calmed.

Then, just as they were able to break through the clouds into the bright, clear sky above, a reverberating quake and a brief glow of light confirmed his worst fears. One plane had collided with another, evidenced by shredding plane parts spinning through the air. Cries of anger and disbelief, and a battery of expletives, traveled through their interphone.

Eddie's eyes scanned the skies, watching in horror as the fire and metal fell like solid rain. He desperately hoped for chutes to open, but saw none. He tried to remember which of his friends were flying in that formation. His mind stopped on one. *Clifford.*

The redheaded airman had been the first to greet him at Bassingbourn. The memory of Clifford's solemn smile filled Eddie's mind, but he forced himself to shake it away, remembering the task at hand.

By the time they crossed into Belgium hours later, flak was heavy in the sky. And they still had a long way to go to make it to the Evere Airdrome north of Brussels, in the heart of the Nazi-occupied lands.

Eddie's stomach tightened as *Destiny's Child* was rocked by nearby explosions. It was the worst flak they'd encountered yet, and bursts of black, greasy smoke hindered visibility.

Then something felt different. Their plane vibrated like a bucking bronco as the copilot's voice filled Eddie's ears: "Problem on two. Manifold pressure's gone. Oil pressure's dropping. Feather the number two engine. Feather the number two engine!"

Eddie had first heard about feathering during training in Texas. When the engine was hit, it was necessary to change the pitch of the propeller blades as a means of stabilizing the plane. If it wasn't done quickly enough, it would cause a terrible drag and a spin.

As he jotted it down in his log, Eddie imagined the pilot's and copilot's hands moving fast, switching off the throttle, fuel, oil pump . . . and dozens of other toggles. The vibration lessened as the blades rotated with their edges facing into the wind.

He let out a sigh of relief, remembering the horror stories of what could happen if the blades failed to feather. It would have caused an almost impossible drag on the plane, making *Destiny's Child* unable to keep up with the formation and a prime target for the German fighters.

Flak continued to burst around them, sounding like heavy rain hitting the aircraft, and he could feel the three remaining engines struggling to keep up. This was it. They weren't going to make it the rest of the way. Eddie knew the other bombers would have to go on without them. Their only chance was to turn around and head back to the Channel.

"Eddie, it's up to you. I need the mag heading to take us home." Marty's voice echoed in his ears.

The burden of responsibility pressed heavier than even the three layers of clothing and the flak jacket Eddie wore.

More pounding of debris, more shouts from the other crew members warning of enemy fighter planes, sweeping down from out of nowhere.

"Germans to the north. The south. They're coming from every direction!" Wally cried through the interphone.

A sharp pain hit Eddie's chest, and at first he thought he'd been hit. But when he looked down and spotted no blood, he realized the pain was caused by the extreme pounding of his heart. Fighting for control, he pushed the fear from his mind and told himself that if he messed things up this time, nine other men would die.

Lord, help me.

"Eddie, are you there?"

"Yeah, Marty. Just doing my calculations."

Eddie reviewed the charted course with his Weems plotter and checked the wind drift on the back side of his E6-B computer to determine magnetic heading. Within a minute or so he blurted the mag heading through the interphone, and the pilot maneuvered the sputtering machine into submission.

"We can make it home on three engines, but we've got to drop the bombs over the Channel."

Eddie glanced at the bombardier, who was close to him. The oxygen mask covered Vinny's face, but he could make out the anxious eyes that peered out through the goggles.

Then, as they turned for home, the German fighters seemed to disappear into thin air, making it seem as if they'd never been there at all. The minutes ticked past, and they waited and watched, hoping the remaining engines would hold. Hoping the German fighters were gone for good. And maintaining silence over the interphone aside from necessary communications.

The closer they got to England, the more the heaviness eased from Eddie's chest. He'd done his job and had gotten them home. He'd never seen a prettier sight than the airfields that resembled dozens of toy triangles tossed out upon a green-and-yellow carpet. In fact, in the thirty-mile radius around Bassingbourn there must have been twenty-five bases. Yet the pilot set his sights on theirs.

When the bomber's wheels finally hit the ground, Eddie sucked in a sigh of relief, yet he couldn't stop his jaw from chattering. When the plane finally stopped and the engines cut, crew members climbed from the bomber and circled around to view the damaged engine.

"Look here," José called, peering into the smoking engine. "We're in luck. The fuel lines are busted, but I think she's fixable. Looks like *Destiny's Child* will be up in the air again soon after all."

Air-raid sirens blared, and Hendrick's gaze met Lydia's worried expression from across the office. They moved to the door, and he grasped her elbow, leading her through the mass of people.

"The RAF?" someone called, cursing.

Hendrick straightened his shoulders, refusing to give in to the panic. His feet maintained an even gait.

"No, Americans," another answered. "I can tell by the sound of those engines."

Shoulders brushed against him. A sob escaped the lips of the woman to his right. To his left, Lydia kept pace, her face fixed ahead.

Good girl.

With swift strides they moved down the long hall, descended the stairs, and moved through the wide doors to the air-raid shelter below their offices.

"Americans, all the worse," Hendrick spat out as they entered the room packed with people and illuminated by two bare light bulbs. Though fifteen years had passed since Hendrick had studied at the Kaiser Wilhelm Institute of Anthropology, Human Genetics, and Eugenics in Berlin, images of the various races of Americans flashed through his mind—Negros, yellow Japs, Jews . . . a "melting pot," the Americans claimed. *Genetic sludge,* Hendrick countered.

He turned to Lydia. "The stronghold of the devil himself, America is." He pointed to a space on a far bench. "Their tainted blood will be their downfall, just you watch."

"Hendrick, do you think they'll hit the city? Or maybe . . . well, my parents live near the airfield—a prime target."

His own thoughts were on Katrine and the safety of his child. *She's fine,* he convinced himself. *I'm sure she's found refuge in the nearest shelter even now.*

The ground shook under their feet in short bursts. Dust filled the air, stirred by the movement of people packed around them and by the shaking of the building's foundation.

Hendrick coughed, swatting at the spinning particles with his hand. "They're fine. Do not worry, pet." He spoke into Lydia's ear only loud enough for her to hear. "After all, the Americans are fools."

His voice grew louder. "They bomb during the day, making perfect targets for our big guns." The ground under his feet shook again. "Feel that? It's our 88s, knocking them from the sky."

Boom. The guns fired from somewhere near the perimeter of the city.

"One aeroplane lost," he said.

Boom. The guns sounded again.

He took Lydia's hand in his own and squeezed. "Two aeroplanes lost . . . "

Lydia attempted a smile, and Hendrick gently chucked her chin with his free hand.

Boom. Another tremor.

"Three," Lydia said, leaning her head against his shoulder. "Bye- bye, GI."

The rest of the day, Eddie's crew lounged around the barracks and played the waiting game. Waiting for word on how many planes and crews had been lost. Waiting for the others to hobble back. Hoping they all would.

As the minutes ticked past, Eddie showered, changed into clean fatigues, and ate lunch. Then, one by one, the planes started arriving. Each one brought a sense of relief, but also strong foreboding for the others who hadn't come back.

By 1800 hours all the planes had returned, or had been counted as lost, except one. Tired of waiting and wondering, Eddie decided to check the mail room. Tugging his cap down over his close-cropped dark hair, he strode out the door of their hut, hoping to find a letter from home. It eased his tense stomach, somehow, to read letters that told about new calves birthed and progress of the crops. At least *those* green fields were untouched by the war.

As he walked toward the mail room, he witnessed the crews as they straggled out from interrogation. After each mission, they had to be debriefed. Some dragged out of the room tired and listless, no doubt having to report their eyewitness accounts of planes shot down. Others were buoyant and loud, wanting to talk and recount the drama in the sky. Eddie'd experienced both before.

"Hey, Ed," Marty called as he jogged in from the airfield.

"Good news. *Lady Liberty* is crippled but attempting to make it over the Channel. Should be here before long."

They caught a ride to the airstrip, where groups of men gathered a safe distance from the edge of the runaway. Fire engines and medics were also lined up, waiting. Eddie couldn't help but notice how everyone spoke in low tones and shifted their weight from foot to foot as they watched the sky.

Then, in the distance, a gray metal speck drifted down through the clouds. Three red flares burst into the air. The message was clear: *The radio's not working, wounded are on board, have an ambulance ready.*

She circled close to the runway. Eddie knew the pilot wanted the emergency crew to view their damaged landing gear and prepare for a "gear-up" landing. Thankfully, the turret gunner had escaped from his Plexiglas bubble on the bottom of the aircraft. Eddie had heard horror stories of men trapped inside the bubble with the pilot having no choice but to do a belly landing in order to save the other men.

The blades of one of *Lady Liberty's* outboard and one inboard propeller were feathered.

"Flying catawumpus," the guy standing next to Eddie said.

Eddie shielded his eyes. "Doesn't look so hot, does she?"

Lady Liberty completed her circle, aligning with the runway, floating toward them impossibly slow, head up and on the verge of stalling. She passed over the runway's near end, her tail just feet above the pavement. Her horizontal tail stabilizers must have picked up some ground-effect lift, because her nose began coming down.

Suddenly she could fly no farther, and flopped onto the pavement, trailing showers of sparks. A second later the sickening sound of metal scraping against pavement hit Eddie. With his mind riding along inside *Lady Liberty*, every muscle in his body tightened even more.

The flying sparks and screeching metal seemed to continue forever as she slid by center field, but the damaged plane finally groaned to a stop.

The ambulances and fire crew were at her side within seconds. Eddie and dozens of others ran toward the injured bird, as much to relieve their tension as anything. A few yards away they stopped to watch, hearts pounding, as medics first passed a man with a gashed thigh through the aft door. Next came a man trying to walk on his own, his left hand wrapped in bloody rags. The men inside passed another injured man out the door, his bleeding head lolling in unconsciousness. More men, pierced and broken, were pulled from the aircraft.

And from the look of the bullet-riddled B-17, Eddie was amazed they'd made it back at all.

CHAPTER SIX

Nothing looked familiar to Eddie, not even the snow-covered ridge nearby. He could see his breath, now that daylight was fading. The clear sky meant a real cold night, but his father and brother would find him before then, wouldn't they?

His father had been unsure about taking Eddie along, but Eddie'd promised, and whined, enough to gain a small space in the pickup beside his brother. The morning had started out fun— bundling up like a real hunter, riding into the hills with the guys, walking along the trail behind his father, imitating his every move. But his eight-year-old legs could keep up for just so long. First, his bratty brother Richard teased him about falling behind. Then he complained that Eddie was holding them up.

His father glanced back at him, annoyed, and Eddie struggled to pick up his pace. That satisfied everyone for a few minutes—until he began asking why they had to walk so far. Couldn't they have driven farther? Couldn't they at least slow down a little?

His father wheeled around, and Eddie felt the heat of his glare.

"Head back to the truck, son. I can see it from here." His father had pointed through the trees toward the blue pickup standing out against the snowy hillside. *"There's hot cocoa in the thermos. We're going to scope out this next ridge; then we'll meet you there."*

They had walked for hours, or it seemed that way. How could the truck be so near? Obediently, Eddie began the short walk back to the truck—at a reasonable pace.

What should have taken a half hour dragged on, and Eddie knew he was in trouble. Everything was white—the trees, the ground, the mountains rising in jagged peaks on the horizon—the only color was the big, blue Montana sky. And when the sun finally dropped below the mountains, he felt frozen to the bone.

Unable to take another step, his jaw chattering and ice caked to his lashes, Eddie hunkered down by a tree and waited. Dad would come, he knew it.

Stars began showing themselves in the darkening sky. If only he'd paid attention when his father had tried to tell him how to navigate by them.

Eddie's nose tingled, and he fought back tears—eight-year-old boys weren't supposed to cry when things got bad. But they came against his best efforts.

Suddenly, he saw bright pink through his eyelids, and he squeezed them tighter. "Ed . . . Eddie!"

The voice didn't belong to his father or brother. "Eddie, wake up . . . the whole barracks'll hear you blubbering."

"Take that blasted light off my face, Vinny." Eddie tried to knock it away, but his hand hit only air. "I was just dreaming."

"Dreamin' with your blanket kicked off. You tryin' to get the Golden Ticket home by catching pneumonia?" Vinny's gruffness couldn't hide the concern in his voice. "Yer shiverin' like a stupid Chihuahua-dog."

"I was back in the Montana hills, getting myself lost again. I remember hunkering down, trying to stay warm, and watching the stars. They could've guided me back to Dad's truck, if I'd known how to use 'em. I promised myself right then that I'd learn to find my way by looking at the stars, just like the old-time explorers."

"Yeah, that explains a lot." Vinny playfully slugged Eddie's shoulder. "Reveille's in twenty minutes. I'm gonna grab a couple more winks."

Eddie thought about his life, and where that early training had gotten him. His knowledge of the sky had been one of the reasons he'd chosen to ride as a navigator. God had designed order to this world, and discovering that design would help him find the right path—whether by night or, as in the Army Air Corps bombers, by day.

"Trust in the Lord with all thine heart; and lean not unto thine own understanding," Eddie whispered in the quiet night. "In all thy ways acknowledge him, and he shall direct thy paths."

On days when weather had kept them from school—which was often in the winter months in northwest Montana—his mom had taught him, his sisters, and brother some book learning of her own design. She'd gathered them around the kitchen table and drilled Bible verses into their heads. He only hoped this favorite verse applied to B-17 bomber crews, and to their scared and lonely navigators.

Lee wandered through the half-empty market, trying to find something to calm her growling stomach. *There's just got to be more to this country than the newsroom.*

"Tea," she mumbled. "Aren't they supposed to have tea around here?"

They'd only been in England a few days, and she'd ventured out to catch the warm rays of spring, gas mask swinging next to the satchel on her arm—even if it did mean someone else would get assigned today's top story. To get to the market she walked through a lot of bombed areas, some blocks completely flattened. Even Buckingham Palace, she'd heard, had an entire wing leveled. She couldn't imagine such a thing ever happening to the White House. Yet instead of moaning about their fate, the English continued on with determined efficiency.

She walked past a white cross someone had planted in front

of a leveled apartment building. *Jonathan, Evelyn, George* had been painted in shaky script, and Lee wondered if perhaps a mother had written the names of her lost children. Yet even if she knew the story, it would simply be one of many. So much loss, heartbreak, and especially change. As she scanned the sea of people walking around the market, it seemed the entire island had been taken over by Yanks.

Unlike home, where she couldn't walk a block without turning at least one head, here Lee moved through the crowd of mostly soldiers and middle-aged women and received barely a passing glance. Officially part of the Women's Auxiliary Army Corps, she wore a khaki shirt and slacks, tie and cap, accented by a green armband with a single C for *correspondent*. There were a dozen different uniforms represented in the Piccadilly marketplace that morning, but somehow they made everyone look the same.

Lee approached a vendor selling an array of baked goods and handed the woman a pound note for fresh bread. The smell reminded Lee of breakfast on Saturday mornings when her father returned from his morning walk with a treat from the corner bakery. Lee smiled, yet the woman didn't even make eye contact as she handed over the small loaf and some change and moved on to the next customer.

Lee's grin faded. She carried the bread to an empty bench, folded back the paper bag, and tore off a chunk with her hands. She shoved it into her mouth and chewed slowly. *Here's to you, Mother,* she thought, realizing how horrified her mother would be to see her eating in such a manner.

Before she realized it, Lee had eaten all of the loaf as she watched the customers interacting with the vendors in a variety of accents—half of which barely resembled English, or at least an English she could understand. She watched young girls batting their eyelashes and flirting with the GIs.

"Feelin' lonely so far from home, aren't ya?" she heard one girl say. "I'm free tonight."

Lee knew what these girls were up to—a free dinner and

maybe a movie show to boot. There was nothing fashionable about them. Faded dresses hung on thin frames, and their oxfords looked as if they'd been patched together one too many times. Yet the GIs didn't seem to mind, and wandered off arms linked with the young women.

Then Lee spotted something that caused her to sit up. Two young girls, barely teens, trotted through the market hand in hand. They were sisters, perhaps even twins. They laughed and carried on as if they had no idea a war was going on.

Lee's throat felt thick, and she folded her arms over her chest, looking away and thinking of Rondi. A smile curled her lips as she recalled their last days together and Rondi helping her pack. Lee had found a couple of designer scarves and small pieces of jewelry that her sister had tucked into her suitcase when she wasn't looking. As if she'd ever have need of those items here.

Lee let out a low sigh and crumbled her paper bag into a tight ball in her hands, refusing to look at the girls again. Instead, she focused her gaze on a woman sitting on a bench opposite her. Lee didn't realize she'd been staring—so intent was she on crushing the bag tighter into her hands—until the woman approached. She was extremely thin and tall, with full gray hair that fell to the center of her back.

"You are an American newswoman, yes?" The woman cocked her head to the side, but instead of meeting Lee's gaze, she eyed the gold chain visible above Lee's collar.

Lee instinctively touched the chain and straightened, realizing she'd been noticed after all.

"I have only seen men in such positions." The woman spoke in perfect English, yet her accent was unmistakably French—so smooth and warm. So different from the choppy, nasal British voices around her.

Lee wavered between answering the woman or bolting for a cab, thinking of the panhandlers in New York who often tried to seduce her. The Frenchwoman didn't provide the opportunity for either choice and settled onto the bench beside Lee. "Yes, I think this is a good thing, to have women in this position. They are natural observers, no? And a more tender heart to tell these stories."

"Yes. I—I'm with—"

"ETO, I know."

A chill traveled up Lee's spine. She stood.

The woman rose beside her and reached out, taking Lee's hand in her own. It was warm, soft, and nonthreatening. Still, Lee took a step back.

"I am very sorry," the woman stated. "I have scared you. One of my sisters, yes, she lives in the States. She sends me care packages when things get bad. This is how I know you. I'd recognize your face anywhere—from the editorial page. Let me just say I am a fan of the magazine."

Lee chuckled. "That's quite a feat. Recognizing me, I mean. Especially in this getup." She glanced down at her uniform; then her eyes met the woman's blue-eyed gaze. "And are you here now, in England, because of the war?"

"For a time. But I wish to go back to France. To help my family, you see." She paused and looked away. "If it were possible I'd be there now."

The woman pulled gently on Lee's hand, guiding her to the park beyond the market. "This is, indeed, a story I wish to share with you. Come. Let us go where there are not so many ears. And as a woman of words and an adventuresome spirit, you will no doubt find my story most fascinating."

CHAPTER SEVEN

The newsroom in London buzzed with men in motion. Like its counterpart in New York, it was no doubt a masculine domain. Yet amongst the sea of khaki green, one bright spot of color stood out. Lee stood across the room, staring at a large map spread onto the wall. Her army cap had been replaced by an orange and yellow chiffon scarf wound around her head.

Mary approached, curious about what held her interest.

"I just have to get some action," she mumbled as Mary stopped beside her. "I swear if I have to write another article about these English politicians, I'll die of boredom." She ran a manicured finger along the wall, tracing an invisible line across the English Channel to the coast of France. "Seems like the only place to see action these days will be to get in on this invasion that everyone knows is coming."

Mary studied the pattern on Lee's scarf, wondering if she'd ever have the nerve to wear something so bold. *Nah.*

"Yeah, but too bad they won't send any female correspondents."

"And why not?" Lee straightened her uniform jacket over her Saks Fifth Avenue slacks. "They worried we might show up some of those men?"

"It's not that, Lee. They won't let us too close to the action. I already asked. To send a lady into a dangerous situation will go against their policy. After all, what would the publicity be like if one of us got hurt?"

"Policy or no policy, I'll just see about that." Lee glanced back over her shoulder to the editor's desk. "I believe my brother has done a favor or two for our editor friend. Let's see if he's willing to cash in." She straightened the collar of her shirt and strode toward the desk. More than one head turned as she glided through the room.

Surely, they wouldn't give Lee a chance for the front lines just because she demanded it. *Would they?*

Mary punched the map, right on the coast of France—madder at herself than at Lee. Mad that she didn't have the guts to do the same.

"Hey, Mary." One of the other reporters approached. "Can you run back down to *The Stars and Stripes*? The guys sent the wrong pack of photos."

"Sure." She cast what she hoped was a believable grin. "I aim to please."

Her smile faded as she turned back to the map. *What's wrong with me? Have I turned yellow since crossing that sea?* She hit the map again with her fist, then yelped as pain shot up her knuckles.

"Ouch," she whispered under her breath, turning away and ignoring the curious stares.

Later that night, after the lights had been turned low in their room, Mary plopped on her unmade bed, pulling a rumpled uniform shirt from under her rear. Lee sat on the floor painting her toenails.

"So, what did Sergeant Perkins say? You never told me."

"I'm supposed to head to the airfield and hitch a ride as soon as they get news of an attack. I need to be packed and ready at a moment's notice. That's what I was doing tonight." Lee patted the army duffle bag sitting next to her. "They said I could only bring this. Can you believe it?"

"No, I can't. You're really going?"

"Anyway." Lee glanced up at Mary from beneath her long lashes. "Lyle agreed—"

"Lyle? You mean Sergeant Milner?"

Lee stopped painting and gave Mary a long stare. "*Lyle* understands that I'm the logical choice to go since I've hobnobbed with those army commanders on social occasions. So, you see, they've already built a level of trust with me."

"I can't believe it." Mary sat up straight. "I've asked for *much* more minor assignments only to be turned down." Her voice rose with each word. "I . . . I . . . I seriously wish I had something to throw at you right now!"

"Really? How very grown up of you." Lee's voice remained even. "Well, at least it's better to be disliked than perceived an unequal."

Mary took a deep breath, realizing how foolish she sounded. "You don't understand." She leaned against the black-draped glass window, pulling her knees to her chest. "I've worked hard *for years* just to see my name in print."

Lee didn't respond, but Mary knew she was listening.

"You knew you were somebody the moment you were born. I had to make myself somebody."

"Are you saying that I'm getting these assignments because of my family?"

"Those weren't my exact words, but yes, that was my point."

"And you think *your father* has nothing to do with you being here?"

Mary bit her lip, wondering how Lee knew. Then again, Lee seemed to know everything and everyone. Mary's voice caught in her throat. "He . . . had nothing to do with it."

Lee screwed the cap onto the nail polish, lifting her toes and nodding at them with satisfaction. "Then, *sweetheart*, you have missed a great opportunity." She rose and pattered into the bathroom, lifting her toes as she walked, protecting the polish.

"Don't blame me if you aren't living up to the truth. Have you ever thought maybe you wouldn't have to *make* yourself somebody if you realized you already are?"

Mary waited just where her mother said. The top of his head was the first thing she noted. Golden brown hair, slightly darker then hers. Her father was sliding one arm into a suit coat, then a second. He straightened his shoulders as he neared the top of the landing, then lifted his head and spotted her.

The man—Donald Miller was his name—paused on the step and cocked his head slightly. Then he continued upward and smiled. At the third step from the landing he stopped and looked at Mary face-to-face.

"I, uh, hear you're enjoying watching the reporters?" His voice was gruff but not angry.

She nodded.

"Do you like to read? To write?"

Mary glanced back for her mother, but saw only the empty hall. She turned back to face her father, and from somewhere she found her voice. "I like profiles mostly. People round town that no one notices but are almost like angels in disguise." She crossed her arms over her chest to stop their shaking. "Like that guy last week, the hotdog vendor, who saved the kid from stepping in front of the bus. That was a good story." She stopped short, afraid she was talking too much.

Donald jutted his chin, motioning down the hall. "Have you seen the photo lab?"

Mary shook her head.

He glanced at his watch. "I have a few minutes, if you want to take a peek."

He headed down the hall, and she quickened her pace to catch up, then widened her own steps to match his stride. A couple of reporters walked toward them, but Donald didn't offer them a passing glance and neither did she. She just kept her eyes on his back, noticing the way his hair brushed against the back of his starched white collar and the gentle swaying of his arms as he walked.

Later that night, Mary tried to recall something about the dark-room he'd shown her. It had a weird, red glow and it smelled something like vinegar, but for the life of her she couldn't recollect how it was laid out or anything about the images hanging on the thin wire across the room.

She lay in bed next to her mother, trying to keep from disturbing her by taking shallow breaths so not even her blankets would rise and fall. Tears came, and she squeezed her eyes shut, afraid of dampening her pillow.

Her mother stirred, tugging on the blankets as she always did, tucking them around her thin body to keep off the chill. Mary knew she was awake.

She ached for her mother to say something. To help Mary understand.

Did he ask to see me? Have you shown him my school pictures? How did he know that was me at the top of the stairs?

Maybe he'd wanted to see her all along, but her mother refused. Maybe he had a framed photograph of her on his desk. Maybe he even stood on the street corner and watched her walk to school every day, making sure she made it there safely.

He'd wanted to know her. She was sure of it now. And he'd be eager to make up for lost time. Maybe tomorrow he'd take her to see the printing presses, then after that they'd venture outside and share a hot dog. Pretty soon she might even join him on his daily walks around the block.

Mary was sure she'd be able to keep up. She'd take long strides. And then everyone would see them—father and daughter together. And they'd say, "Look at that. She has her father's eyes."

"Hendrick, where in the world are you taking me? This isn't a normal jaunt through the countryside, is it?" Though she'd tried to pretend things were still all right between them, Katrine could see a change in Hendrick's eyes. It had been a week since their last picnic, and ever since then she'd felt the distance growing between them. Until this morning, that was, when Hendrick had picked her up promptly at eight o'clock with news that he had a special surprise for her.

They'd been on the road for three hours already. And the farther they drove from the city, the more Katrine clutched the door handle, her hand growing numb from her tight grasp.

"Katrine, I'm taking you to a very special place. And not to worry, my pet, your things will be arriving shortly. I have it all arranged."

"My things? You mean from the Pfizer home? For how long? I don't understand."

Hendrick turned off the two-lane, asphalt road onto a more narrow country lane. Despite his stern face, he'd insisted it was merely an outing. Yet he'd worn his dress uniform, which troubled Katrine from the moment he'd picked her up.

"Hendrick, they need me. Especially little Arthur." Tears formed in Katrine's eyes as she thought of the baby waking to find her gone. She was the only one who knew what songs helped him drift off to sleep. She was the only one he'd allow to bathe him without a fuss.

Hendrick glanced at her with a look of impatience. "Surely you do not believe that I will allow you to keep working in this condition? You're frailer than you let on. You must take care of yourself and my child. In fact, you need people taking care of you—not the opposite."

Birch and aspen trees lined the road. They crossed a small bridge over a creek that wound along roughly parallel to the lane. Up ahead, Katrine made out a clearing. She sucked in a breath as a large castle-like structure filled her view.

They drove closer, and her eyes wandered over the manicured lawns and large brick building. From this view it seemed as large as Prague Castle itself, home of the Czech government!

"Your new home, my pet." Hendrick's words were endearing while his voice was cold. Though his mouth curled into a broad smile, he refused to look her direction.

Dozens of white-trimmed windows faced the roadway. Four towers pointed to the sky, and an arched walkway from the largest tower's center led to what appeared to be a courtyard.

I'd get lost in such a place.

Hendrick slowed the car as they approached the front of the building. A few people milled around the property, but it was mostly quiet, reminding Katrine of the spa in Austria that her father used to take her family to on holiday.

"I'm going to live *here*? Are you joking?"

"I would never joke about your welfare. This is the Führer's gift to the mothers of the Reich. This place is called *Lebensborn*— Source of Life. Here you will receive the best food and care possible."

"A home for mothers? There is such a thing?" Katrine's pounding heart echoed in her ears.

As the car rolled to a stop, she noted two other pregnant women walking along a sidewalk toward the main entrance. They turned, eyeing the car with curiosity. Three other young women sat around a rectangular fountain on the front lawn, all of them at various stages of pregnancy. The girls smiled and waved—clearly at Hendrick. Katrine bit her lip and looked to see his response. He smiled, finally turning his focus back to her.

"Hendrick, they aren't women at all, but more like girls. Do you know them? They seem to know you."

Hendrick laughed. "No. Believe me, my pet, it's the car and uniform they're most interested in."

He parked the vehicle in front of the large double doors, but Katrine's fingers refused to release the door handle. This was really happening. He was leaving her, away from all she knew. Without her permission.

He opened his car door, and Katrine reached across the seat and grabbed his jacket. "Wait, Hendrick, please."

He paused and looked into her face with a questioning gaze.

"I'd rather not stay here. I know you mean well, but I enjoy my work. My mother worked, caring for children through all her pregnancies, and I'll be fine doing the same. Then we'll have a chance to see each other, to be together. You want to be with me, don't you?"

"Do you think I have time to care for you myself?" His gaze narrowed. "I have work. A family. Seriously, Katrine, I do not need to deal with a pregnant mistress on top of all that."

At her shocked expression his face suddenly softened. "Do not worry, my pet. I'll visit often. And when the child is born we will return to the city together. Maybe then, I'll find you your own flat."

"Promise?"

Hendrick gently removed her fingers from his jacket and kissed each one. "Yes, I will return for you. You are my favorite pet, you know. Then the two of us will be together."

Katrine noticed a nurse walking toward them. Hendrick released her hand.

"You mean the three of us."

"Three, of course." And with those words, he was out the door and warmly greeting the nurse.

Katrine's throat constricted, and again she wondered just what trouble she'd gotten herself into. "Pretty is as pretty does," her mother had always told her. And even though she was dressed in fine clothes and soon would be living in a castle, Katrine felt anything but pretty. It was almost as if it were someone else living through the nightmare that had become her existence.

Actually, it was.

The chink of crystal tapping crystal met Hendrick's ears as Frau Schmidt poured him a glass of wine. She handed it to him, patted her blonde coif, and settled onto the sofa beside him.

Hendrick glanced around the room, taking in the tall bookcases, party posters, and a framed and signed photo of Himmler on Frau Schmidt's desk.

"You will give this girl the best. Nothing will be withheld from her care, understand?" He took a sip of the wine, then glanced at his watch, proving to the woman that this was a business call only.

Frau Schmidt cast him a strained smile. "It is how we care for all our mothers, Officer Schwartz. Did I tell you Himmler himself has visited twice?" She stood and strode to her desk. "There is, of course, this matter of her paperwork. I see it has not yet been provided. We must—"

"Did you look at her?" Hendrick downed the fine wine in one large drink. "Do you dare question?"

She placed her glass on the desk and settled in the chair, her hands moving to the top drawer. "No, of course not. But I must have all the paperwork in order before I turn it into—"

"Into me? Into my office?" He cocked an eyebrow.

Awkward laughter escaped her lips. "Of course. I suppose I don't have to worry about getting your required signature." She closed the desk drawer.

Hendrick stood. "I assure you, Katrine's paperwork is in order. You will receive a copy for your files." He straightened his uniform jacket and moved to the door. "While I value your thoroughness, proceed knowing it is all in order."

"Very well, Officer Schwartz. And while you're here, do you wish to examine last week's transport? The children should be heading to calisthenics as we speak."

"I do not have time. With the most recent bombings by the Americans, my dear wife insists I make arrangements for her to return to Germany."

"I understand. It's an honor to serve you in this way."

Hendrick stopped in his tracks. "It is not *I* you serve, woman, but this country's future—of which my child will be one of the greatest. Please do not forget that." He turned and strode out the door.

CHAPTER EIGHT

A fist pounding on her door jerked Lee from a fitful sleep. Before she could pull the satin mask from her eyes, she heard Mary jump out of bed and rush to answer it. Light streamed into Lee's newly uncovered eyes, and she attempted to blink away the brightness.

"Miss O'Donnelly, a phone call just came in."

Though the messenger appeared as a blurry profile against the hallway's brightness, Lee recognized his voice as belonging to one of the front desk clerks.

"Sorry, mum, your editor said to wipe off your face cream and meet him at the airfield. Will you be needin' a driver?"

Lee jumped from her bed, not bothering to slip her robe over her satin nightgown. "Yes, please. I'll be down in a few—ouch." Her toe struck the leg of her desk, and pain shot through her foot. She yelped and hobbled to the wardrobe. "Go, go, find a driver. I'm coming."

"Right, then . . ." He pulled the door shut, mumbling, "You're welcome indeed."

Lee flipped on the room light and threw on her uniform. Then she grabbed up the musette bag she'd prepacked and hurriedly limped to the door. Mary still stood there, arms crossed at her chest.

Lee brushed her hair back from her face and slowed down long enough to look into Mary's gaze. For someone who acted tough, the girl appeared close to tears.

"Don't look at me that way. I *told you* I was going when the time came. I just can't believe today's the day." She hoisted the bag to her shoulder, leaning under its weight. "Can you do me a favor and take any calls that come in for me? I'll make it up to you."

Mary nodded, fingering a coinlike gold pendant that hung from the chain around her neck.

Lee paused, looking at it closer. "I've seen that emblem before. Did you get it at the World's Fair in '39?"

Mary glanced down at the pendant. "You're about to head out to the biggest invasion in history, one we've been hearing rumors about for weeks, and you want to know about my necklace?"

Lee moved the bag to her other shoulder and shrugged. "It's just that I haven't seen you wearing jewelry before."

"I, uh, usually don't. My mom just sent it in a care package. For some reason she thought I'd want it for luck. Okay? You can leave now."

Lee held her bag closer to her side, oddly wishing she could confide in Mary about her own stash of jewelry and other valuable items she'd stored at the bottom of her bag—the things Rondi had slipped in. The face of the woman in the market came to mind. *Wish I could tell her all about that, too.*

"*Tell no one,*" the lady had told Lee. "*You never know whom you can trust.*"

Roaring planes overhead disrupted her thoughts, and Lee knew now wasn't the time to go into the details, even if she did trust Mary.

"Well, then, wish me luck." Lee hurried out the door, then hesitated, feeling suddenly sorry for leaving her colleague behind. "Don't worry, your turn will come. You're worthy of the front page, Mary Kelley."

She ignored her toe's pain while running down the stairs and hurrying to the waiting jeep. Without pausing for the driver to unseat himself and take her bag, she tossed it into the back and jumped into the front. As soon as she hit the seat, the jeep lurched away from the curb.

Racing off to cover the biggest story of her life, Lee realized how true Mary's statement the other night was. *You were born somebody, Lee.* But instead of making her feel better, the thought caused a sinking feeling in the pit of her stomach. She'd never really know if she had what it took to make it on her own.

The door clicked shut, and Mary hurried to the window, pulled back the blackout curtain, and opened it. Though cloud cover blocked her view, from the muted roaring sounds above London, Mary knew hundreds of aircrafts filled the predawn sky.

Her fingers trembled, not from the cold air washing over her, but from the realization that their boys would be fighting and dying today—attempting to invade the beachhead the Germans held with an iron fist.

But that wasn't the only reason they trembled.

Why had she lied about the necklace, which in fact she had worn every day for the last five years? Maybe it was easier being untruthful than cracking open the hard shell surrounding her feelings about her father.

No one called Mary, asking her to come in before her regular time. Yet she quickly dressed anyway and hurried to the office. As the taxi drove her toward Fleet Street, the dark city seemed unaware of the attacks already in motion.

Mary glanced at her watch, then sprinted across the busy street packed with automobiles as soon as the traffic cop motioned for her to walk. Her eyelids felt thick and gritty. She'd been up half the night toiling for a unique angle on the World's Fair, and still the pages in her satchel weren't any better than what she started with yesterday.

Her assignment had been to write a story about the fair from a child's-eye view. She'd attempted to capture the awe—the large crowds, the constant noise and nonstop activity, the amusement park rides, icons, exhibits, and demonstrations, yet something still wasn't right.

She'd played with the words into the wee hours of the morning, only to drop into bed frustrated. And even now her mind moved twice as fast as the businessmen she scurried between on her way to the paper. A better lead? More quotes? Or maybe she should just tell Paul to find someone else—someone who understood childhood innocence and wonder. It was obvious she sure didn't.

"What was he thinking?" she growled to herself as she hustled up the brick steps to the main lobby. "I need to tell him I'm not the right girl for this stupid story."

"I wouldn't do that if I were you."

The voice stopped her. She paused with her hand on the smudged metal door handle. Her heartbeat quickened, and she glanced up to see her father standing not more than two feet in front of her.

"Did I, uh, say that out loud?" Mary readjusted the strap of her satchel over her shoulder and then fiddled with her collar, making sure it was straight.

"Having trouble with the World's Fair piece, huh?"

Mary glanced away.

"What would you say to an outing?" Donald rubbed his clean-shaven chin and looked down at her. "I've wanted to head out there myself. If anything, just to see how they turned that swampy waste-land in Flushing Meadows into this 'World of Tomorrow.' Did I ever tell you I used to explore that area as a kid?"

"No, I missed that one." Mary tried not to sound too sarcastic. Was he testing her? Trying to see if she'd skip out on her work? Or maybe testing her role as his daughter—now that would be a good one.

"I have a deadline. This piece is due in—oh—about three hours."

Donald smiled, wrinkles forming around his eyes. "Then we'd better hurry."

The odor of cigar smoke struck Mary as she hurried into the newsroom. Despite the fact that outside night had surrendered to morning, inside with the blackout curtains still drawn, no one seemed the wiser.

She fanned the smoke from her face as she hurried to the large map spread across the wall and studied the colored pins representing members of their group. A slip of paper and a hand-written note accompanied each pin, providing the location and assignment of each reporter. It looked like Manson had gone with the Rangers. Silvers with the paratroopers. Schmidt had taken off during the night with the medium bombers who were blasting open a way for the land forces on a beach they'd code-named Utah.

And O'Donnelly? Well, she was on a ship just off the landing sites. Had been flown from London to the vessel right before the launch. *Of all the stinking good luck.*

Mary perched her fists on her hips and looked around the room, feeling sorry to be stuck with these guys. Green-shaded lights illuminated tired faces. Many, she guessed, had been here since midnight when Operation Overlord had been announced.

One reporter, who she knew had just arrived from a ship somewhere in the Atlantic, knocked over a chair as he lunged for a ringing phone. Other men hammered on their typewriters as if pounding on German heads with each stroke. And yet another man, whom Mary had seen around the office from time to time, sat behind a desk with a sign that read COMBAT CENSOR. Before any news of the landing was published, it had to get by him first. After all, loose lips—or loose news stories—sink ships.

"M.K., I need you to head down to the airfield in Bassing-bourn." Sgt. Lyle Milner approached with an unlit cigar dangling from his lips. Dark circles rimmed his eyes, and a white residue lined his jaw, highlighting his hurried attempt at shaving. He sighed as a dozen phones rang off the hook and an equal number of reporters called his name.

"Bassingbourn's one of *the* top bomber bases. All the brass are hanging out there. Talk with a few cronies and get their take on this morning's efforts."

Mary resisted the urge to scrape her nail against the dried shaving cream on his face. "Bassingbourn. Isn't that where Clark Gable was stationed and did that documentary? I watched that a year or so back."

"He was stationed at Peterborough in the 508th, but he was filmed at Bassingbourn for publicity and recruiting spots. Bassingbourn was the home of the *Memphis Bell*. And if you know that, most likely there are some Americans out there who will want the scoop."

Mary placed a hand on her boss's shoulder as she'd seen Lee do. "Sure thing, Lyle. Do I have a ride?"

Her familiarity didn't seem to faze him.

"Yup, there's a jeep outside. Patrick Jessup's going with you." Sergeant Milner pointed across the room to a balding man with a camera bag swung over his shoulder.

The photographer was thin and average looking, but he perked up when he heard his name, and moved toward Mary with quick steps and an eager expression. She couldn't help but return his smile.

After being briefed once again about security concerning classified information, they jumped into the waiting jeep. Mary sat in the front seat next to the driver, and Patrick hopped in back, easing his camera case onto the black vinyl seat as if it were a crystal vase. The engine roared to life, and the driver pulled out onto the road.

Though morning had brightened slightly, because of cloud cover they still couldn't make out any action in the sky as they drove the sixty miles toward the air base. Yet the closer they got, the louder grew the sound of aircraft roaring overhead.

"I should be up there, you know." Mary cocked her head and stared into the murky sky. "I could produce much better stories if they'd let me do the job I was sent here to do. I mean, I could have stayed in New York for this type of gig. There's plenty of important people I could've tracked down there."

Mary heard a snicker and turned in time to spot Patrick playing an invisible violin. The driver stared straight ahead, but Mary could tell he was holding back a laugh.

"Are you mocking me?" Her eyes widened. "It's not some sob story; it's the truth."

"Not mocking, just giving my opinion of what it sounds like from here."

Mary turned back toward the front and crossed her arms over her chest.

The driver leaned in closer to Mary. He didn't look old enough to drive, let alone be so far away from home without supervision. "*I'm* listening, lady."

"Thank you." She tipped her chin and raised her voice, projecting it toward the backseat. "That means a lot."

"Hey, buddy. I appreciate you helping the lady out, but I have a favor. Can you pull over for just a minute? This shot's too incredible to miss."

The jeep had just crested a small hill overlooking the base, which was still five or so miles away. Without comment, the driver pulled off the narrow road. Mary opened her mouth to protest, but as she followed the photographer's gaze, she immediately understood. The sun streaming through the thinning clouds reflected off huge silver bombers rising from the airfield in an almost continuous stream. Her stomach flipped as their controlled power overwhelmed her.

As Mary watched, she thought of her complaints just moments before, and heat filled her cheeks. The photographer was right. Her sob story was nothing compared to the sacrifice of those fighting and dying this very moment.

She climbed out and watched the way Patrick tilted his head as he studied the sky. With a knowing smile, he finally hunkered down to brace his Speed Graphic for the perfect angle. He snapped one shot at a time, sliding each plate in and out of the camera manually. Then he straightened up, repacked his equipment, and climbed back into his seat.

"Okay, let's get going," he said, as if he'd been waiting for her.

After they started down the road once again, Mary couldn't help but get the feeling he was studying her. She glanced out the open window, tucking strands of wayward hair behind her ears, attempting to ignore him.

"So why don't you just make the best of it?" He leaned forward in the seat, and she could feel the warmth of his breath on her neck.

"Excuse me?" She continued looking toward the base, refusing to turn around.

"I mean, you're in Europe, for goodness' sake, covering the war. Instead of complaining about what's *not* working, figure out what you want. For instance, if you had the choice, who would *you* interview on this base?"

Mary scrunched her nose and lifted her hand to the door, drumming her fingers on the frame. "Well, personally, I'd be interested in talking to someone that everyone else overlooks— but someone vital to the war effort."

"Like a member of the ground crew? A man who keeps the planes flying, but no one really thinks twice about?"

Mary turned in her seat, facing the photographer. "Exactly! After all, in New York, that's what I was known for. Looking beyond the obvious to stories of the heart." She paused, thinking of Paul. If he were here, he'd tell her the same—follow your gut. Show the people what matters. She bit her lip and imagined what his advice would be. *Go for it, sweetheart.*

Suddenly a bright flash of the glass bulb and click of the shutter caught Mary by surprise.

She blinked. "Hey, what was that for? Are you trying to blind me, or use that photo for blackmail?"

Patrick laughed. "Nah, it was just a good shot, that's all. If someone in Hollywood were to cast the role of battle-ready war reporter, primed for the front lines, you'd be the last person they'd pick for the part."

"Thanks," Mary huffed. "I'll take that as a compliment."

They pulled up to the base and stopped for the MPs guarding the front gate. Mary couldn't help but smile as she handed over her press pass. After all, Patrick *had* called her a battle-ready war reporter. Primed for the front lines.

CHAPTER NINE

After getting permission from the main office to interview the ground crew, Mary hurried through the feathery afternoon fog, past the squat control tower and dreary combat-crew equipment sheds. Up ahead she saw a row of aluminum huts—the tech sites where the oil-splattered mechanics bustled around aircraft in various stages of disassembly.

The high-pitched whine of drills and the banging of sheet metal put her on edge, and she covered her ears against the deafening echo reverberating off the aluminum. She turned, gazing through the opening.

Surely, there has to be someone outside to talk to. . . .

Then she saw him, on a cement pad near the airstrip. A tall, trim man in overalls and sheepskin jacket stood with hands in pockets, his head tilted back as he gazed into the sky. *That's him,* she told herself.

Mary approached, sidling up beside him.

He glanced down, meeting her gaze, and his brows lifted in surprise. "Well now, another first. Whatta day. Can I help you, miss?"

Mary stretched her small hand toward his large, grease-smudged one. "Mary Kelley, ETO Correspondent." She shook his hand vigorously. "I was wondering, sir, if I could ask you a couple questions concerning today's missions? I've already cleared it with the CO. Are you part of the ground crew, Mr.—" She cocked her head.

"Harris. Jack Harris. Crew chief in charge of maintenance of *Destiny's Child*." He shrugged. "Don't know what you'd want to talk to me for. I'm probably the least in the know."

"But you were here this morning, correct?" She pulled her notepad and a freshly sharpened pencil from her jacket pocket. "When did you first know today was the day of the invasion?"

He rocked back on his heels, digging his fists deeper into his pockets. "Well, as usual, the crew left on a mission unknown to us. This morning didn't seem all that different. Same number of planes going up. Same mode of operation. Nothing too unusual. 'Cept for the gliders, that is."

Mary paused from her note-taking and glanced up. "Gliders?"

"We always have a crewman or two who stays in the dispersal area in case a plane has to abort. I was waiting this morning when suddenly there were these planes flying over the base. They were towing gliders. Never seen that before."

He chuckled and readjusted his cap. "Heck, then one of those gliders broke loose and circled the field. It landed off the runway, and right before my eyes a group of armed paratroopers complete with camouflaged faces piled out." He shook his head, chuckling again. "Man, did those guys seem disappointed they'd malfunctioned. But their being here told me—no doubt about it—the invasion was on."

His blue eyes met hers. "I think that's all, really. I won't know more about the mission until the guys return." His smile faded, and he scuffed the toe of his boot to the concrete. "Those who do return, that is. Even when the aircraft comes back in pretty good shape, sometimes the same can't be said of the men."

Mary still didn't comment, but waited for him to continue. While some reporters would jump in with the next question, Rule Number 4 of Paul's Pointers reminded her to give the interviewee time to speak. The good stuff, he always insisted, came after a long pause as the person worked to fill in the silence.

"About a year or so back, I was the assistant crew chief on *Invasion 2*," he finally said. "They'd been out on a mission to Germany. Done a good job too, but were receiving a lot of ground fire." His forehead creased. "They sent a Kraut aircraft whistling to the ground, but not before a stray bullet nicked the radio operator at the base of his spine. He was gone by the time the plane made it back."

"That must've been so hard to witness."

Jack's voice grew thick and raspy. He peered back into the sky as if reading a script there. "Heck, there's a lot we do on these aircraft—engine and prop repairs, aileron and elevator changes, supercharger changes—anything to keep it in tip-top shape. That's the easy part. The hard part is cleaning up messes like that one. I wiped up that radio room." He swallowed hard. "I—I'm not too proud to let you know that my tears flowed into the pail with each squeeze of that sponge." Jack rubbed his pointer finger near his eye, leaving a grease smudge.

Mary pictured the scene in her mind, this big man unashamedly weeping over the lost crew member.

"Not too long later, *Invasion 2* was shot down by fighters and flak over Bremen," he continued. "Our squadron sent six planes out that day and none returned. We found out later that all the men on *Invasion 2* bailed. They're prisoners of war . . . somewhere."

He straightened his shoulders and glanced at Mary, as if remembering she was still there. Then he shrugged. "When you're on the ground crew, you know there's a war on, and that you're a big part of it. But sometimes, I feel bad not being up there myself. I mean, what I deal with doesn't seem much compared to what the crews face—"

"But that's not true," Mary interrupted. "If it weren't for the ground crews, well, these beaten-up planes would never make it back up, fighting for freedom." She could see in Jack's eyes this war had been as painful for him as it was for anybody.

"Thanks, miss. That means a lot."

She tapped the pencil to her lips, amazed that the man had been so willing to open up. Then she glanced behind her and saw Patrick approaching. She was thankful he'd given her the fifteen minutes she'd asked for. That was another pointer she'd picked up from Paul—no cameras during the interview. Nothing made a person's lips clamp down tighter than a camera in his face.

"Thank you, Jack." She placed her hand on his arm. "I appreciate this; I really do."

The crew chief followed her gaze, noting Patrick. He crossed his arms over his chest, the vulnerability of the moment fading. "Do you got what you need, then? I'd like to get back to the shop to see if there's been word 'bout my plane."

"Just a few photos, if you don't mind."

Jack agreed, posing in the same wide-legged stance—eyes skyward—as he'd been when Mary had first approached.

When Patrick was finished getting his shots, Jack hustled away in short, Jimmy Cagney–type steps.

Mary slid her pencil behind her ear and tucked her notepad back into her pocket. "Well? That was the best thing I've done since I've been in England."

Patrick dropped onto one knee and returned his camera to the case. "Get what you were looking for?"

"Yeah." She patted her pocket and gave a contented sigh. "The story's already half-written in my mind. That's a good sign. Let's just hope he likes it."

"Gee, Mary, Sergeant Perkins is an open-minded kinda guy. You're going to give him a great story."

Mary pursed her lips as they began the slow walk to their waiting driver. She didn't tell Patrick that it wasn't her boss's opinion she was worried about.

The roar of the bomber's four engines filled Eddie's ears, and his stomach quivered—both from the rumbling plane beneath him and the nervous excitement about the day's events. Their mission was to bomb targets on the La Havre coastal area, softening up the opposition for troops preparing to invade France.

From the moment they awoke, he and Adam had known something was up. A number of things had clued them in—getting awakened at 0130, the bomb load of 100-pound fragmentation bombs, and the number of aircraft involved in the mission, to name a few. And by the time they'd filed in for their briefing among the other sleepy-eyed officers, the two had come up with a few options: Berlin, a possible raid on Russia, or invasion.

They'd glanced at each other with a knowing look as the CO pulled back the curtain and they spotted the red ribbon that marked a straight line to the French coast.

"This is it, boys. Invasion Day. What I ask of you today must be achieved if we ever hope to liberate 'Fortress Europe.'" The CO placed a finger under his nose and said the words in a heavy German accent, making fun of Hitler's term for his empire.

"Guns will be manned but not test-fired at any time. Gunners will not fire at any airplane unless being attacked. Bombing on primary targets will be carried out within time limits prescribed. Takeoffs will be accomplished according to schedule—regardless."

The CO then informed them that 11,000 planes and 4,000 ships would be taking part in the day's events. It seemed an impossible number until hours later, when Eddie witnessed it for himself.

Dawn was just beginning to break as they found themselves at 15,000 feet. A blanket of thick cloud cover, tinted pink from the first rays of sun, lay under them. Above them, the moon was still high in the sky, the large round orb refusing to give up its position of prominence just yet. And in the space between the clouds and moon, three levels of aircraft circled, each moving into the exact position that would take them to their final destination.

"Gee whiz, they're everywhere! Above. Below. I feel like I'm being surrounded by a swarm of bees," Adam said into the interphone.

Like toy planes being lined up by invisible hands, Eddie thought as he watched, impressed, as they moved from disarray to order, lining up to their exact specifications. By the time they'd all filed into play, they were well over the Channel with only minutes to spare before making a fix on the target.

"Oh, man, can't see a thing," Vinny moaned.

"Can't see a thing? This is one of the prettiest mornings I can remember." Eddie glanced at his watch, jotting down their time and position. Then he looked back out the window, both taking in the beauty of the day and keeping his eyes open for enemy planes.

"He means the ships in the Channel." Marty's voice also hinted of disappointment.

"What a sight that would have been," Chancey stated over the interphone. "The clouds look the same to me as any other day."

"And there are no Germans yet. Not even much flak. Looks like the only thing pelting us today will be the rain when we return below the clouds."

"Let's hope anyway," Vinny added.

Eddie focused out the window on their pathfinder navigator aircraft, which was already dropping smoke bombs, marking the correct bombing location. The bombs dripped from the sky like raindrops on a windshield, marking where to drop their load over the coast of France.

Eddie shook his head, amazed they could even find France. While he most likely would have had to abort the mission due to lack of visual confirmation, the pathfinders used a combination of grid radio navigation and airborne radar to find the exact drop points. The clouds didn't even slow them down.

Vinny's voice was strong over the interphone as he prepared

CHAPTER TEN

The teacup on the lunch tray quivered from Katrine's trembling hands as she walked through the large dining hall. The arched ceiling, high chandeliers, and velvet tapestries reflected an era when this place had hosted the finest families in Belgium. Now only three dozen girls occupied the space as guests, sitting at a small cluster of tables, their laughter grating on Katrine's nerves.

How am I going to last another four months?

She glanced at her plate of sauerkraut and sausage, and her stomach turned grim—almost as grim as the first time she noticed the SS guards stationed at the doors and around the gates. She'd only been here one day, and already Katrine couldn't wait to leave.

Oh, Hendrick, she thought, *how could you leave me here?* The flat he'd promised her was what she wanted most. She didn't need anything grand, just someplace for her and her child. A place where she could come and go as she wished, walking to the park or market. Although the castle and grounds were more grandiose than anything she'd ever imagined, they were like a gilded cage. And she a songbird who'd lost all reason to sing.

Upon her arrival, Hendrick had stayed by her side—holding her hand loosely—as the director, Frau Schmidt, gave her a tour of the facilities. As a mother-to-be, honored by the Third Reich, Katrine was assured her every need would be cared for. Even her spiritual needs were considered by the two nuns who lived and worked at the home.

Tears filled her eyes even now as she realized what they'd think if they really knew her spiritual state. They could offer no help here to ease her loneliness or help her forget what life could have been like without the war.

"Do you need assistance with that, dear?" Sister Josephina in her brown habit approached, holding out her hands for the tray. "Would you like me to carry it for you?"

"No, I'm fine, really. The little one just gave me a swift kick in the ribs, taking my breath away, that's all." Katrine lifted her tray higher and glanced down at her round stomach, feigning laughter.

"Good enough. Enjoy your dinner. And if you'd like to join us in the library we'll be open this evening, reading from Himmler's latest writings."

Katrine thanked the nun and found an open chair at the farthest corner table.

The other lone occupant offered a bright smile. "I don't know about you, but I can't believe the abundance of food, can you? It's far more than I can eat." The girl lifted a spoonful of green beans and sighed. "Of course, I suppose we shouldn't complain. The rations in Berlin have been terrible lately. It's one of the reasons my mother insisted I come here."

"I know what you mean. But it's hard to eat so much—especially when being here makes me not feel like eating at all." Katrine forced herself to take a spoonful of potatoes.

The girl leaned closer to Katrine, glancing over her shoulder to make sure no one was listening. "I understand. I didn't care for it here at first, either. But what could I do? My boyfriend's on the front lines, and my parents have enough to worry about taking care of my sister and brothers. Is your family here in Belgium?"

"No, they . . . they died in a bombing raid in Munich." She repeated the story so believably, it was almost as if it had become the truth.

"I'm so glad you speak German," the young woman continued. "Most of the girls here don't. They're from Belgium, of course, and France. I got in because my mother is Belgian—even though we didn't live here."

Katrine placed her fork on her tray. "I moved to Brussels to be a nanny for a family here. And I met Hendrick the first day."

"Was he the one in the automobile that brought you? I heard the girls talking about him this morning. They say he was *so handsome*. Like one of those screen stars. I'm Inge, by the way." She flipped a blonde braid over her shoulder. "My soldier, Adler, wasn't much to look at, but we're to be married when he returns, which is more than some of the others have. A few of the ones here know nothing more than their soldiers' names and ranks."

Katrine furrowed her brow, but Inge prattled on before she had time to comment. "Are you keeping your baby?"

Two other girls joined them, and Katrine nodded a greeting. One had reddish blonde hair and looked ready to have her baby any day. The other had darker hair, and she—like Katrine—had a small, round tummy.

"Yes, of course. Why wouldn't I keep my baby?" Katrine answered.

"Not all do, you know," the redheaded girl butted in. "One shouldn't just assume. Some wish to be mothers. Others simply feel it's important to do their part for the Fatherland."

Katrine felt her stomach lurch, and she ran a hand down her face, not believing what she was hearing.

Inge nodded her agreement and then turned her attention to the other girls, referring to the redheaded one as Anneliese.

Katrine did her best to choke down her food, wondering

what type of world she'd been dropped into. These girls talked as though having a child out of wedlock was the most natural thing in the world. No, wait—the most *honorable* thing.

Hanging above their table, a large swastika ruffled in the breeze of the open window. And below it, the home's slogan had been painted in neat script across the wall: *Sacred to us is every mother of good blood.*

Katrine felt a sick feeling in the pit of her stomach, and she knew there was no way she'd be able to finish her meal. Rising, she pressed her hand to her mouth and hurried from the dining hall. The voices followed her, as did the sounds of shoes—most likely one of the nurses, trailing to ensure she was okay.

And still Katrine hurried on, trying to remember which hall led to her room, and attempting to figure out just how she could escape this nightmare—escape Germany's gift to mothers.

It had been nearly sixteen hours since Lee had boarded the plane, bound for what she assumed were the front lines of the invasion. *But no. Here I still am on some medical ship—they must've thought it safer for a lady. What's a girl gotta do to see some action?*

After steaming through the waters during the daylight, the ship had stopped barely a mile from the coast. Behind them, a battleship had fired 14-inch guns, nonstop. Overhead the planes had flown over in wave after wave—like freight trains plowing through the skies, delivering their powerful, noisy loads.

Through the day, landing crafts shuttled back and forth from the troop carriers to the beach, and Lee had seriously considered jumping onto one of them as it plowed past. *Should have done it.*

Instead she waited as the daylight gave way to darkness, turning the Channel into a private Fourth of July production with long streams of rockets trailing through the sky. From her place on the deck she could still hear guns firing on the shoreline and smell the pungent odor of smoke and gunpowder.

Still, she was too far away to see any real action and knew more about the war's progression from the BBC playing on the radio than from what she could see with her own eyes. *Wouldn't Mary Kelley love to know I'm so close, but not getting through?*

The doctors and nurses on board finally gave up hope that they'd be landing soon, and disappeared into the hold. Still Lee remained on deck, shivering and waiting, clinging to her musette bag and life jacket. What would happen if a German sub broke through the perimeter and attacked them? Or if a dud rocket fell short of its mark and hit their ship instead? The medical personnel would be on the bottom of the Channel before they had a chance to scurry up those metal ladders. No, it was better to watch outside. Better to wait, despite the frigid night air. She slumped onto the damp steel deck, her back to the captain's quarters.

The clouds cleared slightly, and the moon appeared high overhead. Still unable to sleep, Lee snatched a notebook and pencil from her pocket and attempted to write a piece about her view from the Channel. Her mind worked overtime to come up with the most descriptive phrasing she could think of. But no matter how vividly she painted the scene of the bombers and the landing craft shuttling in, she knew there would be better stories already on the editor's desk from correspondents who had actually made it to shore.

It's all Lyle's fault, making promises he had no intention to keep. Lee grunted in frustration, and then her thoughts turned to Mary, wondering where her roommate had spent the day.

Lee couldn't help but chuckle, remembering the first time she'd seen Mary in that schoolgirl outfit and ponytails. It had infuriated and amused her at the same time. Actually, she was almost looking forward to hearing what feat Mary had pulled off today.

Suddenly a loud clang reverberated through the ship, as though someone had hit the steel boiler with a sledgehammer. Lee shrieked and grasped her life jacket. She waited for the others to appear on deck, sure they'd been hit. Then she glanced over the side and wondered just how cold the water would be—whether she'd be forced to swim to the nearest craft or wait for a pick-up.

At least it would be something to write about. . . .

Another loud clang, then nothing else. She screamed again and then noticed a sailor walking across the deck, perfectly calm.

He winked at her as he sauntered past. "It's just depth charges, lady. The patrol boats are hunting for subs."

"Don't you think I know that? It just startled me, that's all."

Lee looked down at her half-written story on her notepad, and then flipped to the next page.

Dear Rondi,

You'll never believe where I am this very minute. I'm sure by the time you read this letter you'll know all about the invasion and a place they've code-named Utah Beach. I could, of course, write and tell you where we are now and what we're up to, but it most likely will be censored out. I could write about the other war correspondents and the news office here, but that would bore me as much as it would you. What I wish I could tell you is something of the most secretive nature. Something that can't be written about at all. But if I told you, I'd be doomed for sure. And since I'm your only and best sister, I think you'd like to keep me around. I will say, though, that you've had a part in it—even from a distance.

Oh, well, clouds are beginning to cover my writing light (the moonlight, that is), and I may try to sleep despite the horrible conditions. Tell Roger hi, and Mother and Father too. And if you're lucky, I'll write more later, when I make it to shore. At least more action will take place there, I hope!

Forever your sister and friend,

Lee

Lee closed the notepad. Then she unfastened the life jacket and used it for a pillow, curling onto a ball on the deck. She thought back to her assignment—not the one given to her by ETO, but the one given by the woman from the market. Somehow the woman had known about the invasion. When and were it would be taking place.

"Three days after you arrive in France, a messenger will find his way to you. It is then you will pass on the goods."

Lee tucked her fist beneath her chin and sighed. At least she had that adventure to look forward to.

Katrine had just slipped into the cool sheets of the white iron bed when she heard a soft tapping on the door. She pulled the quilt up to her chin, and her mind immediately flashed back to the truckload of young men who'd been dropped off after dinner. She'd watched them from her bedroom window as they boisterously jumped from the trucks with their military bags in hand and huge grins on their faces. She hadn't seen them after that, but just knowing they were loose in the castle somewhere unnerved her.

What are they doing here? What could they want?

Another knock.

"Who is it?" Her voice trembled.

"It's Inge. Can I come in?" The girl didn't wait for an answer. The door swung open, and she scampered across the room, the light in the hall illuminating her long, golden hair. She was dressed in a lace nightgown, with her large stomach making it look as if she'd swallowed a large rubber ball.

"Sorry. I hope I didn't wake you, but I was going for a glass of milk when I heard the delivery boy in the kitchen talking with the cook. The Americans have invaded France. Millions of them are pouring onto the Continent." Her eyes were wide with fear, and she sank down onto the bed next to Katrine, instinctively caressing her stomach. "You don't think they'll get this far, do you? I mean, Belgium is right next to France. Oh, I should have stayed in Berlin. Why didn't I stay there?"

Katrine scooted to a sitting position and placed a hand on Inge's shoulder. "Don't be silly. There are thousands of German soldiers and machines between them and us, and it's farther than you think." She brushed Inge's hair back from her cheek, amazed that someone so young was soon to be a mother herself. And though Katrine was only twenty-one, she felt a decade older than the other girls here.

"Besides, I've only been here a day, and I've heard the same thing over and over. *We* are the pride of the Reich. Our sons will be their future soldiers. Do you seriously think they'd allow anything to happen to us?"

Inge wrapped her arms around Katrine's neck and gave her a quick hug. "No, you're right. Nothing's going to happen to us here." She stood and hurried across the room. "Thank you, Katrine. I'm certain you are going to be my new best friend." And with that Inge exited, allowing the door to click shut behind her.

Katrine placed her hand on her shoulder as if she could still feel the warmth from Inge's hug. Without Hendrick and baby Arthur, her new friend's warm touch would be all she'd probably receive for a long time. Tightness grew in her chest. She'd felt it before. Loneliness . . .

She rose from her bed and moved to the window. Cautiously she lifted the blackout curtain and scanned the manicured grounds that spread as far as she could see in the moonlight.

"The Americans are coming . . . ," she whispered to herself. On one hand, she was thrilled. After all, in their protection she'd no longer have to hide her true identity.

Then again.

Katrine spread her fingers and placed her hands over her stomach.

Then again, what would they do to me, knowing whose child I carried?

CHAPTER ELEVEN

Katrine didn't know she had so many tears bottled up inside. It was the third day after she'd arrived at Wegimont bei Lüttich, and she'd been encouraged to make good use of the vast grounds for exercise.

"We believe all our mothers should keep their bodies in top physical shape to prepare for labor and delivery," Frau Meier, one of the nurses, had announced after breakfast.

She approached Katrine with a firm hand on her shoulder and eyed her. "You appear to be of healthy stock, but one must not slack during pregnancy. Take a walk around the grounds. It is perfectly safe. After you return, we will provide a thorough health exam, yes? Also, there is still much paperwork to be done."

Frau Meier was blonde and big-boned, with her hair pulled back in a tight bun at the nape of her neck, and always smelled of disinfectant. Yet she moved like a prize boxer and frightened

Katrine with her deep voice that seemed always a few decibels too loud.

Katrine slipped on her sweater and eagerly obeyed, sure she didn't want to get on Frau Meier's bad side. As she strolled through the well-kept gardens, the bright summer sun and soft breeze urged her on. Past the fountains, past the benches lined with chattering young women, and past the manicured lawn area, she heard the evocative murmur of water flowing over stones. A few meters farther on she discovered a small creek running through a thinly treed forest. She tilted her head back, closed her eyes, and slowly inhaled a deep, warm breath of pine.

For nearly a minute she breathed in the forest scents, until she remembered that behind her sat the castle—or prison, from her perspective. She opened her eyes and turned around to view the awe-inspiring structure rising from the rolling Belgian countryside like a giant's residence dropped from the clouds. Through the trees to her right, less than a half mile away, the perimeter wall jutted from the earth. Built with rock and mortar, it was too tall for her to climb, too thick to break through.

Abandoning her dreams of escape for the moment, she found a wide, flat rock to sit on. She closed her eyes, feeling the relief of being free from the spying eyes that seemed to cover the castle's very walls, and the dam of emotions broke. She sobbed as she'd wanted to since the moment two years ago when she walked away from the life and family she'd known and loved. She plucked a pale, purple lilac from its bush and crushed the stem in her fingers, not even noticing its sweet scent, as she thought of that day.

Things had been growing worse in Prague for the Jews. Restrictions had increased until one day they were no longer welcomed citizens. Their pink slips, stating their relocation, arrived. Her family was chosen for transfer to a nearby work camp. Nazi guards holding ledgers told them to report to a holding center, where they'd board trains for the trip east.

They walked to the assembly center that day, dragging a few meager possessions and leaving everything else they owned behind. Even then, Katrine had no idea those would be her last moments with her family. How quickly life can change.

She wiped her tears and pictured the faces of her parents, sisters, and brothers. According to the calendar that hung in her new, private bedroom, it had been almost two years exactly since she'd made that long walk with her parents toward Messepalast—the large hall that was the first holding cell for their relocation. Despite the fact that SS guards urged them along as they walked, a tall, blond man approached Katrine as if he hadn't a care in the world. It was a man she recognized as one of her father's gentile friends.

He leaned close as she walked and spoke into her ear. "The papers are in order. You're coming with me, Rebecca. When the crowd turns to the left at the next street, you will hand off your suitcase and keep walking." His voice was low in her ear. "As we walk, remove your hat. Allow them to get a look at your blonde hair."

Her father's voice was the one she heard next, to her right side and slightly behind. "We have been planning and hoping the papers would come in time. Your sisters and brothers—well, they have not been kissed by the golden angel as you have. Obey, girl. Do as the man says." His voice quivered, and she started to turn her head.

"No, keep your eyes forward. Our family's line will live on through you. These camps . . ." He sighed heavily. "Remember us."

Katrine's throat tightened at the memory—just as it had that day.

Then her father had gently slid her suitcase from her hand, replacing it with a small book. His voice was hurried and closer to her ear. "As you know, when we met, your mother believed differently about our God. Through our years together I attempted to prove her wrong. Yet . . ." His voice grew serious. "Read these words, my precious daughter. Trust them as I have learned to. They will be your comfort when we can't."

His face still close to her, he slipped her a kiss on the cheek. "Good-bye, my dove. Good—"

The road turned before he could finish. Katrine slowed her steps. She wanted to cry out, "Papa, Mama, Leah, Joel . . . Please, I can't leave you." But the man beside her pressed his hand to the small of her back and hurried her forward.

Obediently she pulled off her knitted cap, shaking out her blonde hair.

"Rebecca! Where—"

It was her young brother Abram calling her name, but her mother shushed him.

Oh, Abram, I'll come back to you. I promise. Inside her heart was breaking, but she kept walking. Face set, eyes focused ahead, fingers clutching the small book in her hand.

Katrine plucked more wildflowers—tearing off their petals and tossing them to the ground. *How could God allow this to happen?*

She'd acted bravely at the homes of her rescuers. She'd held back tears for fear they'd confuse her heartbreak with lack of appreciation. But now, perched beside the stream, Katrine lifted her face and allowed the tears to fall. Her sobs filtered through the canopy of leaves overhead.

"Why?" she cried. *Why have I been chosen to live when I feel so dead inside?*

She'd lived a mock happiness for a time. Her life with Hendrick. How could she have fallen in love with . . . She couldn't think about it—couldn't face her failure. She glanced at the round bulge under her dress. There it was, accompanying her every moment, the evidence of that selfishness, pride, and lack of self-control that had led her to this point, this place. Yet, somehow the child growing in her womb gave her a sense of purpose. She'd protect this child, no matter who the father was. This baby was hers. *Mine.* And suddenly she felt a love more intense than any she'd known before.

And as she imagined the little one curled in her womb, protected and safe, her understanding of her parents' love that day made sense. Yet with that understanding came a flood of shame. *And look what I did with such a gift. Look at what I've allowed myself to become. . . .*

She lifted a hand to wipe her face and heard the sound of footfalls behind her. A branch on the forest floor snapped under someone's weight. Leaves rustled as the person pushed through the underbrush.

Katrine's thoughts raced. Would she be in trouble for wandering so far? Was it a guard coming to force her back? She quickly wiped her face and pulled her father's book from the pocket of her sweater, opening its pages at random.

The person stopped beside her, and Katrine glanced up. The nun in the brown habit offered a small smile and held out a white handkerchief in her extended hand.

"You must miss him, I know. He's so far away. Here, wipe your tears."

"Yes, I do," Katrine whispered. "I can barely remember his face." She flipped through the thin soft, pages, thinking how he'd touched them, embraced them, taking in their words of hope.

"Child, it's been less than a week. Your officer will be back soon."

"My officer . . . oh, Hendrick, yes." She closed the book on her lap and patted it. "But his face, his smile." She waved a hand in the air. "Hendrick always said I'm a bit too dramatic and sentimental."

Sister Clarence squatted beside her, plucking a tall blade of grass from the warm, moist earth and frowning at the massacred flowers spread at Katrine's feet. "But the words of that book will help, won't they?"

Katrine glanced down at the book in her hands. She traced her fingers on the gold lettering. *Holy Bible.* "I believe so."

The nun patted Katrine's knee and stood. "As for me, I may read the words of Himmler every night to make Frau Schmidt happy, but the words in that book are the ones I believe in. They're the truth . . . about our Lord Jesus."

Lee blew out a quick breath, turned, then gingerly climbed down a net toward the landing craft that would take her to shore.

It wasn't a fancy ladder or steps, oh, no. Just a wet, slimy, stinky mess of rope, of all things.

A flatboat—the same type she'd seen hauling troops during the invasion—had been sent to bring her and the others to Utah Beach. Even now, field hospitals were being set up to care for the numerous wounded already flooding in, and she was the correspondent assigned to the story.

The motor vibrated the pitching, filthy deck on which she stood. Black diesel exhaust washed over her in waves, the stench nearly making her sick. Still, the craft plowed through the waves toward the unseen horrors of the war-torn beach.

The landing officer had assured them the landing was safe, although the distant booming of big guns caused Lee to tighten her helmet strap. *This is it.*

Over the last two days she'd wanted nothing more than to be carried to this shore, to witness the action on the beach. Yet now that she was actually moving in that direction, she wasn't too certain. Broken crafts of all descriptions littered the water, and the acrid odor of gunpowder was heavy in the air.

Is it too late to change my mind? But she heard a muffled grinding sound as the craft slid to a lurching stop in the shallow water. She grabbed up her bags, put on a strong face, and felt the deck jerk as the landing bridge fell onto the sand. *I've come too far to turn back now.* She leapt onto the sand without even getting her feet wet.

"Dear God, help us all," a nurse with short-cropped, black hair said in a strained voice as she jumped onto the sand. "I knew it would be bad, but I never imagined . . ."

Lee followed her solemn gaze, and her stomach churned at the sight, and even more at the combined odors of torn and burned flesh, seaweed, and burning rubber and oil.

Pocked with bomb craters, scattered and discarded weapons and vehicles, the beach looked like an army convoy that had exploded, scattering parts from one end of the shoreline to the other. She used her hand to shield her eyes and noticed the German defenses still smoking on the cliffs above. But even more troubling than the half-submerged tanks and exploded shells were the little things, like the lone boot and the bloodied helmet cast aside, lying near her feet.

Lee spotted something else—the body of a man half-buried next to a bomb crater. Her first instinct was to look away, but she knew that wasn't her duty.

A GI who couldn't have been older than seventeen lay flat-backed in front of her. The nurse simply stepped over his body, but Lee paused. His red hair was caked with sand. A thin line of blood stained his neck from his ear to his army-green fatigues. He had freckles. Freckles like those her brother had when he was a kid. Lee pictured this kid's sister at home, praying, worrying, wondering.

Hey, kid, she said in her mind. *I will be your voice, yours and the others. With my words, I'll show folks back home what happened. What you did for them—for all of us.* She reached down and closed the boy's eyelids.

She watched the others trudge up the now-secure beach. But she lingered and removed the camera from her case. She hoped the quick lesson Craig at the paper had given her before she left would be enough.

Freely snapping pictures those first few minutes seemed eerily surreal. Yet the ever-present stench as she walked farther inland reminded her it wasn't just a bad dream.

"Bodies not yet buried," she said to herself, letting the camera hang from the strap around her neck. "More young men whose families have no idea they're dead." She closed her eyes and sighed heavily.

"Miss O'Donnelly, you coming?" one of the soldier-escorts called back.

"Coming," she answered, grabbing up her bags and trotting behind him along the sandy road recently carved into the hillside. If only she had a free hand to pinch her nose from the stench.

Catching up, they marched past fields marked with German signs. Lee didn't need to read the language to understand that they warned of mines. Also, dotting the fields like model airplanes scattered in the wind were dozens of wooden gliders. Was it just two days ago that she'd watched them being towed across the Channel? Some gliders had seemed to land in one piece, while others were so broken and battered by artillery that little more than twisted frames remained.

How many soldiers died after touching down in those flimsy craft? She paused just a moment to jot this question in her notebook, determined to find out.

And how many American lives were lost for this one little strip of beach?

At the top of the hill, jeeps waited to take them to the newly constructed field hospital near Montebourg. By the time they arrived, four big tent hospitals boldly occupied a large, open field. The canvas structures all looked alike—long, dark, and greenish-brown with white tape to outline the stakes and entrances during blackout. The area surrounding them was pitted with trenches—used for cover. And beyond that were fields, acres of whole, transplanted trees sharpened into spikes against the Allied landings. From where she stood she could see the bits of white parachute silk still stuck to some of the spikes, and the black smears she knew were dried blood. A shiver ran down her spine.

As she climbed out of the vehicle, other jeeps roared past with litters tied onto the hoods. An ammunition truck also rumbled by. YOU'VE HAD IT, KRAUTS was painted in bold letters on the back cargo doors.

She quickly lifted her camera and took a shot.

"Did you get it?" one soldier asked.

"I'm not sure. I suppose I can cross my fingers."

"If you didn't, another one should be coming through soon. All of them are painted up with some type of message. I suppose it helps with morale."

Before they even had time to rest or eat lunch, the medics had already set to work on the casualties. Rows of men on litters lined the field next to the surgical tents. Most of them had been patched up the best they could. Others lay limp under dirty blankets, and Lee knew it was too late for them.

And as she stood there, playing the part of both photographer and reporter, it suddenly felt like too much. *I should be with* Vogue *right now writing stories about what people are wearing in air-raid shelters, not writing about this scarred landscape and these brave doctors. Not snapping photos of soldiers who might or might not make it.*

This is it. They're going to figure it out this time. I'm a fake and a phony and. . . .

"Can you help me, miss?" A young soldier lying on a litter held out his hand to her. "Can you get me a drink of water? Please?"

Lee hurried through the rows of litters and lines of walking wounded to the water supply area. She found a spare canteen, filled it to the brim, and took it to the needy soldier. He closed his eyes and swallowed the best he could. With the cuff of her sleeve, Lee wiped his moist cheeks where the water had spilled onto his face.

When he finished swallowing, his brown eyes fluttered closed. She hoped that was a good sign. His chest rose and fell with each breath, so at least he was still alive.

"I need help here," one medic called to no one in particular. "Someone grab the handles and help me carry him inside."

Lee didn't give anyone else a chance to respond. Immediately putting the lens cap on her camera and sticking the notebook in her pocket, she grabbed the two handles. The man's unmoving body was heavy. She strained, her arms trembling under the weight. Inside, she handed her end of the litter off to another medic. With smooth movements the two men transferred the injured soldier onto an operating table. It wasn't until he was moved under the lights that Lee noticed his uniform. It was a German soldier they were now working furiously to save.

Taking the lens off the camera once more, she walked the rows of beds. Mazes of rubber tubes hung over them, feeding life-giving plasma into their torn bodies and swaying with the movement of doctors and nurses bustling about, working with clear efficiency and skill.

Bandages were tacked to the ceiling of the tent, curling down like flypaper rolls. Lee lifted her camera to get a shot of a doctor working furiously over a soldier, and then paused.

"Is it okay if I take a photo with a flash?" she asked the nurse.

"Honey, he doesn't even flinch under gunfire—have at it."

She snapped photos of these physicians who just hours before had worn olive fatigues, waiting with her on the ship. Now dressed in white gowns, face masks, and coifs, they went about their work with determination—their discarded helmets littering the floor. Lee carefully stepped over them, making sure not to trip.

One doctor probed a deep wound with a common flashlight. "Nurse, if you don't apply more pressure now, we're going to lose him!" The flashlight flickered, and he shook it furiously. "And will someone please get me more light!"

A second and third nurse hurried to his side, one adding pressure to the soldier's wound and another holding up a second flashlight.

Lee's stomach grew queasy at the sight of the blood, and she turned away. She saw an arm reaching out to her, flagging her down. Cautiously she approached.

As she neared, she realized the man hadn't been signaling her after all. Instead he moaned and pulled at the bottle of plasma that dripped into his outstretched, splintered arm. She stepped closer, noting sulfa powder that sparkled on the edges of the wound. Then her eyes turned to his face.

The young soldier's closed eyelids fluttered. He must have felt her presence, because as she neared, his eyes popped open— two light blue orbs amidst a face caked with dirt and dried blood.

"Hey, soldier," Lee whispered. She leaned down to let him see her face more clearly. Her heart seemed to swell in her chest, aching for the handsome boy. "You're gonna be okay, you know that? You better keep that hand still, though." As gingerly as she could, she touched his fingers, and his arm stilled. "You've done a good thing here. I'll go see if someone can get you something for that pain."

His lips parted, but no sound emerged.

"Shh. It's fine. You don't need to say a thing."

Lee found a medic to provide a shot of morphine, and once the drug took effect the young man's eyes fluttered closed once again. She tucked the khaki blanket to his chin, and as the blanket pulled up, she noticed he still wore muddy boots.

Putting down her camera, she untied the boots and pulled them from his feet. Then she found warm water to wash him down the best she could. She let out a slow breath as she worked a towel over his skin.

"You're gonna be okay," she whispered again. "They're gonna fix you." She stepped away, knowing it was up to the medics to do the rest.

It was just a little thing, washing his face, his neck, his feet. But suddenly it seemed like the most important thing she'd ever done—far more important than striving to get her name on a newsprint page.

CHAPTER TWELVE

Daylight hit Lee's face as she lifted the hospital tent's flap. Uncounted hours of broken bodies, frantic doctors, and young men hovering between life and death had physically and emotionally drained her.

She glanced down at the traces of blood that had dried on her fingers, reminding her of the hands of the young soldier she held as he slipped into eternity. "Tell my mom I love her," he said before his last breath gurgled out of him. She'd sat with his body for a while, looking at his now-peaceful face and trying to imagine his family back home.

Lee also thought of her own mother and wondered how she was taking the separation. Did she and Rondi still make their weekly visit to the salon? Did she order a new wardrobe from the fall collection and host yet another dinner party for her "closest friends"? Those memories seemed somehow distant, even unreal, as if they were simply a dream.

She ran her fingers through her tangled hair, sucked in a

breath of fresh air, and blew it out slowly. In front of her, a soldier with dark hair climbed into a dusty ambulance that had backed up to the tent. She stepped over to the back windows and stretched to see inside. It was empty, and the driver was on his way to the front for another load.

Despite the ill feeling in her stomach, Lee saw her opportunity to get closer to the action and hurried to the open window. "Hey, there. Do you mind if I ride up with you?"

The soldier's eyes widened as he eyed her uniform. "Lady, what the he . . . eck are you doing here? You a nurse?"

"No, Lee O'Donnelly, ETO Correspondent. I'm writing a story on the field hospitals and thought you should take me to . . ."

"To the collection station?" He scratched his head. "You sure it's allowed?"

"Hey, they said to get a story. Don't you think they want me to get the best one I can?" She flipped out her notebook. "And your name is?"

He straightened in his seat. "Bill Day, from Kentucky. Yeah, lady, jump in. I'll give you a ride. But you know the front's not secure. In fact, I had some Kraut taking pops at me not a half mile from here. Good thing he was a lousy aim."

"It wouldn't be a war zone without some danger, now, would it?" Lee tightened her helmet strap as she jumped in.

They bumped over potholed dirt roads, past scattered farms separated by rock walls. A serene setting if it weren't for the bullet holes and heavy-artillery wreckage. Pockmarked terrain spread in every direction, and the big guns boomed louder as they drove on.

To their left, the crashing sea was littered with half-submerged vessels and debris. Lee soon filled one page of notes, then two, as best she could considering their bouncing over the gullied road.

As they drove along, she noted more truck convoys headed to the front. Bulldozers prepared to clear the land for the American tents and control centers to follow.

"As for this collection station . . . what's the difference

between that place and the field hospital?"

Private Day scratched his head. "Well, that's where the triage is given to the boys. The medics—"

"Triage?"

"Oh." He glanced suspiciously at his passenger. "That's the first diagnosis, where the medics decide who lives and who dies. I mean, they do their best on the front, but . . . you know, some of those poor guys would never make it to the hospital alive. They're the real heroes of this war, the medics. I swear I've seen those Krauts target their red cross just as much as anybody."

The ambulance shook as they drove over a rough spot. The soldier swerved hard to get around it, smashing Lee against the door. The bumpy ride didn't seem to faze him.

"Anyway, they don't get the chance to do the best bang-up job out there, so the wounds need to be redressed and splints refitted at the collection station. They also give plasma to the boys in shock. The worst off are sent back to the field hospital. Others who can travel farther are sent to an evacuation hospital."

Lee jotted his words in her notebook then leaned her head toward the open window, catching her reflection in the side mirror. She took in a breath of the sulfur-smelling air and noted more hedges and more signs: *attention aux mines* and *gefhr minen* hung near fields blooming with poppies and daisies. She wrote down those descriptions too. *Unhindered beauty in the midst of heartache.*

Then she paused, realizing the note may have as much to do with the changes she felt within as the surprising beauty of the war-torn land around her.

The ambulance bounced under her. She looked up and saw that the road was now full of potholes—big ones. She imagined the smoke-tailed bombs whistling through this blue sky and landing here, on this road, in those fields. How many had there been?

She tucked her notebook in her pocket and clung to the metal doorframe, certain one large bump would toss her out the window.

Overhead a scattered formation of B-17s was returning to England after a bombing run. The driver gave them a silent salute as they flew over.

Then the ambulance turned a corner to an area even more shattered than what they'd just driven through. Where once farms were thriving and prosperous, now was only scarred crimson soil. Where once stood a forest of mighty pines, as old as the Continent, now were slit trenches and foxholes. Lee pictured the battle—our boys hunched in foxholes firing on German boys in theirs. Many had died, for a cemetery spread out before them, row after row of fresh mounds of dirt.

Lee weakly pulled out her camera. She thought about the redheaded soldier on the beach. *I promised.* And despite wanting to curl into the seat like a scared child, she lifted her head, pointed the lens, and—

"Get down!" the driver shouted, pushing her head to the seat, making her drop the camera onto the floor. He stamped on the gas, and the ambulance surged forward as bullets pelted the side.

Lee screamed as her forehead hit the dashboard.

"Hold on!" the driver yelled. "And shut your trap."

She moved to the floor of the truck, squeezing her body as tightly as she could beneath the dashboard.

"Dear God, help!" she cried out. *I promise I won't be this stupid again.*

More gunfire erupted. There had to be multiple shooters out there. A stinging sensation shot up her ankle. "I've been shot!" She instinctively grabbed for the spot, anticipating blood gushing out. The ambulance shook with the boom of nearby artillery fire.

"Hold on, lady!" The driver's rugged hands gripped the steering wheel and made a quick jerk to the right; then he slammed on the brakes.

The vehicle spun and skidded to a stop. Without even asking if she was okay, the driver jumped out. The gunfire had lessened, but maybe the Germans were just waiting for the perfect shot. The back doors of the ambulance opened, and she heard voices outside.

"How many?" the driver asked over the clacking of gurneys being loaded and the patients' moans.

"Six. This one's the worst." It was a medic's voice, and she knew she should get a shot . . . see the collecting station. Her fumbling fingers attempted to retrieve the camera from where it had slid under the seat. A pit grew in Lee's stomach. Unable to reach it, she buried her head in her hands. *I'm pathetic. My father was right . . . I'm not cut out for this job.*

The driver jumped back into his seat. "Ready, lady?" He didn't wait for her response before he turned the rig around.

"What are you doing?" Lee shouted at him. "We're not driving through that again, are we?"

The driver punched the gas. "Got to. These guys are hurt bad. If we don't get them into surgery, they're not going to make it."

The ambulance rumbled again over the rough road.

"Oh Lord, oh Lord, please," she muttered over and over as the truck picked up speed. They hit one bump after another; fast enough for her to know they were still in danger, but slow enough not to jolt the wounded passengers.

An explosion sounded to the right.

"That's the big guns," the driver said. A hunk of shrapnel hit the hood of the truck. "Lousy Krauts!"

"Hurry, hurry." She grasped her helmet as they hit another hole, and her head slammed into the dashboard again.

The ambulance finally slowed, and she was certain they must have blown a tire. Every muscle in her body was tensed, waiting for what would happen next. She was sure the Germans were advancing on the ambulance. They'd grab her out and push her to the dirt. Would they take her as a prisoner of war? Or would her body soon be one of those buried in that field?

"Is it a flat tire? Are they close?"

Another explosion rocked the ambulance, though farther away than before.

The driver cursed. "Lady, calm down, will ya? We're out of the danger zone. There's a truck up ahead, so I had to slow down. You can look now."

"But the explosions. They're still firing on us."

Another burst rang in her ears, and she crouched even tighter into her knees. Suddenly, tears began streaming down her face. "They won't stop, will they? Not till we're dead!" She sobbed even harder. *Oh, God, why did I come here? Why did I do this?*

The driver reached over and touched her back. "Look, lady." His voice was gentle.

But then came another explosion.

"Take a look. Those aren't the Krauts. Those are cows."

"Don't!" she cried. "You're making fun of me."

Another explosion sounded.

"See?"

"Really, lady. Cows. Not even German cows."

"Cows?" She dared to lift her head to peek out the window.

"Yeah, they've been sent out in the fields to find the booby traps and mines."

"They're blowing up cows?" She scooted on her knees, brushing off her pants.

The vehicle started to move once more. "Better than blowing up people. Look, the hospital's ahead. You better get off those floorboards."

Lee didn't listen, but instead turned to check her ankle. It was bleeding, all right, but not from a bullet. Instead, a piece of sharp metal on the door had dug in good.

The ambulance stopped, and the driver cleared his throat. "Uh, lady."

Lee glanced up from her place on the floorboard to see a handsome, gray-haired man staring into the cab.

"Colonel Stiles!" She scooted onto the seat, already feeling the heat rising to her cheeks.

He cracked the door opened and motioned for her to climb out.

"I came to check on you, Lee. Or should I say Correspondent O'Donnelly? One of the nurses said she saw you heading to the collection station, and I have to admit I was a bit worried. I mean, what would I tell your father if you had been hurt?" The colonel laughed. "But I see, dear, you were taking the necessary precautions."

Lee's hand shook as she tucked a wayward strand of hair back into her helmet. She didn't know what bothered her more—being in a vehicle that had just been fired upon, or being found on the floorboard by the very person who'd allowed this assignment.

Her mind searched for an explanation, and she turned to watch the driver and another medic open the doors to unload the men. The first man they pulled out was a sergeant. His clothes had been cut away, and his face was stricken and pallid under the dirt.

"I, uh, wanted to experience the system of retrieving injured soldiers from near the front. I thought it would add to my story." She turned back to the colonel, pulling together all the poise she could muster. "But you were right." She laughed. "It unnerved me more than I imagined."

The colonel winked and placed a hand on her shoulder. "Your mother wrote and told me to keep an eye on you. How about a boat ride back to England? It's been a tough four days. Then, when we reach the outskirts of Paris, I'll send for you again. Deal?"

Lee knew four days ago she would have fought for the right to stay. She would have insisted on being taken to the front and argued that a woman could do a man's job equally as well. That was before seeing the beachhead. Before washing the face of that unconscious soldier. Before having the Germans shoot at *her*.

She crossed her arms over her chest, feeling the pounding of her heart, and realized that fear was even more powerful than any pride she could muster.

"Just make sure I can be there when you take back Paris." She attempted to hide the quiver in her voice. "I suppose I could be ready to leave in . . ." Suddenly Lee remembered the French woman's assignment. " . . . in two days. There's still some more nurses and such I'd like to interview around here."

"Two days, and a boat ride will be ready for sure." His gaze softened. "You're doing okay, aren't you?"

"Yes, Colonel Stiles. You can write my mom back and let her know I'm just fine."

Eddie followed Vinny and José into the Knightsbride Studio Club. They had a forty-eight-hour pass and had gussied themselves up in their class-A uniforms in preparation, catching the train to London.

Eddie couldn't help but feel handsome and distinctive in his pinks and greens, with his crushed hat set at a jaunty angle. He even swaggered a bit, wondering if a cute English girl would spot his 8th Air Force patch on his sleeve and the crew wings and ribbons on his jacket.

"Have a Scotch, Eddie? My treat." Vinny turned a chair backwards and straddled it, leaning up to the café-type table.

"Nah, soda's fine. Gotta get you two lushes back to the hotel, after all." Eddie chuckled. "Heard about the time you two dopes went on liberty without me, and ended up snoozing at the park when the bombs came in."

José leaned back in his seat, then folded his hands behind his neck and closed his eyes. He bobbed his head gently to the melody of the cocktail pianist. "Yeah, I remember that night in the park. I was dreaming about the Fourth of July. Never occurred to me that the dream was a bit *too* real. The Fourth is when Maria and I met, you know, at a barbecue at her brother's house."

José smiled, and Eddie knew he was thinking about that night, reliving it in his mind. José didn't go into details, and he didn't need to. The content grin on his face told all.

Eddie glanced around the room casually, so Vinny wouldn't catch him scoping the scene. As much as he insisted he didn't want to find a girl in England, Eddie always kept his eyes open just in case God had a different idea.

The song ended, and Eddie stood up. "Hey, Sam," he called over the café's noise. "How about 'And the Angels Sing' by Benny Goodman."

"Sure thing, Joe," the pianist answered, his fingers gliding across the keys. As the melody played, the pianist leaned into his microphone. "We meet, and the angels sing. . . ."

The music filtered into his ears, yet Eddie felt as if the song were playing for everyone but him. It was his favorite. Or at least it had been back in high school. He looked at Vinny and José as they each ordered another Scotch, and he could see it in their eyes too. The song took them back to days of innocence and safety. Days unlike today.

"Here's to Danny O'Harlen's crew. God rest their souls." Vinny lifted his Scotch and took a long swig, his face showing a slight pinch as he swallowed.

The image of the plane flipping in awkward angles toward the ground came to Eddie, but he focused instead on the musician's voice, hoping to wash it away.

He glanced around the room at the pretty girls and soldiers. And he knew that if anyone were to study the three of them, they'd never suspect what they'd just lived through. Oh, sure, they could most likely guess they'd been on a raid recently, but their personal experience—the Kraut fighters they shot down, the bombs dropped, even the aching fear was known only to them. It made it sort of special, that way. Like their little secret.

"Kinda strange, isn't it?" Vinny commented.

"They have no idea, do they?" Eddie added.

"Our other world five miles high." José reached for his glass.

"We kiss, and the angels sing," the pianist continued, and Eddie closed his eyes, wishing he could remember this time and place forever. Yet also wondering if there'd ever be a time when others would be here toasting him.

———————————

By the third day at the field hospital, Lee had already sent enough material back to Lyle for two stories, but still she waited. With security as tight as it was, she had no idea how the French-woman's contact would ever find her.

She'd eaten breakfast in the mess tent with the "fellas"—if

you call dried eggs washed down with coffee as thick as syrup breakfast. But she liked eating with the others. Helped her to get to know who she was writing about. In the past couple of days she had grown more relaxed. In fact, as long as there weren't bullets flying her direction, she was fine. Still, she was glad to be going back to England today—with the wide Channel separating her from the big guns.

After breakfast she'd taken the first shower since she'd arrived—in a portable unit with ice-cold water. Who cared that it was so chilly it sucked out her breath. It felt good to be clean.

Now she sat in the cluster of nurses' tents, propping herself against a log in the sun and letting her damp hair dry. Around her, off-duty nurses also lounged. The worry lines that had creased their foreheads inside the medical tents had faded as they slipped out of their starched white uniforms. A few nurses rolled up the sides of their wall-tents. They wore only long handle, GI underwear. Others lounged in their khaki uniforms.

As she relaxed, Lee noticed one of the farm boys who'd been delivering food to the camp. *What is he doing near the nurses' tent?* From behind a tree, he was studying her. When her eyes met his, he lifted a loaf of bread, motioning her to come. Lee slowly rose and approached. She kicked a pebble across the packed dirt as if her heart wasn't pounding in her chest.

He leaned close as he handed her the bread. "Comet says leave dees bag near de trench."

"The slit trenches, as in the toilets?"

The boy nodded.

"What if someone finds them?"

"No. My sister she wait. She watch." The boy shook his head. He was young, not more than twelve or thirteen, with light brown hair that flopped on his forehead as he spoke.

How did you get involved in this? Lee wanted to ask. *Do you have your mother's permission?*

For the first time, Lee questioned if she was doing the right thing. That day on the bench she had wanted something, anything, to fill the ache she had inside for those back home. And when this woman approached, telling Lee she was involved in helping to support needy, hungry people in France and Belgium—and even those in the underground—it seemed so simple.

Lee had agreed to become an unpretentious courier, and she even offered to throw in a few items of value to support their cause. But now? Now that she was actually here, Lee wondered what she'd gotten herself into.

Still, what could she do? She'd come this far.

"Okay, it'll be there in five minutes." Lee took the bread and hurried to the tent she shared with three nurses. She glanced to the door to ensure no one was watching. Out of the musette bag she removed a smaller bag made of coarse black fabric. She opened it and peered inside. Playing cards. A board game. A belt buckle. She'd been told they contained special maps used to help Allied airmen escape from German-occupied territory. And along with those items, Lee threw in her sapphire necklace, a pearl bracelet, a gold ring—things Rondi had packed for Lee so she wouldn't be caught without when "dining with the important generals."

Lee scoffed at the memory of her sister's note, then pulled out a scarf. It had been an expensive gift from her brother Roger, hand-painted silk. It was her favorite, something she'd packed herself.

"All for the cause." She double-tied the knot on the top of the bag, bunching it as tight as it would go. Then she slipped it under her uniform shirt, pushing out the image of one of the last times she'd seen her brother—at the crime scene, investigating the death of an alleged spy. The blood. The body. *Is that what happens to those who try to butt in where they shouldn't be? What have I got myself into?*

No one paid any attention as she hurried toward the slit trench, hidden behind the roses and hollyhocks that grew naturally in the cratered field. She shooed away a bumblebee with her hand and forced herself to use the latrine, then left the black bag sitting to the side, nearest to a small cluster of trees.

Tucking her shirt back in, Lee strode over toward the tents

once more. A nurse whose blood-splattered uniform and dark-circled eyes gave evidence of just getting off duty trudged toward the trench.

Lee hoped the woman wouldn't notice the bag. She couldn't help but glance back, then paused, her jaw dropping. It was already gone.

The train whistle blew, causing the girl in Hendrick's arms to tighten her grasp around his neck.

"There, there, Stella. Papa will come for you soon." He placed a kiss upon her cheek, stroked her fine, blonde hair, and adjusted the collar of her red blouse before handing her back to Onna. The girl glanced up at him uncertainly, then pushed her thumb into her mouth, resting her head on Onna's shoulder.

"She's coming along well," Hendrick stated, patting Stella's back.

"No thanks to you. Seriously, Hendrick, is your work so important that you rarely make it home at night? So important you cannot accompany me for the ride back to Berlin? I'm not asking you to stay; just help us settle. Besides, it's not safe—"

The train's whistle blew again, and Stella's shoulders quivered.

"I will not answer that, woman. I believe the child in your arms and at your side should be confirmation enough of the importance of my work." His tone made it clear the conversation was over.

Hendrick squatted so his face was level with Sabine's. His voice softened. "You will care for your mother and sister, won't you?"

Sabine nodded and smiled, clutching the two china dolls he'd purchased for their trip.

"You're doing well caring for your sister's baby and your own." His gaze lifted from Sabine's face toward Onna's. "And next time you see me we'll have our own baby to care for. *My son*. Won't you like that?"

"Yes." Sabine wrapped her arms around Hendrick's neck. "A brother!"

He unwrapped Sabine's arms and led her toward the train, merging with the other passengers now boarding. "Good then. The time will come sooner than you think. And no worries. Even now our soldiers prepare for final victory. One battle lost has only strengthened our resolve." He said the words more for Onna's sake than the girl's.

Onna paused before stepping onto the train. "Hendrick," she stated flatly. She placed a kiss upon his cheek; then she took Sabine's hand and led her forward.

Hendrick touched her arm, and Onna paused, turning to him. He studied her eyes, attempting to read her look—weariness, fear, hurt . . . abandonment.

"Do not worry." He caressed her cheek. "This will get better, you'll see. I've done this for you. *For us.* This is the child we've longed for."

"No, Hendrick. It's the child *you've* longed for. Don't you understand? I didn't need a baby. I didn't need these . . ." She jutted her chin toward Sabine and Stella. "All I needed was you. But that's something you've never understood."

Onna boarded the train and didn't look back.

CHAPTER THIRTEEN

Mary couldn't believe nearly three months had passed since the Americans first landed on the coast of France. No one imagined they'd be in Paris so soon, crushing four years of Nazi strongholds in under three months.

And it hadn't been a slow three months either. It all started with Mary's interview of *Jack, the Crew Chief*—as he was now referred to by the London crowd and apparently those back in the States. "The man behind the men," they called him. The photo of the man's face peering into the sky had grabbed folks' interest.

That one interview led to more, until she'd traipsed from one shore of England to the other, interviewing more unsung heroes. Clerks typing Eisenhower's secret memos. Red Cross workers handing out hot coffee and doughnuts to early morning air crews. Even the ETO girls who sang and danced across the American bases, taking the GIs' minds off the war for even a few hours.

And while England had been jolly good about elevating Mary's name and face, she waved her last good-bye to the green English countryside this morning when the transport plane carried her to the new frontier of the recently liberated Paris.

As she climbed into the army jeep sent to give her a ride into the city, she chirped to the driver, "Can you imagine this, Joe? We're in Paris."

"Name's Harold, ma'am. But you're right. Sometimes I feel like pinching myself." He flashed a tired smile, showing off the dimples in his cheeks.

Mary thought he should still be a boy—at home fishing and inviting girls to school dances. But like so many others, he was a man now, with tired brown eyes and worry wrinkles creasing his pimpled forehead. She tapped his uniformed shoulder. "Hey, what do you say we do a quick spin around the block before you drop me off at my hotel?"

He looked at her out of the corner of his eye. "I never was good with directions." He grinned. "And I'm still not sure how I got this job, seeing as I always end up lost."

"Turn right, Harold. I have my eyes set on the Eiffel Tower and need a closer look."

Yet getting there wasn't as easy as one would think. Barricades still smoldered, blocking the streets. Even the fluttering French flags couldn't hide the names of German offices painted on buildings. The scents of urinals, gunpowder, and burnt castor oil still hung in the air.

As they turned down one narrow street, Harold pointed to a side alley. Mary followed his gaze, spotting a group of children swarming an abandoned German tank as if it were a toy. They were thin waifs in ill-fitting clothes, and she realized that these were their first experiences of freedom.

After attempting to find a path through the maze of open streets, they finally made it as close to the tower as they dared.

Mary gazed up at the iron structure spiking into the light blue sky. "I can't wait to write home and tell my mother about this. She always said I could achieve anything I put my mind too. Go anywhere I dreamed of going. I guess she was right."

She snapped a few souvenir shots; then Harold turned their jeep around, apparently determined to get her to the hotel by the Place de la Concorde before a search party was sent out for them. As they drove, a woman hurrying down the sidewalk with her shoulders slumped and eyes downcast drew Mary's attention. Unlike the other women in the street who were dressed in their finest, with their long hair twisted on their head in braids, this woman's head was shaved completely bald.

"She had a Kraut boyfriend," the driver scoffed. "The French citizens marched a group of them down the street and shaved them in broad daylight."

"Were there a lot?" Mary thought of the numerous Piccadilly Commandos, as the prostitutes were called in London.

"Oh, yeah, there were a bundle. Those were the ones who had done it for love. The rest did it to survive."

"Of course," Mary said, thinking of her own mother. "It's so much more reasonable and acceptable to give one's body and soul for food. Love is such a trivial thing, after all." She released a disturbed sigh. "Okay, Harold. I'm ready for my hotel."

Fifteen minutes later, when Harold pulled the jeep up to the Hotel Scribe, a smile filled Mary's face as she spotted a passel of people dressed just like her in khaki uniforms with large C patches on the sleeves. Jeeps, trucks, and army cars lined the adjacent streets, and a hotel attendant guarded the door against anyone not in uniform.

Mary had heard about this hotel even before heading overseas. Eighty years ago, it had been built and named for Augustin-Eugene Scribe, a popular writer of comedies and operas. Only weeks ago, the Germans had used it for their press center. Now the good ol' Americans had liberated it for their own purposes—war correspondents.

Through the front glass doors, Mary discovered khaki duffel bags and bedrolls lying in heaps topped by gas masks. Guests strode by in field clothes and mud-caked boots, thinking nothing of proper attire. She felt as if she'd entered a "Who's Who of

American Journalism" convention.

Many of them glanced at her with curiosity. Then a wave of anxiety hit her. *What was I thinking coming here? These guys are the real thing.* She hoped she hadn't turned her back on a good situation by leaving her niche in England. Not to mention the fact that she was the only female in the room.

She moved to the front desk, squeezing through groups of men swapping stories of what they'd witnessed on the field. Her driver followed, and at the desk she thanked him for his help, taking her large musette bag from his hands and slinging it over her shoulder.

Then she spotted a familiar face—a thin man with a receding hairline, dressed in a too-baggy tan shirt and slacks. He waved and approached.

"Hey, you don't happen to be Mary Kelley, do you? America's Sweetheart reporter?" He pointed across the room. "I made a bet with my friend over there that you were, but he'd assured me that there wasn't such a person. He's certain the *Sentinel* used a beauty queen's photograph, but it was really an overweight bald guy writing the reports."

"Patrick!" Mary's eyes widened and a chortle burst from her lips. She gave the photographer a quick hug. "Patrick, it's great to see you. It was your photo that took my story to the top. But really—an overweight bald guy?"

She patted her side, and a layer of dust from the jeep ride puffed up. "I'm surely no beauty queen these days, but tell your friend I'm the real thing. Heck, if I'm hanging out with all the behind-the-scene guys, hearing their stories and being treated to powdered eggs, I surely want to get the credit for it."

"Thanks a lot, Mary. You've just won me a beer." Patrick turned toward the man waiting and watching from an elegantly upholstered chair. "See, Poppa, it's Mary Kelley after all."

Mary's laughter was cut short when she saw the "Poppa" Patrick was talking to. "Oh, I think I'm going to faint." She pressed a hand to her chest. "That's Ernest Hemingway."

"Yeah. I suppose you're a fan too. Everyone seems to know

that guy." Patrick patted Mary's shoulder. "Your paper's smart for sending you over. I've read some of your recent stories. Those guys see your sweet face and imagine they're talking to their girl from home." He paused, and then glanced down at her bag. "Here, let me get that. I'll carry it to your room."

Mary allowed the bag to be lifted off her shoulder. She offered a shy wave to Hemingway before they headed toward her room. He nodded and lifted his glass to her in return.

Patrick led her to the room number she'd been given. "See you tomorrow." He tipped an invisible hat as he set the bag by the door.

"Tomorrow?"

"General Eisenhower's daily press conferences are held downstairs every morning. Unless you're heading out to the field."

"No, I'll still be here tomorrow. So I'll see you there."

After unpacking her things, she decided to check out the first floor of the hotel consigned to the ETO press offices. She quickly strode through the joint, peeking into a room with bare tables where censors worked all day and much of the night. A few doors down she found the transportation room, where the beds had been pushed against the wall to make space for the cans of precious gasoline. Beyond that was the mail room, with thin V-mail envelopes spread out more or less alphabetically on the red quilts. And finally the correspondents' mess, which featured K rations, coffee, and champagne—all a reporter's basic needs— located next to the kitchen in the basement.

As she walked she looked for Hemingway, but spotted only men in from the field and couriers who came and went. She even looked around for Lee, imagining she had quite a few stories to share about being at the front.

Finally realizing she should follow the example of the other correspondents and head to bed for the night, Mary settled into her room. But she was too excited to sleep. She pulled the blackout curtain to the side and glanced out the window at the intersection of the Rue Scribe and the Boulevard des Capucines below, still wanting to pinch herself. The moonlight shone down on trees lining the streets—Parisian trees. And tomorrow she'd get an update from Eisenhower himself.

She slipped out of her filthy traveling clothes and started the water for a hot bath. Yet even as she dipped into the steamy water, only one thing was on her mind. *If I can only get to the front lines . . . then I'll really find a story.*

Katrine hurried down the hall toward the nursery. Ever since she'd been registered for the child-care classes, and discovered the wing where the children lived, she wished she could spend all her free time there. She opened the doors to the sunny room lined with cribs. Two nurses rocked newborns to sleep, and a wet nurse gazed down at an older baby as she fed her. Katrine rubbed her stomach as she watched a half-dozen toddlers running and playing with assistants. Being here, seeing the amazing gifts of life, made this place bearable. No, even enjoyable.

The sound of a baby's soft cry drifted across the room. "May I?" she asked a nurse who had just entered the room behind her.

The nurse looked up impatiently. "Class is not for an hour, but go ahead."

Katrine hurried to the infant, scooping the small girl into her arms. She kissed the top of the soft bald head, breathing in the infant's scent. "I know, but I thought I could help. As my mother always said, many hands make light work."

"This is not work, Katrine. This is destiny. The future of the Reich rests within these children."

This fuss about birthing and special infant care seemed strange to her. She'd been the oldest of six and had also spent time with many aunts and cousins when they delivered their babies. Did these people really believe that bringing up a child in this strict, institutionalized facility would produce better children than a loving home?

"Someday they may be soldiers and mothers. But they're children first." Katrine sighed. "And I can't wait to see what my little one will look like. I want nothing more than to hold my baby in my arms. I don't think I'll ever let go."

Lee sat in the newsroom at the Hotel Scribe, surrounded by a dozen other reporters writing an equal number of stories. She pushed back her chair from the desk, unable to believe she was back in France so soon. After receiving the call from the colonel a few days ago, she'd been one of the first correspondents into Paris. Yet her tension had returned as soon as she set foot back on this continent. In England, the closest action she'd experienced was a buzz bomb that fell from the sky, exploding on the same block as the private apartment a friend of her parents had found for her. And that was too close for comfort. After quickly moving her things to her new London flat, she'd spent most of the month writing society-type pieces and interviewing famous figures of the war. The assignment fit her well, like a satin glove.

A headache began forming at her temples just to think that soon she might be asked to head to the front lines where the pounding sounds would come from her typewriter *and* artillery shells. But she couldn't think about that now.

Focus, Lee, focus on the one thing you need to work on next. Forget about what might come after that....

Her most recent piece was about the liberation itself, and how all Paris had streamed into the center of town, to the Arc de Triomphe, the Place de la Concorde, along the Champs Elysees, and even past the Hotel de Ville to Notre Dame Cathedral. If it were not for the bullet holes in the windows or barbed wire lining the dignified avenues, Lee would have never believed the Germans had occupied the city only the day before.

Of course, "streamed into the center of town" was an understatement. The truth was, Paris had thrown a party unlike anything she'd ever seen—and that was saying something. Joyful groups cheered and screamed, waving flags that had been hidden away with hope of this day. And Generals De Gaulle, Koenig, Leclerc, and Juin were the centerpiece, leading the procession.

She'd met the famous men, of course, and she'd been honored when General De Gaulle approached with an outstretched arm and devilish grin.

"Such a beautiful lady. Why, I should be the one honored."

She'd spent the rest of the day at his side, getting the inside story—the envy of dozens of journalists—and some of which was strictly confidential. Keeping the classified stuff to herself, she wrote the detailed article, checked with the censor, and telephoned to the editorial office where she knew the rewrite man would record it with headphones and a typewriter—not that she needed much rewriting. She felt more confident about this piece than she had for months.

But who knew how long this confidence would last? She seemed to be a dozen different people these days, all occupying the same body: The confident reporter. The fearful correspondent. The homesick American. The delicate female in need of an open door or steady arm to help her cross the busy Parisian street.

No mood lasted more than a couple of hours. Her biggest struggle was to be a professional in a great big war.

Just then the doors opened, and Mary Kelley strode into the room. "Well, look who's here. Let me guess; you've been here for days, and even rode into the center of Paris inside some officer's private limo?"

Lee stood by her desk, leaned against it and crossed her arms, her gold bracelets jingling. "A *general's* limo, Mary dear. How did you ever figure it out? Did you read about me in England?"

"Oh, I heard about it from one of the other correspondents. He couldn't stop talking about the beauty he spotted near the parade route. I knew it had to be you. What story were you working on, Lee? Something edgy, like which general was attending which celebration party?"

Lee shrugged, noting Mary looked as unkempt—yet as perfectly darling—as ever. "What can I say?"

Mary glanced at her watch. "Can't stay long. I just heard you were here, and wanted to stop by for a quick hello to my roommate."

"Former roommate. Were you disappointed we had separate billets this time? It's harder to fight for the top with no one around to step on on the way up." Lee smirked.

Laughter pealed from Mary's lips. "See you at the front, I'm sure. Maybe we'll even share a tent sometime."

The more Katrine wandered around the halls of Wegimont, the more she understood why she'd never heard of the place before. Why, the whole *Lebensborn* program was a secret from even the most patriotic German citizens. The home wasn't merely a nice place for German women to wait out their pregnancies, but rather a breeding lab experimenting in creating perfect Aryans. Though only three hours from Brussels by vehicle, it was as if she'd been transported to a new world.

"You should be thankful to be here," Frau Meier said as she measured Katrine's stomach during her checkup.

The cloth tape was cool against her skin, and Katrine tried not to flinch.

"Half of the women are not accepted. Some do not have good Aryan genes, and others not sufficient papers. You are privileged, Katrine, with the opportunity to honor the Reich."

Katrine thought of her own papers, which she carried with her at all times. Hendrick had only asked to see them once, and he'd been satisfied. Yet no one had asked for them here. She wondered why they hadn't probed into her history. Was it due to Hendrick's position? Surely it would be foolish to question the mistress of someone who worked for the Office of Racial Purity.

The nurse pushed hard against Katrine's stomach, checking the position of the baby. "He's a big one, isn't he? I'd say you might be further along than you thought."

"He?"

"Officer Schwartz wishes for a son, does he not?"

"Yes, but it's not as if I can determine that."

"That is true, but you can always try again. Another child after this would help them to reach their quota."

"Quota?"

"Girl," Frau Meier scoffed. "Were you just born yesterday? All officers receive great rewards when the fourth child is birthed into their home. Any financial debt to the government is canceled. Plus, they receive many additional benefits from the state."

Katrine's limbs grew cold. She pulled her thin examination gown tighter around her. "But this child, or any future one, will not be in *their* home. He, or she, will be in mine. In the flat Hendrick has promised for me."

Frau Meier finished the exam but refused to meet Katrine's gaze. "You can dress now."

Suddenly the door burst open. Inge stood there panting. "Frau Meier, come quick. It's Anneliese. She's having horrible pains. I think it's time."

"It can't be; it's far too early."

Inge placed her hands under her stomach, wincing under the weight. "Oh, yes. Well, you should tell her that!"

Katrine dressed quickly, then followed Frau Meier down the hall. Even before they reached the delivery room she could hear Anneliese's screams. She moved to open the door, but a hand caught her arm. She turned to find the nun.

"No. You wait here." Sister Clarence's eyes hinted of her concern. "It's too close to your time to disturb you this way."

"But what if she needs someone to hold her hand? Surely, she shouldn't have to be alone."

"She's not alone, Katrine. Remember what the Good Book says. The girl is in God's hands. He has her in His care."

Katrine allowed Sister Clarence to lead her outside into the afternoon sunshine. Though the air was breezy, causing her to pull her sweater tighter around her frame, the sun felt warm on her hair.

"I'll be fine, here. Really." She made her way to the closest bench. "I'll wait . . . and pray," she added for the nun's benefit.

The nun hurried off, and Katrine indeed attempted to take Anneliese's needs before God. Yet every time she tried to picture

God's hands holding Anneliese, another image came to mind—
Frau Meier clenching the girl's hands and screaming in her ear.
"Push, girl, push. Push me out a soldier for the Reich!"

CHAPTER FOURTEEN

Katrine spotted Anneliese sitting as still as a statue at the front of the small chapel. Though they'd been more like acquaintances then friends, Katrine felt Anneliese would need extra support during her child's naming ceremony, especially since these would be her last moments with the baby.

Frau Schmidt sat on one side of the young mother, an SS officer and his wife on the other. The Nazi flag hung over a small altar with a cushioned cradle, still empty. Next to the cradle stood a higher-ranking SS officer in full military dress. He held a small oak box in his hands.

Katrine's blood ran cold as the man's eyes followed her into the room. She looked away, focusing instead on the dozens of candles that lined the altar—their light flickering on the framed photos of Himmler and Hitler, proving this was indeed a supreme rite.

As she strode to the pews behind Anneliese and sat, she couldn't help but think back to the naming ceremonies that took place in the Jewish Quarter of Prague. Held eight days after a child was born, the observance was a time for the family to gather together to celebrate the new life, to dedicate the child to God, and to perform the ceremony of circumcision. In the silence, she closed her eyes and imagined her father's prayer over Anneliese's infant. . . .

Creator of the Universe, may it be Thy gracious will to regard and accept this naming ceremony as if I were bringing this baby before Thy glorious throne. And may Thou, in Thy abundant mercy, through Thy holy angels, give a pure and holy heart to . . .

The prayer in Katrine's mind was interrupted by a baby's cry as he was carried into the room, wrapped in a white blanket, and laid before the altar.

The man at the front spoke. "Welcome to the *Geburtsfeier*, the naming ceremony of the child of Officer and Frau Kaufmann. In my hands I hold this oak box, used to illustrate the thousand-year destiny of the Reich. Who presents this child for naming?"

The officer and his wife rose and strode to the front of the room. Then together they descended to their knees before Anneliese's baby.

"We do," they spoke in unison.

"Very good. Do you have a special prayer or blessing over this child?"

"I do," the woman said, pulling a slip of paper from her jacket pocket. "It is a poem for such an occasion." The woman cleared her throat and began.

"Now I live in you.
You shall and will live on
In times I will not see.
How wonderful that is!
It is as wonderful as in the old sagas,
When each tribe strove
To ensure its bloodline did not perish.

"Still, you are yet small.
How could you know
That you are a branch on a large tree!
But the day will come
When I must tell you
That not only you,
But your fathers also will be judged by your deeds.

"No, you do not yet understand that.
You dream and play throughout the day.
But when you understand,
Then I will know
That in each heartbeat in you and me
That keeps us living,
Also flows a drop of eternity."

The woman finished, and the officer overseeing the ceremony lifted the child into his arms. "It is our greatest concern, our noblest duty, to raise these future generations for our Fatherland and our blood. It is for these generations we toil and struggle. It is for a pure race we strive." He returned the child to his bed.

"Heil Hitler!" the officer cried.

Automatically, as she'd been trained to do, Katrine lifted her arm with the others. "Heil Hitler!"

Then, one by one, the witnesses approached the child to murmur their individual oaths. Katrine couldn't help but ache when she looked down at the now-sleeping infant—the child Anneliese had carried but would not care for.

"I promise," Katrine whispered to her own child that moved inside her, not loud enough for anyone else to hear, "I promise to remember your birth and make sure you have a mother who loves and cherishes you."

After they all made their pledges and returned to their seats, the officer removed an SS dagger from the oak box, raising it high above the baby. Katrine sucked in a breath. Her heart pounded as she eyed the glinting blade in the candlelight.

"In naming you today, we call you to a lifetime of service to protect and promote the Aryan blood that pumps through your veins. For the Fatherland you were born, and for the Fatherland you shall live. You shall henceforth and forevermore be known as Claus Kaufmann."

When the ceremony ended, the couple retrieved the child and hurried out of the room to the party prepared for this occasion. Anneliese remained seated.

Katrine also remained as the others exited.

Frau Schmidt paused at her side. "We have refreshments in the dining hall. Will you join us?"

"I'll be there in a moment. I—" Katrine paused. "I would like to meditate for a time on this glorious event."

By the large smile that spread across Frau Schmidt's lips, she could tell her answer pleased the director.

When the sound of Frau Schmidt's footsteps had moved down the hall, Katrine hurried to Anneliese's side, taking the young woman's hands in her own. "I am so sorry. It must be difficult. I mean, after carrying a child for so long."

A single tear trickled down Anneliese's face. "It is not him that I cry for. It's my daughter."

"Your daughter?" Katrine placed a hand on her friend's forehead, checking for a fever.

"I had twins, Katrine. A boy and a girl. At first the nurses rejoiced at such luck, and then they noticed . . . my daughter's left hand. It hadn't developed completely. Yet the rest of her was perfect. Absolutely perfect." Anneliese's voice drifted off.

"Where is she? In the nursery? I'm sure she is beautiful just like her mother."

Anneliese's shoulders began to shake. "They—they said she died in the night. Of breathing complications. But I know that isn't so. I must leave." She turned to Katrine, eyes wild. "They said they are going to give me an operation. To make sure I don't have any more children. It does not matter that I gave them a perfect son. My daughter was not according to their standards. First, they took her from me. Then this."

Anneliese rose. "I wonder where they buried her." She rushed to the door. "Can you help me find my daughter?" Her voice took on a haunting tone. "I just pray your child is perfect, Katrine. A perfect Aryan to meet their satisfaction."

When Katrine did not make it to dinner that evening, or breakfast the next day, Sister Clarence brought her a tray.

Katrine sat up in bed, not caring that it was noon and she was still in her nightgown.

Sister Clarence set the tray on her lap. It was Katrine's favorite—bacon, cheese, carrots, and fresh rolls. Still her stomach lurched at the sight of the food.

"We've missed you, dear. Aren't you feeling well?"

Katrine poked at a carrot with her fork. "No, it's not that. It's just . . ." She took a bite and sighed. "Sister Clarence, what are you and Sister Josephina doing here? I mean, why would you want to be in such a home?"

"When the home opened just over a year ago, I felt drawn to offer my services. Every consideration was taken for the care of these mothers, except for their spiritual welfare." She offered a sweet smile, the wrinkles around the corners of her eyes spreading and deepening. "Since that is my area of expertise, I thought I could help."

"You're from this area?"

"From Soumage. Our parish is only one mile away. Most people in town still do not understand the purpose of this place. The property has many walls, ponds, woods—it's easy to keep the true activities hidden. Himmler's Experiment with Life— that's what Father Fritz calls it."

Katrine pushed the lunch tray aside and caressed her stomach. *You are more than an experiment, my child.*

As if reading her mind, the nun pulled up a chair next to Katrine's bed. "Oh, I'm sorry, dear. I meant no condemnation. Please do not take that the wrong way." She turned toward the window and gazed out to the grounds. "In fact, I tend to speak too liberally around you, which I should not do. It's your purity and innocence, I imagine, that opens my lips."

Katrine thought about her moments with Hendrick. Their closeness, the bond that continued to draw her to him, despite his faults. "Innocence. I think not. I am anything but innocent, sister."

"Maybe you have ventured further from the path of righteousness than you'd ever imagined possible, yet I see a desire in your eyes to do what is right—for yourself and your child. If you seek truth, you will find it. Keep searching out the Scriptures as I've seen you do."

"That, well . . . I'm not sure how much of it I believe. I mean, from a child I've always believed in God. It's . . ."

"It's just the Jesus part that makes you stumble?"

Katrine shook her head, suddenly realizing what the nun was implying. "I didn't mean that. All good Christians, which I am of course, believe in Jesus. It's only the Jews who accept God without believing the Messiah has come." Katrine's voice quivered, and she rose from the bed and hurried to the window.

"Katrine," a voice behind her said. It was not the voice of Sister Clarence.

She turned. "Frau Meier. I'm sorry, I didn't hear you coming."

"Yes, it *did not* appear as if you heard me. Seriously, Katrine, you need to watch your words. Especially with one of the holy order. To speak of the Jews in this honorable place is unacceptable. Apologize to Sister Clarence."

Katrine fell to her knees before the sister, and she did not need to fake her apology. Her hands trembled as she placed them on the sister's lap. "Sister, forgive me. Forget I ever spoke those words. They were foolish. I had turned my back on my family's faith, and I didn't understand what that meant until I considered my child being raised without it. Forgive me."

"Do not ask for my forgiveness, child. It's your heavenly Father who needs to hear those words." Sister Clarence brushed back a strand of hair from Katrine's cheek.

Frau Meier cleared her throat. "Fine then. Rise, Katrine.

Dress and hurry to lunch. You *can* eat in the dining room. I refuse to let you be pampered like an ill child. We'll give you your medical check tomorrow. You do, after all, have a baby that needs nourishment. A beautiful *Aryan* child."

The foolishness of her comments hung heavy on Katrine's mind during lunch. Unable to deal with Inge's constant conversation, she sat down next to two new girls who both appeared to be in their late teens. They were blonde and slim, and Katrine glanced to their flat stomachs and frowned. One of the girls noted Katrine's gaze.

"I'm Lotte, and this is my sister Gustel. This is our first night here in this beautiful place. Have you been here long?"

"Oh, four months, but it seems much longer. Maybe that is due to the fact I cannot wait for my child to be born. I have still a month to go."

"I heard the last month is the hardest part of pregnancy—the waiting, of course. I do look forward to finding out."

"Finding out?"

"What it's like to be pregnant, of course."

"You mean you aren't already?"

Lotte broke off a piece of bread with gusto, dipping it in the gravy on her plate. "Oh, no, we've been chosen to come for that purpose. Didn't you see the SS soldiers arriving this afternoon?"

"Yes." Gustel looked to her sister and laughed. "We are eager to meet them—and to fulfill our duty for our country. Himmler is a friend of our family, you know, and he says not every young woman is given this opportunity. Most have to be pregnant first before they come, but thankfully he's already placed so great a trust in us that we could be part of populating the New Order."

"What more could we do for our country? *Kuche, Kinder, Kirche*, as the saying goes," Lotte added.

Kitchen, children, church, Katrine repeated in her mind. *What more indeed.*

Hendrick stalked through the front door of the castle, making a beeline path to Frau Schmidt's office. He strode in, not bothering to knock, and saw her quickly pushing on the bookcase as one would close a door.

She turned at the sound, surprise and fear clear on her face.

"What in the world did you do to the girl?" Hendrick crossed the polished floor with quickened steps. "A request passed my desk yesterday that a psychiatrist has been requested for Katrine's care? A *psychiatrist*? She was perfectly fine and healthy when I brought her here—"

"Officer, please." Frau Schmidt faced him. She crossed her arms over her uniformed chest and moved away from the bookcase. "She hasn't left her room in days, is convinced we're murdering children within our walls, and is eating little . . . thus harming your child. Do you not think something must be done?" She emphasized her words with the toss of her hand. "Besides, it's not as if you have need for her after she gives birth—from the papers in our files, you've already made that quite clear."

Everything within Hendrick urged him to strike this woman. He'd had enough of females like her. Females who no longer knew their place. Who dared to speak to him as if *he* were a fool.

He clenched and unclenched his fists, then strode to the window. The peaceful setting below seemed to contradict the rage building in his chest. He sucked in a deep breath and turned his focus upon a group of young women strolling across the lawn. Anticipating where their path led, Hendrick's gaze moved toward the fountains where a dozen young SS soldiers lounged on red and black blankets on the bright green grass, and for an instant he considered joining them.

"You're right. She is of no consequence," he finally stated without hint of emotion. "My wife and I plan to adopt the child once he is born."

"He or *she*." Frau Schmidt strode to his side, her eyes also surveying the scene below. A smile curled on her lips. "We can provide the opportunity for conception. And we can supply a young woman with all the material comforts available to the highly valued in our Fatherland." She turned to him, placing a hand upon his arm, as if attempting to soften the blow. "Yet we cannot design the child. You understand, of course. Boy or girl, it is not in our control. Nor can we ensure a woman is fit to be a parent . . . if she's not genetically disposed."

Hendrick brushed Frau Schmidt's hand from his arm. "And what do you suppose I should do?"

Frau Schmidt sighed. "We've attempted to console her. We've catered to her every whim, and it's accomplished little. I think she needs to see your force. To know this is a serious matter. Katrine needs to understand if she continues on this path, she will lose the child for good."

"What do you mean, *if?* The child is mine, and I will claim him from the moment of his birth."

"Yes, but Katrine doesn't know that. Let her think she still has a chance to make it right. Let her believe it is so. As the proverb goes, 'It's the whole, not the detail, that matters.' And the whole of your situation is that you will walk out of here with a healthy, strong child in your arms."

CHAPTER FIFTEEN

After being found digging around in the garden with a shovel and pick late one night, Anneliese was taken away and never heard from again. Katrine wanted to think she'd been sent home now that her child was born, but she knew better than to ask.

As the time neared for her delivery, she secluded herself from the other girls and staff more and more. And after three days of refusing to leave her room, she heard a knock on her door.

"Go away," she called, flipping the blanket over her head. "I'm not hungry." She heard the door open.

"Katrine?"

Hendrick.

She pushed back the covers and was on her feet in seconds, despite the bulkiness of her frame. With two quick steps, she was in his arms, their child pressed between them.

"Hendrick. Thank goodness. You have to take me away from

here. I can't take it anymore. You wouldn't believe what happens within these walls, even if I were to tell you."

"Katrine, calm down. Please. You're endangering my child —and yourself—behaving this way." He pulled back and took her by the hand. "Come, sit. We need to have a talk."

She followed him to the bed and sat upon the rumpled sheets. Katrine ran her fingers through her hair. When she sought Hendrick's gaze she realized he was staring at her round stomach and full breasts.

"It's our child." She rubbed her stomach. "Look how much the baby has grown."

"Which is exactly why I'm here. The time is getting close, and there are things we need to discuss."

She looked into his face, expecting to see the adoring man she knew. Instead his features were hard. There was no love in his gaze.

"Hendrick, is something the matter?" She scooted close and placed her head on his shoulder. "I've missed you so much."

"Katrine, please stop." He pulled his shoulder back. "Now is not the time. I've heard there is a problem. You must take care. You must give your full work to this baby's health. Otherwise, we need to make a plan for the baby once he is born."

"A plan? We have a plan. You promised to find a flat for us in the city." She swallowed hard, fear building in her unlike anything she'd ever known. "You are getting a flat for us to live in, aren't you?"

"I have no better way than just to say it. I've heard from the nurses you have been found mentally unstable. Unfit to care for a child."

The blood in Katrine's veins seemed to run cold. She stood, wrapping her arms tightly around her. "They say I am the unstable one? Do you know what they do around here? How they breed girls like cows? How they dispose of imperfect children?"

Hendrick stood, grabbing her arm. "That is exactly what I'm talking about. You must stop these horrible rumors." His grip tightened on her arm.

Katrine jerked away. "Stop. You're hurting me. Hendrick, I love you. Why don't you believe me?"

"I hate to tell you this, but I have no choice. You have forced my decision. You have done well in caring for our child before his birth. And I will assume responsibility after."

"You're taking my baby away?"

"Surely, you don't think I would trust my child to a young woman with no home, no family, and no future? Especially one in your mental condition."

"Hendrick, look at me. It's Katrine. You love me. You've told me over and over. It's just this place. If you take me home, I'll be fine. I promise I will."

He turned away, refusing to meet her gaze.

"All I want is to be safe. I know you are a good man. I know you will fulfill your promise to take care of me."

He strode to the window, and she followed. "Did you hear me? Look at me. And tell me what you see."

He turned, his gaze cold. "A beautiful woman. One I chose specifically to be the mother of my child. You think it's by accident you became pregnant? It was my plan all along. To gain honor, position, I need to be seen as the perfect officer. And to do that I must have children. Lots of children."

He approached and placed both hands on her shoulders. "When I saw you that day on the trolley, I knew you'd give me a child that would be the envy of everyone. Your beauty couldn't be ignored."

"Then . . . you really didn't love me. You were just using me?"

He dropped his hands from her shoulders. "Well, I have to admit it was an enjoyable process. But really . . . you were of no consequence in my planning."

Katrine felt her knees give, and she sank to the floor. "You don't want him," she said almost in a whisper. "To think I felt safe with you. After all, if I could fool you, I could fool anyone."

Hendrick looked at her in confusion. "What are you saying?"

"This baby." She sat up straighter from her position on the

floor, unable to keep from blurting out what she knew she should not say. "You will not want this baby once you know the truth." She dared to look directly into his eyes. "His grandfather, my father, was the great Samuel Lodz, a teacher in the Jewish Quarter of Prague. My family lost their home. We were forced to wear yellow stars. I was given a pink slip—"

"Stop it, woman! Cease these lies."

Katrine knew she'd be taken away now, just like Anneliese. She'd be taken to the camps after all . . . but even that was better than this place, with this man.

"I was given a pink slip to be deported to a relocation camp like all the other *Jews!*"

Hendrick's hand swung at Katrine and struck her face before she could block it. Her head jerked back under its force. Pain coursed through her jaw and tongue, yet she continued. "But I fooled them. I walked away from my fate. And I fooled you. You think you used me, but it was I who used you. After all, who would question the purity of a woman loved and honored by a Nazi officer?"

Katrine didn't see his hands grabbing her until her body was sliding across the room under a powerful force. She hit the wall, and a pain shot through her abdomen.

She curled into a ball, sobs racking her body. "I've been dead from the moment I met you. Maybe that's why I embraced you so—an officer of death. My rescuers took me, hid me, but couldn't save me. And now maybe it's just time my body catches up with my heart."

"Enough!"

Her tears flowed freely now. From pain. Fear. And from the release that only comes with the agonizing truth.

She felt a kick to her side, a pain greater than she'd ever experienced, and she huddled to protect her child, wrapping her arms around her stomach.

"You don't want this child!" she shouted. "And your country will not want you—an officer defiled!"

Another kick, to her back this time. A scream tore through

Katrine's body. She felt a gush of warm water, and she knew the time had come. With the water, another pain shooting through her loins.

Hendrick must have realized it too, for his frantic movements ceased. And she imagined for a moment that perhaps he'd changed his mind—that someplace deep inside him an ounce of compassion was found. But when she heard the click of a magazine being loaded into the gun, she realized that was a lie too.

She sucked in a breath—trembling, hurting, waiting—and praying for the end to come quickly. What had been planned for her from the beginning would now take place. She'd walked away from her people, but not her sentence. Katrine tasted blood seeping from her tongue. The tongue that lied for the last time. The blood she had mixed with that of the enemy, dishonoring the memory of her family. *Father God, forgive me.*

"Do it," she sobbed. "Send me to my family. I want them. My father. My mother. All I want is my family. . . ."

Suddenly the door swung open, and heavy footsteps hurried toward her.

Katrine opened her eyes to see Hendrick slipping the gun inside his uniform jacket as Frau Meier hurried to her side.

"What is wrong? Did you fall? It is not yet time."

Katrine couldn't speak. She rocked back and forth where she lay, the pain shooting through her, tearing the child away from her body and attempting to expel him onto the floor.

There was commotion then, as Frau Meier called for help. Before she knew it, Katrine found herself in a white and stainless birthing room—the jab of a needle sticking into her leg, giving her an injection to ease the pain and help her relax.

If the nurses around her saw the bloody lip or noted the bruises already forming on her pale skin, they said nothing. Instead they worked around her, poking her, prodding her as if she wasn't a person at all.

The room grew black, but Katrine fought for consciousness. She had to see him, if only for a moment. More than anything she wanted to see her child.

She opened her heavy lids and lifted her head. Frau Meier's face came into view.

"Hold on. You can do this. You're from healthy stock. Do not give up."

She screamed as another contraction seared her stomach. Hendrick walked into the room and strode up to her, grasping her hand. Katrine tried to pull it away, but she was too weak.

"You cannot be here. This girl is in trouble." The other nurse's voice was frantic. She pushed on her stomach with a force so strong Katrine thought she was going to pass out.

"Katrine, you need to push *now*," the nurse cried.

Behind them Sister Clarence hurried into the room.

"Rebecca. My name is Rebecca Lodz. My fa—!"

Hendrick squeezed her hand tighter. "Do not listen. She is ill. She has lost her mind."

Frau Meier's face hovered over her. Her voice rose with astonishment. "She is a Jew?"

"Silence, woman! This is my child you speak of."

Another sharp pain hit, and Katrine screamed once more.

Hendrick stalked out and a moment later returned with two guards.

"Push, Katrine, push!" someone shouted.

Then she felt the baby slide from her body.

"It's a boy!"

"We're losing her."

Sister Clarence's face drew near. Tears ran down her cheek. "Your work is done, Rebecca. Go to your people."

CHAPTER SIXTEEN

By age sixteen, Mary was the best gopher the newsroom had ever seen. She made great coffee, ran memos up and down staircases— which was faster than waiting for the slow elevator—and even brought back lunch orders.

By eighteen she was writing regularly, but had come upon the chance quite by accident one especially busy afternoon. Most of the guys were out covering their beats. A few were pounding out stories, attempting to make deadline, when the phone from the city news desk rang.

"Hey, Mary Christmas, you mind getting that for me?" Paul had been calling her Mary Christmas ever since she'd baked cookies for them for the holidays.

Without hesitation Mary answered the line. The reporter on the other end rattled off facts about a big warehouse fire in the shipping yards. She jotted down the notes and then hung up the phone.

Later, Mary claimed she'd decided to type out the notes because her handwriting was too difficult to read. But she also admitted the *keys did feel good under her fingers. She'd been practicing for months to get faster—retyping old stories and sometimes even rewriting them just for fun.*

Ten minutes later when deadline arrived, she handed her notes to Paul.

"Here, sir. Something just called in. I'm not sure there's time to work on it . . . but maybe the editor in chief will get you a few more minutes."

Paul scanned her notes, his hunched form straightening in his chair as his eyes scanned the page.

"This is the one just called in?"

"Yes. You asked me to take it. I'm sorry, but I thought if I typed it, it would be easier to read."

"I see. Let me just call and check a few things."

Paul hurried to the phone, talking to someone for a few minutes. Then he resumed his seat, slid her "story" into the typewriter, added a few words, and pulled it from the rollers.

Mary rose. "Um, Mr. Bramley, sir. Were my notes useful?"

"Notes? You're kidding, right? Sweetheart, you've written your first story." He turned the stack of papers so she could see hers. Under the headline Warehouse Fire Destroys Famed Shipping Yard, *he'd typed her name:* MARY KELLEY, ASSOCIATED PRESS.

He opened the door and strode away as if it were an everyday occurrence to have her story submitted in the stack.

Mary hadn't been able to sleep all night, and the next day she hurried to the office an hour early just to get a first glimpse of the morning paper.

A copy waited for her next to one of the typewriters, already opened to page three. Mary let out a whoop. Then she noticed a note scribbled in the margin. Too melodramatic. Next time don't editorialize the facts.

Mary read the two lines twenty times, feeling nearly twenty different emotions. It was her father who'd written those words. She recognized his handwriting. Finally, acknowledgment. Finally, a note from the man who paid little attention to her presence. Who passed her in the halls with no more than a nod and a smile. Elation, disap-

pointment, anxiety . . . in the end she settled on hopeful determina-
tion, focusing solely on two words: "Next time."

Mary opened the newspaper on her desk in front of her and flipped to the second page, which held her article. The phone receiver was tucked tight under her chin. Paul was on the line, and she knew she should keep it short—emergency communication only. Yet she had to know.

"Well, what did he say?"

"Fine, Mary, thanks for asking. Good to hear your voice too."

"C'mon, Paul. You know I don't have a lot of time."

"Yeah, I suppose. Well, your story about the Marines moving into Antwerp harbor? That was pretty amazing. I mean, I thought *Did Mary really write that?*"

Mary laughed. "Stop it, you."

"Plus, the buzz on the street is that your stories are the all-time favorites."

"Whose all-time favorites?"

"Our readers, Mare. And some artist has done this fantastic pen-and-ink drawing of you in your combat suit, and I've seen copies hung all over town. I have to admit you look pretty cute, sweetheart."

"That's America's Sweetheart, to you." Mary smiled and leaned her head into the phone.

"Oh, sorry, America's Sweetheart. Did you know the BBC's even silly for you? Even the English can't get enough of you, Mary."

"Yeah, but you're ignoring the question. What did *he* say?"

The line was silent, except for a thick buzzing, and Mary was afraid she'd lost the connection.

"Paul?"

"I'm still here."

"Hey, listen," she said. "I don't need a glowing report here, but a half-decent compliment will do. I mean, he must have liked it, because most of my words made it to the page."

"Well . . . he threw a fit he didn't get it in time to wield his red pen."

"What?" Mary's smile faded.

"He says that you should have broadened your focus. Y'know, beyond just the experience of the individual men. You should've included more information on the importance of the harbor. Big-picture stuff. You know how he likes that."

"I know. But this story didn't call for—"

"He feels your weakness is you're not going after big enough stories, just interviewing the average joes."

"My weakness?" Mary's voice trembled. She was beginning to draw attention from other reporters in the room. "My weakness is that some people don't let me do my job. It's hard enough for me—a dang female—to get clearance onto the bases and the harbors, which are relatively safe. What does he want? For me to sneak onto the front lines?"

The line was starting to break up, but Mary strained to listen.

"I don't understand it either," Paul said. "You've put out far better stories than Manahan, Ryan, or a lot of the guys. Stop torturing yourself. Think about it; you're continually making A-2. You're the talk of the town, and, hey, your old friend here likes your stuff. It makes me wonder, though. Are you in this for the love of journalism or the love of a father?"

"Paul, you're not being fair here."

"Just a minute; I wasn't through."

More static was making it hard to distinguish his words.

"You know Donald's always had a higher standard for his own writing. I think . . ."

"Paul? You there?" She pressed the phone tighter to her ear. "Paul?"

The line was dead. Mary set the phone in its cradle, then rested her forehead on the cool surface of her desk.

What did Paul think? That Donald's standard wasn't obtainable? That he would never be satisfied? Or . . .

Mary headed to the front door for some fresh air and privacy, but halfway there she stopped, leaned against the hallway wall, and slid down, hunching over her mud-covered boots. Maybe she too was judged at this higher standard because of who she was. And if word ever leaked that journalism's most eligible bachelor and Pulitzer Prize–winning writer had a daughter, wouldn't they judge him by who she was too? But few people knew, and so far they hadn't told. Which meant, it would only be she who revealed it to the world.

She stood and walked out to the quiet sidewalk, stopping just outside the door and brushing off her filthy olive-drab uniform, attempting to shake away the thoughts that clung to her just like the dirt and mud. But it didn't work.

Mary stomped her feet on the sidewalk, then returned to the lobby. The room was alive with conversation, yet she suddenly felt alone—so far from Paul, so far from her mom—the two people who cared the most.

If word ever got out, everyone would think I got where I am because of who I am, not because of what I've accomplished. Mary grabbed her duffel bag and trudged up the long stairway, remembering the first time she ever met her father, the first time she realized who she was.

Mary hurried to her room, pulled the key from her pocket, unlocked the door, and kicked it open. *If he's hard on me, makes me do better than the best, well, no one will be able to accuse him of favoritism. Plus, they'll know this girl from the German quarter really worked hard for whatever she got.*

She dropped her bag, spread her arms, and fell backward onto the unmade bed. *So he wants to be impressed, does he?* She stared at the photo pinned to her wallpaper—the image of *Jack the Crew Chief*, staring into the sky. And an idea hit her.

The only problem is, I'll need Donald's help to accomplish it.

Hendrick kneeled before the cradle, and anger stirred within his chest to hear Lydia's humming from the other room. "Get out! Get out now!" he called to her.

"Hendrick, what's wrong?"

He stood as she entered and grabbed her by the hair, forcing her head backward so he could study her face.

"What are you doing? Hendrick, you're hurting me!"

It was almost as if they were Katrine's words in his ear. Beautiful Katrine.

"Tell me the truth, is your blood Aryan? Are you pure, or is it simply a lie?"

"What do you mean? You know to work in the RuSHA office I've been thoroughly checked. No woman would dare to sleep with an SS officer without complete documentation."

"Oh, yes, but what if she lies and says she's a refugee—the last of her family? What if someone in the main office believes her, without realizing she has tainted blood?"

"You mean sleep with someone unclean? Like a Jew?"

He yanked her head back farther, forcing her to the floor. "Of course not a Jew! Officers of racial purity have standards. We can determine Jewish characteristics. . . ." A cry burst from Hendrick's lips, and he sank onto his knees. "I want you out by tomorrow."

"But my things . . . I just moved in. It's not like you need this space. You have your own house and your own apartment."

"Your things. I said I want them out! You're worthless anyway. Just like Onna. I'm wasting my seed on trash like you."

Lydia's hands instinctively covered her stomach. "Well, at least I'm alive. What do you think, you're going to get another chance to have a child with your dead mistress? Do you think you're going to bring your dead son back from the grave?"

As the newspaper headline flashed in her mind, Mary realized what she'd known deep inside for a very long time. She was going to make the front page, forcing her father to put her name on the *New York Sentinel* masthead whether he liked it or not. She'd nab a story that would catch the world's attention. Because by catching the world's attention, she would catch his . . . if even for the briefest moment.

Thankfully, she was able to get her mentor on the phone the following afternoon.

"Paul, I'm going to shrivel up and die if I spend one more day in this joint. I've got to do something meaningful. I want to go back to England. I've got *Destiny's Child's* crew chief trusting me; that means her air crew should trust me as well. I want to join the crew on a bombing raid over Germany."

"You're joking, right? Mary, you're sure to be the death of me."

"I know the risks, and I'm willing to take them. I wouldn't be on this side of the pond if I weren't. Do you think you can get me clearance with the base? Will Donald let you?"

"Well, I'll ask, Mare, but it could be a few days. . . ."

"Forget it. Let me talk to Donald myself."

Mary's heart slammed against her chest when, within a few minutes, her father's voice came on the line.

"Hey, uh, Da—Donald. I know you've read every one of my stories, because—well, I know you."

"What's this about, Mary? I have a meeting in five minutes, and I'm sure this call is costing my paper a fortune."

"I know my stories are good," she said hurriedly. "You push me harder than anyone. I also know how *you* got where you are. You've taken chances and refused to be held back. And because you are where you are, I also know you have connections. If I was to ask you for an assignment, and you thought it was a good one, you'd find a way for me to have it the next day, right?" She took a deep breath, not waiting for an answer. "So I'm asking you. I want an exclusive. I want to be the first female war correspondent to fly in a B-17 bomber on a bombing raid . . . over Berlin."

The line was silent. Then a chuckle. "You do, do you?"

Was he taking her seriously? "Yes, sir, I think so."

"Good. It's about time. I've been waiting for this."

"What?"

"It scares me to death to give you this assignment, but I've been waiting for you to use my position to get what you want."

"I don't understand."

"A lot of people don't receive because they don't ask. And what kind of father would I be if I turned my back on my kid when she needed something from me?"

"Then why didn't you offer? Why didn't you just make it happen?"

"I had to know you needed my help. Prepare yourself, sweetheart, and I'll get back to you with all the details."

Then the line went dead. Mary glanced at the receiver, unsure if Donald had hung up on her or if they'd lost their connection. It didn't matter, though.

Did he say sweetheart? She gazed at the receiver. *He wants me to need him. He was just waiting for me to ask.*

CHAPTER SEVENTEEN

Adam's groan made Eddie stir from his sleep. Then the noises of the air base coming to life warned him of what the day held and dragged him to full wakefulness. He turned his head to notice Adam pressing the flimsy army pillow over his head.

"Looks like we're going up today."

Adam pulled the pillow down harder. "Couldn't they just give us a break and let us sleep in? After all we've done . . . "

"It's not over till it's over." Eddie stretched, feeling the chill of the morning hit his arms, then curled to his side. "Tomorrow we can sleep in."

Adam tossed the pillow to the floor and sat up. "Hey, I like the sound of that."

Eddie reached over, lifted the blackout curtains, and peeked out, but only saw darkness and fog. *This is it. Last mission. I can't believe I've lived—we've lived—to see this day.*

Somewhere outside their barracks, the airfield was alive with men, each with his own small part of the big job of getting the planes ready. Ground crews, he knew, were assembling at the hardstands. He could picture old Jack's muscular arm yanking at the starter of one of the portable gasoline-powered generators. They were what provided the electric power to the airplanes and the muted lighting, which made the ground crews' work possible.

There it was, the first engine puttering like a hard-starting tractor; and then others joined it, until they formed one continuous hum saturating the foggy air throughout the base.

"I hate that sound." Marty leaned up on one elbow, pulled a pack of cigarettes from his boot, and smacked it against his hand until one slid out a half inch from the rest. He stuck it between his lips and drew the pack away, leaving one white stick hanging there.

He dug again into his boot and withdrew his Zippo lighter, clicked the lid open, and flicked the wheel against the flint. When it produced a flame, he held it against the end of his cigarette and drew in deeply.

Marty gestured with his cigarette toward the barracks wall and beyond. "That sound means men are going to die today. Let's hope not too many."

"Amen to that," Vinny said.

At 0330 came the call for breakfast. "DeBorgia's crew. Grab your socks!"

Sleepy groans filled the room as the sergeant and his flashlight beam moved from bed to bed, rousing the officers.

Within thirty minutes they emerged from the barracks dressed and as ready as they could be under the circumstances. Outside, winds of the North Sea stung their clean-shaven cheeks. Eddie had only missed shaving once before a mission, and soon learned that eight hours with a rubber oxygen mask rubbing against stubble wasn't a pleasant experience.

From the barracks beside them a window slid open, and a half-naked man leaned out. "Drag the dang Luftwaffe out of bed, and blow 'em a kiss for me!"

Eddie glanced around at the faces of those walking beside him. They gave the guy in the window a courtesy chuckle and a wave, yet lacked enthusiasm. No one had slept much.

Before leaving his room, Eddie had grabbed his pocket-sized New Testament with its gold-finished steel cover—a parting gift from his brother, Richard.

Just yesterday, Vinny had given Eddie his own method of dealing with the fear: "At first you try to forget it. If you can't, deny it. And if you can't do that, pretend."

But Eddie found the words of the Bible worked better.

Large mugs of coffee, thick toast and jam, and eggs waited for them, prepared by the mess sergeant, Williamson, whom Chancey lovingly referred to as their ugly mother.

By 0430 the men separated—enlisted men being briefed first, followed by the officers.

After thirty minutes, the six enlisted men of Eddie's crew filed out of the large Quonset hut, their faces grim. The pilots, navigators, and bombardiers anxiously scanned their faces for clues to the nature of the mission.

Adam paused in his tracks after he entered the room for the officers' briefing, and Eddie bumped into him.

"Come on, what's holding ya up?" Eddie glanced over his friend's shoulder and spotted the distraction. A girl . . . in the briefing room. She sat erect in the chair, looking straight ahead. Blonde and petite, she looked no older than sixteen. Eddie glanced to the officer in the front of the room for an explanation.

"Come in, boys, she doesn't bite." The intelligence officer stood before the curtain-draped board at the head of the room. "Have a seat."

Murmurs erupted, and Eddie noticed that every row of seats was filling except for the one where the girl sat. Her eyes were intent on the notebook in her lap, and she fiddled with the pencil in her hand.

Eddie moved toward her row and plopped down with a seat between them. Close enough to give her a little support, but not so close as to make her feel he had any wrong intentions.

He leaned over the empty seat. "They're just a bunch of big oafs, the whole lot of 'em. Don't take it personal, but you're the first lady we've ever seen in a briefing room."

"Yeah, well, it's not like I have horns protruding out of my head or anything," she whispered. She tucked the pencil behind her ear and turned, giving him a view of a second one tucked away in the same fashion—like two yellow antennae emerging from her golden curls.

Eddie erupted in laughter before he had time to hold it back.

The intelligence officer cleared his throat; his eyes met with Eddie's and locked in a serious gaze. Eddie slid down in the seat and pressed his lips tight, focusing straight ahead.

"Tenn-hut!" one of the airmen called out as the commanding officer entered the room. Everyone in the room jumped to his feet.

The commanding officer reached the front. "Be seated, gentlemen."

The airmen nervously took their seats, and the G2 intelligence officer scanned their faces, as if trying to remember each one, and then pulled the cloth from the map.

Eddie felt a tightening ripple through his stomach. Their mission was Berlin. Their obstacle, the 750 flak guns that surrounded it, not to mention the Luftwaffe.

The elongated flight paths showed them traveling from England over the Channel, through France, and into the heart of Germany. The return trip was nearly the same path but farther north, heading over Belgium instead of France.

Berlin meant a thousand miles round-trip under attack by enemy fighter planes and antiaircraft guns on the ground. They'd flown practically the same circuit before, with disastrous results.

"You will leave the coast of England at this point." The officer spoke in a cold, emotionless tone as he moved his pointer along the red-ribboned route. The concentrations of enemy flak were marked by cellophane overlay. "One group of P-51s will join you at the IP and take you past the target."

Eddie scribbled a quick note and showed it to the girl. *IP = Initial Point.*

She nodded. "Thanks," she mouthed.

"You will have escort all the way to the target area and all the way back to the coast of Belgium," the speaker continued.

As the navigation officer briefed them in detail on their course, airspeed, altitude, and alternation, Eddie jotted down the information on a piece of paper that he would tape to his upper pant leg when he was seated at his flight station.

"You're going to hit a flak gun factory just at shift change, which will give us the maximum number of workers on site. This target is of vital importance. Which means, boys—I want you to give Jerry a headache."

Next he pointed out the main areas of concern for antiaircraft fire. Then the lead bombardier approached the front of the room, showing them pictures of the IP, of the bomb run and the targets. His pictures showed rivers and railroad tracks in relation to the IP and target to help the crew identify them.

"Gentleman, look to your right," the intelligence officer said. "That man might not be coming back."

Eddie shuddered because to his right . . . sat a girl.

Mary took notes, not of the bombing run, but of the men. The eyebrows of the airman closest to her almost touched in the middle as he focused on every word. He scribbled down notes too, glanced up to confirm what he'd written, then added more.

When the aircrew had entered the room just moments before, scents of shaving lotion, hair oil, and sweat entered with them. Even though they'd obviously just showered, Mary knew sweat still clung to the jackets they'd worn into battle time and time again.

When the briefing officer concluded, another officer stepped forward.

"Men, I know you've heard this a dozen times at least, but today it's especially important we go over escape and evasion procedures." He glanced at Mary, then back to the notes in his hand. A new map was pinned up as he discussed escape routes in Holland,

Belgium, and occupied northern France.

"You can find locations of rescue ships in the North Sea, here, here, and here."

Mary shuddered, remembering the statistics she'd read concerning the number of crews that bailed into the Channel and were never found. She squirmed in her seat.

"Wear your dog tags and carry your black leather shoes with you. Nothing else. And if you're captured, give only name, rank, and serial number."

When he finished, the meteorologist took center stage and gave the weather reports for the trip there and back. Visibility and ceiling were currently poor, but he had hopes they'd clear by the time they reached the target. And when he was through, more men came forward—the radio officer providing procedures and the group navigator explaining the order of takeoff, assembly, and the position of each plane and squadron in the group's formation. Hearing them gave Mary a new appreciation of the formations she'd seen flying east on numerous occasions.

Finally, the last order of business was something the lead navigator called "time hack." Each man grasped the tiny dials on his watch. The navigator cleared his throat. "Seven, six, five, four, three, two, one, hack." The men clicked the dials so they were all in unison, then rose stiffly from their chairs.

And Mary—preparing herself for what she had to do—took a deep breath and stood with them.

Ten minutes later, Mary slipped off her combat boots, bouncing from foot to foot on the bitter-cold concrete floor of the small, unheated storage shed.

"These guys couldn't give me a warmer spot?" she muttered as she stripped down to her long johns. "Are they hoping I'll get frostbite and not be able to join them? They're out there laughing. I know it."

But despite the cold—and her racing heart—she was glad to be here. This was it. Her big chance.

Donald had called her back a mere one hour after their phone conversation, telling her arrangements had been made for her to return to England. For a week she'd practiced how she would operate inside the big B-17. The flight had its own equipment, its own rules, even its own morals—but she'd learned fast. She was ready. With Patrick's help, she also learned how to use a professional camera to capture shots of the mission.

Since she insisted on being treated no differently from any other crew member, she stayed the night at the base and was awakened at 3:30 a.m.—or 0330. Under complete blackout, she dressed—but too slowly to make it to breakfast, so she'd met up with the others in the briefing room.

As she dressed, she replayed in her mind the briefing and what happened afterward. As they filed out to leave, many of the men formed into a line. There, a Catholic chaplain stood, praying over any crewman who wanted a blessing before the mission. That line of men—tall, handsome, capable—kneeling before the priest had shaken her up even more than the CO's anticipation of heavy opposition or the estimates of crew losses.

These men apparently knew what they were going to face. And they knew whom to turn to for help.

Hendrick didn't need to sleep for the nightmare to flash before his eyes. Even in the waking hours, the image of Katrine's limp body on the birthing table refused to leave him.

Heavy steps took him through the flat, toward the nursery, where the cradle still lay on its side. He righted it, then leaned against the wall, letting his legs soften and sliding onto the floor.

With one extended finger, he pushed it. Rocking the empty helm.

Blood was everywhere. On her. On the child.

Cries. *His* son's cries had pierced the air, then faded for some unknown reason. The nurse had glanced at Hendrick, her eyes wide with fear; then she had whisked the child away. He knew then his son would not live, and that the nurse feared telling him so.

Katrine, a Jew. A sick feeling rose in his stomach, and pain shot through his skull. He of all people should have known. *How could I have missed it?* He'd helped to design the racial purity posters. He'd written the text concerning the requirements for claiming Aryan lineage. It was a matter of science and genes. How could he not have realized?

Hendrick dropped his forehead into his hands, wondering if he dared return to work. That day at the castle, he'd been so troubled by Katrine's words and the thought of his child's death that the realization that others had also heard her words hadn't hit him until he'd reached the outskirts of Brussels.

Hendrick heard the front door open and cocked his head, noting the footsteps leading down the hall. He could tell it was Lydia. She still hadn't removed her things, but rather acted as if they'd never exchanged words. Yet he also wondered how much she'd figured out.

He stiffened, and fear coursed through his chest. *Uniting with a Jew is cause for imprisonment. Conceiving a child with one, punishable by death.* Would she lead the guard here? Would the very laws he'd written be enforced on him?

She paused outside the bedroom doorway, sucking in a breath. "Hendrick. I wanted to let you know that I understand. I'll stay if you still want me."

Her footsteps neared, and Hendrick lifted his head, focusing on her slim ankles and high-heeled shoes. Would she give him away? Tell of his location? *Just how much does the office know?*

Lydia stopped before him. "I'm sorry to hear about your son . . . and the girl's lies. She did lie to you, didn't she? From what you said, I guessed that she claimed to be a Jew. I've never heard of such a wicked woman. She knew what to say to hurt a man in your position the most."

Hendrick's eyes trailed up Lydia's legs, body, finally resting on her face.

Lies? Of course, lies! Katrine knew she'd already lost the child. He sat up straighter.

With four words—I am a Jew—Katrine attempted to strip me of my position, my pride, my life.

Lydia hunched down and took his hand in hers. "Surely all you need to prove her words were untrue is inside her file. I'll help you, Hendrick. I know just where to look. Tomorrow, in the office, I'll help you. I know you are hurting. I know you don't truly want me to leave."

She stood. "I'm going to the market now to get some things for dinner. I'll be back shortly."

Hendrick listened as she exited, the front door clicking shut. He rose to his feet and spoke aloud into the empty room. "The problem is, my dear, I won't be in the office tomorrow. In fact, I won't be here by the time you get back." He slowly unbuttoned his uniform shirt and tossed it to the floor.

He was no fool. The Americans were nearing by the day. The others from his office would soon be abandoning their posts. He would simply be leaving sooner than the rest.

He unbuckled his belt. *Gott Mit Uns*, it read. *God is with us.*

"Katrine lied." He removed the last of his uniform and stepped into civilian clothes. "The nurse lied." He thought back to the fear on the nurse's face and now understood clearly.

"The child lives." He slipped on his hunting jacket and tucked his pistol into his pocket, his mind working out the plan to retrieve his child, while at the same time ensuring their safety in case the Americans gained any more ground.

And with the same intensity with which he'd preserved the blood of the Reich, Hendrick knew he must fight for his own bloodline, that pumped through the veins of that child.

"I will find him, no matter the cost. Our government may retreat from this soil for a time . . . but I will not abandon my son."

CHAPTER EIGHTEEN

A camouflage-painted army truck crunched through the thin layer of ice forming on innumerable puddles as it neared the airfield. The inside of the truck attacked Mary's senses with the rattles and clanks of loose gear and the odors of petrol, dirt, and man sweat. The dimly lighted B-17 coming into view distracted her attention from her sensory feast. *Oh, well, this is all worth it.* Mary had scribbled in her notebook that military folk referred to the B-17 as a "Flying Fortress." And she could see why.

"Jeepers, you're a big one," she said as she stepped out of the truck.

She took a breath of the fresh, crisp air and gripped her equipment under her arm—a leather helmet like those she'd seen WASPs wearing in the magazines. She eyed the ten crew members hustling around, preparing the plane for flight. She recognized a few of them from the briefing room.

The plane, named *Destiny's Child*, was battle-scarred with

hundreds of flak holes. Jack the Crew Chief approached with his James Cagney steps and warm smile.

"Yup, this ol' bird, she's seen her share of action." He pointed to three riveted patches of metal on the fuselage.

Mary laughed at Jack's silly German jokes for a few minutes, then targeted the man she wanted to talk to next.

The navigator, who'd sat beside her in the briefing room, leaned over the hood of a jeep that had just brought him in. He was studying some type of map. She brushed a stray lock of hair aside as she strode toward him, feeling confident in her army-issued leather flight jacket.

She was just about to say, "Excuse me, may I ask you a few questions," when her feet nearly slid out from under her on the ice-coated runway. She wobbled and reached out, accidentally grabbing his arm.

He let her steady herself. "Are you okay there?"

"Uh, yeah." Her cheeks grew warm despite the bitter cold. "Thanks." She let go of his arm.

"No problem." He gave her a slight grin; then the intense look he'd had when she first spotted him returned and his eyes went back to the maps.

"Hey," Mary muttered, "I just wanted to thank you for sitting next to—"

Another crew member sauntered over. Mary tried to hide her smirk at the man's confident swagger and the slight smile she assumed most girls found charming.

"Sergeant Vinny Rosario at your service, miss. Do you need a hand with anything?"

From the corner of her eye, Mary noted the navigator straighten. He laid down his papers and crossed his arms over his chest, leaning a hip against the truck.

Mary lowered her head and gave the man her most fearsome glance. "Need a hand with anything? Like what, with my pencil?"

"Well, no, of course not. I mean, if you need someone to show you around." He raked his fingers through his dark, greased-back hair. "To assist you during the flight."

Mary rolled her eyes and grinned. "Thanks, flyboy, but I'll be all right—"

"She's with me," the navigator piped up. "Uh, the CO asked me to watch over her on the mission."

Mary noted the surprised look on Vinny's face.

He scratched his head, maintaining his wickedly handsome grin. "I didn't hear him say that."

"Oh, yeah. He called me back in, right after the briefing, and said to set up an extra ammunition box in my area for her seat. It's the only place with enough space for two."

"Sure, cowboy. Fine with me." Vinny backed off and pointed his finger as if pointing a pistol. "Good for your initiative, Eddie. Good for you."

The Vinny guy walked away, and Mary turned to the navigator, flashing what she hoped was a sweet smile. "I'm sorry. I didn't get a chance to introduce myself. I'm Mary Kelley with the *New York Sentinel*. Maybe you've heard of me?"

He shook his head. "Sorry, lady. Can't say I have." He folded his papers and tucked them into his jacket pocket. "I'll go get an area set up for you. I'll be just a minute."

He walked toward the nose of the plane to an opening. Then in one quick movement he grabbed the sides of the hatch and flung his body inside, but not before Mary noted the hint of pink creeping up his cheeks.

She'd witnessed a lot of bold advances, like Vinny's just a minute ago. After all, she was one of the few women many of these guys had seen in days. She had a dozen ways to let them know she wasn't interested. But this . . . seeing the shy kindness of the navigator caused her heart to warm.

Without waiting for him to return, she strode up to the open hatch. She was just tall enough to peer inside and could see him moving equipment around to make room.

"Uh, I don't mean to interrupt, but can I ask you a few questions, you know, before we get started? Since I'll be positioned near you, it will help to know what your tasks are during the mission. I'm sure it won't be easy to answer my questions up in the air."

He shook his head. *That's* an understatement if I've ever heard one." Then he glanced at his watch. "Five minutes is all I have. I need to get this place ready—and get my things together before we take off."

He slid back down through the hatch so they were standing face-to-face.

Mary cleared her throat, taking on her reporter's tone. "Name and hometown?"

"Edward Anderson, but everyone calls me Eddie. Whitefish, Montana. I'm the navigator of this crew, which I assume is your next question."

"Yes." She wrote frantically in her notebook. "And just what does a navigator do?"

"There's a whole lot that needs to be done in preflight planning and debriefing that I won't go into, but once we take off, the navigator directs the flight to the mark and then back home. It's my job to know our exact position at all times. And just so things don't get boring, I also man a .50 caliber machine gun at my station in the nose of the plane."

She flashed him another smile, wishing for Vinny to return. Eddie seemed to pay her more attention with him around. "That should be interesting to watch. And what are those?" She pointed to the pile of objects in his hands.

"Communication maps, my logbook, and these here are mission flimsies." He held one up so she could get a closer look. "These give the call signs and frequencies I'll need."

"They look awfully thin."

"They're made of rice paper. And must be eaten if we ditch or bail." Eddie pressed a hand to his face, as if trying to warm his cheeks. "Now, you'll have to excuse me, Miss Kelley; I really need to get back to this paperwork. I'm not sure if you understood what was happening in the briefing room, but we have orders to bomb Berlin today."

Mary's opinion of him was beginning to change. Who was he to assume the cute little lady reporter didn't understand? "Yeah, I got that."

"Well, I'm also not sure who signed you up for this mission, but let me lay down the facts. During our first run to Berlin in March, sixty-nine B-17s were lost. Considering each has a crew of ten men—well, do the math. The 'Big B,' as we like to call it, is one of the most dangerous missions possible . . . and why they decided to put a lady up there is beyond me." He shook his head.

"Listen here, bub. I know the risks, and I'm proud of our boys who died." She poked his chest with her pencil. "That, my friend, is why I wanted this mission. Someone needs to tell the story. Show folks back home the boys, like you, risking their lives. Do you copy that?"

The flyboy had the nerve to roll his eyes. "Fine, miss. I don't have much choice anyway."

Frustrated and angry, she milled around with the other crew members, asking a few questions and forcing herself not to glance at the hatch every two minutes. Finally she was motioned to board the plane.

She watched as a few of the guys climbed through the nose hatch by grasping the hatch edge over their heads, lifting their weight, and swinging their legs up and through.

Mary glanced down at her bulky layers, certain she'd not be able to pull herself through the hatch . . . even if she could get a good handhold on the opening.

The navigator peeked his head back through and pointed to a set of steps rising through the underbelly of the plane. She climbed them, then turned and walked up another half level from the bomb bay.

She jotted down notes about the engineer's position right behind the cockpit. Since he also was the top turret gunner, he had a 360-degree field of fire for his .50 caliber guns. An upright bulkhead—the funny name they used for internal walls—separated him from the bomb bay.

Another bulkhead closed off the bomb bay from the tiny compartment of the radio operator and the left and right waist gunners. In the cockpit itself, controls seemed to cover every available space.

"Would you like to look in the nose area?"

It was the navigator. His handsome face peeked around the corner.

"Sorry about what I said before." He smiled and guided her toward the nose. "I always seem to tense up before missions. But I talked to Marty—the pilot, and you'll be sticking by me. We even fashioned a little seat for you."

Standing next to the engineer's station, just behind the pilot's and copilot's seats, Mary peered through a narrow tunnel under the cockpit's floor, into the nose area of the plane. "Sounds good."

She bent down to climb between the two cockpit seats and under the bank of instrumentation, and into the navigator's domain. She'd never had a fear of tight places, but the air was thick with the fumes of grease, paint, solvent, sweaty seats, and who knew what else.

How am I gonna fly for hours in this tight spot? The nose of the plane had barely enough room to contain the navigator and the bombardier, and the navigator didn't even have a real seat—just ammunition boxes.

When Mary finished looking around, she found her spot—an extra ammunition box just behind the bombardier, José, and opposite the navigator.

"You realize, don't you, there's a chance we won't make it through this one," a voice said from behind her.

It was the small guy—no bigger than she was—that Mary knew would ride in the ball turret under the belly of the plane.

"There are many guys who don't. More than I can count. We've seen it all, you know, and it's not pretty. No one should see what we've seen." His eyes were serious, concerned, like a father's.

Mary's heart sank. She'd been trying not to think about that. Instead she'd focused on her mission. "But don't you understand? That's why they've sent me. Readers need to know. We'll be bombing Berlin today. Berlin! There are songs about this. It's what everyone's been waiting for. It will be a huge morale boost to our friends and family back home who are waiting to see Hitler ousted."

She brushed off her helmet and faced forward, ready to get going. "Besides, they need to know about you guys. You've beaten the odds, haven't you? Twenty-nine missions with your whole crew intact. What are the odds of that?"

"Yeah, but you're a girl." Eddie's fingers ran up and down the wires connecting his electric suit to the plane. "They never said they were sending a girl. I mean, if something happens . . ."

"Well, sometimes it's a woman's perspective that gets the job done."

"Maybe," the ball turret guy said. "But there's so much we can't prepare for. Be careful, lady. Do what we tell you, okay?"

She glanced back over at José. "Besides, this is *my* job, just like yours is bombing the smithereens out of the Nazis. You're willing to die, and so am I. What I could tell all your families back home makes the risk worth it."

Mary did know the risks. She'd done her research. Even if the aircraft made it back, she knew about the many crewmen who'd been killed by shrapnel that cuts its way through the walls of the plane. Pushing those thoughts out of her mind, she finished getting set up in her station.

Eddie helped her with the winter flying helmet with built-in earphones as the engines began starting up. He looped the snap-on oxygen mask and connecting hose around her neck.

"I'll help you when it's time for these," he stated. "It's important this oxygen is hooked up right. It only takes a few minutes for someone to asphyxiate. Oxygen's needed at 12,000 feet, and we'll be going up to 24,000."

She could barely hear him over the two engines that had already fired off.

Over the helmet, he adjusted her flying goggles, and then he paused, holding his mouth close to her left ear. "I'm sorry, miss, but you're gonna have to put that notebook away. We need to get these layers of gloves on, and I'm certain that pencil will be totally useless once you do."

She was sure he saw the panic in her gaze even behind the goggles, because he smiled as he gently pulled the notebook from her hands. "It'll be okay. I'll stash it over here with my maps. It'll be safe there, and I can help you with the details when we land."

Eddie tenderly layered three pairs of gloves over her hands. Silk ones next to the skin, electrically heated gloves over the silk, and a pair of heavy RAF fleece-lined mittens over the other two.

She held them up, struggling to wiggle her fingers. "How do you move your hands in these things?"

Just then, the engines roared, and though he said something else, Mary couldn't make out the navigator's words. He quickly grabbed her notebook and jotted down a few words.

Temperature—up to 55 below zero.

Winds—clocked at 200 miles an hour.

She nodded her thanks as she watched him return the notebook to his pile. Then he topped her bulky layers and parachute harness with a Mae West inflatable life vest. By the time he finished, she could feel the sweat rolling down her knees and pooling in her socks.

Mary thought of a dozen things to comment on—the bulkiness of the gear, the horrible screaming of the turbo-charged engines, even the rumble of her stomach caused by the vibration of the aircraft. Yet she knew it would do no good to talk. So she nodded to the navigator, gave him two thumbs-up, and forced herself to remember every sound, every smell, every emotion, and every physical response as the plane began to move.

Lifting the large camera, she took a shot of the navigator, fumbled with the film advance knob until she locked another frame in place, then shot a picture of the bombardier. She was thankful for the roll-film adapter that Patrick had thoughtfully installed, and for the dawning daylight filtering through the bomber's Plexiglas nose. Some of her shots might even come out.

From her position, she could see the fogged-in runway through the glass nose. Despite the limited visibility, the engine revved to full power, and *Destiny's Child* began taxiing.

Then she spotted something—a jeep was moving down the center of the runway only a hundred feet ahead. Mary guessed it was helping the plane to establish a straight course. She focused the camera on it and snapped a shot, hoping that she was doing it right, trying to remember everything Patrick had showed her. Soon the jeep pulled off the runway, and the plane sped at full power.

The plane lifted off the ground, and Mary let out a whoop. The laughter of ten men, flowing through the interphone, filled her ears.

"Sorry about that," she said, hearing her own voice echo in her ears. "I had no idea I was connected."

"Ah, don't worry about it," someone said. "A woman's voice over the phone isn't something we hear every day."

"Although I wouldn't mind one bit. . . ."

It was Vinny's voice; she had no doubt. The navigator glanced her way as if determining her response.

"I want to do the very same thing, every time," someone else said.

Mary believed it was the friendly voice of the copilot she was hearing.

"And I usually give in to my whim when we touch down, making it home. Can you believe it, guys? Today's the day, our last flight."

"You've made Uncle Sam proud," the pilot said with a fatherly tone. "Now let's do this thing and get home. I'm sure the little lady has more important things to write about than a bundle of old crew members who've danced with Lady Luck and successfully completed the tango."

When they finally climbed far enough to break through the cloud cover, the image of hundreds of B-17s rumbling all over the sky took Mary's breath away. Gradually the formations began to take shape, each one moving into place. She saw them clearly for a few minutes, but lost them as they soared into a second layer of clouds.

Once they approached the Channel, Mary discovered her flight gear had one final layer before it was complete.

"Here, put this flak jacket on." The bombardier handed her a thick gray vest.

Mary took it from his grasp, and it immediately hit the ground, its weight slipping through her fingers. A tinge of pain shot up from where the "jacket" landed on her foot.

"You're kidding, right?" she said over the interphone. "Is this thing lined with steel or something?"

"Basically, yeah."

She could see the navigator's smiling eyes even through the goggles.

"It's to protect you from projectiles."

Mary wrinkled her nose at the word *projectiles*. It was such a civilized way for saying stray bullets and shrapnel.

"You don't understand." She tugged at the jacket, but it refused to budge. "There's no way I'm going to be able to wear this."

"Here, let me help." The navigator leaned over and lifted it ,and placed it around her like a cloak. She wiggled her arms the best she could to fit them into the armholes.

He topped the outfit with a steel infantry helmet. "There. Comfy?"

"If comfy means doubling or tripling one's body weight— yes, I'm fine. Thank you."

"Wonderful. It's time to plug you in."

Eddie hooked her up, explaining the oxygen tubes and wires for the electric heat suit. Then he plugged in his own gun positions by electric wire.

Mary breathed in, feeling the cool flow and tasting the slightly metallic oxygen. Then she gave a thumbs-up and glanced at the notepad still among Eddie's things. She longed to record this experience as it unfolded, and made a mental note to herself.

I feel burdened, weighed down. Not only by the numerous layers of clothing, but also with the knowledge there's no turning back. This is it. We're entering enemy territory. The next group of planes we come up against will have one thing in mind—making sure our Fortress never returns home. But I trust these guys. They've completed so many missions. Yeah, I'm scared. Shaking in my boots! But I've got to be in the safest plane in the great blue.

She sighed and looked out the window. They were flying across the Channel with fighter escort. Vapor trails appeared like white wakes from the Thunderbolts.

Suddenly smoky bursts filled the air around the plane, with their thunderous reports following almost instantly. A few small plunks hit the metal frame.

Oh, dear God. Oh, Lord, help us. Mary didn't know where the prayer came from. Yet here, as shells continued to burst around the plane—like Fourth of July rockets gone bad—prayer felt like the right thing to do.

CHAPTER NINETEEN

Eddie glanced over at the reporter sitting in the makeshift seat. His crew had come so far, had fulfilled so many missions together—now this. What was the commanding officer thinking? Eddie had enough to worry about with his own duties, and this time he was in charge of a woman too?

It will be over soon, he told himself. *Before I know it, we'll be back, and she'll be out of the picture.*

It would be a good thing to have her gone. Just being near her made his stomach ache even worse than it normally did on missions. And the way he'd lied—he hadn't been that bad since the fourth grade when he'd nearly flunked his math quiz and meticulously worked with the red-ink pen to transform the D to a B. He'd got caught though—he hadn't counted on his mother counting up the red check marks on the page.

The fact was, Eddie *had* heard of this woman. Her black-and-white image in the newspaper had made her look older, more mature than she was in person, but he'd read her stories just the same. He'd even cut out the interview from the *Sentinel* about their crew chief on D-Day.

So why had he lied to her, saying he didn't know who she was? And why did he lie to Vinny, stating that the CO had put him in charge of her?

Yes, it would be a good thing to have her gone, to end his confused feelings. *But why does she have to be so pretty, and smart, and nice?*

The rumble of the plane reminded him this was no time to relive past memories or get flustered by the girl sitting beside him. *Edward Anderson*, he thought to himself in the same way his father had spoken when he'd been in trouble. *Listen up, boy. It's time to get mad. Fighting mad.*

Thinking of D-Day would help him do just that. He'd read another story by a different woman reporter. The way she described the beaches and the wounded men stirred his anger. So many American lives lost because of a few madmen.

Think of the German killers. The bodies lining the beaches. Even the citizens—mothers and children—killed by those Krauts who've decided to take over the world.

Soon Eddie felt his body heat up—more than simply the electric coils at work. Sweat poured down his back and chest, and his eyes burned. He'd used this tactic before, after reading that only one emotion could reign in a person at any given time. Now it had to be anger.

But then he glanced to his right once more and spotted Mary Kelley. Fear rushed in again faster than he could control it. Fear that she'd be the one hurt this time.

I'm going to club the person who ever placed her pretty face on this mission.

"Check your guns." The pilot's voice spoke over the interphone once they were well over the Channel.

The navigator jumped from his seat, nearly tripping over

Mary's feet, to one of his machine guns. She heard him mumble something, then listened to the small bursts of bullets and the replies.

"Tail guns, okay."

"Left waist gun, okay."

She heard her navigator report, "Right cheek gun, okay." Then a moment later, after crossing to the other side, "Left cheek gun, okay."

The process continued from the rear of the aircraft to the nose.

They finally leveled off, and it appeared as if they were suspended in the air—fixed in place. Huge metal machines jockeyed into position around them like toy planes hanging from a mobile in the sky.

The only hint of their motion was the white garlands left by the wingtips. Mary tried to imagine just who they were flying over, another world away. She'd been through enough bombing alerts to remember the alarms and sirens that sounded when bombers roared overhead. She could almost hear the women screaming and the children running for safety, then crouching in darkness as tense as a taut wire as uncertain minutes ticked by.

Oxygen flowed cool into her mouth. Awe of these men and fear of what lay ahead tussled for control of her emotions. She spotted movement from the navigator. He glanced at her, then pointed to the window to the south. She sucked in a breath and saw the snow-covered Swiss Alps. How majestic they looked, even from this distance. But then she spotted something else. Four B-17s swung out of formation and headed toward those mountains.

"They must be having problems and are aborting the mission. That leaves the rest of us in a tight spot. I hope they make it."

The crew members must have realized Eddie was talking to her, because no one else responded.

"Flak! Flak at three o'clock!"

The antiaircraft fire from the ground burst high and just to the left, but clicked closer with each explosion, as if someone were dialing in their position.

They're trying to hit us! Mary tightened her grip on the ammunition box.

The flak exploded, showering glimmering fragments—burning steel spinning through brown smoke.

"Those aren't just 88s. Some are the big ones—the 105s," someone said through the interphone.

Suddenly big, black bursts of smoke flowered in front of them. And it seemed as if they were instantly alone, like a rocking ship in a black sea, with no sight of the other ships.

Mary heard the clank of metal hitting metal and now understood why she'd been turned away from frontline work for so long. The battle was already raging, and they were hours away from their target. How could they possibly make it there and back without a serious hit? Even more than that, how had this crew done it twenty-nine times already without losing one crew member? The image of them on their knees before the chaplain came to mind.

Another missile—or whatever it was—burst right outside of the window. The concussion from the blast seemed to shoot through Mary's whole body. She heard her own scream echoing in her ears.

"Shut that girl up, will you?" a voice called out. "Heck, that hurt my ears more than the explosion."

Mary wasn't sure which of the men had spoken, but she bit her lip and tried to comply. She closed her eyes, squeezing them tight. But it only took a large bounce and another loud explosion for her to realize not knowing was worse. She opened her eyes, gripped on to the metal wall the best she could, and looked forward over the bombardier's head to the action outside. Mushroomed puffs of smoke marked the sky where the shells had exploded around the planes. A cinch of fear tightened around her chest, making it hard to breathe.

From her previous interviews, Mary knew that with each shell that burst, thousands of shards of metal bulleted in every direction. If direct hits exploded inside the plane, the results were fatal. But even a close explosion could seriously cripple a plane or injure crew members.

Over the interphone, the men kept each other updated on what they saw coming at them. Before her, Eddie and José were busy at work, each one knowing his part.

"Copilot to crew," she heard over the interphone. "Check-in."

She knew he was confirming the status of the crew and checking for battle damage.

"Top turret, okay."

"Right waist, okay."

"Left waist, okay."

"Radio, okay."

"Navigator, okay."

"Sage, okay."

"Bombardier, okay."

"Tail gunner, okay."

Their voices rattled over the line one by one.

"Mary, how about you?"

"Tagalong, okay."

Laughter echoed through the interphone despite what seemed a desperate situation outside.

Mary saw that since those other bombers left, they were now in an outside position. And just when she thought the shells exploding around them were bad, she noted German planes bearing down on them, ready to tango. And soon the dance began.

As the aircraft bounced around, she also realized that the duties of the pilot weren't only to stay on course, but to also keep out of the way of the other planes . . . and take evasive actions when it came to the Germans, especially the Me-100s that were firing rockets from their rear.

The level aircraft dropped suddenly. And just when her stomach returned from her throat, the Fort shifted to the right. Through the interphone, she heard the two pilots talking to each other, keeping watch over their half of the plane and any enemy threats.

"Kraut at four o'clock. Looks like a Me-410."

"It's in my sights," someone said.

Machine-gun bursts sounded from somewhere behind Mary. The rounds continued, until a "yee-haw" sounded through the interphone.

"The Kraut's outta control. I see him dropping. Look, a parachute!"

"Nice kill," Eddie shouted. "Now watch out, here comes his buddy!"

Although she couldn't see the action behind her, more machine-gun fire erupted from the two waist gunners and from the gunner in the top-turret bubble.

How long does it take to get to Berlin? Mary wanted to ask, feeling helpless as she pulled her arms tight to her chest. *How soon can we drop these stupid bombs and head home?*

Hours passed, yet the crew members of *Destiny's Child* had few breaks from the assault. It was nearly a constant stream of antiaircraft fire and enemy fighter aircraft. Yet surely they had to be getting close.

"The right, watch out for the Kraut on the right!" one of the men screamed. The plane jerked to the left.

"FW 190s!" someone shouted through the interphone.

Mary tried to remember what she'd read last night about the distinctive markings of the planes. She'd studied them in order to impress the crew, but now she understood that nothing she could ever say or do would impress them. These aircraft were more than just something to memorize facts about—this was their life . . . or death, if their number was up. Which she sure hoped wasn't today.

A flash of yellow zipped past her window, the black-and-yellow checkered paint on their tails and engine cowlings blurring by. She couldn't believe how close he was to their plane. *Get 'em, guys!*

The Fort continued to vibrate from nose to tail, and there

was a steady staccato from machine guns and constant clank of shell casings spewing everywhere.

"Little friend, little friend. We need some help up here," either the pilot or copilot said.

The P-51s, their fighter support, were indeed helping, but there weren't enough of them to go around.

"IP coming up." It was the bombardier's voice in her ears.

Mary remembered reading that originally the IP had meant a point thirty miles from the target where the bombardier would lock into the crosshairs and fly straight and level until bombs away.

Unfortunately for previous crews, thirty miles gave the flak gun ten minutes to concentrate on the approaching Fort, zeroing them into the sites. Many crews were lost. So instead, the new system was to make a minor change of direction every minute, until the last one ticked down. Then they would run straight and level toward the target.

As Mary's body shifted with the aircraft's adjustments, she lifted the camera from where it hung around her neck. She ignored the flak bursting around them in every direction, ignored the desire to scream, and instead set her jaw with determination, knowing this is what she'd come for.

"Bombs away!" she heard through the interphone.

She knew they'd released when *Destiny's Child* bounced up, due to the lightened load. Then suddenly the plane made a sharp turn to dodge the flak. Seeing her opportunity, Mary turned her camera to the window tilted to the ground. She focused and shot as a large plume of black smoke billowed from a refinery.

"You got it. You got it!" she squealed. Then it was time to turn home.

The flight home went faster than the trip there, and Eddie cleared his throat, speaking into the interphone. "We're only an hour from the Channel, gentleman. But keep your eyes open. Sometimes the worst part of the ride is at the end."

Mary sighed. They'd made it. Once they crossed the Channel, just a couple of hours and they'd be back on Allied ground.

But just as Eddie finished, his voice was cut off from an explosion that rocked the plane, and Mary's screams weren't the only ones filling the interphone.

"Oh no, oh no. The wing. Half of the wing is gone!" Reggie shouted. "The wing hit the tail. I'm going to check it out."

Mary's chest constricted, and she grasped her oxygen mask, breathing in and out, attempting to stay calm. She didn't dare look out the side window—didn't want to see the plane with half a wing.

This was it. She imagined the story now. *AMERICA'S SWEETHEART DEAD. Reporter for the* New York Sentinel *killed while stupidly joining a B-17 bombing raid. Just when they thought they'd made it home . . .*

She placed a hand over her pounding heart and imagined the London office waiting for her transmission, and Paul waiting for theirs.

Would her father be waiting and wondering too? What would he do if she didn't show up?

The plane bounced and shifted beneath her as the pilots attempted to stabilize it. She could tell they were backing off from the rest of the formation.

In her mind flashed images of an African safari story she'd read in *National Geographic*. The lions of Kenya always singled out the weakest in the rear, picking them off first. Feeding their hunger with those who couldn't defend themselves . . .

"We're losing oil," someone called. "This doesn't look good. If there was ever a time to pray, guys, this is it."

Just then, Mary's body pitched toward the ceiling as the plane dropped sharply.

"Abort flight plan. Our goal is to ditch in the Channel," the pilot called through the interphone.

"The wing. I was right," came another frantic voice. "It hit the tail; there's a big hole back here. . . ."

Mary glanced at Eddie. An oxygen mask covered his face, yet

still she could see his fearful eyes peering through the goggles.

"He's gone! No, no! Chancey's gone! Blown out with the tail!"

"Where's his chute!" another voice said, louder. "I don't see any chute!"

The plane turned and continued to shudder. Mary wished that she could ask where they were. Had they made it out of Germany?

She glanced up just in time to see the bombardier making the sign of the cross.

Other B-17s around them were hit. Mary's wide-eyed gaze watched three chutes emerge from a bomber before it made a slow spiral to the ground. *What about the others?*

Another aircraft exploded, leaving a smoky cloud. Below it parts of machinery fell to the ground, and Mary looked away, realizing there were most likely parts of men falling too.

"Sorry, guys, the ship's not going to hold for the Channel." It was the copilot's voice, jerking with the shuddering of the plane.

"Pilot to crew. Prepare to bail out."

Bail out? No, this can't be possible. It has to be a bad dream.

Mary tried to remember the instructions she'd been given before she boarded the plane. Did the three short rings mean to prepare to bail or actually go?

She remembered the CO saying that when they were over enemy territory to bail out individually—that way, if someone was captured, it wouldn't be all in one bunch. Yet hadn't Eddie said that he'd watch after her?

The navigator. Stick with the navigator.

Eddie was out of his seat in a matter of seconds, tearing off his flak suit and hooking on a chest pack parachute. Then he pulled Mary to a standing position, stripping off her flak jacket and hooking a chute on her too. He yanked the oxygen mask from his face and yelled into her ear.

"We're going to jump! Follow me. Count to ten after you clear the plane; then pull the rip cord."

Mary froze, wishing desperately that she had never taken this assignment. She closed her eyes and pictured herself back home at the City Desk, answering calls. *If I get out, I'm going back.... I don't want to do this anymore.... Please, if there is a God up there somewhere, fix this plane.*

The ground neared at an amazing speed, and she could feel the pilots attempting to level the plane.

"Do I really have to do it? Do I have to jump?" she said into the interphone. There was no response, no echo in her ear, and she knew the interphone was dead.

More flak erupted around them. Then three short rings. The navigator grabbed her hand and pulled her through the tunnel door. He grabbed the emergency latch to open it, but nothing happened.

One long ring.

He took her hand and rammed his shoulder against the door. She never actually felt herself leaving the aircraft. Yet within seconds she was by herself, hurtling head over heels through space.

Then everything quieted. The shouts, the sounds of the plane's engine, the flak explosions. Mary saw only white. She knew she was supposed to count to ten, but by the time she got to eight, in a panic she pulled the cord. The white umbrella chute slowly trickled upward. *Please open, please . . .*

The parachute opened with a terrible jerk. Above her the bloom of silk made it hard to see what was happening with the other ships in the air. But she did spot a German Focke-Wulf swooping down like a rogue eagle, heading straight for a cluster of five chutes in the distance.

Who are they? Men from Destiny's Child? *But where are the other chutes?*

As she glanced around, she saw one other parachute lucky enough to continue down unscathed. One close enough to make out the man's face . . . the navigator.

CHAPTER TWENTY

From the moment the cold air hit his face, Eddie had been planning their means of escape from enemy territory. He noted the lady's chute next to him—a good thing. But the others . . . they drifted north on an unseen breeze.

"Oh, please, no," Eddie muttered when he spotted the Focke-Wulf sweeping down toward them. "God help them." A simple prayer was all he could offer. He knew getting this woman to safety would take his complete concentration from this moment forward.

As he drifted downward, his mind's eye tried to form a picture of the terrain. *Sun to my back. Winding river over left shoulder. Large forested area to the right—adequate camouflage. Beyond the forest—fields bordered by hedgerows.*

His arm and shoulder ached from where he'd slammed against the door. No time to think of that now.

In the distance, two villages and a larger city formed a triangle. Eddie closed his eyes and pictured the map hanging over his cot. From his best guess, the larger city was Liege.

I should have spent more time studying that booklet of Dutch phrases so I can talk to someone in this country.

The fact was, they were in Belgium, hundreds of miles from free France, with little food and no shelter. If he were alone it would be more manageable. *Will the underground resistance find us? How can we ever find them?*

The ground neared, and he spotted the woman already sprawled on the white snow. She was moving, attempting to get up.

Oh, Lord, help me here. I'm in way over my head. Send us a protector. Please, God. If not for my sake, then for Mary's.

Mary floated down, eyeing the frozen field beneath her and the forest beyond. She wished she knew where they were. In Germany? She scanned the roads, expecting swastika-marked jeeps or guns pointed. Instead, everything seemed still, quiet.

She was about thirty feet above the ground when the parachute seemed to fold inward, dropping her like a rock. She squealed and attempted to get her feet under her, but instead twisted and landed with a hard thump on her rear and thigh.

She moaned and lay there for a moment, whimpering. Then suddenly a man loomed over her. "Well, Miss Kelley. I'm sure that's something you don't write about every day."

"They worked," she managed to mutter.

"The chutes? Of course they worked."

She panted loudly. "No. My mother's prayers."

He tilted down, resting hands on thighs. "You okay?"

"Yeah, I think so. Ouch." She rubbed her leg, hoping to ease the pain.

He reached a hand toward her. It was covered with blood. "C'mon, get up."

"Okay, but I can do it myself. Just give me a second to catch my breath." She noticed his jacket sleeve was shredded, and a chunk of flesh on his upper arm had been torn open.

"Ugh. What happened?" Her stomach did a flip, and she looked away.

"It's nothing. Come on, hurry. We have to get out of here."

Mary's chute stretched behind her. She sat there as Eddie hurriedly unbuckled her straps and pulled the silk into a bundle.

As she watched, he stripped down faster than she thought possible, rolling up his electric suit into a tight ball—except for one piece he'd ripped off and wrapped around his arm to stop the bleeding.

She struggled to her feet as he took their chutes, harnesses, and Mae West life jackets, darted to the opening of the forest, and quickly hid them under a pile of brush.

He came back with quick steps, again reaching for her hand. Mary swallowed hard as she noticed the pistol on his shoulder holster. Next to it were two extra clips of ammunition.

Mary slid her gloved hand into Eddie's. "Your gun. You knew all along this could happen. That we might wind up here, on the ground, fighting for our lives." She shivered, missing the heat from their electric flight suits.

"I told you that before you ever boarded the aircraft." He winced, glancing down at his arm. "Come on."

He pulled her along. The snow was so packed it was like walking on ice, but Eddie seemed to know how to dig in his boots for balance. Mary slipped and skidded behind as they darted into the woods. Pain shot up her leg with each step.

"Yes, of course," she whispered. "I heard the words . . . but you *knew*. You've seen it, haven't you? The planes, the chutes."

"Shhh . . ." He placed a finger over his lips and continued on.

She looked back, thankful they left no footprints, no drops of blood, on the hard-packed snow.

Then she heard it. The sound of vehicles approaching on a nearby road—Germans who no doubt had seen their chutes billowing in the cloudless sky.

Eddie tightened his grip on her hand, increasing his speed.

What a fool, she thought. *What a fool I am. And all for a story. Why did my father let me do this?*

"Here." Eddie whispered the single word, and then motioned to a dry irrigation ditch surrounded by thick shrubs.

She curled onto the cold dirt bottom, and Eddie slid next to her, pulling the shrubs over them as best he could. Her whole body quivered. She couldn't stop the shaking. She looked to see Eddie. They were face-to-face, but he was gazing upward, peering through the thin layer of brush covering them.

Are they coming? Will they find us?

She wanted to ask, but it was almost as if she wasn't there at all—he was so fixed on keeping watch for any sign of danger.

Minutes passed, then Mary was sure she heard a noise. Footsteps nearing. She held her breath, and Eddie's gaze finally met hers. Yet instead of fear, she saw a deep sadness—almost an apology.

He pulled the gun from his holster and aimed it upward. The footsteps came closer, and he cocked the trigger.

Outside their den, she heard the scraping of more brush; then the bits of blue sky turned into blackness. Then more brush, and a heavier burden covering their bodies. Finally a voice.

"Comrade. You safe. Germans follow my friend, wrong way. I return. Be still."

"Thank you," Eddie answered softly, but the man was already gone, his quick footsteps hurrying away.

Mary leaned close until her lips nearly touched Eddie's ear. "What if he's on the wrong side? What if he's going to turn us in?"

"No, I trust him." His breath was warm on her cheek. "We're in Belgium. The people help us. They hate the Nazis. Besides, I've been praying for a rescuer from the first sound of the alarm. Praying for someone to lead us home."

With a soft sigh, he uncocked his gun and slid it back into its holster.

Eddie didn't know how many hours had passed as day twilighted into night, but he was chilled to the core. And his arm.

He'd ripped the sleeve off his shirt and had Mary tie it into a bandage, but still he was losing feeling in it. Before, it had been warm and sticky with blood; now it felt like a cold, dead thing hanging from his shoulder. Ignoring the pain, he wrapped his good arm aground Mary. She eagerly pulled her body next to his.

Go figure. Never imagined this is what it would take to get a girl under my arm.

Eddie sighed and gazed at the feisty blonde. If captured, he knew he'd be taken to a POW camp, but what would they do with her? He shivered. *Lord, please keep her safe.*

"Eddie," she said in the gentlest whisper. "What if they find us? What if . . . ?"

"Shh, don't say it. We'll be okay."

He heard the slightest noise and lifted a branch. It was the man with the cap, stealthily moving toward them in the dimness, ducking and hiding behind trees, shrubs—every bit of natural cover the earth offered.

Eddie crawled to the edge of the ditch. *"Bonjour."*

The man pushed back the brush and shook his head as he noticed Eddie's arm. "You have escape kit? Yes?" He moved his hands to emulate a needle going into skin.

Morphine. Eddie knew the man was telling him to use the morphine from his kit. He shook his head. "No, I will be fine. I need to save it. For later."

The man shrugged his shoulders. "Then we go now." He helped Eddie out of the ditch first, then reached a hand to Mary. Seeing her face, the man leapt back in surprise. Obviously with her flight helmet and bulky clothing, he'd not noticed she was a woman. "Lady flyer?" their rescuer said in a loud whisper. "No. Cannot be."

"A women re-port-er." Mary motioned as if opening a newspaper.

"You on plane?" He pointed to the sky.

"Yes. We were shot down."

Their rescuer stroked his chin as if unsure whether to believe them. "We help flyers. We do not know about this."

Eddie took Mary's hand and pulled her to his side. "Both of us. We are together." He felt her give his hand a warm squeeze.

Then the man stepped close, studying Mary's face. His eyes brightened. "Yes! I know this face from paper. *Jack the Crew Chief*! Come, come."

It took nearly an hour to steal through the forest, darting from tree to tree, careful to keep the snow-crunching sounds to a minimum. Their eyes peered through the naked elms, branches reaching to the myriad of stars. Mary was glad for the moonlight that reflected a lavender hue on the snow.

Soon they were led into a small barn. Mary held her nose at the stench, and a grunt from the corner told her they were not the sole occupants.

The man shut the door behind him, and Eddie collapsed onto the ground as if unable to take another step. The man lit a lantern and hung it from the rafter. The swaying light bounced around the room, illuminating their guide's face. He was older than she imagined. He was so quick and agile.

"I am Roger. Dis my barn. And dis—" He turned to the pig in the corner. "Dis my darling Eva. If Hitler have such a woman, I do too. Yes?"

Eddie leaned up on his good arm and pulled a silk map out of his flight suit. "Sir, can you tell me where we are?"

"No, first we fix that arm. I be back."

Mary glanced around the barn. A rickety ladder led up to a loft. Not counting the dirty hay the pig slept on, there was nowhere else to hide. No place to keep warm. With all the coats and the traipsing through the woods, she wasn't really cold. But she knew she would be. Soon.

"Eddie, do you think we'll be okay here? I mean, is this our best option?"

His face was pale, even in the golden light. "I don't think we have a choice."

He gripped the part of his sleeve that was soaked with blood, then winced. "I think my arm caught on something on the hatch door when I was trying to get it open."

She knelt beside him and gingerly tugged on the fabric. *Be strong, Mary. You can do this.*

She succeeded with getting a tear started. She was so grateful he'd helped her, so grateful they hadn't been shot out of the sky. She thought about the others. Marty, the pilot who was so fatherly. That Vinny with his wickedly handsome grin.

"Eddie, the other guys. Do you think . . . ?"

He looked away, his voice quivering. "I don't want to guess what happened to them. I saw some chutes, but not enough . . . I just don't know."

Within a few minutes, Roger returned with a basin of water, some strips of cloth, and a pair of scissors. A few handmade quilts hung over his shoulder.

He handed the blankets to Mary and waved her out of the way. Then he quickly went to work cutting off the torn fabric, cleaning the wound, and bandaging it with fresh cloth. A pool of blood had soaked the hay under Eddie's arm.

"You rest now." Roger rose to his feet. "I keep watch, but I think the Germans got cold and tired too."

Eddie once again pointed to the silk map.

"Liege." The word rolled off the man's tongue. "It is that city. Filled with Germans, yes. But do not worry. We have a way . . ." He paused and looked at Mary as if remembering. Then he pulled out torn pieces of newsprint from his jacket. The paper was stained and smelled of fish, but sure enough—there was her face, smiling in black-and-white.

"Yes, that's me." She pointed to herself.

The man grinned broadly and nodded. "Then we find a way for airman and America's Sweetheart, yes?"

The man motioned for Mary to lie next to Eddie. She obliged, and he covered them both with the intricately sewn quilts. Seemingly satisfied, the man blew out the lamp and closed the door behind him. She heard him hunkering down outside the door.

"I think your prayers were answered, Eddie. Can you believe

it? A barn *and* a pig." As if agreeing, the sow snorted from her corner.

"And can you believe your pretty face in the paper saved your life?" he whispered.

"Well, if it weren't for that paper, I suppose I wouldn't be here. What was I thinking?"

"Still . . ." Eddie's voice was strained, most likely from the pain. "What a smart way to smuggle information—in newspapers wrapped around smelly fish."

"I feel honored." Mary curled closer to his side, a warmth flooding over her as if she'd known Eddie for years, not just one day. "I just hope they're as smart in smuggling us out."

Hendrick leaned back in his office chair and studied the locked door. It was after hours, and his plan was to slip in and slip out without anyone knowing he was here.

The image of the nurse whisking the baby away came to him again. The child had lain limp in her arms, but had it just been Hendrick's imagination or had he seen the infant's chest rise and fall? He'd replayed the image in his mind so many times that now he was sure it had.

He wished he'd asked to view the body. At the time, his only thought was to flee. To try to make sense of Katrine's words. But now . . .

I will find him.

Yet first, Hendrick had a job to do. He must find Katrine's file before Lydia did. While she expected all Katrine's paperwork to be in order, Hendrick knew differently. He'd been foolish for not going through the proper procedures, but honestly, how could anyone look at the girl and not believe she was pure Aryan? Genes do not lie. The blood of the pure and impure could be evidenced by one look at a person's face. Couldn't it?

Over the next hour, Hendrick shuffled through four large filing cabinets . . . but with no success.

He slammed the last one shut, curses flowing from his lips.

Does Lydia have the file already? Does she assume the worst?

Hendrick's heart pounded, and his legs felt as if they were going to give way. On the radio that someone had left on down the hall, German marching songs played over the airwaves, as if all were well in the world.

"I have to travel down there again. There's no time to waste." Hendrick strode from one end of the room to the other and back again. "To find my son. And to do so before the Americans push any farther north."

While the extent of the enemy's advance was not mentioned much over the state-run stations, Hendrick knew the truth. The Allies were pushing to the north, advancing more day by day. Bombers never ceased to find their way over Belgium, and more German-run factories were getting knocked out by the week.

With one glance back over his shoulder, Hendrick eyed his office for the last time. Eyed the photos of the children, stopping on the captured images of Sabine and Stella.

He'd given his skill, sacrificed his time and energy, to reclaim Aryan blood. Now it was time to leave it all behind and recover his own.

CHAPTER TWENTY-ONE

The barn door slowly opened, and Mary shielded her tired eyes from the morning light filtering in. She yawned and shifted her hip once again. She'd tried all night to get comfortable, at least comfortable enough to sleep. Finally, she gave up and just listened to Eddie's breathing and the pig's snorting. She'd snickered, imagining they were talking to one another. *Hey, boy, don't get too comfortable. This is* my *hideout,* she imagined the pig was saying.

But her mind couldn't help replaying all that had happened—from the early morning briefing to the late-night hog cohabiting. Gone were her notebook and the camera. *Come on, memory. It's up to you now.*

Roger, like a black shadow against the gleaming dawn, stepped through the doorway.

"I bring food."

Mary scooted to a sitting position as the rugged farmer handed her two sandwiches wrapped in waxed paper. "Eddie, wake up. Sandwiches."

"Is that eggs I smell?" He stirred beside her.

"Didn't you hear those dang roosters? Real eggs, not those wooden ones you're used to on base. Can you sit up? I'll help you eat."

"I be back." Roger grabbed a bucket from the wall. "I bring water for drink."

Eddie sat up, favoring his bad arm. His short hair was plastered down on his head, his eyes were still heavy from sleep. "But this man, he's so thin. I can see the hunger in his eyes. He shouldn't be feeding us."

"True, but there's something else in his eyes too. Appreciation. You represent freedom for him and his country."

Suddenly a soft whistling sounded from across the field. Seconds later they heard voices, shouts, and dogs.

The Germans.

Roger ran into the barn. "Hide!" He pointed to the loft. "Go. Go!"

Mary helped Eddie to his feet and pushed him toward the ladder. He climbed the best he could with one arm.

"Hurry, faster," she whispered, hearing the voices growing louder, closer.

Eddie climbed onto the loft and Mary followed, scampering behind him to the far corner, diving next to him under the loose hay and punishing her hip in the process.

Then she remembered the blankets, the sandwiches she'd tossed aside, and the stain on the ground where blood from Eddie's arm had seeped. *They'll know. They'll find us.* She placed her hand over her mouth to stop the trembling.

Even louder than the shouts of the German soldiers came the sudden squeals of the pig. *Eva.* Roger shouted something to her, and sounds of wrestling filtered up. Her squeals increased, and then there was silence.

The dogs' barking grew louder. Next came sounds of the barn door being kicked open.

"What's going on in here?"

"Sir, I am slaughtering my pig," Roger said in German. "To

feed my family, of course. It has been a hard winter, even though it has just begun."

Mary could hear the quiver in the farmer's voice.

"Are you alone in here?"

"My wife is in our house, sir."

"I mean in the barn."

"Yes, well, me and this dead pig. You are free to look around."

Eddie's hand took hers, and Mary squeezed, holding her breath.

"What is up there?"

"Nothing much this time of year. I store some hay, but everything has been lean this year."

The German cursed. "Stupid dogs, come. Do you not know the difference between man's blood and that of a pig? Carry on, imbecile. But know I'll be back. Tell your sweet wife pork roast is one of my favorite meals."

"Yes, sir. We will have dinner waiting, sir."

And only after the sound of the barking dogs filtered into the distance did Mary let out a slow breath. In soft whispers she translated what had just happened.

"Mary, how do you know German?" Eddie's brown eyes were still filled with fear.

"I grew up in a German neighborhood in New York. I learned some German words even before English—at least in song."

"We've gotta get out of here." Eddie's voice was raspy. "It's too dangerous."

"But you're injured. I don't think you'll have the strength to make it."

"You're the one who told me the German said he'd be back. We don't have much time."

Lee rose from the chair, leaned forward, and placed both hands on the polished wood of the commander's desk. She'd been packing to leave Paris for the front lines in northern France when she'd heard the news. Within an hour, she was on a plane to Bassingbourn, England—the home airfield of *Destiny's Child*.

"You know their plane crashed somewhere in Belgium, but you have no idea if any of the crew survived? No idea if Mary Kelley is dead or alive? Excuse me for being so blunt, sir, but I just can't accept that."

The commanding officer cleared his throat and leaned forward, folding his middle-aged hands on the desk in front of him. His light blue eyes looked weary; puffy bags hung below them. The vein in his neck thumped so hard she could see it, just like her father's.

"I'm sorry. But I told Miss Kelley this would in no way be a safe situation. If she went up, she would be doing so at her own risk. These crews deal with extreme combat on a daily basis. We prepare them as much as we can, but once they leave our field they are no longer under our control."

"But someone has to know something. Did another plane see them go down? Were there chutes reported?" She paced to the window and looked out to the tarmac where more Forts were lined up. *A new day. A new mission.*

But not to her. She wasn't going to let this go as easily.

"We've briefed all the other crews involved, but no one was close enough in the vicinity to give us any more information than what I've already told you. We'll simply have to wait until we get word."

"From the German POW camps? Is that who you're expecting to hear from?"

The CO shrugged. "I'm not at liberty to say."

"Surely there are underground workers in the area. We both know what I'm talking about. Can they get word to you?"

"We don't discuss these things openly, Miss O'Donnelly." The man stood, pushing aside his chair with his foot. "If we receive word, we'll let Mary's father know."

"Excuse me, Colonel, but this is a different situation. We're talking about a female correspondent here—surely, this is a unique case. Surely *someone* knows something."

"I can tell you this," he finally answered. "Sometimes we get requests—to check information, to ensure that the people who are being helped are not Germans attempting to infiltrate the escape system." He sighed. "But I can say no more. Again, I'm sorry. We're just going to have to wait and see."

Lee placed her hands on her hips, her gold bracelets jingling. "I'm sorry, sir. I'm afraid if I can't get help from you, I'll find it someplace else."

The man shook his head, and a surprised chuckle escaped his lips. "You are your father's daughter, aren't you? I'd recognize that stubborn set of your chin anywhere."

"Yes, and my mother's daughter too. And . . . if you remember, my mother pushes and pushes until she gets what she's after. Good day, sir. You'll be hearing from me again . . . and if you get a letter from my mom, tell her I'm fine. And that I'll contact her *after* I find my friend."

Roger's wife, a red-cheeked, plump woman with calloused fingertips and bitten-down nails, had thrown civilian clothes into the barn fifteen minutes after the Germans had left. Roger now led them along a dirt road toward who knew where. It grated on Eddie's nerves not to know his exact location at all times.

He glanced up at the German planes circling overhead, and it took everything within him not to continue to watch them as they looked for signs of him and his crew.

His arm ached, but he refused to use the morphine. If it wasn't sewn up soon, infection could set in. Then . . . well, he didn't want to think about it, but then he might need the morphine more.

On the outskirts of town, Roger led them to a small shed. A young couple peered from the window but did not come out to welcome them.

Could they be trusted? Was this place safer than the barn? Eddie wasn't sure, but what could he do? His head was spinning, and his legs felt weighed down as if by concrete boots. He had no choice but to trust. *Lord, You know. You see all. Only You can hide us under the shadow of Your wings.*

"Wait here. I come back after dark. After dinner."

"And if you don't come?" Eddie searched Roger's tired, sad eyes.

"Then someone else will. Yes. I promise this."

The door closed behind him. Eddie slid to the ground, leaning against a lumpy bag of potatoes. There wasn't room to extend his legs, so he pulled them tight to his chest. Mary sank down beside him.

"And to think I gave up my lovely room with private bath in the Hotel Scribe for this. I could be sharing drinks with Ernest Hemingway right now."

Eddie stretched his arm around her shoulders. "I'm sorry, ma'am. I'm not Hemingway. I can't compare when it comes to charming the ladies, but I am awfully cold."

She slid next to him, tucking her head under his chin. "Yeah, navigator. If it weren't for your quivering I'd think that was simply a new pick-up line—one that would make Hemingway proud."

He felt his eyes growing heavy, and he let his chin rest on the top of her hair. She smelled like the hay from the farmer's barn. Her closeness made his heart pound faster, despite his aching arm.

"Poor Eva," Mary whispered. "Roger loved that pig."

"Yeah, I knew we'd be safe then. I mean, if he was willing to sacrifice that . . ." He let his eyes close and felt his body relax. "I wonder where they'll take us next?"

"I just hope we won't be stuck in dark places like this for weeks, or maybe even months."

"Could be." He blew at a strand of her hair that was tickling his nose. "Just as long as we get out."

"It doesn't matter how long it takes. . . . We'll make it, Eddie, I know we will."

Eddie sighed, wishing he were as confident. *Lord, please.*

Just when they'd found a content place—asleep in each other's arms—Roger had returned to lead them on another night excursion. But that was hours ago. Now the edges of dawn threatened to spill over onto the cold earth as they walked over the hard-packed snow. She could tell by Eddie's shuffled footsteps that he wouldn't be able to make it much farther. They came across a large rock wall, and Mary glanced up. *How are we gonna get over this big boy?*

Roger tugged at her arm. "This way. We follow the wall to the gate."

Mary turned to Eddie, noticing the sweat pooling at his temples from pain. "Can you make it?"

"My arm's throbbing. I really need to lie down. But, yes, I'll do my best."

When the gate opened up, they came upon a narrow road. In the spots where the snow had melted was pavement. They had walked a few hundred feet when the road turned and a large shadow loomed in front of them.

Mary paused at the sight of a huge structure rising up from the snow. It may have just been her imagination, but the fortress—or whatever it was—looked as if it would take up an entire New York City block.

She gasped when she spied Nazi flags still fluttering from the first row of windows. They'd been betrayed. They'd trusted this man, and he'd led them straight into the hands of the enemy.

CHAPTER TWENTY-TWO

G et out of bed. Now!"

A screech and a flood of light interrupted Eddie's sleep. He blinked. A woman with waist-long gray hair glowered over him in the antique bed he'd been so grateful to collapse into last night. The slit through the heavy curtains showed that it was still dark out.

"Did you not hear me? Out of bed now!" Although she spoke in English, the accent was strong. He thought she sounded French, but couldn't tell if she was from France or Belgium.

In the doorway stood a broad-shouldered man, his frame blocking the view to the hallway.

Eddie scanned the room—tidy furnishings, Turkish rug, private bathroom. *Where am I now?* He tried to sweep the cobwebs from his memory. It had been dark when Roger led them away from the shed, but even that memory was blurred by the pain.

The castle. The kindly nun who welcomed us in. And Mary . . .

"Mary!" he shouted, struggling to his feet. "Where's Mary! What have you done with her?"

The woman's outstretched hand and intense gaze stopped Eddie in his tracks. *"Nem."*

"Excuse me?"

"I said *nem!*"

The man from the doorway, fists clenched, took a step closer. Eddie, struggling to stand and meet the threat, hardened his face and straightened his shoulders.

"Don't touch him!" Mary squeezed under the big man's arm. Darting into the room, she ran to him, protectively standing in front of his injured arm.

This was it. They'd been captured. Unless . . .

Suddenly it hit him: He was being interrogated. He knew the procedure—what information to give and what to hold back—but he dared not glance at Mary. *Lord, keep her silent.*

"Lieutenant Edward Charles Anderson. 0-565390."

The woman nodded. "Base? Squadron number?"

"I'm sorry, I cannot give that information."

"Do you not realize? I am Magda. You have heard of me, yes? I have come to take you on the next leg of the journey, but I cannot do so without your base and squadron number."

"I'm Lieutenant Edward Charles Anderson. 0-565390."

"Squadron?"

Eddie tightened his lips.

"Base?"

He dared to fix his gaze on the woman's dark brown eyes. "I cannot!"

"Do you not understand? I am here to help, but I cannot do so unless you give me the information I need." She motioned to the man standing behind her.

"Eddie, please." Mary took his hand. "Tell them. They're here to help."

"Quiet. This does not concern you."

"Yes, Miss Kelley. We know who *you* are." Magda pulled a folded newspaper from her pocket. The words had been torn away, but Mary's face smiled up at them.

"At least tell us this. When is the day of your birth, Edward Anderson?"

"July 12, 1923. But you have to leave Mary out of this . . . she is no use to you."

The woman's face broke into a smile, as did the face of the large man standing behind him. "You are checked out, yes. This line has been infiltrated by German spies before, and we must ask these questions, you see? True American flyers know never to answer those other questions, and good thing you did not . . . for we would have to kill you."

The woman's laughter filled the room, and she unwrapped her heavy coat, revealing a black dress with a patterned red scarf she used as a belt.

"Eddie, I need to talk to you. Alone." Mary tugged on his good arm.

"Not now," he said through clenched teeth, still unsure if he could trust the woman standing before him. When he tried to move Mary out of the way, pain shot through his arm, and he pulled it tight to his chest.

He approached the woman. "Where is the nun?"

The woman motioned to her bodyguard. "In the dining hall. In case we were forced to kill you. We would hate to have a bride of God witness such a thing."

Mary's thin hand grasped his forearm and squeezed. "Eddie . . ."

He turned and noticed Mary's wide eyes, realizing she was serious. "Can you excuse us?"

"But of course." Magda playfully glanced between the two. "I never want to intrude on lovers' conversations." She motioned to the man, and they stepped out and shut the door.

Mary sank onto the bed on top of the sheet still wrinkled from his sleep.

"That scarf. I know that scarf."

"Excuse me?"

Mary ran her fingers through her matted hair, and Eddie

couldn't help but grin at her wide-eyed expression. Her fingers played on her lap, as if she were attempting to type out the right words across her mind.

"Eddie, I know this sounds nutty, but that scarf. There's this friend—rather, a fellow reporter I know. She owned that very scarf. How could Lee have made this connection with the Resistance? Still, I wouldn't put it past her." She stood and clasped her hands in front of her chest. "We have to see if Magda can get word to Lee. She can help us."

"Gee . . . this seems awfully far-fetched to me. And I don't see how it would help. *If* this woman is a leader in the underground, she'll know what she's doing. These people are specialists. They've pipelined hundreds out before us."

"Yes, but you don't understand Lee. She's got connections even the queen of England doesn't have. If anyone can find a way to get us out of here, it's her."

"I don't know . . . it might be better not to bring it up. From what I've heard, these underground workers make sure that everyone involved knows as little as possible—that way, if they're ever captured and tortured, one person can't do much harm. She might not like it that you've figured out this connection." He lifted her chin so their gaze met. "But it's something to think about. If things don't turn out like we think, we'll try to get word to your friend, okay?"

"You're right." Mary shook her head as if brushing away her wild scheming. "Besides, who knows *how* she got that scarf. Lee could have cast it off, if she tired of the style. The woman drives me crazy sometimes."

"I thought you said this reporter was your friend."

"Did I say that? She's more of an acquaintance, really." Mary let out a low sigh. "But I have a feeling I'd be able to count on her if it really mattered."

Eddie and Mary were taken to the dining hall, where the nun sat waiting, and the priest beside her. They were two people in a room designed for two hundred.

Magda motioned for them to sit, and she paced as she spoke. "The Germans are looking for you, you see. They have searched all the homes near the crash site. The closets, beds, everything pulled apart and destroyed. They even looted, taking what little valuables the people still held on to."

"Just for us?" Mary tucked a strand of hair behind her ear and met Eddie's gaze. His face was pale, and his eyelids only opened halfway.

He let out a low breath. "And have they found anyone?"

Magda strode to a Nazi flag that still hung from the wall. She paused before it, reached up, and took the fabric in her two fists, pulling on it with strength that surprised Mary. The flag broke free and fluttered down, falling to the ground around Magda's feet.

Words painted on the walls in German still remained. Mary couldn't make them out, but one word stood larger than the rest: *Lebensborn.* She'd almost forgotten Eddie's question when Magda turned.

"Five." She clenched her fists to her sides. "With the body, and you two, that leaves only three unaccounted for. Unless the other airmen connected with a cell of my workers farther south, I have little hope for them remaining free—I am still trying to know this. I have sent a messenger to my cell."

"Body?" Eddie whispered.

Magda hunched before Eddie, placing a hand on his knee. "I am sorry to say. He was one without a parachute."

"Chancey." Eddie looked to Mary. "The tail gunner. When the wing hit the back he must not have had time to snap on his chute."

He turned back to Magda. "So what's the plan? What's going to happen to us?"

Mary's stomach growled, and she realized it had been nearly a day since they'd had anything to eat besides the candy bar from their kits. She thought of the sandwiches they'd been given but never had a chance to enjoy.

"We have a secret room here." Magda motioned down the hall with a toss of her head. "You will remain there for a few days, hidden. I know a nurse, too, who will tend to your arm."

"This place?" Mary glanced up at the writing on the wall once more. "What is this place?"

"*Lebensborn*. Source of Life. The Germans used it for their own evil schemes. A scheme to create a bloodline that would carry on for one thousand years. But it is abandoned now. Safe for you." She hurried on, refusing to meet Mary's gaze. "But first we must feed you. Make certain you are strong for the journey. Nothing is worse than an airman unable to keep the pace."

Mary noticed Magda had said nothing about her.

"And Mary?" Eddie asked. "She's coming with me, right?"

Magda looked away. "I am sorry. Not at this time. She will remain here. No one is searching for a woman, after all. And this home will be the perfect place for her to hide."

"No way. I'm not going without her."

"Do you think so?" Magda folded her arms over her chest. "And your life is worth risking for *hers*?"

"Of course. I promised to protect her."

"Yes? Well, then you can do it yourself." Magda motioned to the man, and he rose. She hurried out of the room, not giving Eddie a chance to respond.

The man lingered, a puzzled expression on his face. Mary wasn't sure why he hadn't spoken, but she guessed it was because he didn't know English.

She hurried toward him. "Sir?" She spoke to the man in German. "Convince them to include me too. I know this airman. He won't leave me behind. In order to save him, you will have to take me."

The man cracked a smile and shrugged. "I cannot, miss," he answered in English. "You do not know my mother. She is even more stubborn than he." Then a grin curled on his lips. "But do not worry. She will be back. In a few days, when he is well. I doubt she will abandon the airman for long."

They ate a hearty breakfast of sausage, eggs, and biscuits, and then the nun sent Eddie to bed with a promise that someone would be there in the afternoon to check his wound. They were taken to their private rooms, still wondering about the secret ones that Magda spoke of.

Mary helped Eddie to his room, where he collapsed into the bed once more. Now she had a choice—a bath or a bit of exploring. She lifted her arm and sniffed under it. "How did Eddie stand to be around me?" But still her curiosity won out. "I can hold out a few hours."

As she slowly walked down the long corridor, Mary wondered what the woman had meant by "Source of Life." Had it been a command post for top Nazi officers? Barracks for German soldiers? Surely such a beautiful place would be occupied by the most valued members of the Reich.

"And why was it abandoned?" she whispered to herself. She knew the American front lines grew closer by the day—but wouldn't this be perfect ground to hold? An ideal location for boarding troops for the fight?

The castle consisted of three floors with bedrooms running down two sides of the courtyard. Mary opened one door, then the next, but instead of rows of bunks, each room had a single bed with a flower-patterned duvet. Clothes had been tossed aside and items remained in the bathrooms as if someone had packed in a hurry. *Women's things . . .*

In one room Mary discovered the photo of a handsome blond Nazi officer on the dresser. She couldn't make out the other words, but it was signed for a woman named Katrine from a man named Hendrick.

A brush and mirror rested next to the frame as if a woman had looked into the face of her beloved as she primped herself for his return. Yet Mary frowned. Some type of skirmish had apparently taken place in the room. She stepped closer to a wall. Tiny drops had splattered the wallpaper, and they looked like blood.

A chill ran down her spine, and she thought of the horror stories Paul liked to read, checking them out by the armload from the New York City library. *A perfect setting for murder and mayhem*, she thought, hurrying toward the door. She let out a squeal as a person stepped in front of her.

"The Castle of Wegimont itself was first built in the fifteenth century, but modernized later," said the nun in English.

"Oh, my goodness, you nearly scared me to death, sister. . . ." Mary placed a hand over her pounding heart.

"Sister Clarence, please. The moat, courtyard, and four towers date from the seventeenth century. I learned this growing up as a girl, living not too far away." The nun hurried down the hall, and Mary assumed she was supposed to follow.

"It was the coal mines, you see, that supported the local people. Yet this place . . . " She motioned about her with a sweep of her arm. "This place is darker still. Come, let me show you."

Mary's peasant shoes echoed as she was led past the dining hall, through a separate wing, and into another set of rooms.

The nun paused before a closed door. "This is the chapel."

Sister Clarence opened the door wide, and an eerie chill hung in the air. It was dim, but Mary could make out a white altar, framed photographs of Hitler and Himmler, candles, and . . . was that a cradle? "What is this place? The women's things. The cradle. I don't understand."

"Come, come, there is more."

They walked farther until the nun swung open the doors to what appeared to be a nursery. Rows of cribs lined one wall, some knocked over on their sides. Bottles, toys, children's things. They were scattered everywhere.

"Where are they? Where are the children?" Mary hurried over to the nearest crib, picking up a stuffed doll, and pressed it tightly to her chest. "Just what has happened here? Or do I want to know?"

"It's a birthing home, for German mothers. They come here to have their babies, you see."

"And where are they now? Did they return to Germany?"

"Yes, most of them did. In mid-November, when the war drew closer. They were taken to Steinhoring, in Bavaria—the safest place possible, so the blood would not be lost."

"The blood?"

"The blood of the children. The so-called lifeblood of the thousand-year Reich. Aryan blood. They birthed these children to carry on what they started."

"Sister, you said *most* escaped. And what of the others?"

The nun lowered her gaze. "A few did not make it. It's very sad, but some . . . well, I will tell you later. But first, we must check on the airman. The nurse should be here shortly to tend to his wounds."

Mary had many more questions, but now was not the time. The nun was right. Getting Eddie well was the most important thing they could do. Only then would they be able to escape this country. This place the Nazis still held, refusing to lose any more ground.

She glanced around the room one more time, and then followed the nun. *Nazi blood, bred to carry them on for a thousand years. Now that would be an interesting story.*

CHAPTER TWENTY-THREE

Eddie found himself tied to what appeared to be some type of examination table, as the dark-haired nurse gingerly unwrapped the bandages on his upper arm. She tugged when a piece of the bandage stuck to his wound. He let out an involuntary moan. Hot pain swelled through his body, and he felt like he was going to pass out.

Mary had knocked on the door to his room, awakening him just an hour before, telling him some crazy story about this place being a Nazi breeding facility. He hadn't believed her at first, until he'd been taken to the delivery room to be cared for.

What did she say? Nazi women had come here to give birth? He tried to remember her words, but his throbbing arm wouldn't allow it.

A stench rose as the nurse cut away the bandage layers closest to his skin. The strips of cloth were caked with dried blood.

He looked to Mary and saw her eyes wide with fear. "I'll be

okay," he whispered. "Just you watch."

"Sure, Eddie. I know." She took his right hand and placed it to her lips. "They're going to fix you up."

The nurse hurriedly said something to the nun in German, and the nun placed a finger to her lips, silencing her.

Eddie looked to Mary for an explanation, but her brow was creased in a puzzled expression, as if she was trying to figure out the words herself.

Am I going to lose my arm? He pulled his fingers from Mary's grasp and covered his mouth, willing his stomach to calm.

You'll be fine. Think of something else, Eddie, he told himself.

The nurse moved around the room with practiced efficiency, and he knew he'd have to ask Mary about this place. Ask her to tell him again what it was all about. *Yeah, focus on that instead.*

The nurse approached him with a large pair of scissors and a needle. His eyes widened as she removed the cap from the long, thin syringe and aimed it toward his arm. He moaned and forced himself to hold still as she plunged it into his broken skin.

Mary was saying something, and though he stared at her lips, her beautiful lips, he didn't understand one word.

Then everything faded to black.

A cot had been made up for Mary on the opposite side of the secret room, yet she sat on the floor, her head resting on the mattress next to Eddie. She watched the rise and fall of his chest. Listened to his soft breaths and prayed as she had seen him do.

He should be awake by now. What's wrong? God, please help him.

On her lap was the small Bible she had found in one of his jacket pockets. She'd opened it, finding a spot he had underlined in pencil in the first chapter of Luke. She held the Bible near the lantern and cleared her throat.

"Through the tender mercy of our God; whereby the dayspring from on high hath visited us, to give light to them that sit in darkness and in the shadow of death, to guide our feet into the way of peace."

She thought of Sister Clarence's words, *What happened in this place made it even darker than the coal mines in the hills nearby.*

"It is pretty dark here, uh, Lord. If it's okay with You, could You help us to get away? Do like that Bible verse said; guide our feet into the way of peace. I don't really know what that means, but peace would be a good thing about now. And please, God, heal Eddie. Take the infection away. . . . "

A moan escaped Eddie's lips, and a chill traveled down Mary's spine. She'd prayed before, mostly when she was a child, but she'd never felt anything like the warm heat that filled her chest now.

"Eddie." She leaned close, her lips inches from his ear. "Can you hear me?"

He nodded once, then smacked his cracked lips.

"I'll get you some water. Hold on."

Mary lifted the glass from the side table and held it toward his lips. His eyes opened, and he took a small drink.

"Thanks, Mom. Can I stay home from school today?"

Mary hesitated. *Oh, no, he's worse than I thought.*

A smile formed on his lips. "Just kidding, Mary." He opened his eyes wider, studying the room around him. "Where is this place?"

She returned the glass to the side table and scooted back, creating space between them. "It's the secret room that Magda lady was talking about. It's off one of the main administrative offices. The door is hidden behind a bookcase."

Her eyes darted around the windowless room. Silk hangings hung on the wall. Silver candleholders lined a long shelf. And Eddie's bed had satin sheets. She felt heat rising to her cheeks, remembering the intimate undergarments she'd found in one of the dresser drawers.

"It looks like a fancy hotel room or something," he said.

"Something like that." Mary's finger traced the pattern on the Oriental rug beneath her. "For important German clients, I mean, officers."

"You said something about that earlier. Is it true this place was for German babies to be born?"

"And obviously conceived." She swallowed deeply, trying not to think of what had taken place in this room, and scooted back even farther. She'd never even kissed a man, let alone . . . Mary cleared her throat again. "But we're safe here. You can get more rest. It's the middle of the night, after all."

"I've really been out that long?"

"Yeah. You had me worried."

She rose and placed the Bible on the table next to Eddie's bed. He lifted one eyebrow as he watched her, but didn't say a word. She stretched. "I think I'll catch a few z's." She pointed to the small cot made up for her against the wall.

"Really, Mary, you should be the one sleeping here. I'll take the cot." He attempted to sit up and then winced, falling back onto the sheets.

"I don't think so. I'm fine, really." She laughed. "Besides, you haven't had a bath in days. Do you really think I want to sleep on the sheets you've been sweating all over?"

Eddie sniffed, wrinkling his nose. "Nah, I guess you're right."

She moved around the room, blowing out all the candles except one, and then climbed onto her cot, lying on her back.

She could tell by Eddie's breathing he wasn't sleeping. She turned to her side and pressed her eyes tighter. *Men are trouble,* she told herself. *Don't let your weaknesses pull you down.*

"Mary." His voice was no more than a whisper. "Are you awake?"

"Yeah, what's up?"

"I just have one question. What did that nurse say to the nun? It must have been in German or something."

She turned toward him, noticing how handsome he looked in the flickering candlelight. "I didn't quite catch it. She said something like, 'These are the ones—an answer to our prayers—we must send him with them.' "

"Him? Who do you think they were talking about?"

"I'm not sure." Mary let out a sigh. "But if the underground doesn't want *me* to go along, good luck to the other guy."

With no windows, Eddie had no way of knowing if it were day or night, except for the meals Sister Clarence brought. He and Mary had spread one of the blankets on the floor and were having their own indoor picnic. His arm still throbbed, yet it wasn't as bad as the heat that had coursed through it before. The nurse's sewing job had worked, and he knew within a few days he'd be well enough to set out.

Still Magda's words bothered him. Did she really think he would leave Mary? He glanced across the room and watched her eat. She broke off pieces of her bread and then closed her eyes as she placed each piece in her mouth, as if savoring every bite.

Poor thing, he thought. She was losing weight. He could see it in the hollowness of her cheeks. *There's no way I could leave her.*

He rubbed his gut, realizing the ache didn't come from hunger, but from trying to figure out their next plan of action. *I have to get my mind off this. Think of something else, Eddie. Talk to her about anything.*

He glanced at the Bible on the nightstand. It was as good a topic as any. Really, the best topic.

"Have I told you I want to be a preacher when I get back?" He smiled at the shocked look on Mary's face.

She sat crossed-legged, then pulled her knees to her chest. "Eddie, are you pulling my leg?"

"No, ma'm, I'm serious. A preacher or a farmer. Both, in my opinion, nurture new life. When I joined the military, I told them I liked the stars, but that they could put me where they wanted me. I ended up being a navigator. It was sort of a confirmation, and you know what that says to me?"

"That your head's always in the clouds?"

Mary took a drink from her cup, but he could still make out her grin peeking around the edges of the glass.

"I'll just forget you said that. I mean, seriously, a navigator finds the way. He doesn't plan the mission; he doesn't fly the plane. He just has to keep track of true north." He patted the Bible.

"I never thought of it that way before." Mary chuckled. "I think my tendency is to want to fly the plane." She looked around the room. "Gee, smart idea, Mare. And look where it brought you." Her look softened as she glanced at him. "Of course, it could've been worse."

Eddie felt his cheeks grow warm. "And you know," he started in again, "the Bible says God put the stars and planets in the sky to distinguish the seasons and the times. All that just for us. As I figure it, if God's willing to give us this universe, how can we think He won't take care of our smallest circumstances?"

"Even the circumstances of us getting out of here?"

"Yeah. I just need to keep reminding myself of that."

They sat quietly for a moment, and Eddie watched the light of the candle flickering along the wall.

Mary pushed aside her empty plate. "Do you think anyone else got out? It's been nearly a week. How long would it take them to make it back?"

"I suppose, if things worked out, they could be pretty close by now. Three guys can travel pretty fast if they have no injuries, especially if they find creative ways to use the transportation systems, like the train. Since free France isn't too far away, maybe they've already made it."

"And we'll make it out too, right?" Mary's blue eyes pleaded with him. "Both of us."

"Of course both of us." He scooted closer to her, taking her hand. "We're not alone. God is carrying us in His arms of deliverance." Eddie gave a soft laugh. "I think He did it on purpose, you know. He held me up there until the last mission to drop you down here with me. Heck, I think He figured if I was too busy worrying about getting you out, I wouldn't have time to fret about myself."

"Oh, you don't have to worry about that." She gently arranged one of the bandages on his arm. "I've been fretting enough about you to last a good long while."

Later that night, as Eddie snored, Mary couldn't help but think back to their conversation. *A navigator only has to keep track of true north*, Eddie had said. And for the first time, something concerning God made sense to her.

Could it be possible that I don't have to figure out this world and my place in it on my own? Could it be that I only need to focus on You?

Mary slipped out of bed as quietly as she could and took Eddie's Bible from the small table near his bed. She scooted across the floor to read near the flickering candlelight. She tried to find the verse she'd read before about the peace of God, but instead another underlined verse caught her eye.

"Jesus saith unto him, I am the way, the truth and the life: no man cometh unto the Father, but by me."

The way. The truth. The life.

She thought about her own limited church experiences, and also the few moments those flyers spent kneeling before the chaplain. While those things were fine, it seemed that only believing in Jesus would take a person down the right path.

She thought of Paul's Pointer: *It's not what you know; it's who you know.* His words were apparently more accurate than she first realized.

Mary closed the Bible, pulled her knees to her chest, and let her chin drop onto them. She glanced around at the finely decorated room, amazed that God could meet her even here. Then she closed her eyes.

Dear Jesus, I never knew what living life for You could look like, until I saw it in Eddie. I want what he has, Lord. I want You in my life like that. Somehow I feel it deep in my soul that accepting You is the first step and committing myself to following You is the next . . . no matter where it leads.

A scattering of thin, shriveled leaves lay over the two mounds in the garden. One large. One small. Hendrick scanned the three stories of windows, looking for any sign of movement before stepping from behind the tree and walking toward the mounds. Two wooden crosses had been planted where spring and summer flowers had previously nodded in the wind. A cold breeze hit his face, and Hendrick pulled his civilian jacket tighter around his frame—his chin dropping to his chest as he read the markers.

Katrine Mueller.

Baby Boy Schwartz.

Reading the marker was like a fist to his gut. He moaned, then noticed movement from the front door. He was about to bolt back to the trees when he noticed it was the nun who hurried down the front steps as if she were on a mission. The nun who had been there that day. Who'd heard Katrine's lies.

"Sister!" The word burst from Hendrick's lips. Though there was always the nagging feeling that someone would come for him—come to imprison him for abandoning his post—he had no reason to fear a nun.

With long strides, he jogged across the frozen ground toward the woman. She paused and turned, her eyes wide. Hendrick halted his steps and stroked his beard, realizing she knew who he was despite his new look.

"Herr Schwartz." Her voice caught in her throat. "I never expected to see you here."

"I should say the same. This place has been abandoned for weeks, has it not?"

"Yes, well. Of course. I was just checking on a few things I left behind." Her thin fingers reached up and fumbled with the cross hanging around her neck. "Is there anything I can help you with?"

"My son. I have come for him." He watched as the color drained from the nun's face, making it as ashen as the gray sky overhead.

"I'm afraid that's not possible." She paused, closing her eyes as if trying to find the right words. "I was there when his body and soul were committed to the Lord."

Lee pressed the phone into her ear as she read the latest story to Lyle, back at the news offices in London.

"That's right, Lyle. It's Eisenhower's official statement about the U.S. Congress giving him his fifth star. He's only the third one after Marshall and MacArthur to receive that rank."

Lyle's voice was breaking up, and she closed her eyes to focus. "No word on . . . but we should know . . . "

Suddenly she felt a hand on her shoulder and opened her eyes, annoyed. She frowned at the young soldier standing next to her. He had black hair and a handsome face. He looked tired, though, and a bit confused. Lyle was still rattling in her ear, and she realized she'd just missed everything he'd been saying.

She covered the mouthpiece with her hand. "Can't you see I'm on the line? It's sort of important."

"I'm sorry, ma'am." He slipped his cap off his head and twisted it in his hands. "My name is Vinny Rosario. I got word from my commanding officer to come talk to you as soon as possible. He said—"

Lee glanced down and noticed the silver wings on his uniform and a patch on his sleeve reading *Destiny's Child*.

"It's you, you were on the plane. . . ." She placed a hand on the airman's arm, then shouted into the phone. "Sorry, Lyle. Gotta go." She quickly hung up the receiver.

"It's you; right? You were on the crew of *Destiny's Child*. Did you escape from Belgium? Of course you did, you're here." She grabbed his arm and pulled him out of the room into a quiet corner in the lobby of Hotel Scribe.

"I got into Paris just last night. Two buddies and I . . . " He lowered his head. "We're the only ones who made it out that I know of."

"But there were others who made it to the ground?" She pulled her notepad from her pocket. "Mary Kelley made it to the ground, right? Do you know what the name of the closest town was? How many chutes where there? Were they clustered together, or did they fall separately?"

The man's face was red, and tears filled his eyes. Unashamedly, a sob emerged from his mouth, and he covered his face with his hands. "I saw them go out. Eddie and that girl. I tried following them, but my chute caught on my stupid seat." He blew out a quick breath and looked at her.

"I was too far away to see exactly where they landed. I tried to find them. Adam, Marty, and I, we looked around for a few days, but the Germans wouldn't let up, and we had to make it out on our own—those few phrases in Dutch we learned were enough to let us catch a ride in a wagon heading to France."

Lee had never seen a man cry before. She didn't know what to say. She tucked her pencil behind her ear, a habit she'd acquired from Mary.

"Ma'am, Eddie was my best friend. And I swear, if something has happened to him . . . if he doesn't make it out . . . why, I don't know if I could ever forgive myself."

She opened her arms, and he crumbled into her embrace. She squeezed him as tight as she could. "I promise you, I'm going to do everything in my power to see that we find them, understand?"

A tear threatened to trail down her cheek, and she brushed it away. "Mary was, *is*, my friend." Lee laughed and stepped back. "At least I'd like to let her know she is. And I know some people who can . . . Well, let's just say, you give me every single piece of information you have, and I'll see what I can do. Deal?"

Vinny sniffed loudly and wiped his nose with the back of his hand. "Deal."

CHAPTER TWENTY-FOUR

Lee and Vinny found a quiet table at a café not far from the Hotel Scribe. Not too long ago, the Parisian owners had been serving coffee and biscotti to German officers, and it was clear from the smiles on their faces they were thankful it was now the Americans they catered to.

The two spent hours poring over every possibility—capture, help from the underground, possible injury, until Vinny's eyes glazed over.

"Are you sure you saw both Mary's and Eddie's chutes?" Lee asked again, glancing at her notes.

Vinny rested his forehead on his hands and closed his eyes. "I don't know. I think so. I could be wrong."

A man in uniform approached their table. Lee glanced up, perturbed at the interruption. Tall, thin, and balding, he looked vaguely familiar.

"Sorry to interrupt." The man extended a hand to Lee. "Name's Patrick Jessup. I'm a photographer. I—"

"Of course!" Lee stood, taking his hand and giving it a warm shake. "You worked with Mary, didn't you? I remember seeing your name on the *Jack the Crew Chief* photo. I've seen you around the hotel."

"That's me. I worked with Mary Kelley quite a bit." He nodded to one of the empty chairs at the table. "Mind if I have a seat? I contacted the CO in charge of *Destiny's Child* today. I'm nutty with worry about Mary." He rubbed his eyes. "Can't sleep thinking about her over there by herself, hurt, scared. And the newspapers are a waste of time. Not a word . . . I think they're afraid of the public's response to losing their sweetheart."

"I know. It's so frustrating, but please." Lee swept her hand toward the chair. "Mr. Jessup, this is Vinny Rosario, one of the men from the flight."

The two men shook hands.

"Call me Patrick. I don't want to get in the way, but I'd like to help if I could. I suspect I was one of the last people to see Mary—working with her to figure out that camera, you see." He turned to Lee. "Did you know she was taking one up with her?"

"No, but I'm not surprised." Lee turned to Vinny, placing her hand on his. "I know you're tired, but can you tell the story again, just one more time? Maybe Patrick here will pick up on something we missed."

"Sure, lady, but can I have another black and tan first?" Vinny lifted his finger and motioned to the bartender. "What's one more gonna hurt?"

"I should've said something, Eddie." Mary paced their quarters, which seemed to grow smaller by the day. "I should've asked Magda about Lee. I'd know that scarf anywhere. Lee used to tie up her hair in it, looking like she just stepped out of the pages of that fashion magazine she used to work for."

"You have quite the imagination. I mean, the same scarf? Really, Mary . . ."

She tossed a cushion at Eddie, smacking him in the face.

"You can blame my mother for that!"

"For your good aim?" He brushed down his hair where the cushion had ruffled it.

Mary couldn't help but smile. The beard he was now growing helped him to look more like a Belgian farmer than an American flyer. The clothes helped too—the white shirt with brown buttons, baggy trousers, black suspenders.

"No, for my wild imagination, silly." She placed a hand on her hip.

"How so?" He tossed the cushion back at her, but she ducked and it sailed over her head. She stuck out her tongue.

"Since my mom worked at the paper, she'd always bring a copy home. Then she'd make up her own fanciful tales to go with the pictures. Instead of reading about someone else's plight, she'd put me in the story."

"No wonder you're such a natural . . . actress."

Mary picked up the cushion and lay back on the rug, tucking it behind her head. "I agree. In fact, I've been thinking about that too. Yeah . . . sometimes I wonder if this whole reporting bit has just been a role I'm playing. Maybe it's just real-life dress-up."

"I don't think so. You have a gift. A talent for seeing the stories no one else sees, and pointing out the hero inside each of us."

She leaned up on one elbow. "How do you know, mister? I thought you said you'd never heard of me. Never read my stories."

Eddie affected a wide-eyed, innocent look. "I said that? I don't think so; you must be thinking of someone else. . . ."

Mary frowned, jutting her jaw forward and squinting in a threatening manner.

Eddie rolled his finger around the white collar of his farmer's shirt. "Uh, I sort of lied. I didn't want you to get a big head and all."

Mary sat up with a start, grabbing up the pillow. "Edward Anderson!" Within a few seconds she stood over him, striking his face with the cushion gently enough not to hurt, but quick enough that Eddie couldn't swipe it away with his good arm. As hard as she tried to maintain her stern countenance, she felt it breaking into a laugh.

Finally he caught her wrist and held tight. When she paused, looking down at him, she felt a knot forming in her throat.

His eyes were warm. "This is one thing I won't lie about. Mary Kelley, I think I'm falling—"

Suddenly the door swung open, and Magda and her henchman, as they now referred to her son Hans, entered. Eddie dropped Mary's arm, and she turned toward the door, the heat of embarrassment rising in her face.

"The Germans, they have opened up on American army in Ardennes—not far from here." Magda was panting, and her eyes were wild. "Tanks—men, they are in town, everywhere moving to the east. I am afraid more will be coming. It seems they will throw everything into regaining lost ground. They might even seek to board in this place."

Magda approached Eddie, reaching up and patting his sore arm.

He flinched slightly. "Hey, what was that for?"

"I see you did not pass out. You are well enough to travel. Pack your things, both of you. I'll be back tonight with the plan."

Magda stalked out of the room. Hans turned, winking at Eddie and casting Mary a knowing smile. Her jaw dropped, and she felt like hurling the cushion at *him*, but Hans hurried from the secret room, shutting the door behind him before she had the chance.

Mary folded her hands over her chest, and a cold chill washed over her. *If things were bad before, what chance do we have of getting out alive now?*

"Did you hear that?" She looked into Eddie's face. "There are even more Germans around here. Are we really supposed to leave this place with *them* out there?"

Eddie sank onto the bed but didn't say a word.

She tugged on his ear. "Eddie, are you with me? Did you hear what Magda said?" She sat on the bed next to him, feeling the warmth of his leg against hers.

"Of course." He swung his arm over Mary's shoulder and drew her close. "She said 'both of you.'"

———————————

The nun led Hendrick into the castle. To Frau Schmidt's office, and then to the bookcase. The nun pressed on it, and it swung open, revealing a secret room. They walked through, and there among the rows of cribs lay a cradle just like the one he'd purchased with the swastika on the headboard. And in the cradle, his son . . .

A cold wind blew on his face. I have to find shelter and food. How will I care for him? Where can I find help? Hendrick glanced down at the child in his arms. His feet were heavy as he slogged through the thick, wet snow. He pulled his jacket tighter, looking down at the baby's face, amazed how similar it looked to his Stella's. Same blonde hair. Same wide, blue eyes. Yet there was also Katrine's resemblance in the baby's features. Poor Katrine.

He spotted a sign at the crossroads and frowned. The words were in Polish. He recognized the city names from those on the files of the children in his shipments. The words seemed to fade in and out, and he looked around, realizing he was no longer in Belgium.

Suddenly Hendrick heard the rumbling of trucks approaching. German trucks driven by SS soldiers. He waved them down with one arm, cradling his child with the other. The truck pulled to a stop, and Hendrick noted faces in the back. Children, so many children. Those he'd processed. Those he'd placed into good German homes. Faces from the wall in his office.

"Another one!" The soldier in the passenger's seat jumped from the truck. "Another son for the Fatherland."

"No, wait. That's my son," Hendrick called. "I'm a German officer. I—"

The soldier placed a gun to Hendrick's head and without another word, swept the child from his arms.

"My son!" Hendrick screamed. "You cannot take him!"

Hendrick sat up with a start, his heart pounding. His blanket was pressed to his chest. It took a moment for him to remember where he was. In a rented room, in the city of Liege. He'd come for his son, but found only a grave.

Another dream. The children in the transport. Had Stella, sweet Stella, been pried out of her father's arms in such a manner?

A shiver ran down his spine, but Hendrick refused to accept those thoughts. It was a dream, nothing more.

Yet . . . he remembered Frau Schmidt's office . . . and the bookcase. He'd vaguely remembered her pushing against it, as if she were shutting a door.

Is this a message from the gods? Is my child there?

Hendrick jumped to his feet, knowing he could not return to Brussels, or even attempt to make it back to Berlin, without knowing for sure. He remembered the ashen look on the nun's face when he'd mentioned his son.

"She's hiding something," he mumbled to himself, pulling on the civilian clothes, now wrinkled and dirty. "And I must find out what it is."

Magda and Hans had brought a small table into the room, around which the four of them now sat.

Magda held Eddie in her unblinking gaze. "You will go into the town of Verviers. There are many refugees, and you will not be noticed." She placed two white handkerchiefs on the table. "Go into the church in the center of town. Airman must carry one handkerchief with the corner peeking out. With the other one, you must blow your nose like this."

Magda lifted it to her face and blew loudly. "Over and over like that, yes?"

Eddie slid on the peasant's jacket. It was too short in the arms and waist, and he hoped no one would notice. "Yeah, I can do that."

He glanced at Mary, noticing how pale she looked, how small and helpless in the flickering candlelight. *I swear if anyone touches her . . .*

"A man will approach you. He will ask in French if you have

a cold, and you will follow him to a safe place on the edge of town."

"But I don't speak French. How will I understand him?"

"Listen carefully: *Je vous vois avoir le rhume*. Now repeat."

"*Je vous . . .*"

"*Je vous vois avoir le rhume.*"

He tried it again, and got it right.

"Very good. Now keep repeating it in your head."

"And Mary?"

"At first she was refused. They told me they would come at another time for her."

Eddie felt Mary slide her small hand into his. "I'd stay rather than leave her. You told us both to get ready." Eddie tightened his grip.

"This is what I told them. So they found a way. She go too."

"When do we leave?"

"In the morning. At first light."

Mary pulled her hand from Eddie's. Then she rose and gave Magda a quick hug. "I can never thank you enough. I don't know what I'd do if I had to stay."

Tears filled the older woman's eyes, and she quickly wiped them away. "These airmen. They risk their lives to help our people. I know you both would do the same"—Magda pointed to the sky—"if I had been the one who had fallen down to you."

"The shadow of wings." It was Hans who spoke this time.

Eddie turned to him in surprise.

"They fall over us many time. And for each one I pray. By this we find our own freedom. To help you is to help our people."

Lee and Patrick were the last ones remaining in the café, except for the bartender, of course, who cast them impatient looks as he wiped down the polished wood bar yet again. Vinny had left hours before, his head down and shoulders sagging as if he carried the weight of *Destiny's Child* upon his back.

"Okay, Patrick. Let's go over this again. Vinny remembers

seeing five or six chutes, and he is pretty sure that Mary and Officer Anderson were two of them—the two floating down closest to each other. If that's the case, why haven't we received word? Vinny was able to get out rather quickly. So do you think it's because one of them is hurt? Could it be Mary, and the navigator doesn't want to leave her? Or maybe he's hurt, and she doesn't know where to go. Or maybe she doesn't want to leave him. That sounds like Mary—unless she was alone. I mean, just because they went down close to each other doesn't mean they're together. Would she have any idea how to get out of there? Would anyone help her?"

"Lee, stop." Patrick raised both hands like a traffic cop. Yet his eyes were sincere, and she knew he cared as much as she did.

Maybe there was more than just friendship between Mary and this photographer? Lee couldn't stop the thought from crossing her mind, and she suddenly looked at Patrick with fresh eyes. *He is handsome in a Benny Goodman sort of way, except with less hair, of course.*

Patrick sighed. "You're going to drive yourself crazy with all this worrying and wondering. Sit there and catch your breath. All your fretting isn't going to help your friend one bit."

"You're right. But I know something that will. Do you have enough film and supplies to last you a week or so?"

"Lee, I've seen that same determined look in Mary's eyes. What in the world are you up to?"

She cocked one eyebrow. "What do you think about heading for the front lines? I have a friend who can give us permission. Do you think Lyle will let you?"

"Let me? As if he had a choice." Patrick rose, then tucked the chair back to its place under the table. "Can you give me an hour to pack?"

Eddie and Mary were attempting to get a few hours' sleep when a knock sounded at the door.

Mary glanced at Eddie and sighed. "Well, navigator. It looks like they've come early. You ready for this?"

The door opened, but instead of Magda and Hans, the priest stepped through.

"Oh, boy, we're dead now," Mary muttered, feeling the knot in her stomach cinch tighter. "You know things are bad when they send in the big guns."

Eddie moaned. "Mary, *stop*. You've got me quaking in my boots."

Mary started to stand, but the priest gestured for her to remain seated. He glanced out the door, motioning to someone, and seconds later the nurse and Sister Clarence appeared with a white bundle.

Then the package moved, and they heard the softest coo. Mary jumped to her feet.

"Sister, a baby? Is it one of the ones born here? One who didn't make it out?"

Without waiting for permission, Mary lifted the blanket to see a sweet face staring up at her. The child had the most brilliant blue eyes she'd ever seen and amazingly thick, dark hair.

"Oh, can I hold him?" She turned to Eddie. "Look, a baby."

Eddie moved to her side, his brow furrowed as if trying to make the connection.

Mary reached out her arms and swept the baby up, pulling him close. "He's so beautiful. Oh, little guy, what have *you* already faced in this big world?"

The nun and nurse gave each other a knowing look.

"What?" Mary asked.

Eddie placed a hand on her shoulder. "Mary, we'll be leaving soon. He's a cute kid, really. But I don't think now's the time."

The priest said something in Dutch, and the nurse motioned to the bed.

"Sit, please. There is something we must talk to you about," Sister Clarence said.

The priest shut the door behind him, and they moved to the bed.

Mary sat with the infant on her lap. He looked up at her, bobbing his head as he did. "What's his name, sister?" she asked.

"Samuel. His name is Samuel."

CHAPTER TWENTY-FIVE

As Lee walked up to the colonel and took his arm, she—for an instant—felt it wasn't really her treading over the rough, wooden floorboards, but her mother. Her mother's charisma. Her mother's charm. Her mother's sly half smile.

The colonel was talking to her about a dinner party he would be hosting the following evening. She nodded and grinned without truly hearing. *I've come three thousand miles to escape my mother, only to realize I've become her.*

Lee knew her charm was for a purpose. Her poise was focused in a different direction than her mother's—news instead of niceties. Helping a friend instead of climbing the social ladder. Still, she knew what it took to turn a man's attention. To get what she wanted from him with a nod, a smile, and an attentive look. But her time for playing the doting companion was about up. Mary needed her.

"Excuse me, Colonel, but I won't be able to join you for dinner after all. I have a photographer waiting outside. We're going to the front lines in Belgium to get a few stories. I think the guys on the front will go to bed tomorrow night with a smile on their faces, knowing their mamas will be reading about their exploits in next week's paper."

"Of course. Maybe some other time. I'm eager to read your stories, Lee. Let me know how it goes." He ran his fingers through his graying hair and winked.

She patted the colonel's arm and offered him a warm smile. Getting permission to head into a dangerous situation had never been easier. "I'll be sure to do that, sir. When I return."

Mary gently rocked the baby. Sister Clarence sat next to her on the bed. The nun placed her finger to baby Samuel's hand, and he curled his fist around it. She continued the account she'd been telling. "I heard the screams and knew something was very wrong," she said. "I sent for the priest so he could offer last rites and then hurried into the delivery room."

Mary focused on Samuel's face, while picturing the scene in her mind. The baby's eyes were growing heavy.

The nun shook her head, tears gently trickling down her sad face. "It was too late. Katrine was slipping away."

Katrine. Mary's mind went to the photo she'd seen in that room. It had been inscribed to Katrine. *The blood splatters on the wall* . . .

"The nurses in the delivery room were fired and sent away. They were told if one word of this was leaked, they were as good as dead. They had overheard the young woman's confession. She had tricked him, you see. She was a Jew in hiding. The officer knew that if word had gotten back that he had slept with someone unclean, *he* would be jailed. And the fact that he'd had a child with her—that was worthy of the death penalty."

"Then what happened?" Mary asked, peering down at the now-sleeping infant.

"We hid the baby. We told the officer he too had died. He left for a time, and a few weeks later showed up again, looking for his son. He didn't believe us. Thought the child still lived." She wiped the tears from her cheeks with her creased hands, and a slight hint of sternness shown in her eyes.

"We knew if he found him, he wouldn't kill the baby. Not right away, at least. It would be too hard to explain. He would use him, own him, like any other object. But the baby would always be evidence of his defilement. Hatred would grow and eventually . . ." The nun sighed. "Love and hatred cannot possess the same space."

The priest said something in French, and the nun kneeled before Eddie, taking his hands in hers.

"This is why we must ask you to take the child with you. We have prayed much for a deliverer. And when you came . . . well, you are the answer to prayer."

"You want us to do what? To try to escape . . . with a baby?" Eddie stood and paced across the room. "Don't you think it will be hard enough just to get ourselves out?" He looked at Mary, studying her. Her stomach knotted. She knew he was worried— worried he'd not be able to protect her as he'd promised.

Sister Clarence stood, and Mary returned the baby to her. She pressed her fingers to her temples, wishing for the hundredth time since she'd strapped on that parachute that she'd never asked for this assignment. *Who cares what my father thinks? Who cares if my stories never make the front page? I just want it all to be over. . . .*

"Do you not think that God has made a way?" Sister Clarence rattled on. "A man and a woman, falling from the sky. A woman who speaks German. A loving couple. Does this not seem like destiny? Like our great Lord's hand is over us all?"

Eddie seemed deep in thought as he turned and walked to the far wall. He stood there for a full minute, then turned to face them.

The features on his face had softened, and he stepped toward Sister Clarence. He reached out with his large hand and stroked the baby's head. "You've been praying for a protector?" He took the child in his arms and approached Mary.

The priest lifted his large golden crucifix from his chest and began fumbling with it, rubbing it as if attempting to gain strength from the emblem.

"Mary, do you realize?" Eddie's voice was low, as if not to wake the baby. "My plane. Its name—drawn from a hat—*Destiny's Child*."

Tingles traveled up the back of her neck, yet something still didn't feel right. If the priest and nun loved the child, which was clearly evident, why did they not keep him and raise him themselves? She looked closer, peering into Sister Clarence's face. She thought of one of Paul's Pointers. *A good reporter can see the truth in someone's eyes, even if his or her mouth is saying something completely different.*

"Sister Clarence?" Mary approached the woman, meeting her eye-to-eye. "Is there something else you're not telling us?"

Sister Clarence hesitated, then nodded. "The officer . . . he's been back again. People saw him around town a few days ago. We thought the grave marker had convinced him, but it seems he is still searching for his son."

Mary turned to Eddie, who now held the infant against his chest, curled up in a little ball under his chin. Her heart sank with regret, but what could she do?

"It's not bad enough that we need to escape the country?" she said. "It's not bad enough there are Germans all around; now we're going to be hunted by a Nazi father who wants his son? You know how they feel about their heritage, a thousand-year Reich and all that. I'm sorry, but we can't do it."

She turned to Sister Clarence. "Eddie is a navigator. Do you realize how important his job is? Do you know how many times he's risked his life to help your people?"

Eddie interrupted. "We'll do it. We have to try."

"But what about getting out? Getting home? Eddie, this is not your responsibility." *But I am*, she wanted to add. *What about me? What about us?*

"Look, Mary, when I read the Bible, I see a lot of times when God called people to do things they didn't want to. Take Joseph, for example. God told him to take care of Mary, and care for the child not his own."

"Eddie, I know the Christmas story, but that's different. That was God's Son, and this . . . this child is the son of a Nazi."

Eddie lifted the baby and swaddled him close. "Every human is created in the image of God, no matter whose blood pumps through his veins. God knew this child from conception and has a special place for him. It's no accident He brought us here, at this time, for this purpose."

Mary shook her head. "But—"

"Destiny's Child made it back after twenty-nine missions, yet on the last one, we end up here. And not just me, but *you* too."

Eddie spoke with an earnestness that Mary would never have imagined. Yet she loved it.

"Besides, what kind of life could I lead if I returned home safely, but had to turn my back on a child to do so?" He stroked the baby's back and kissed his head. "I may fulfill every dream I set for myself, but if I fail at this God-given task, what good would I be?"

Mary cocked her head, looking at him. Studying this man with this child.

"Besides, Mary," he added. "Consider what it would be like to have a father who didn't truly care for you. A father who felt you were never good enough. Especially when we could most likely find a couple who would love to have a child . . . or I could even raise him myself. We've got to do it. We've got to try."

What kind of crazy thinking is that? She was just about to say so, but she paused. *How did he know?*

Then another thought seemingly came out of nowhere. *This is the man I'm going to marry. And this will be my child.*

Hendrick found the office door unlocked. He entered and stopped short, noticing that the bookshelf was partly open. He swallowed hard and pulled his pistol from his pocket, crouching down and approaching with slow steps. He heard voices—a man and woman talking.

He rushed into the room and saw them sitting at a small table, heads bowed close as they spoke. The man jumped up in surprise, and Hendrick fired a shot, hitting the young man's thigh. The man screamed and crumbled to the ground.

"What are you doing? Who are you? What do you want?" The woman stood and hurried to the man. "Hans, are you okay?"

Hendrick glanced around the room. It appeared to be some type of hidden bedroom. Yet it smelled of soiled diapers and . . . yes, he noted an empty bottle on the table.

"Where is he? Where is my son?"

The woman stood, tossing her gray hair over her shoulder. "What are you talking about? I don't understand."

Hendrick looked to the man on the floor, his face constricted in pain. He pulled a knife from his pocket and moved to the woman. "Oh, don't worry. You can play stupid all you want." He nodded his chin toward the man, then pointed the knife at the woman's chest. "But he'll tell me all I need to know."

Morning's orange arms were just beginning to penetrate night's gray leftovers when Mary and Eddie bade good-bye to the castle and their friends. Each carried a bundle as they set out across the frost-covered grounds. She clutched a cardboard box with their lunches, and he held baby Samuel wrapped up tightly and tucked inside his already too-small jacket. With each step the pain in her leg seemed to be renewed, reminding her of the injury that had lain dormant during the time hidden in the safety of the castle. But she refused to say anything to Eddie. They had a mission, after all.

Mary glanced up at a bank of clouds floating in. She wondered if they carried snow. With a smile, Eddie reached over and took her hand.

They left the castle grounds and stepped onto the road. Snow had started to fall, speckling Eddie's black hat with white crystals. Gray frost had covered layers of mud on the road, but soon it would be covered with white again. Fields between the towns lay quiet, taking their winter rest and accepting their slow white blanket from the sky. Mary imagined the fields in late summer, bursting with crops, with life.

They walked a few miles, and Mary's feet already ached from the cold seeping through her peasant shoes, adding to the pain in her leg. *How will I make it?* Soon they passed by a quaint cottage. Smoke rose from the chimney, and an old truck sat in the front.

Mary saw the curtain lift, and she remembered what Magda had said. She kept her eyes forward, not daring to meet the gaze of the person inside. *Keep walking. You're a family seeking refuge in Verviers. You've lost your home and are looking for loved ones.* Still her heart pounded, and her knees felt weak.

Magda had told them to steer away from people. And, surprisingly, she agreed they should take the child along.

"The greatest dangers do not come from the Gestapo, but from homegrown Fascists known as the Black Brigades. Yet, no one will suspect," Magda had said as they prepared to leave. She handed Eddie extra bullets for his pistol. "They are looking for one or two flyers—they would not think to suspect a man, wife, and child."

Eddie's eyes had met hers, and Mary was almost certain she'd seen his lips part, mouthing the word *wife*. Fresh snow now crunched under Mary's feet, yet somehow she felt warmer remembering Eddie's look of adoration.

They'd yet to see any sign of the German troops that Magda spoke of. And at this moment, as the snow-covered world still seemed safe around her, Mary imagined she and Eddie were in his home state of Montana. They were a family, out walking through a blanket of untouched snow, searching for the perfect Christmas tree on their property.

A twig snapped under her feet, and she came back to reality. "So, were you serious when you told them you'd consider adopting this baby?"

"Sure," Eddie said, adjusting the baby in his grasp, then kissing his bundled head. "I'm just glad to be able to take him away from that Nazi. Can you imagine having him for a dad? Having your father hate you because of his own shame? Besides, I've always wanted kids."

Mary coughed nervously. "And what about a mom?" she asked, turning the conversation back the direction she'd intended. "A child needs a mom too."

Eddie looked at Mary, and his eyes locked with hers. "Maybe before I get back home I'll find myself a good woman." His serious expression softened to a slight smile, and he gave her a wink. "Someone who will love me, love Samuel, and maybe will want to give him three or four brothers and sisters."

"Three or four? Doesn't that seem like a lot?"

"Nah, my mom had four. Sure made for a lot of fun times as a kid." Eddie glanced at a tree with a long branch stretched out like an arm. "See that?"

"That tree? Yeah."

"Reminds me of the one me and my brother used to jump from into the lake when I was a kid." Eddie laughed and brushed snow from his shoulder. "There was this one time. Richard was getting ready to jump when Sally Brown came walking up saying, 'Hi, fellas! I brought some lemonade for ya.' My brother was so sweet on that Sally. He fell backwards into the lake with such a jerk, his shorts got stuck on a branch. He was so embarrassed he swam all the way to the other side of the lake and waited for me to bring him his shorts."

Mary laughed. "That's quite a story."

Suddenly Eddie's gaze peered through the falling snow toward the rolling, frosted hills. Mary detected a layer of tears creeping over his eyes.

"Boy, I miss that guy," he finally said. "My sisters and mom and dad too."

"You surprise me, Eddie."

"Why?"

"I never pictured a strong army airman being so sentimental."

"I've never been sentimental, not until waiting for so many planes to come back from missions—and learning they weren't ever coming back. Not until looking through my window straight into the face of a Kraut pilot firing on us, smiling with each hit. Not until hiding in a dark hole in the forest for a whole day, not knowing if I'd be safe—or the girl with me." He caressed her hand as they walked. "It's times like these when a man realizes it's the simple things that matter most—a caring wife, a bundle of kids, and a little place to call your own."

"I never thought about it like that. You surprise me again."

"How's that?"

"Because you have a way of making me long for things that have nothing to do with front-page news."

"I hope that's a good thing."

Mary turned to face him. "Yeah, I'd say it's a good thing. Very good." She reached up and touched a snowflake on his cheek, brushing it away.

A deep contentment filled Eddie's gaze, and he took one of her curls between his thumb and forefinger. He looked like he was going to say something, but the baby started to fuss. "We'd better keep moving."

He pulled out one of the bottles Sister Clarence had packed for them, and frowned. "It's a little cold. I hope it doesn't give him a stomachache." He pulled back the blanket just enough to put the bottle in the baby's mouth.

Mary's heart warmed to this man with each step. Someone who would love and care for a child who wasn't his own. *A child of the enemy.*

"How do you know so much about babies? Look at you. It's as if you've been doing this all your life."

"Nieces and nephews. I have six of them." He shrugged his shoulders. "I was the favorite uncle."

Up ahead, Mary saw another cottage coming into view. She pulled her hands from her pockets, blowing on them. *Keep walking. You're just an average family.*

"I'd like to hear more about your family," she said.

"It sounds like you're interviewing me for one of your stories. Do you have a notepad hidden in one of those pockets?"

"Oh, I don't need a notepad. It's all right here." She tapped the side of her head. "And I *do* have to admit this would make a great unsung hero story.'"

"My folks are hard workers, that's to be sure. In fact, I can hardly remember my mother's hands idle. She has a large garden, mainly green beans, tomatoes, and squash, because of the short growing season. She loves to crochet the prettiest things too. Not that I understand why each table and shelf needs so many frills, but they do look nice."

Samuel let out a contented sigh as he finished the bottle. Eddie tucked it back into his pocket.

"My dad, he's a mechanic. Works on cars, tractors, anything with an engine. His hands are always caked with grease or bandaged up. In fact, thinking about it, it seems I remember their hands even more than their faces, especially when they were folded."

"I thought you said their hands were never idle."

"I don't mean they were idle. I picture them in prayer. That's the best work of all, when you think about it. Most important, anyway." Eddie glanced up. "And what about you? I've been telling you everything, and I know so little about your dad and mom."

"Well, there's not much to tell. I grew up with my mom, just my mom," Mary hurriedly said. "We were poor in the pocket but rich in words. I told you earlier how she made up stories, but I didn't tell you why. She never learned how to read.

"One night, in the second grade, I could sound out enough words to see that the headline story was about men out of jobs all over the city. But when I asked my mom to read it, she told me that the men lined up were actually actors auditioning for a part in Gary Cooper's latest movie. She said she'd seen the filming on her way to work. I couldn't believe it. I couldn't sleep all night, and in the morning I made her confess the truth. She stopped reading to me after that. But now I regret I found out."

"Because the truth hurt her?"

"My mother? Are you kidding? I was sorry because her stories were much better than any I read in the headlines."

Suddenly Mary noticed a black army truck moving toward them. A red swastika was painted on the door.

"Keep up the pace. Don't freeze." Eddie took her hand as the truck moved closer.

Yet instead of continuing on, the truck stopped in front of them.

You are a German refugee. This is your son and husband . . . no, brother.

Mary waved and glanced up at the truck. *"Guten Morgen allerseits!"*

CHAPTER TWENTY-SIX

The German soldier leaned out the window. "What are you doing on the road in this weather? Do you need help?"

"A ride would be nice." Mary spoke in German and looked to Eddie, pursing her lips and hoping he understood not to speak.

Trust me, she wished she could tell him.

"Just down the road to Verviers—that is where we are headed. My brother, he is deaf and dumb, and I must get him to my sister's house. Taking care of him and this new baby is too difficult."

"And where did you come from?" The soldier eyed her with suspicion.

"From Soumage, just up the road. I didn't realize how cold it was until we set out."

He opened the door and motioned them inside. Eddie's feet didn't move. Mary made a fist and knocked it on the side of his head. *"Dummkopf!"*

Eddie glanced at her, let his jaw go slack, and climbed inside the truck. Mary followed, squeezing in.

"Thank you. We appreciate not having to walk." Her mind hurried to think of what Magda had said—where their next contact would meet them.

"Just drive us to the market in Verviers, please. We can walk from there."

The bouncing of the truck woke Samuel, and he started to cry. Eddie didn't budge.

Good job. Yes, you're deaf, I remember.

She took the infant from Eddie and held him to her chest. Her mind thought back to the music filtering through the thin walls of their apartment back in New York. *Thank you, Cousin Velma. God rest your soul.*

"*Schön ist die Welt, drum, Brü-der, lasst uns rei-sen wohl,*" Mary began to sing. "*In die wei-te Welt, wohl in die Wei-te Welt.*"

Fine is the world, so brothers let us travel, all through this wide, wide world, all through this wide, wide world.

The men in the cab joined in.

We are not proud; we don't need any horse to go from here to there, to go from here to there.

When the song ended, the man seated next to her smiled. "I have not heard that song since my father sang to me as a child." He pointed to Samuel. "Where is this babe's father?"

Mary lowered her gaze. "He is dead. He died, fighting against the Americans." Her voice caught in her throat.

"Do not worry." The soldier reached past Eddie and patted her shoulder. "We will avenge his death, yes? This is where we are going now. To Sankt Vith. To take back the ground lost from the American devils."

St. Vith. Wasn't that their next destination? Where they were to cross over into American-held territory?

"In two days, yes, we will attack. And the city will be ours once more," the soldier boasted.

Two days. That wasn't very much time. She and Eddie could most likely get there by then, but could they get out? Just because the Americans held the Belgian town didn't mean the Allied soldiers would be able to give them a ride out to safety—especially if they were fighting to hold the city.

Lee. I must ask our next contact to find her. Mary knew she was their best chance of making it back alive. If she were anywhere close to the front lines, Lee would find a way to get them out.

They'd arrived hours before they were due, so Mary and Eddie hurried from the market to the parish church, pushing the doors open to find warmth within its walls. Mary unbundled baby Samuel.

"There you go, sweet one," she said as the baby emerged from the mass of blankets. "Does that feel better?"

Samuel cooed as they walked into the sanctuary. A nun was praying near the altar, but paid them no mind as they slipped into the second seat from the rear.

Eddie leaned close. "Hey, what was that about *dummkopf*?"

"Well, we couldn't have you speaking to them, now could we?" she whispered.

"We should have just let them drive past."

"But we're here, and we're warm. I think it was a blessing in disguise."

The nun turned and walked toward them. Eddie made the sign of the cross, and they immediately sank to their knees and bowed their heads.

She moved past them, slipped a coat over her habit, and exited. They slid back onto the pew.

"You won't believe what those soldiers were saying," Mary whispered, brushing her fingers across the infant's downy soft hair. "They're heading for St. Vith and plan to attack in two days."

"That's where we're heading." Eddie's eyes grew wide. "Didn't Magda say the area was under American control?"

"Yes, but we don't know for how long. I know Magda believed just getting us there, behind the American lines, would be good enough, but we need to make a plan to leave. And I think I have one. But we're going to need the help of our next contact."

Her eyes looked to the stained glass window showing Jesus gathering the children around Him.

"Let's pray for His help," she said. "Let's pray my plan will work."

Eddie walked around the church. He gazed at the altar candles—a hundred, flickering, dancing prayers. He'd never been in a Catholic church before, but he'd had a friend who'd described it to him. He glanced at the pictures on the walls—Christ's journey to the cross. At the same time, Eddie's senses were poised as he listened for any sound of someone coming. He checked the door once more, then gazed at Mary and the baby.

She wore the dress and coat of a peasant woman. Her cheeks and nose were smudged with dirt she'd most likely picked up while climbing out of the German truck. But she was no peasant. He had to hand it to this big-time reporter from New York; she handled herself like a pro. Samuel sat on her lap, gurgling as she tickled him with one of her blond ringlets. Mary's giggle echoed through the empty church, and the candlelight made her smile seem even more attractive.

Eddie sighed. *Man, I think I love this woman.*

"You know how to handle this little guy pretty good yourself," he said as he slid into the pew beside her.

"Oh, I love babies. But I want to tell you about my plan."

"I'm listening."

"I told about my friend Lee. I'm guessing she's at the press camp closest to the front lines."

"How in the world do you know that?"

"If it's the closest to the action you can get, Lee will be there. She has connections, and she's not afraid to use them. It's a lesson I'm learning."

Mary turned her back toward Eddie, held the baby with one arm, and lifted her hair from the nape of her neck with her free hand. "Can you unclasp this chain for me? Lee will recognize this, I'm sure of it."

Her neck was creamy white, and Eddie was not prepared for the effect it had on him. He studied the gold chain for a minute before lifting it from the warmth of her skin and fumbling with the small clasp. Finally, it released.

Mary dropped her hair, and his arms wrapped over her shoulders as he lowered the chain into her upraised hand. He breathed in the scent of her hair and smiled.

Mary seemed to lean into his touch. Her eyes closed just for a moment—then back to business.

"This necklace was a gift from my father. When we meet the contact, I think we should ask if he'll take it to the nearest Allied press center and ask for Lee. Maybe I'll write a note—"

"No, you don't want to do that," Eddie interrupted. He took the necklace from her, then studied the pendant souvenir from the World's Fair. "If he gets caught—well, it won't be good. It'll be dangerous enough having something clearly American with him." Eddie shrugged his shoulders. "It sure seems like a long shot, but I'm starting to trust your instincts. It's worth a try."

The door opened, and two pairs of shoes clomped along the wooden floor in their direction. Neither of the refugees dared turn around. In seconds, the nun stood beside them with another person, a priest, who approached Eddie and pointed to the two handkerchiefs in his pocket. He took one of the handkerchiefs and loudly blew his nose.

He then turned to Mary and said something in German. When he finished, he motioned for them to join him.

"Mary, what did he say?"

"He said we're early, and we'll be staying with a family in town. They're expecting us.'"

Mary rose to follow the priest, but Eddie paused, reaching for her arm. "I'm not sure. This isn't the plan. He didn't say that French phrase."

"Eddie, he knew the sign and countersign. And he's right, we're early, which would explain a lot. It's a priest, for goodness' sake. Come on. I'm ready for a warm bed and some food.

Besides, Samuel will be hungry again soon, and we want to have a chance to warm his bottle this time."

The short winter day was already turning to dusk as they walked over packed snow through the sleepy town of Verviers. They finally came to a beautiful house toward the edge of town. It was made of brick, and dried, snow-covered ivy draped the front. They were led down the cobblestone drive, but instead of turning toward the front door, they kept walking beyond the house to a small caretaker's cottage.

The priest knocked twice, then without waiting said, "The eggs are in the basket."

The door opened, and a short, slim man with hunched shoulders and brown scraggly hair peered out. After seeing them, he smiled a toothless grin. "In. In."

As they walked in, the caretaker, priest, and nun left. At the caretaker's rough wooden table waited their contact, Julien. He was a young man, yet serious enough to make him seem older. He greeted them in English.

Mary explained what she'd heard from the soldiers, and Julien agreed to go ahead to the American front lines, to warn them of the German attack and to try to find the female correspondent named Lee.

"Only one problem," Julien told them. "If this I do, I can no join you to St. Vith. You go alone."

Mary turned to Eddie. "What do you think?"

He wrapped an arm around her shoulders. "I trust Mary's judgment," he said to Julien. "Go ahead as she asked. I don't think it will hurt to try, and I definitely don't think she's going to let this one go." He winked at her. "Besides, if you talked German soldiers into giving us a lift, surely we can make it safely on a twenty-kilometer wagon ride."

"Fine then." She spoke to Julien in German, making sure he clearly understood the directions. "Take this necklace to the press office closest to the front and ask for a female correspondent named Lee. Tell her to meet us in St. Vith on the 17th at the U.S. command center, and warn her that the Germans will be attacking the front lines soon, so our troops need to be prepared."

Julien slipped the pendant into his pocket. "I will pack my things and leave shortly." He tugged on his cap and opened the door. "The wagon will be waiting in front of the parish at eight o'clock in the morning. Tell your man to be there to pick it up."

"Yes, I will." Mary turned to Eddie, knowing he didn't understand a word she was saying. "I'll have my man do just that."

Despite the filthy blackout curtains and the layer of dust covering everything from the stone mantelpiece to the wood floor, the cottage was dry and warm. The fire in the small fireplace glowed softly and crackled as Eddie threw in a log from the stack left for them.

Eddie sat down in front of the fire and spread out the silk map from his kit and compared it to the hand-drawn one Julien had given them.

As she watched him, Mary felt an odd peace settling over her. Tomorrow they would have to figure out how to get to the American lines, but today they were warm and safe. Today they were together in this simple place.

"What luck to be rescued by a navigator." She plopped onto the floor next to him. Samuel lay on a blanket between them, his blue eyes fixed on the dancing flame. Mary caressed his plump baby belly.

She looked at the figures Eddie was writing on the back of the sheet. His eyes were focused intently, like that morning before the flight. How long ago was that? Just a few weeks? It seemed like forever.

She watched his finger trace a route toward their destination. He'd have them go one direction, then shake his head and start over. Mary knew she could trust his skills. She knew he'd find the best back roads, rivers, trails to follow to keep her and baby

Samuel safe from the flood of German troops moving in the same direction. By his mumbles, she figured he was also trying to determine how long their journey would take.

"How do you do it?" she asked when he'd sat back like he was done. "All this math stuff. It's all gibberish to me. Now if it were a news story . . ."

"Some things are easy to calculate," Eddie said. "Like the time it will take to get from one destination to another." The sound of planes roared overhead. He paused, cocked his ear to the ceiling, and sighed. "Then there are things harder to calculate, such as the price of fear, or the cost of seeing your buddies' chutes going down without knowing what happened to them."

He reached over and caressed Mary's cheek. "Do you trust me, Mary?"

"Of course. Why do you ask?"

"Well, for starters, we're always talking about me, but you never say much about yourself. I mean, you said you were raised by your mom, then later said the pendant was a gift from your dad. . . ."

He placed a comforting hand on her shoulder. "I wish you'd trust me not only to help rescue you, but trust me with your story, too."

Mary crumpled the edge of her peasant dress in her hand. "I don't know where to start. It's confusing even to me. I didn't meet my father till I was twelve. And when I did, I'm not sure if it made things better or worse. I guess it's better, because I can see him in person now. I'm sorry; listen to me. This isn't making any sense."

She wiped her face with her sleeve, then lifted Samuel onto her lap and cradled his head with her hands. She took a deep breath, hoping Eddie would let the conversation drop.

He brushed her hair from her face. "So has he been part of your life since then?"

"Well, sort of. It's not a relationship that's been allowed to grow naturally. Instead, one day we knew each other, and it was like, 'Okay, here we are, now what?'"

The baby cooed, and she kissed the top of his head. "I sound so stupid. *Dummkopf.*" She took her fist and softly knocked the side of her head, casting him a sad smile. "I've never shared any of this with anyone before."

"But would you feel different if your father acted how you've imagined a dad should act? Seems it's not so much 'what could have been' as 'what should be.' What you wished the future could hold." Eddie paused, and the last phrase just hung there—in her mind and in her heart.

What should be. Yes, Mary supposed that's what had bothered her most all along. She still felt like that gangly twelve-year-old who so desperately wanted her daddy's approval. So desperately that she'd risked her life to get his attention.

"Yeah, Eddie. I think you've figured out in five minutes what's been bothering me for thirteen years. 'What should be . . .' It's not like Donald hates me. But maybe he's just as unsure about me as I am about him."

Eddie leaned over and peered into Samuel's face, running his finger down the baby's cheek. "So the question is . . . what are you going to do when you get back?"

She thought for a moment. "No, the question is, what am I going to do *now*? If you haven't figured it out, I have a whole world of ideas and thoughts swirling around my head every waking moment. Maybe I need to pray about it." She looked at Eddie, seeking the reaction in his brown eyes.

Then she felt the tears coming. "If God is everything you say He is, then . . . then I need His help figuring this out. I believe in Him, Eddie. I didn't when I first walked through the doors of that aircraft. I didn't know enough about God to even consider what He was all about. But the last few weeks have been like a crazy, bad dream that I keep thinking I'll wake up from."

She scooted closer to him, refusing to allow the fear of rejection to stop her from what she'd wanted for so long. "But you know what? I'd do it all again. Well, I don't think I'll ever step into a B-17 again. . . . but you know what I mean."

Then she told him about her prayer in that secret room—her

prayer to accept Jesus and learn to trust God as Eddie did.

Now there were tears in Eddie's eyes. "That's amazing, Mary."

She offered him a shy grin. "You've shown me every day, through the little things you do, the small ways you seek God, how He works with people who love Him. I'd go through this again to learn that . . . and to be with you."

Eddie's face was only inches from hers. He lifted his hand and brushed her tangled hair back from her face. "I told myself that I wasn't going to *look for* a girl." His voice was thick with emotion. "I mean, I always knew God had someone special in mind, and He'd bring me to her in His time. But I had no idea what He had up His sleeve."

His voice lowered into a whisper. "I care about you, Mary. And it's more than just the fact that we've been thrown together and have had to depend on each other. It's the idea, well, I was chosen for you. You were put into my plane. And we were given this crazy mission." He glanced toward Samuel. "One so incredible that nobody's going to believe it when we finally make it out."

"It is quite a story, isn't it?" Her fingers found his and intertwined.

"Are you kidding? If *this* story doesn't make the front page of every paper, I don't know what will."

They studied each other's eyes for a long moment, as if memorizing the color, texture, and tears ready to spill any second. And then she slowly, hesitantly, leaned in and kissed him. His lips, his scent, his stubble were somehow all soft and sweet, and in her arms Samuel cooed as if giving his approval.

CHAPTER TWENTY-SEVEN

Mary and Samuel slept, but Eddie couldn't. His mind was filled with so much awe of how God had worked among them.

The infant, wrapped in a tight bundle snuggled to Eddie's chest, was the child of a Nazi and a Jew. Two people of "chosen" blood—one chosen by God, and the other by madness.

And for some reason, God had picked *him* as a protector of this woman, now snuggled in a ball under a wool blanket beside him, and this baby, both of whom he was growing to love more each day.

He'd heard stories back on base that the underground would stop at nothing to move navigators through the lines. They were so important. *Shoot, I was proud of that. But now* . . . He glanced at his maps, neatly folded and ready to take tomorrow. Then he looked at Mary.

What map brought me to this place, Lord? To this lady? He inhaled a bit of Samuel's sweet baby smell. *And to this child. All my navigational skills would've never brought me here. A father. And a husband, if she'll take me, all in one. Just a downed plane and a crazy journey.*

Mary stirred, and he fixed her blanket over her.

But the journey's not over, Lord. If I'm to protect them, I need You to guide me.

He laid the baby down on the makeshift crib and walked to the window to whisper a prayer. "You are my rock and my salvation. You are my fortress; may I not be shaken." Then he gazed anew at the two next to him. "Lord, I'm so small. Somehow, make me a fortress for my . . . my family."

Mary sang to try to still little Samuel's squeals. "Boy, you don't like getting your diaper changed, do you, little one?" She lifted Samuel's tiny bottom and slid a clean diaper underneath. She pinned one side, thinking of Eddie.

Maybe I should have gone with him to get the wagon. What will he do if anyone tries to talk to him?

The pounding on the door interrupted her thoughts. Mary quickly pinned the other side of the diaper and turned to the door. Eddie had only left fifteen minutes ago—he couldn't be back already.

She hurried to the window, peeked out, and let out a little gasp. Sister Clarence!

Mary opened the door and pulled the nun inside. "Sister Clarence! Come in."

The woman was panting heavily. "You must leave at once. Take the child." Sister Clarence grabbed her side and hunched over, wincing.

"Are you all right?"

Sister Clarence nodded. "You must leave."

"Eddie's gone to get the wagon—"

"No, now!" Sister Clarence hurried to where the baby lay. "He's coming."

"Eddie?"

"The baby's father. Somehow he has learned where the baby is."

Mary's heart was ripping open—the thought of a madman taking this child. She'd heard what he'd done to the child's poor mother. She'd seen the blood-splattered wall. There was no way she would let the Nazi have this baby.

"If he finds Samuel, what will he do?"

"What he has done to so many others."

Mary scooped the baby into her arms. "Sister Clarence, what do you mean?"

"He was an SS officer responsible for the deaths of thousands of children, in the name of racial purity. I didn't want to tell you." She moved to the window and peered out.

"But how did he find out the baby was alive?"

"Someone must have gone to him with the truth—perhaps another nurse, or even one of the young women, hoping to gain his favor. All I know is he's on his way here." Sister Clarence pulled an envelope from her pocket. "I came to warn you—and to give you this. It is a letter from Samuel's mother."

"A letter from Samuel's mother? But why didn't you give it to me before?"

Sister Clarence kissed the baby's cheek. "Because she only told me what to write last night. She's still alive, Mary."

"Then why do we have Samuel? Why doesn't she care for him herself?"

"Well, there is Hendrick, of course. The baby is not safe here. And . . . Rebecca is not well. She had a stroke and is mostly paralyzed, and unable to care for her son. She prayed for two parents for him. We prayed with her. Then you came. . . ."

Mary's head spun. "Can you thank her for us?" It was all she could think to say. Her voice quivered. "Thank her for this gift?"

She kissed the top of the baby's head. *What incredible courage your mama must've had to give you up. Oh, Lord, thank You.* She turned to the window, noticing a wagon approaching.

"Eddie's here. We must go." Mary threw on her coat and gathered her things. "Tell Samuel's mother we will love and care for him," Mary called behind her as she hurried out the door.

"Samuel?" a man's strong voice boomed. "The baby's name is Hendrick, after his father."

Before Mary realized what was happening, two strong arms grabbed her. She clutched the baby to her chest.

"Thank you for taking care of my son." A deep voice, filled with contempt, assaulted her ears. "He will be my responsibility now."

"No!" Mary attempted to pull away; then she froze. The man before her held a pistol in his hand. His face was the same face as in the photograph on the dresser at the castle, but he now had a beard. His eyes were even colder and darker than the photo had revealed.

"You will come with me." He dragged her to the wagon. "I need a mother for my child, and you're a pretty pet, aren't you? I've yet to impregnate an American." He ran his finger down her cheek and along her jawbone.

Mary dared not look back to the doorway as he forced her into the wagon, not wanting to draw attention to Sister Clarence. *Go find help, sister. Get Eddie. Samuel and I again need a rescuer.*

The wagon plodded on at a quickened pace, its rocking motion lulling the child to sleep. In the hour since she had been abducted, Mary plotted her escape while her fear rose. Where was Eddie? Why hadn't he come for them?

"I don't understand why you want this child. Doesn't he represent everything you tried to destroy?"

"Darling," Hendrick's voice purred. "You do not believe what they told you, do you? I expected you to be much brighter than that." He sighed. "After tormenting myself about this very thing, I realized the girl spoke lies. She knew I had planned to take my son, to raise him without her; and she knew there was only one thing that would change my mind—to say this child was not pure. For me to believe she was a Jew." He spat the last word as if it caused a foul taste in his mouth.

"At first I believed her. But then . . ." He turned and looked at Mary. "Then I realized the truth, and I knew I had to do whatever it took to get my son back. Even if it meant abandoning my work, my uniform, and setting off to find him. And it was easier than I thought. Hans didn't handle the sight of his mother's torture well." Hendrick clicked his tongue. "To think of such weakness in such a large man. It is a shame."

Mary felt sick. She bounced the baby even more, trying to get her mind off poor Magda. Yet even more prevalent in her thoughts was worry about Eddie. *Where are you? Are you okay? Please be okay. Please save us from this madman before it's too late.*

Just then she heard the sound of a vehicle approaching from behind them, heading back to Soumage.

The large army truck stopped just ahead of them, and two German soldiers jumped from the cab. "You there," one called.

Hendrick slowed the wagon and stared up at them, annoyed. "What is the problem? Can't you see I'm on my way home with my family?"

"Friends of ours fell for your ploy once, but not twice. Get down from that wagon seat, flyer. We have a nice prison cell we've been saving for you. Your friends have been waiting."

"You have the wrong person, idiots! I am an officer of the Reich." He stood on the floorboard of the wagon, staring down at them.

Mary looked to Hendrick's hand in his pocket, and she knew the pistol was still in his grasp.

"Eddie," she said in German. "Please don't. They will hurt you. Give yourself up. For my sake and the child. Think of Samuel."

"Silence, woman!" Hendrick pulled the pistol from his coat pocket, turning to her.

"Halt!" The German soldier pointed his gun and lunged at Hendrick.

Mary saw her chance. She pressed Samuel tighter and jumped to the ground. Her feet sank in the snow, and her bad leg gave out. Samuel let out a cry from the jolt, and she crouched into a ball around the baby as gunfire sounded.

She looked up to see Hendrick slumped on the wagon seat with multiple wounds in his chest. His eyes were wide open in surprise, and blood spread through his peasant clothing, dripping onto the white snow. She turned away. *I'm next.*

The soldier approached, his boots crunching through the snow. He stopped before her, raised his gun, then slid it into his jacket pocket.

"The nun," he said curtly. "She made me promise if she told me where the flyer was that I wouldn't hurt you or the child." He squatted down, helping her to a sitting position.

Mary struggled to catch her breath. She rocked the baby, willing him to calm.

"I will keep that promise." His voice was firm. "But I *will not* risk my position or my life to help you. You'll have to find your own way out of here."

The two soldiers took Hendrick's body, leaving a trail of red dots in the snow, flung it in the back of their vehicle, and drove off.

Mary cuddled Samuel closer to her chest. He stopped crying as he snuggled under her neck; and she rocked back and forth, letting the tears fall.

Mary felt a hand on her shoulder. She jerked back, and fear rushed through her. Then Eddie hunkered down before her.

"Eddie, what happened? Where were you?" She folded into his arms, the baby pressed between them. "Oh, thank You, God. I'm so glad you're okay."

His trembling fingers brushed the hair back from her face. "Shhh . . . we're all right now. I've been following in the distance in a truck Sister Clarence managed to commandeer. She's a smart one, all right." Eddie wrapped his arms around her and baby Samuel. "I'm so glad you're okay too."

After a minute, he pulled her shoulders back and looked into her face. "God is watching over us. I know that now more than ever. Not only did we get rid of that officer, but the Germans will

no longer be hunting us. They think they got me, Mary. And"—
he waved with a flourish at the old truck parked behind them on
the side of the road—"we have a vehicle and fuel that will hope-
fully get us as far as St. Vith."

Mary stood and looked at Eddie. "Well, I suppose things did
work out . . . but from now on I'm not letting you out of my
sight. I can't handle this escape business alone."

CHAPTER TWENTY-EIGHT

Lee stood watching the sleek, streamlined press pumping out news stories to be sent to the front lines—updating the boys of the war, encouraging them to keep up the good fight, and informing them to look out for a very important person.

At least the Germans did something right as they fled this part of Belgium, leaving this beautiful machine behind. Makes our search for Mary easier.

The scent of paper and ink was heavy in the air. Around Lee, circulation men took the paper as it slid off the rollers, and bundled it. Within the hour, she knew, it would be packed into jeeps and trucks and carried off in the early morning darkness, toward the flickering red of gun blasts in the northern sky.

And just maybe someone somewhere will have news about Mary. Surely she didn't simply disappear into thin air.

Lee pulled one paper from the stack. The top story was written by Donald Miller, telling about his daughter lost somewhere in Belgium.

"Hey, mister, you can't go in there!" Shouts emerged from behind, and Lee turned to see a thin man running into the room. His arms were stretched out to her, and his face was set in determination.

"What's going on?" She took a step back, and two soldiers who manned the news office caught the man, grabbing him by his arms.

"No, no!" the man shouted, dragging his feet. "A-mer-ri-ka Sweet-heart. Lee, talk to Lee."

Lee cocked her head, unsure if she'd heard right. Yet her heart pounded with hope. She hurried to him. "Sir, what did you say?"

Instead of repeating himself, the man shook free and un-buttoned his shirt collar. Glimmering on his filthy neck was a gold chain and a pendant from the 1939 World's Fair in New York.

Lee took the man's hand in her own, heat rising to her cheeks. "A woman with blonde hair. She gave this to you?"

The man nodded.

"How long ago? Where is she?"

The man pulled his hand free and hurried to the map spread on the wall. He found Belgium right away.

"She is here."

"Here? She's here in Belgium?"

"Yes." The man nodded, then his brows furrowed.

"Where, tell me where?"

He shrugged and looked at her with confusion.

"It's the map," one of the office workers said. "It's in Eng-lish. Here . . ." He hurried to the dusty shelf and pulled out an atlas the man could read.

The man's face brightened as he took it and flipped through the pages, then turned to Lee and pointed excitedly.

St. Vith.

"St. Vith. Is that where?"

"Yes, yes. Going there," he said.

Lee studied the map. "That's only thirty miles from here. How long ago was she there?"

The man looked at her, confused.

"How long?" she said slower, pointing to her watch.

He studied her lips, as if hoping she'd say something he'd understand.

Lee hurried to the calendar on the wall, pointing to December 17. The man nodded his head and smiled.

"Today? She will be arriving there today?"

"Yes. Today."

He nodded again, unclasping the necklace and holding it out to her. Lee took it in her hand, sure she'd never seen a more beautiful piece of jewelry in her life.

Lee hurried to find Patrick, who was packing film and other supplies in another room. "It's Mary! She sent for me."

Patrick swung the camera bag over his shoulder and hurried to her side. "Mary? You found her?" He whooped and lifted Lee up in a bear hug. "You're amazing. I knew you'd find her."

"But how did she know where I'd be?"

"She has you figured out; she knew you'd be in the thick of the action . . . despite your fears. She's a reporter, after all. Knowing people is part of her job."

The journey to St. Vith was worse than Mary had imagined. Panzer tank divisions filled the main roads, spreading as far as they could see. Thankfully, no one paid too much attention to the small truck weaving through the country roads that cut through the thick forests.

Eddie drove as fast as he dared, and she could tell his arm was bothering him by the way he favored it—and by the beads of perspiration forming on his brow. They were down to their last bottle for Samuel, and the sky had begun to lighten with the dawn. She didn't want to ask him again how much farther, so instead, Mary sat holding the baby, glad the motion made him sleep and praying as she never had before.

"Eddie?" There was one thing that bothered her, one thing she had to ask about. "It's bad enough we're racing panzers to the front lines, but what will we do when we get there? I mean, will there be American guards posted on the roads? Will they shoot at us as we approach? Or worse, what if we get in the middle of the attacking Germans and defending Americans?"

Their truck turned a curve, and he slowed. "I guess we're about to find out."

Up ahead an American tank halfway blocked the road; the other half had slid into a ditch due to the ice and snow. Mary's heart raced. Americans!

Eddie stopped the truck. Someone from the tank shined a flashlight toward the cab, and Eddie raised his hands so they could see them.

"Mary, I need you to lay Samuel on the seat and climb from the cab as slowly as possible. Keep your hands where they can see them. Keep quiet; I'll handle it."

"Who goes there?" an American soldier called, approaching them with a gun. He squinted against their muted headlights. "Password?"

Eddie climbed from the truck. "I don't know the password. I'm an American B-17 navigator. Our plane went down—"

"Don't listen to him, Charlie," someone called from his position behind the tank. "He could be a German in disguise."

"Password!" Charlie called again.

"My name is Edward Anderson. 0-565390. I was part of the crew for the B-17 *Destiny's Child*. I was the navigator. I—"

"Don't listen to him, Charlie," the man from behind the tank said again, his rifle pointing at them.

Mary stepped forward, her feet crunching in the snow. "Yes, listen to him. He's telling the truth. And I'm Mary Kelley, ETO war correspondent." She continued forward despite the fact the man's weapon was now trained on her. From the cab behind them, Samuel started to cry. "Our plane was shot down, we—"

"Wait," said the soldier called Charlie. "Did you say Mary Kelley? Are you the daughter of Donald Miller?"

Mary's knees buckled, and she lowered her hands. "How—how did you know?"

Samuel's cries escalated. She turned, wondering if she should get him. And still questioned if she'd heard the soldier right.

"Heck, lady, it's all over the radio. And in the paper that just arrived. Your daddy's looking for you. He's offered a big reward. Hey, Howie!" he called back. "This here is Mary Kelley. It looks like we'll be rich soon, my friend."

Eddie lowered his hands too and approached. "Wow, I wonder how much the reward is?" He pulled her into his embrace with a chuckle. "I just might have struck gold here."

Mary punched his chest softly and pulled back, hurrying to get the baby. "Forget the reward!" she called. "My dad is worried about me. More than that, he's looking for me!"

Deciding the tank was stuck for good, Charlie piled into the small truck and headed back to St. Vith with Eddie and Mary to get more help. Samuel's bottles had run out, and his diaper was soaking.

Soon they were pulling into St. Vith, just as the sun crested over the tall trees on the edge of the city. German planes flew low overhead, appearing to be the main threat, and drawing the attention away from the men and machines that Eddie knew were filling the forest.

The soldier directed them to the command center. He ran inside to report the mounting attack while Eddie and Mary parked the truck. In the distance they could already hear the sound of a big gun firing on the sleepy town. Fog had begun to roll into town, and the snow fell in large white flakes as they hurried inside.

"Our orders are to hold the town," the CO was saying to the soldier. "I don't care what your sources told you about the amount of metal heading this way. We're going to stay and fight."

Eddie handed the screaming baby to Mary and strode up to the CO, explaining who they were and their current situation.

"That's quite a story. Welcome back to friendly territory, but I have a mounting situation here I need to take care of. I'll make sure a report gets sent back to England with news of your safe return."

One of his officers approached, and the CO excused Eddie with a nod.

"Sir, if I can interrupt again, you may want to ensure the road leading out of here is held. I know you're going to fight to defend this town, but we don't want to get trapped here. In fact, I'm trying to find a way out for the war correspondent with me."

Eddie didn't mention Samuel, and he wasn't sure if the CO had noticed the infant in Mary's arms.

"I'm sorry, Lieutenant." The CO's voice was terse. "But your needs are at the bottom on the list of my concerns. The battle's waging out there, and you're—"

Suddenly an artillery shell exploded not too far from their building. The foundation under Eddie's feet rocked and tilted. Glass from a far window shattered, blowing in on screaming men. Eddie found himself planted on the cement floor. He got to his feet and found Mary, and the baby protected in her arms. "You okay?"

"Yeah." She moaned and allowed him to pull her up. "I found some milk in the kitchen, and a towel I could rip up for a diaper. But there's no one who can give us a ride out. Looks like we've gone as far as we can for now."

When Patrick failed to talk the soldier guarding the road into letting them pass, Lee climbed out of the vehicle, flipping her wool scarf over her shoulder and stomping up toward the guard.

"Sir, is that St. Vith I can see in the distance?"

"Hey, lady, what are you doing here? Don't you know these are the front lines?"

"Actually"—Lee pointed to the small village ahead—"*that* is, and I need to get there, understand?"

"Yes, ma'am, but I can't let you through. Orders say authorized personnel only."

"I am authorized. Authorized to report on this battle." Lee focused on the young soldier's eyes and smiled. "Of course, I fully understand you are only trying to follow orders, and I commend that. GIs like you should be applauded for their duty."

She pulled a notebook from her pocket and motioned to Patrick. "Pat, can you get a photo of this brave young soldier?"

Patrick nodded. "Yes, ma'am." He pulled his camera bag from the vehicle.

"Does your father read the paper?" Lee asked the soldier.

"Every day."

"And what is your name?"

"Willy. Actually William Bookman. Are you going to put my name in the paper?"

She placed a hand on his shoulder. "I'd love too, I really would, but in order for me to do that, I need to get into the town for just one hour—otherwise I'll have nothing worthy of writing a story on. Will you let me in?"

Willy looked back over his shoulder. "One hour?"

"Yes, and whatever you do, hold this road. From the look of things the battle's heating up, and we're going to need a safe way out."

Mary hunkered down in the corner of the command center. Next to her, Eddie was attempting to rock a content and clean Samuel to sleep. Her eyes were growing heavy despite the pounding of the guns outside. She let them drift shut.

Suddenly she felt a kick to her foot.

"Hey, sleepyhead."

Mary recognized the voice and smiled. "Lee! I knew you'd find me!" She reached up a hand, and Lee grasped it and pulled Mary to her feet.

Lee cocked one eyebrow at Eddie and Samuel. "My, have we been busy. How long exactly have you been missing?"

Mary slugged Lee's shoulder. Dirt puffed off her field coat. "Did I just see that?" Mary took a step back and shook her head.

Lee's hair was tucked underneath an army cap. Her face was smudged with dirt.

"Lee O'Donnelly, you're a mess. What have you done with yourself?"

"Hey, coming to a fellow reporter's rescue isn't the most glamorous work, you know." She pointed outside. "Especially under these conditions."

Another shell hit close, causing the room lights to flicker and plaster dust to fall from the ceiling.

Eddie climbed from the floor in slow motion, so as to not wake the baby.

Lee extended her hand. "You must be Edward Anderson. You have a buddy back in Paris who's going to be mighty happy to see you again. Vinny Rosario. Does the name ring a bell?"

Eddie's face broke into a grin. "Vinny? He made it out? Hallelujah."

Patrick strode through the doors. "Hey, I found someone to watch our truck." He quickened his pace to Mary, sweeping her up in his arms. "There you are, kid. Glad you're alive. Lee wouldn't give up. You've been her main assignment these past few weeks, you know."

"Well, we won't stay alive for long if we don't get out of here. Ready to go?" Mary turned to Lee.

"Hold on, will you, gal?" She was striding over to the kitchen. "Let me grab us something for the road. I don't know about you, but I'm starved."

Eddie approached Mary, and she slipped her hand into his and gave it a squeeze. "Boy, has Lee changed since I've been gone."

Patrick chucked Mary's chin. "So have you, kid. I can see something different in your eyes. A beautiful glow." He reached a hand to Eddie.

Eddie slipped his hand from Mary's grasp and shook Patrick's hand.

"Edward Anderson? I'm Patrick Jessup. I can't wait to hear *your* side of the story, especially how you ended up with that little one. Is he a refugee?"

"Not anymore," Eddie answered.

The two men strode to the door while Mary waited for Lee.

"It's quite a story," Eddie continued, "but let's wait until we get out of this place and I'll tell you all about it. If I could, I'd stay and fight, but I'm afraid my current assignment isn't over."

"Don't worry." Patrick placed a hand on Eddie's shoulder. "Lee made sure the road would be held for us. And no one—I mean no one—messes with that girl. I've never met a woman like her."

Eddie glanced back over his shoulder, winking at Mary as they headed for the door. "Oh, I know someone who could give her a run for her money. Has Lee ever caught a ride with a group of Nazis?"

Their voices faded as they hurried outside.

Lee came back, handing Mary a stack of K rations. "What was that about?"

"Well, if you room with me when we get back I'll share all the details."

Lee placed her arm around Mary's shoulders, and they moved toward the door. Then she paused and pulled something from her pocket. "Oh, and I think this belongs to you." She held up Mary's necklace.

Mary paused, clasped the necklace around her neck, and patted the pendant against her skin.

"You're going to share *all* the details?" Lee asked.

"Of course. I don't have anything to hide. Not anymore, that is."

"Okay." Lee sighed. "But I might have to hear the story in pieces. I'm heading back to the front as soon as I drop you off."

"Seriously?" Mary pulled her jacket tighter around her as they stepped into the chilly air. "I don't think I ever want to see danger again."

"Funny thing," Lee commented as they jumped into the vehicle. "I feel just the opposite. I've realized lately that these stories aren't about me or what I can prove being a woman in this business. They're about these guys fighting and dying and making heroes of themselves."

They climbed into the truck, Lee in front and Mary onto the backseat next to Eddie.

"Hit it, Pat." Lee placed her hand on the photographer's shoulder. "I have a story to get back and write. There's one Willy Bookman whose daddy needs to hear how he was the hero of the day."

CHAPTER TWENTY-NINE

Lee jumped out of the vehicle as soon as it stopped at the command center at the edge of Paris. She glanced in the back and noticed Mary curled against Eddie, fast asleep. The baby softly snored on Mary's lap.

"I'll take this film inside to get processed; then I'll come back to help you with your things, Lee," Patrick said as he climbed out and headed toward the building.

Lee opened the door to the backseat, then ducked her head to peer inside.

"Hey, Eddie. Before you wake Mary, I have just one thing to tell you. She deserves the best, you understand? I don't want you breaking her heart."

Eddie grinned. "Yeah, well, I was going to tell you the same thing about Patrick there. I'll promise to give Mary all my love for all my life. But that guy's falling for you hard. Promise not to break *his* heart?"

Lee crossed her arms over her chest. "Really? Think so?"

She turned to the building and smiled. "Yeah, well, I'm sort of taken by him too. I'll keep my end of the bargain if you keep yours."

Eddie nodded. "It's a deal."

With a wide grin, Lee reached in and shook Mary awake. "Hey you, lazybones. There's some bigwig inside who wants to debrief you. But first, we need to get you out of those clothes and into something with style."

Mary opened her eyes, kissed the top of Samuel's head, and stretched. She climbed out of the backseat. "Speaking of style, you wouldn't happen to be assisting some certain French people, would you?"

Lee felt her jaw drop. "How did you know? You *are* a good reporter."

"It was a scarf. One of the underground workers had this red scarf that she used as a belt. As soon as I saw it, I knew it was from you. I just knew you'd found a way of helping."

"What? I don't get it, Mare. I did have an orange-and-yellow scarf. But I gave it to this lady. She approached me in Paris, you see, told me her sister and her children were nearly starving. She wondered if I could make a few . . . how can I say it? . . . donations to their cause."

Mary's eyebrows furrowed. "So your stuff didn't go to the underground?"

"Well, there were a few things I carried over for the underground, but all my personal things went to the family."

"And you didn't have a red scarf?"

"Nope." Lee wrapped her arm around Mary's shoulder. "But hey, whatever worked to put me on your mind, I suppose."

"God works in mysterious ways," Eddie chuckled. "You see . . . I told you it was too much of a long shot to be true."

"Yeah, but you have to give me credit. I got us out of there."

"Ah-hem? Who got you out of there?" Lee squeezed Mary's shoulder tighter.

Mary laughed. "You're right. Thanks, friend. I owe you one."

It wasn't until she was safely back in her room at the Hotel Savoy, back in England, that Mary remembered the envelope that Sister Clarence had given her. It was the letter from Samuel's mother.

Dear Eddie and Mary,

My words cannot express how difficult it is for me to ask Sister Clarence to pen this letter. During the month after his birth, I prayed for arms of deliverance for my son. Unable to even lift my own arms to hold him, I prayed for loving ones to carry him away where he would be safe and would have a hope for the future.

As Sister Clarence told you, I almost lost my life—twice. Yet for some reason my loving God spared me.

My father and mother gave me a chance to live when they placed me into the hands of another to care for me. And I know the extent of their love, as I am now doing the same with my son, Samuel.

My son is named after my father. In the following pages is a short list of our family history. As far as I know, I could be the last of my family's bloodline. Please let Samuel know that he comes from a long line of people who served God with all their hearts.

Sister Clarence assures me you are loving people. Thank you for caring for Samuel as you would a child of your own flesh. And know that every day that passes, I will be lifting you in my prayers.

It is with tears streaming down my face that I ask Sister Clarence to close this letter for me. Tears of missing my baby, but also tears of hope. And perhaps someday, if my heavenly Father chooses to heal me, I will come and see my son again . . . see the good man I know he'll grow to be.

With all the love a mother's heart can hold,

Rebecca

Mary wiped her face where her own tears had already begun to fall. She couldn't imagine such a sacrifice. She strode to the cradle and knelt before it. *May I be found worthy. May I be the mother this child deserves.*

Samuel slept in the small cradle Mary and Eddie had purchased for him. Since Eddie's arm was still being cared for at the base hospital, they agreed Mary would take care of the baby until after his discharge. Then . . . Mary didn't know what would happen after that, but she hoped they'd find a way to be together. And although he didn't say it, Mary could see from Eddie's teary-eyed gaze as he gave them one last kiss good-bye that he felt the same.

She knew she'd be able to raise Sammy with help. From her mother. From Eddie. Auntie Lee had even volunteered to baby-sit now and then, after she made it back from the front lines. And then there was Paul and . . . her father.

She'd already talked to Donald twice since making it to safety. And a smile filled her face as she realized they both hoped to move past the "what should have been," focusing instead on "what can be."

She unfolded the newspaper article she'd read over a dozen times already and scanned it yet again. The photo was one of her and Donald that they'd taken at the World's Fair. As they stood side by side, posing for a guy with a camera who hoped to make a buck, Donald's hand held her elbow. Each seemed unsure of how close the other was willing to lean in. Still, it was clear from their eyes that they were both happy . . . and hopeful.

Mary touched her pendant and read the opening paragraph once more.

A Daughter Lost
By Donald Miller

The old adage is true that a person doesn't realize what he has until he loses it. And I feel that way about my daughter—the one most of this world never knew I had. I suppose fear was the very thing that kept us apart all these years. My fear I wouldn't be the father she deserves. But now, I suppose, my greatest fear is that I will never again be given the chance to try.

My daughter, Mary Kelley, was an ETO correspondent reporting on the bombing raid over Berlin in the aircraft Destiny's Child. . . .

The article gave information about the mission, a plea for help from ground crews, and even a reward. Mary smiled, wondering just what Charlie and Howie were doing with all that money. At first, she'd insisted Eddie should get some too. He was her navigator, after all. But he'd refused.

"You're kidding, right?" he'd said, placing a dozen kisses on her forehead. "I have all the reward right here wrapped up in your love."

What a sap.... *Oh, how I miss that guy.*

"Just a few months and we'll see him again," Mary whispered to Samuel, who was beginning to stir. "Then after that, who knows? Maybe we'll all be together for a lifetime." She lifted him from his cradle, and Samuel rewarded her with a smile. "Would you like that, Sammy, would ya? I know I would."

Eddie woke with a start, his heart pounding. *Samuel, Mary, where are they?* Then he remembered. *They're safe....*

They're gone.

Though hundreds of men still lived on the airfield, Eddie felt a huge void somewhere around his heart. He had never felt lonelier. Or more timid. *I thought I was the strong one. Maybe the strength wasn't mine all along, but Mary's.*

"Hey, Vinny," Eddie called, tossing his pillow across the room. "If you were to propose, how would you do it?"

"Propose? To which one? I have a half-dozen girls I can't live without...."

"No, stupid. Me."

"You want me to propose to you?"

"Vinny, come on. Any idea how I should propose to Mary?"

Vinny moaned and rubbed his sleepy eyes. "I was wondering when you were going to ask that question." He thought for a moment, then grinned. "I know. I'd re-create the first moment you met. Or the first time you knew you'd fallen for her. Get it ... *fallen* for her ..."

"Ha, ha. Very funny." Eddie sat up straighter on his bed.

"Think of something she'd never expect. What would mean the most to her? Is there anything special she talked about when you were together?"

"I think you're on to something." Eddie rapped the side of his head with his knuckles. "Not something, but *someone*. Yeah, Vinny, that's the perfect plan."

Vinny groaned, turned over, and pulled his blankets over his head. "*Now* can I go back to sleep?"

A short knock sounded at Mary's door, then it opened. "Hey, little lady? Are you interested in a really great story?"

Mary was rocking the baby's cradle with her foot as her fingers busily pounded the typewriter keys. She continued a few seconds longer as if finishing a thought. Then she suddenly froze, the sound of Eddie's voice finally wending its way to her consciousness.

"Eddie? Is that you?" She jumped from the chair and flew into his arms. "Oh, my goodness. What are you doing here? You said now that your arm was better, you were going home. Being shipped out."

"Heck, I figured, what's the use, when every thought would still remain over here with you? Now that my arm's nearly good as new, I've signed on for just long enough for you to wrap things up. And maybe enough time to throw in a wedding here in England."

"A wedding? Eddie, are you serious? I— I don't know what to say."

There was another knock at the door, and a smiling face peeked around the corner. *Donald.*

"Say *yes*, of course. And will you give me the honor of walking you down the aisle?"

Mary's trembling fingers covered her mouth. "Yes—yes to both of you!" Then she swung an arm around each of their necks.

"Thank you," she whispered into Eddie's ear, then kissed his cheek. "You've just made me the happiest girl in the world, twice over."

One month to the day that Mary Kelley, ETO Correspondent, had joined the crew of *Destiny's Child* on a bombing raid over Berlin, Eddie stood at the altar of a small army chapel back at Bassingbourn, waiting for his bride to walk down the aisle. He knew some would question how after such a short period of time they could know for sure they were meant for each other. Yet, he knew if he and Mary could escape enemy territory with a madman chasing them and an infant in tow, then they could weather anything this world would toss them.

Vinny, Adam, and Marty stood by Eddie's side. Jack the Crew Chief had made it too.

Word had it five other crew members from *Destiny's Child*, including José, were "safe" in a POW camp, waiting out the war. Eddie prayed every night for the end to come quickly. He knew he'd only feel relief once he saw those guys' faces and hugged each one—well, at least gave each a slug in the shoulder.

The organ started, and his heart pounded as Mary appeared on her father's arm. She glanced at Eddie adoringly; then her father leaned down and whispered something in Mary's ear, making her smile broaden even wider.

They'd thought about waiting until Lee could be here, but last they heard she was on the front lines reporting on the Battle of the Bulge, with no plans of heading back to England anytime soon. Still, thanks to her, the front of the chapel was so filled with flowers that Eddie and the chaplain barely had room to stand. And his bride strode forward in a satin designer gown that only someone with connections could find in war-torn London.

He thought of his own family back in Montana, knowing they'd give a shindig like the county had never seen once they made it back. And as for Mary's mother . . . well, somehow Donald had used his influence to get her across the pond for this blessed event. She sat in the front row, bouncing Samuel on her knee and beaming. Eddie couldn't wait to pull her aside and thank her for raising such a wonderful girl. But now, his bride approached. And his heart swelled as he reached out his hand for hers.

"My bride," Eddie whispered, taking her hand. "My beautiful bride."

CHAPTER THIRTY

Patrick drove their jeep through Weimar—just one of many cities they'd passed through as they kept pace with Patton's Third Army. Lee remembered reading somewhere how the German town had been known for centuries for its cultural life.

"Did you know Goethe lived in Weimar? Bach too," Lee said as they drove through the streets now controlled by the American army.

"Well, if you ask me, they've really let the place go," he said, glancing around at the bombed-out buildings and roads pocked by artillery shells. Following the directions they'd been given, he drove them out of town to a forested area high above the city.

The narrow, battle-scarred road was lined with bodies—both American in their army-green fatigues and Germans in their black uniforms. Yet their faces looked the same. Boys from Kansas, California, Vermont. And the last available males from the Nazi empire.

Lee's heart sank to see the boys from Hitler Youth, the shining stars of the Reich, lying dead in the mud. Most looked too young to even shave. Lee thought about their mothers, sisters. Yeah, they were the enemy, but the human pain was the same.

She took out her notepad and tried to jot things down, but she couldn't take her eyes off the sight before her. It's not like she would forget anything. The war showed promise of ending soon. Yet she had a feeling this was just the start of her looking at the world in a whole new way.

She and Patrick had seen a lot already, spending hours together in this jeep. They'd witnessed German cities reduced to rubble and swarming with recently freed slave laborers—Polish, Russians, and French, whose scarecrow-like bodies were consumed with the idea of returning home.

The two had been a little too close to the action for comfort a time or two, finding themselves in artillery barrages far worse than the one witnessed at St. Vith. And now they were on the way to a different type of horror. The nearby Buchenwald camp had been liberated only hours before, and they were being called in as witnesses for the world.

Lee had learned to travel light and now carried only her typewriter, a sleeping bag, and a few extra clothes. She glanced down at her fingernails and grimaced, wondering what her New York manicurist would say if she saw them in such a condition.

She wrinkled her nose, thinking of what she'd come to refer to as the old Lee. The human courage, sacrifice, and selflessness she'd seen in the scores of young soldiers and nurses had changed her. The carnage, the deaths—they weren't simply something to investigate for a story, to prop up her career. These were real lives. Dying men, wanting nothing more than to see their mothers' faces one more time—they had shown her that.

Mary had shown her too. Seeing her fellow journalist waving her off from the hotel lobby, when Lee could have been setting off for the story of a lifetime, had affected her. And so had seeing Mary cuddle that small child in her arms. It caused a yearning Lee hadn't known existed until now.

She glanced over at Patrick Jessup, realizing how much she cared for the guy. He was a simple man but kind. A good man. One she could imagine spending the rest of her life with.

The jeep slowed, and the new April grass and flowers seemed to fade the closer they got to the tall, gray walls of the camp. Though the sky was blue overhead, a dimness hung over the camp that was hard to describe.

Patrick looked to her with a questioning gaze. "Sure you wanna do this, Lee?"

Her fingers fiddled with the door handle. "Do you think it's as bad inside as they say?"

A heavy, putrid order filled the air, smelling of rotting meat.

Patrick brushed away a fly that attempted to land on his face. "If that stench has anything to do with it, I believe it might even be worse than what we've heard." He grabbed up his camera from the space between their seats and climbed out. Lee followed.

When they approached the gate, a weary-looking American GI waved them forward. "You the reporters?"

Patrick nodded.

"Commander's been waiting for you."

Lee took two steps inside the gate, and wasn't sure she'd be able to go on. Thin bodies moved toward her, their arms outstretched. Smiles cracked on skeletal faces, and a compassion Lee didn't know existed flooded over her. She slipped her notebook into her pocket and extended her hands to the frail man closest to her. He jabbered on in a language she couldn't understand, yet she knew the meaning. Tears streamed down her face as his cracked lips kissed her hands over and over again. The next man did the same, and soon a line began to form.

"I never imagined . . . Never thought . . . How am I to help the world to understand?" She turned to Patrick.

"This is what we've been fighting for," Patrick answered. "That's what you're going to tell them. They've sacrificed a lot. Their sons. Their way of life for a time."

Lee approached the next frail prisoner in line and opened her arms, letting his head fall on her shoulder.

The world needed to know, and she would be the voice to tell them. There was no pride in that. She'd been through too much to believe she was anything special. But there was honor in knowing that she'd been chosen, despite her frailties and fears.

Or maybe because of them.

"Rebecca, you've received a letter. It's from Mary Anderson." Sister Clarence hurried into the side room of the church— Rebecca's room—the fabric of her habit swooshing with every step. She stopped at the side of Rebecca's wheeled chair.

"She's sent a photo of Samuel, all the way from Montana, America. Look, he's sitting on a pony!" Sister Clarence pulled another slip of paper from the envelope. "And here's a newspaper clipping too. It looks like she's an editor of a paper in Montana. She's translated it for us. Would you like me to read the story?"

Rebecca tilted her head so the light from the window kissed her cheek. Outside the maple leaves were beginning to turn into golden red, and as they dropped from the trees they danced like the ballerinas that used to perform at the National Theater in Prague. Running through the leaves was a group of ten Belgian children, laughing and shouting.

"Or would you like me to read the letter? Oh, look, Eddie wrote a short note too."

"I can't wait to hear the news, but we'd better wait until after story time," Rebecca laughed. "I don't think the kids will be patient enough to wait. But can you prop Samuel's photo up on this table so I can see it better? I do think he has my smile."

Rebecca's throat grew thick, and she felt her eyes filling up with tears, until the smiling face of her son was no longer clear.

She closed her eyes, and Sister Clarence brushed her tears away. In her mind's eye Rebecca remembered her father's hand in her own. And remembered how he had released it, sending *her* away.

"I think, Sister, I'll tell them the story of Hannah today. And of the son she dedicated to God. It's a story of hope."

"Good choice." Sister Clarence readjusted Rebecca's hands on her lap, then pushed her wheeled chair to the schoolroom where the children waited.

"Hope is a good thing, Sister. Hope that one's child will be safe and loved. It's all a parent really wants, is it not? My father would be proud, I think, to know where I've placed my hope. My body is broken, but my heart is well, Sister."

"Well? Yes, it is well. You bore Samuel, then gave him over to a godly couple, that his destiny, and theirs, might be fulfilled. But remember, Rebecca, your Samuel is not the only child of destiny. You are too."

HISTORICAL NOTE

Destiny's Child is the name of a real B-17 Bomber that was shot down by Luftwaffe fighters on July 20, 1944. The crew was on a mission to Leipzig, Germany.

As described in this novel, Destiny's Child had an illustration (painted by crew chief Jack Gaffney) portraying the little baby in the hillbilly cartoons, wearing diapers and carrying a shotgun. The name of the bomber was chosen by those tossed into a hat.

Destiny's Child was on her 53rd mission when she was shot down. The story of this bomber was told to me by its Ground Crew Chief Jack Gaffney—one of the wonderful veterans who helped me with this novel. Sgt. Gaffney later was awarded the Bronze Star for the excellent maintenance he and his crew and performed on her, keeping her combat-ready and in the air without an abort.

While the demise of Destiny's Child has been altered in this novel for fictional purposes, both Jack Gaffney and original tail gunner Jack Paget (who did not make the July 20th flight) encouraged me to use the name as a way to honor this crew, and the numerous others, who were shot down during their time in service. Little did the two men know the aircraft's name would tie in perfectly with the story God had placed on my heart.

The crew consisted of the following individuals and indicated their fate.

KIA—Killed in Action
POW—Prisoner of War

Pilot	1st Lt. Charles Van Ansdall (KIA)
Co-Pilot	Flt Officer Joseph Sammon (POW)
Navigator	2nd Lt. Richard Loomis (KIA)
Bombardier	2nd Lt. John Butler (POW)
Engineer/Gunner	TSGT Charles Sullivan, Jr. (KIA)
Ball Turret Gunner	SSGT Anson Riley (POW)
Waist Gunner	SSGT Winton Blevins (POW)
Tail Gunner	SSGT Vernon Winters (KIA)

May these men and their courage never be forgotten.

ACKNOWLEDGMENTS

Psalm 96:3 (NLT) states: "Publish His glorious deeds among the nations. Tell everyone about the amazing things He does." The following people made it possible to share this story from my heart:

John, my other half. You make it easy to write stories of love and hope.

Cory, Leslie, and Nathan. For all the days you made me lunch, encouraged my progress, and bragged on your mom. You're the best.

My grandma, Dolores Coulter. Seeing you with your open Bible and bowed head every morning makes me thankful for my godly heritage.

My mom, Linda Martin. You always said I could do anything I set my mind to. You were right. Thanks, Mom.

My heart-friend Joanna Weaver. For all those times we

escaped away to write, encouraged each other, and prayed. You're an awesome cheerleader.

More forever-friends Twyla Klundt, Tara Norick, and Cindy Martinusen who listen to my heart time and time again.

My prayer friends from One Heart, AWSA, and Blessed Hope. Thanks for the faith-lifts!

My Coeur d'Alene retreat buddies. Brandilyn, Janet, Sunni, Nikki, Karen, Robin, Tammy, Ruth, Sharon, Gayle, and Bev. Great minds unite!

My agent, Janet Kobobel Grant. I'm thankful for your wisdom and dedication.

My editors, Andy McGuire and LB Norton. You make me look brilliant.

My "unofficial" editors, Ocieanna Fleiss, Jim Thompson, Bev Hudson, and Kathi Mathias. You're the best!

Finally, this book wouldn't be written if not for the wonderful men and women who help with my research:

Veterans from the 91st Bomb Group who lived what I wrote:

Jim Bard, Frank Farr, Don Freer, Jack Gaffney, Ed Gates, Lowell Getz, Joe Harlich, Marion C. Hoffman, John Howland, Asay Johnson, Conrad L. Lohoefer, Philip Mack, George Parrish, Robert M. Slane, and Verne Woods. Also, the late Rodney Demars, B-17 gunner. Thank you for your stories.

Mike Banta, 91st Ring. Thanks for connecting me with these amazing veterans!

Historian Roger Marquet from Belgium. Thanks for all the information about the castle and your country.

Mary Lou Wilson, ETO. Thanks for your input on London during WWII.

May the men and women who served never be forgotten!

More from Tricia Goyer . . .

From Dust and Ashes
A Story of Liberation

Nazis flee under cover of darkness as American troops approach the town of St. Georgen. A terrible surprise awaits the unsuspecting GIs, and three people—the wife of an SS guard, an American soldier, and a concentration camp survivor—will never be the same. Inspired by actual events surrounding the liberation of a Nazi concentration camp.

ISBN: 0-8024-1554-7

Night Song
A Story of Sacrifice

Young Jakub finds himself in the prisoner-led orchestra of Hitler's Mauthausen death camp. Engulfed by evil and weakened by starvation, he learns more than music from the world-renowned conductor imprisoned with him. Meanwhile, outside the camp, the beautiful daughter of an Austrian diplomat aids the resistance movement while her brave American fiancé risks everything to find her. Will they be able to survive the Nazi evil that hunts them?

ISBN: 0-8024-1555-5

MOODY
PUBLISHERS

THE NAME YOU CAN TRUST®

1-800-678-6928 www.MoodyPublishers.com

Dawn of a Thousand Nights
A Story of Honor

ISBN: 0-8024-0855-9

Pilots Libby Conners and Dan Lukens are torn apart by the onset of WWII but promise they will wait for each other. Bound by duty and buoyed by hope, Dan and Libby face grueling tests on opposite sides of the world. Libby is pressed into service as one of the first female pilots to serve in a time of war, while Dan endures what would become the legendarily brutal Bataan Death March in the Philippines. With tragedy around every corner, the couple must find the stamina and faith to endure the nightmare of war.

Environmental
Overkill

Environmental Overkill

Whatever Happened to Common Sense?

Dixy Lee Ray
with Lou Guzzo

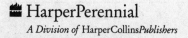 HarperPerennial
A Division of HarperCollinsPublishers

ENVIRONMENTAL OVERKILL. Copyright © 1993 by Dixy Lee Ray and Louis R. Guzzo. All rights reserved. Printed in the United States of America. No part of this book may be used or reproduced in any manner whatsoever without written permission except in the case of brief quotations embodied in critical articles and reviews. For information address HarperCollins Publishers, Inc., 10 East 53rd Street, New York, NY 10022.

HarperCollins books may be purchased for educational, business, or sales promotional use. For information please write: Special Markets Department, HarperCollins Publishers, Inc., 10 East 53rd Street, New York, NY 10022.

First HarperPerennial edition published 1994.

Library of Congress Cataloging-in-Publication Data

Ray, Dixie Lee.
    Environmental overkill : whatever happened to common sense / Dixy Lee
Ray with Lou Guzzo. — 1st HarperPerennial ed.
        p.   cm.
    Originally published: Washington, D.C. : Regnery Gateway, c1994.
    Includes bibliographical references and index.
    ISBN 0-06-097598-9 (pbk.)
    1. Environmental responsibility. 2. Environmental policy. I. Guzzo,
Louis R., 1919–   . II. Title.
GE195.7.R39   1994
363.7—dc20   93-42982

94 95 96 97 98 RRD 10 9 8 7 6 5 4 3 2 1

Dedication

One of the most profound obligations of scientists is to provide factual information about basic science, technology, the environment, and human health in a manner that can be understood by policy makers and the public at large. We feel this obligation very deeply, as do many of our fellow scientists. But too few have the unique talent required for this very special kind of communication. Paramount among those who do are two great men—both physical scientists.

One is Dr. Petr Beckmann and the other is Dr. Edward Teller.

Although these two accomplished scientists have had strikingly different careers, each in his own specialty, they share many attributes. Both are foreign-born; they chose America. Like so many adopted citizens, they display an unabashed patriotism that reminds us native-borns that, whatever her faults, America is a unique and wonderful country, one that continues to be receptive to good science.

Through their research and writing, Dr. Beckmann and Dr. Teller have demonstrated their passionate devotion to truth in science and their unshakable belief in its remarkable power to improve the lot of human beings. Above all, they have used their considerable skills to make complex science understandable to the common man.

For all these reasons—and with profound gratitude—we dedicate this work to Petr Beckmann and Edward Teller.

—DLR and LRG

Contents

Preface

FIRST, a few words about what this book is not. It is not a scientific treatise. It is not a report of original work. It is not an encyclopedic treatment of all the environmental ills that plague the Earth. It is not an apology for modern civilization; nor does it seek to condemn human progress. It takes the position that good intentions are not enough in developing public policies; we need scientific facts.

We have chosen to give special attention to the uncertainties in science and to those policies that favor action above understanding. Unless they are based on a solid body of established facts, widely accepted perceptions may be faulty. We therefore emphasize many of the often-neglected consequences that result when actions are taken, even though evidence is missing or overlooked.

In taking this approach, we are aware that some may conclude that we are "anti-environment." That would be wrong. We acknowledge that there are problems of pollution and other environmental assaults, but we believe that they are amenable to solution when we use the knowledge that science can provide.

We believe that it is just as wrong to exaggerate the seriousness of environmental issues as it is to downplay the remarkable resilience and recovery powers of nature. We also believe that intrusive, punitive government controls are self-defeating. In sum, we believe in the basic goodness of our fellow humans; we believe that problems should be proved to be real before we lavish money on them. And we believe that it's important to demonstrate that a proposed solution is appropriate, practical, and affordable.

That's what this book is about; it is called common sense.

—DLR and LRG

PART ONE

The Air Above Us

CHAPTER 1

The Future According to Rio

UNCED Proposes to Save the Planet

In the first two weeks of June 1992, thousands of people converged on Rio de Janeiro, Brazil, to attend the United Nations Conference on Environment and Development (UNCED). Most of the 20,000 to 30,000 participants were there for the "Global Forum" part of the conference, which was billed as a "world's fair of environmentalism." This consisted of motley exhibits and short programs on every conceivable environmental and social program. It occupied a tent city that was erected in Rio's downtown Flamingo Park. Global Forum provided an opportunity for individual expression and for special interests to demonstrate environmental technologies, but was otherwise unrelated to the official conference agenda.

UNCED's serious work was done at the "Earth Summit" meetings. There the government representatives of 178 nations and the official delegates of hundreds of nongovernmental organizations (NGOs) met in separate sessions to consider a program of wide-ranging measures. The overall goal was to "Save the Planet." Save the planet from what? From human beings, of course!

The tone for these discussions was set by Maurice F. Strong, the UN's official spokesman and secretary general for the conference.

In his opening remarks on June 3, he referred repeatedly to serious deterioration in the natural world and to the pressing need for action. He spoke of "patterns of production and consumption in the industrialized world that are undermining Earth's life-support systems. . . . To continue along this pathway could lead to the end of our civilization. . . . This conference must establish the foundations for effecting the transition to sustainable development. This can only be done through fundamental changes in our economic life and in international economic relations, particularly as between industrialized and developing countries. . . . This planet may soon become uninhabitable for people."[1]

This theme—that nature has been irreparably damaged by industrialization and that the only remedy is to reduce progress and economic growth in the industrialized world—was one of the two underlying principles that guided UNCED. It was repeated over and over. The United States was generally singled out as the primary culprit. Curiously, the other guiding principle for UNCED was that the industrial nations, accused of causing all the problems, must now pay for them by transferring large sums of money and technical know-how to the Third World.[2] How this is to be accomplished by the industrialized nations while they simultaneously lower living standards and retrench economically was not explained or even discussed.

The year before, 1991, Strong had set the tone while the UN agenda was in preparation:

In this transition to a more secure and sustainable future, the industrialized countries must take the lead. They have developed and benefited from the unsustainable patterns of production and consumption which have produced our present dilemma. And they primarily have the means and responsibility to change them. . . . It is clear that current lifestyles and consumption patterns of the affluent middle class—involving high meat intake, consumption of large amounts of frozen and convenience foods, use of fossil fuels, ownership of motor vehicles and small electrical appliances, home and workplace air-conditioning, and suburban housing—are not sustainable. A shift is necessary toward lifestyles less geared to environmental damaging consumption patterns.[3]

It appears that no proof is needed for these assertions and that simply saying so establishes their validity. Throughout the entire period of the conference, they were repeated like a mantra.

Planning for the Earth Summit began at the 1987 Stockholm conference that produced the report *Our Common Future*.[4] That meeting was chaired by Norway's Prime Minister Gro Harlem Bruntland, who was also the vice president of the International Socialist Party. *Our Common Future* is a green internationalist manifesto that brings the political philosophy of socialism into the environmental movement. The socialist approach to problems, along with the kind of remedies proposed, was evident in Mrs. Bruntland's remarks at Rio. She told the delegates to the Earth Summit that "We in the North consume too much."[5]

As reporter Ron Bailey of *Reason* magazine observed drily, "Fortunately, the activists at Earth Summit have a solution for this problem: Let the government divest you of your excess goods, such as your carbon dioxide-emitting automobile; your alienating, too-big house or apartment; and foods imported from outside your 'bioregion'. . . . The assertion by many Third World representatives that 'because you are rich, I am poor' was never doubted in the discussions. . . ."[6]

The Honorable Mrs. Bruntland, who served as vice chairman of UNCED in Rio, reinforced such attitudes in her opening remarks. She spoke of "the burden they [industrial nations] impose on the carrying capacity of the Earth's ecosystems by their unsustainable consumption and production patterns." In a stunning answer to a question from a Brazilian reporter following her prepared remarks, Prime Minister Bruntland freely acknowledged that the Earth Summit agenda was based upon the International Socialist Party's platform. This went largely unreported, although more than 7,000 journalists covered the conference.[7]

A few, however, dissented from the prevailing socialist propaganda. Again, Ron Bailey, contributing editor to *Reason* magazine, wrote:

Although I am generally not much of a nationalist, the patience of even the most laid-back, even-tempered American (excuse me, *North* American) wore thin under the unrelenting onslaught of virulent anti-Americanism at the Earth Summit. Even the ultraliberal Representative Gerry Sikorski, Minnesota Democrat, lashed out after a Zambian made a particularly vicious attack on the United States for not giving more money to the South. Sikorski told the Zambian that he would "feel a whole lot better about asking my consituents for money for the Third World if you would clean up your corrupt governments first."[8]

It would be interesting to know how Representative Sikorski's constituents feel about providing any of their tax money to Zambia. And, indeed, why should they?

In contrast to the predictions of impending ecological doom from Strong, Bruntland, and other UN leaders of the Earth Summit, more than 250 of the world's leading scientists, including 27 Nobel laureates, released a statement on June 1, 1992, called the Heidelberg Appeal.[9] It was directed to the heads of state that were attending the Rio Conference and appealed for the use of common sense and reliable science in making recommendations for action on environmental problems. As background, the scientists pointed out that it is neither reasonable nor prudent for major political decisions to be based on presumptions about issues in science, which, in the current state of knowledge, are still only hypotheses. They pointed out that in the more than two years of preparation for the Earth Summit, there was no significant involvement of scientists who specialize in the specific problem areas under consideration, nor were the competent scientists even informed. The Heidelberg statement, now signed and supported by hundreds of scientists worldwide, says, in part:

We are worried, at the dawn of the 21st Century, at the emergence of an irrational ideology which is opposed to scientific and industrial progress and impedes economic and social development. We contend that a Natural State sometimes idealized by movements with a tendency to look toward the past does not exist and has probably never existed since man's first appearance in the biosphere, insofar as humanity has always progressed by harnessing nature to its needs, and not the reverse. . . . The greatest evils which stalk our Earth are ignorance and oppression, and not Science, Technology, and Indus-